"Fans of the author's books will absolutely not want to miss this one. This sweetly angsty novel . . . will appeal to anyone who enjoys reading opposites-attract romances with found family subplots."

—*Library Journal* (starred review) on *We Could Be So Good*

"When Cat Sebastian is creating romance, every serve is an ace. . . . [The] slow-burning sparks are organic, joy inducing and earned."

—NPR

Praise for Cat Sebastian

"Cat Sebastian writes about love in all its forms with the care, warmth, and effortless mastery of someone putting a home-cooked meal in front of you. I don't know how she keeps getting better, or how she managed to make me care so much about a sport I know literally nothing about, but this one is—again!—the best yet. A truly wonderful and heart-healing romance about community, grief, perseverance, New York bakeries—and baseball."

—Freya Marske, bestselling author of *A Marvellous Light*

"Cat Sebastian is a queen of queer historical romance. . . . [She] never disappoints."

—*Entertainment Weekly*

"It's not about the events [of the plot], it's about the going through [them]. And the going through is wonderful: At one point a character makes some soup, and then later a different character makes more soup, and here I am weeping and prostrate because the reader knows what that soup means. . . . Queer oppression, the civil rights movement, white supremacy—these are tangible contexts in this novel, but they are not the subject. The subject: joy as praxis, love as liberation. You can't do the big rebellions if you can't start with the small ones."

—*New York Times Book Review* on *We Could Be So Good*

"A spectacularly talented writer!"

—Julia Quinn, *New York Times* bestselling author of the Bridgerton series

You Should Be So Lucky

Also by Cat Sebastian

We Could Be So Good

THE LONDON HIGHWAYMEN SERIES
The Queer Principles of Kit Webb
The Perfect Crimes of Marian Hayes

THE SEDUCING THE SEDGWICKS SERIES
It Takes Two to Tumble
A Gentleman Never Keeps Score
Two Rogues Make a Right

THE REGENCY IMPOSTORS SERIES
Unmasked by the Marquess
A Duke in Disguise
A Delicate Deception

THE TURNER SERIES
The Soldier's Scoundrel
The Lawrence Browne Affair
The Ruin of a Rake
A Little Light Mischief (novella)

You Should Be So Lucky

A Novel

CAT SEBASTIAN

AVON

An Imprint of HarperCollinsPublishers

YOU SHOULD BE SO LUCKY. Copyright © 2024 by Cat Sebastian. All rights reserved. Printed in the United States of America. No part of this book may be used or reproduced in any manner whatsoever without written permission except in the case of brief quotations embodied in critical articles and reviews. For information, address HarperCollins Publishers, 195 Broadway, New York, NY 10007.

HarperCollins books may be purchased for educational, business, or sales promotional use. For information, please email the Special Markets Department at SPsales@harpercollins.com.

FIRST EDITION

Designed by Diahann Sturge-Campbell

Library of Congress Cataloging-in-Publication Data has been applied for.

ISBN 978-0-06-327280-4

24 25 26 27 28 LBC 6 5 4 3 2

For V, who knows what she did

You Should Be So Lucky

Part I
MAY

CHAPTER ONE

1960

After a year of doing basically nothing—although Lilian is forever clapping him on the shoulder and earnestly telling him that survival is something, it's *wonderful*, darling, a testament to his *strength*—Mark Bailey finds that it's a bit of a shock to the system to discover he's in the middle of a meeting with his boss.

Sure, they're in a grimy Irish bar instead of the *Chronicle*'s wood-paneled conference room, and they're drinking watered-down gin instead of coffee, and nobody's there to take notes or waste time by talking about golf, but it's still a meeting no matter how Mark looks at it, God help him.

"So here's the problem," Andy says. Andy is—well, when he isn't busy being Andrew Fleming III, the *Chronicle*'s publisher, he and Mark are friends, or whatever you call it when you're both queer and work at the same place and keep one another's secrets.

"We need to convert weekday commute readers to Sunday subscription readers," Andy goes on. "The Sunday paper is where we make money."

Mark's been hearing versions of this for months. After three drinks, Andy's capable of delivering an entire lecture, complete with pie charts drawn on the backs of cocktail napkins, about return on investment, dwindling ad sales, and how television will be the ruination of the free press. It's all unspeakably boring, and the only reason Mark hasn't put a stop to it is that it would take an awful lot of energy that he simply does not have.

"A new Sunday magazine is going to replace the old pullout supplement starting in July," Andy goes on. "It'll be glossy and in full color, and we want it to attract a different set of readers. I was looking at those articles you wrote a couple years back for *Esquire* and *The New Yorker*, and even some of the longer pieces you used to write for our arts and culture section. That's exactly what I want."

Andy's being tactful by not saying something like "back when you used to do actual work instead of writing book reviews every few months for fifty-dollar checks that you forget to cash." Technically, Mark resigned in February 1959 but never quite got out of the habit of coming in to work. This may be pushing the envelope on eccentricity, but he's pretty sure that ship has sailed; he's firmly in Miss Havisham territory now, haunting the dusty and half-empty fifth floor of the *Chronicle* building, an eldritch entity that junior reporters warn one another about.

"According to market research," Andy goes on, "sports coverage is one of the top reasons people buy the paper, so I'm thinking the magazine needs stories with a sports angle."

All this strikes Mark as exceptionally pie-in-the-sky; he's not optimistic by nature and even less so where newspapers are concerned. If Andy didn't look like a man about to ask a favor, he'd assume this had nothing to do with him. His magazine features were mostly profiles of architects and fashion designers. He hasn't written a word about sports since he was on his high school newspaper, nursing an ill-fated crush on the quarterback.

Mark drains his gin and waves the bartender over for some more. "You need a highbrow sports feature for the magazine, and you want me to write it."

"Yes," says Andy, drawing out the syllable and looking at his drink instead of at Mark. "You know when a paper publishes a weekly diary by an athlete over the course of a season?"

Mark scoffs. "I don't think any of those have ever actually been written by the ballplayer. It's always some poor bastard in the sports department . . ." He trails off as Andy's meaning makes its way through the haze of gin. "No. Absolutely not. I'm not ghostwriting a ballplayer diary. I can't think of anyone on your entire staff less qualified."

"Nonsense. You follow the game. You and Nick complain about the Yankees every time we see you, and I know you were pleased to hear about the Robins coming to New York, because you said so, in my own kitchen."

Mark glares at Andy. Surely, using his own words against him counts as emotional blackmail. He and Nick have been paying attention to the trials and travails of the city's new baseball team—Nick because he loves baseball, and Mark because he loves drama. But Mark doesn't follow the game; a passing familiarity with baseball is something he caught, like the measles, not something he did on purpose.

"Why can't you have one of the junior sportswriters do it? Or someone else who can be motivated by an extra ten dollars a week?"

Andy goes back to swirling the ice around in his glass. "Well, the player I was thinking of might need special treatment."

"What player do you have in mind?"

"That new shortstop. O'Leary."

"You think people want to read a diary by a guy who threw a tantrum in public after he was traded here? And who's barely managed to hit the ball since then?" Mark cannot think of anything more likely to get someone to throw their paper directly into the nearest trash can.

"There has to be more to him than that," Andy suggests.

"He called the manager a drunken psychopath, the team a bunch of talentless layabouts, and the owners a couple of debutantes." Mark has seen these phrases printed in every paper he reads and has heard them repeated everywhere from the subway to the *Chronicle* break room.

Andy shrugs. "Is any of that wrong, though?"

Mark snorts. "Probably not," he concedes. "There's no way the Robins will let him within ten yards of a reporter."

"They're operating under the idea that any press is good press if it gets people to the stadium."

"Still, it ought to be a sportswriter who does it."

"Well, that's the problem. Half the sports desk staff have publicly insulted O'Leary. The other half, well. Nobody's going to believe O'Leary wrote this diary if it's filled with aw-shucks earnestness. It would have to have an edge."

"Andy," Mark says, laughing despite himself. "Are you calling me mean?"

"No," Andy protests. He's a terrible liar. "Just—cynical, maybe. When you want to be. Anyway, writing the weekly diary would get you access to the team, which you can use to write the magazine feature. I'd like to run it the first Sunday in October. If you're up to it, that is." He's offering Mark a graceful out, and Mark's tempted to take it. "But with the magazine about to take over the fifth floor, it would be nice to have an excuse for you to keep that office."

At the idea that he might lose his office, Mark feels a faint stirring of panic. Where would he go all day? Where, other than that office on the semi-deserted fifth floor of the *Chronicle* building, could he be allowed to hide away, spending what Lilian persists in calling the Best Years of His Life organizing paper clips by size and hoarding all the best pens?

The *Chronicle*—the familiarity of it all, from his typewriter with its sticky *F* to the people he sees in the elevator—has kept him afloat this past year. He has to get out of bed because he has to brush his teeth; he has to brush his teeth because he has to go to work. There's a rhythm to his day that he doesn't exactly enjoy, but at least it exists, and it carries him along until it's the next morning and he does it all again.

That afternoon, when he unlocks his door, Lula lets out a single sharp bark, as if determined to let him know there's another reason for Mark to get out of bed every morning, and that's to be a wire-haired terrier's indentured servant.

Mark leans down to scratch the dog's head, and she gives him a sad look. *I'm not angry, I'm just disappointed,* she communicates with every bark, every look, every nap spent slumped against the door, waiting for someone who's never going to come home. But honestly, it's an unspeakable relief that the dog hasn't moved on, either.

Everyone—well, the handful of people who actually *know*—has been telling him that eventually he'll go back to normal, but after a year of this, Mark's increasingly certain that everyone is full of shit. Or, more likely, they simply don't understand, and good for them. Mark's genuinely happy for them.

He slips Lula's leash on and lets her drag him back outside. It's warm and breezy, the sort of weather that makes people in the city flirt with the idea of sidewalk cafés and picnics, before remembering that exhaust fumes don't go with most meals.

The dog leads him along the same route she's taken for the entire eight years Mark's known her: around the perimeter of Gramercy Park, then south on Irving Place with a pointed digging in of the heels in front of a bakery. "No, Lula," he says, just like he always does. "We're not going in today."

Back at home, Lula takes up sentry by the kitchen cupboard that houses the dog food. It's the stuff that comes in cans, which is both unreasonably expensive and unfathomably smelly, but that's what William always bought, and it isn't like Mark is about to ruin this poor animal's life even further by purchasing substandard dog food. William raised Lula to have *taste*, and far be it from Mark to second-guess either of them.

The fact that he can calmly formulate that thought surely has to count for something. But it turns out that what's on the other side of last year's brittle fragility isn't *normal* but something grayscale and hollowed out. Mark is . . . fine: he paid his taxes on time and he went to the dentist when his tooth hurt. He isn't in any danger of throwing himself out of windows or acquiring interesting new habits of self-destruction.

It's just that when he tries to figure out what the point is in getting out of bed every morning, he doesn't have the answer. Even work—which had always been *an* answer, at least—feels flat and dull, like there's nothing left in the world worth writing about. He's made sure not to tell Lilian about this or she might get that terribly sad face again, and then he'll have to endure her and Maureen having him over for dinner and relentless sympathy while the whole time they look at him like he's the ghost of Christmas yet to come.

The dog barks, and Mark realizes he's paused with his hand on the can opener. He opens the can and dumps its appalling contents into the little bowl with the dog bone painted inside that they picked up on vacation in Marseilles years ago.

He ought to do something about his own dinner, but instead he turns on the television with the half-formed intention of smugly watching a quiz show—he takes his thrills where he finds them, these days. The television is tuned in to a baseball game, though. The commentators are going on about how O'Leary's been batting literally zero since getting traded. That's almost impressively terrible. Hadn't there been talk last season about him being rookie of the year?

Mark kneels in front of the television until O'Leary's at bat. He knows from occasional glances at the sports page that Eddie

O'Leary has been talked about as having the prettiest swing in base-ball. What Mark sees today doesn't have anything pretty about it. It is, frankly, a mess. It looks like it physically hurts, like O'Leary's body is doing something it has no business even trying.

O'Leary strikes out and then—Mark winces—snaps the bat over his knee. What an absolute *infant*, having tantrums in public. Mark isn't sure how much you can tell about someone's demeanor from grainy black-and-white television footage, but O'Leary looks defeated as he returns to the dugout.

Mark spreads the *Chronicle*'s clippings on O'Leary across the dining room table in chronological order. They make a depressing tableau. You can almost hear the hushed, reverent awe with which reporters last spring talked about O'Leary's future. By the fall, columnists who ought to know better were openly comparing him to Ted Williams and Joe DiMaggio, throwing around rookie-year stats and acting like starry-eyed children. When O'Leary went and started this season by batting .500 in the month of April, an embarrassing array of superlatives began appearing alongside his name.

He was good, Mark will give him that, no question. But what's probably just as relevant is that he's good-looking. He looks like he fell out of a Renaissance painting, all golden curls and blue eyes and excessive muscles. He really is very handsome, but in a way that feels obvious, like if you asked an artist with no imagination to draw you an attractive man.

And he's white—that still matters, even a decade after most base-ball teams integrated. There are plenty of people who *of course* aren't prejudiced, how *dare* you suggest it, but who are demonstrably reassured by the existence of talented white athletes. Eddie O'Leary must have seemed like an answer to their bigoted little prayers.

Mark turns his attention to the final section of clippings, by far the most abundant, those dating since O'Leary's early season trade from the Kansas City Athletics to the Robins. Mark knows what happened—everyone who pays even casual attention to New York sports knows what happened. News of the trade broke toward the end of a game; O'Leary, when informed by an opportunistic reporter in the locker room, proceeded to insult everyone on his new team. It's bad luck that television cameras were in the locker room, but that's all the more reason for O'Leary to have made an effort to control himself. He had to know that once the cameras picked up on his tirade, the newspapers would have no choice but to write about it, however loath sportswriters usually are to tarnish the heroes their readers demand.

Mark has little patience for people who can't muster up a minimum degree of self-control. They're spoiled children. Most people would be arrested, beaten, fired, or disowned if they didn't keep a tight leash on their emotions and reactions, but the Eddie O'Learys of the world think they can do whatever they please.

But a stray phrase catches his eye, something from a Kansas City paper—whoever's in charge of news clippings at the *Chronicle* has made a thorough job of it. It's the beginning of O'Leary's rant—or, rather, what preceded it. "That can't be," O'Leary told the reporter who had broken the news to him. "That can't be right."

Mark reads the rest of the article. O'Leary shared a house with three teammates, and every few weeks his widowed mother drove out from Omaha to see her only child play.

That can't be now seems to carry a decisively mournful note. O'Leary was having his life uprooted, his life as he knew it taken away, and it was happening on *television*.

Mark is being, he realizes with a shudder, *soft-hearted*—an alarming new tendency. The other day he found himself looking charitably upon the hellion upstairs whose violin practice used to make him long for the quiet of the grave. Whatever cracks in his psyche the past year left in its wake, there's plenty of room now for this sort of thing to creep in.

Still, though. This is an angle for the magazine feature Andy wants. A broken-hearted Eddie O'Leary whose game fell apart at the same time his life fell apart is a far fresher story than a badly behaved child who isn't playing his best for the straightforward reason that he resents his luckless new team; there are six of those articles sitting right now on his dining room table. And Mark remembers the palpable sense of doom that O'Leary had radiated, even through a television screen. The idea that this kid is grieving isn't entirely in Mark's head, even if O'Leary *is* a spoiled brat. On any other team, he'd be on his way to the minors to endure this slump in relative private, but the Robins are bad enough that one more lousy hitter won't make a difference. Whatever happens to O'Leary is going to happen in front of the nation's largest television market.

It occurs to Mark that what he's witnessing is a disaster. This is a shipwreck, a funeral pyre, a crumbling ruin. What's happening to Eddie O'Leary is an *end*. That's something Mark knows about; that's something Mark can write about.

Part II
MAY

CHAPTER TWO

At first Eddie thinks he must have misunderstood. When he's called into Miss Newbold's office, he's expecting, best-case scenario, to hear that he's been traded again, not that he really thinks any decent team could be persuaded to trade for a player who hasn't gotten a single base hit in the past fifteen games. More likely he's going to be sent down to Triple-A. Either way, he's expecting to be yelled at, because people don't get called into the owner's office for compliments and a good time.

What he isn't expecting is—

"Interviews?" Eddie repeats. He's sweaty, and he did something to his hamstring diving for that line drive in the fourth inning. All he really wants is to hit the showers, take some aspirin, and fall onto his lumpy hotel room mattress.

"A series of interviews," the owner says, very slowly, as if the problem here is that Eddie's too stupid to understand what she's saying, and not that the idea of Eddie sitting for a bunch of interviews is objectively nuts. "You'll talk to him from time to time throughout the season," she adds helpfully, in case Eddie doesn't understand what an interview is. "You can do that, can't you?"

Eddie'd like to know how divorced from reality this lady has to be to think that Eddie can't talk to reporters. Eddie's entire problem—well, part of his problem, honestly Eddie has a lot of problems—is that he talks too much to reporters. Ask anyone in the locker room. Ask anyone who reads the sports page in any of the city's newspapers.

Sportswriters are the reason everybody hates Eddie. Okay, Eddie's big mouth is the reason everybody hates Eddie, but he might have been able to keep it a secret if it hadn't been for the reporters.

"Okay," Eddie says. "What do you want me to say?" Because that's the point, isn't it? They must have some reason to ask Eddie, of all people, when the roster is stuffed with guys who'd love the chance for some good press while also getting their bar tab picked up. The team must want him to deliver some canned lines.

The owner frowns, like Eddie's being slow. Constance Newbold and her sister inherited majority ownership of the New York Robins when their father dropped dead about five minutes after the expansion draft—a perfectly reasonable reaction to finding out what kind of players he'd been saddled with. The younger sister ran off to Paris or someplace where they've never even heard of baseball and is therefore living the dream of everyone associated with the Robins. As far as Eddie can tell, Connie Newbold hasn't smiled once since inheriting the team, and he can't blame her. She's about forty, has a Katharine Hepburn accent that he did not know people had in real life, and every time Eddie sees her, he wants to straighten a tie he isn't wearing.

Eddie turns to the other person in the room, the head of public relations, looking for help. He really wishes the manager were here, because even though Tony Ardolino hasn't been sober for five consecutive minutes during the two weeks that Eddie's been in New York, he'd at least be somebody else in a uniform.

The PR man clears his throat. "You're happy to be here, you love being a part of this team, New York is a great city, you see a real future for the Robins," he says, not looking up from his notebook.

"Okay." Eddie still has about a dozen questions and twice as many comments, but he bites them all back. He's been biting a lot of things back, which is pretty much a brand-new experience for him, and not one he cares for. "Which paper?" He hopes it isn't the *Post*.

One of the *Post*'s columnists has been tearing Eddie to shreds ever since the trade was announced. To be fair, every sports columnist and beat writer in the tristate area has spent the past two weeks tearing Eddie to shreds. *Eddie* has spent the past two weeks tearing Eddie to shreds. That ghoul at the *Post* seems to really be enjoying himself, though.

"The *Chronicle*."

Eddie frowns. "George Allen?" George has to be eighty. He's been writing about baseball since 1909. He wears a bowler hat and a pair of suspenders that pull his pants up to his armpits. He's interviewed everybody from Babe Ruth to Jackie Robinson, and Eddie can't imagine why he'd willingly sit down for an interview with the likes of Eddie O'Leary, can't imagine why he'd want to.

"No," the owner says, all slow and patient, like Eddie's dumb for asking. "His name is Mark Bailey." The PR guy's pen has gone suspiciously still, probably because he's never heard of Bailey, and neither has Eddie.

Eddie knows better than to ask what the hell is going on, so he just grits his teeth, says "Yes, ma'am," and returns to a locker room that falls ominously silent as soon as he walks in.

When the reporter doesn't show up after the next game, Eddie lets himself hope that the plans fell through. In his mind, the phrase *series of interviews* has taken on the same gloomy cadence as *rain delay* and *batting slump* and *strained hamstring*.

The next afternoon, Eddie doesn't get on base, but he pulls off a pretty slick double play with the second baseman. Buddy Rosenthal might hate Eddie's guts and certainly doesn't have a civil word to spare for him, but he's a goddamn professional and throws the ball where it needs to go. A couple more double plays like that, and maybe he'll start speaking to Eddie in something other than grunts, but Eddie's not getting his hopes up.

The win that they manage to eke out owes more to pitching and fielding than it does to hitting, and some of that fielding was Eddie's, so he's in something that might pass for a good mood when the reporters corner him in the locker room. The reporters are in a good mood, too, a Robins win a rare enough occurrence that it must give some variety to their days.

But when Eddie beckons Rosenthal over—which is what he'd have done for his second baseman in Kansas City, and what anyone would do when they're congratulated on some fielding that was half somebody else's work—Rosenthal *walks away*.

The silent treatment is Eddie's punishment for what he said to the press after getting traded, and he knows he deserves it—he's seen guys get worse punishments for doing less, and the silent treatment is almost quaintly old-fashioned. He should be able to handle it, but instead he's desperately—*homesick* can't be the word, because what he wants is his old team, any team he's ever played on. He feels like his face is pressed up against the glass, watching something he's never going to get to have again.

So Eddie smiles at the press. He makes the usual noises about teamwork, and he thanks the fans. He's been repeating these phrases in front of the mirror on the theory that if he memorizes his lines, he's less likely to mention that nobody on this team can throw left-handed, or that the manager's office is blockaded by empty whiskey bottles.

All the things he isn't saying sit heavy in his mouth. He isn't used to holding his tongue like this. In Kansas City, he used to babble almost nonstop, but now the memory of being surrounded by people who wanted to hear him run his stupid mouth, or at least didn't hate him for it, feels like something he probably dreamed up. But he's trying to behave—he knows how badly he fucked up when he mouthed off to the press, and he knows his teammates all hate him, so he's really, really trying to make it up to them and *nothing is working*.

He bends to unlace his cleats, trying not to watch as one of the outfielders cheerfully whacks the starting pitcher with a rolled-up towel. The third-base coach comes over to take the towel and shove both players in the direction of the shower, then sneaks up behind the manager and smacks him with the towel. It's like every locker room Eddie's ever been in, except Eddie knows that if he tries to join in, everyone will either ignore him, or—worse—silently disperse, leaving him alone in the room, the smell of stale sweat and tobacco the only sign they were ever there.

When the cluster of reporters clears away from his stall, Eddie peels off his sweaty undershirt and is ready to retreat into the showers when he catches sight of an unfamiliar face. Well, it isn't so much the man's face that's unfamiliar as it is his suit. Eddie doesn't pay much attention to clothes beyond what it takes to make sure he looks reasonably normal, but there's something about this man's suit that stands out from the other reporters'. It's . . . softer, maybe? It's definitely better tailored. Also, he doesn't look like he's spent the past three hours sweating in a press box. He's leaning against the piece of plywood that makes up the end of a row of stalls. His feet are crossed at the ankles, and he's reading a book, not paying any attention whatsoever to the chaos that's unfolding around him.

Eddie's gaze travels up from the soft-looking gray wool to the man's face. He's a bit older than Eddie, maybe somewhere between twenty-five and thirty. His hair is a dark enough brown that it looks black under the shitty fluorescent light and is long enough that he's got to be two weeks overdue for a haircut. The glare off his glasses makes it so Eddie can't quite see his eyes.

But—he's pretty. Pretty enough that you can't help but notice. Well, Eddie can't help but notice, and Eddie's gotten really good at not noticing men, especially in locker rooms. Eddie is leading the National League in not noticing men in locker rooms.

Eddie's only been here for two weeks, so it isn't like he knows every single reporter on the Robins beat by sight, but he's never seen this guy, and he'd bet nobody else here has, either. There's nobody standing near him, which is strange, because sportswriters and athletes are both garbage at keeping their hands to themselves even under the best conditions, and anything like manners goes straight to hell in the locker room. It's almost like the other reporters are bouncing off some kind of invisible force field around this guy, like he's a magnet charged the wrong way. And he's not making any effort to fix things—he isn't introducing himself to the other reporters, he isn't asking ballplayers any questions.

There's a notebook and pen in the guy's shirt pocket, peeking out from his unbuttoned suit jacket. But he isn't writing anything down or even pretending to; he's just reading that book. He's definitely a reporter, though—Eddie's never seen anyone other than a newspaperman carry that type of notebook.

The man's gaze darts away from his book and toward Eddie's stall, so fast that Eddie wouldn't have noticed if he hadn't been looking. When he drops his book to his side and strolls over, it hits Eddie that he'd been waiting for the other reporters to leave.

Eddie perks up at the prospect of having a conversation with another human being, even if he really ought to know better than to be happy to see a reporter, even a handsome one. Especially a handsome one.

"Sorry to bother you," the man says, as if it isn't part of Eddie's job to make nice with reporters in the locker room. "But I'm Mark Bailey from the *Chronicle*. I thought I'd introduce myself." He holds out his hand, and Eddie is suddenly very conscious of the fact that he isn't wearing a shirt and his pants are unbuttoned, even though he doesn't usually think much about talking to reporters while he's half naked.

The man's hand is warm and dry. "Eddie O'Leary," Eddie says, like a complete fool, because obviously this guy knows who he is. Jesus Christ.

"A pleasure." Bailey does not sound particularly pleased.

With his free hand, Eddie brings his towel up to his chest in a deranged attempt at modesty. He forces himself to drop the towel. "What's that you're reading?" he asks, partly because that's another ten seconds he isn't fielding questions about the three times he struck out today and also because he kind of wants to know how good a book has to be to keep someone's attention in a loud locker room. Locker rooms are always a bit loud after a win, but when you lose as often as the Robins, a win means that all hell breaks loose.

Bailey blinks. "I . . . beg your pardon?"

"Never seen someone that into a book."

"Not a surprise, with the company you keep," Bailey says, snotty as anything, as he flicks a glance toward where Ardolino is pouring beer into the relief pitcher's mouth and two outfielders are having what looks like a slap fight regarding the radio station. They are, in fact, a bunch of idiots, but that doesn't mean it's any of Bailey's business to say so. Bailey seems to realize what he's said the minute it's left his mouth, and boy does Eddie know that feeling. "I only mean—"

"I know what you meant." Most reporters think ballplayers are stupid, but it's not every day they come right out and say so. He almost admires the balls on this guy.

"Wondered if you'd like to get some dinner?" Bailey asks.

At the word *dinner*, at least four of Eddie's teammates drop their conversations and don't even pretend not to be eavesdropping. Eddie isn't going to have dinner with a reporter. Hardly anybody has dinner with reporters, and Bailey should know that. A drink at the hotel bar during road trips, sure. Not dinner. And especially not Eddie, who's already gotten into enough trouble for blabbing to reporters. His teammates hate him plenty without thinking he's the kind of guy who actually wants attention from the press.

Eddie has to be careful, otherwise he's going to open his mouth and give this man five paragraphs of lunacy, starting with "You're pretty" and ending with "Are you always this bad at your job?" with maybe some "Can I touch your suit?" thrown in there to maximize the horror.

"No," Eddie says, which is enough. A single syllable, a complete sentence. He can't get himself into trouble with one word. Then he imagines his mother whacking him with a rolled-up newspaper in open despair at his manners, and he decides he'll have to manage a few more syllables. "No thank you, Mr. Bailey."

Bailey's eyebrows flicker, and for a minute Eddie thinks it's relief he sees on Bailey's face. Like maybe Bailey doesn't want to be involved in this any more than Eddie does. Bailey straightens his glasses, and his expression settles into something like neutral professionalism. "First, please call me Mark. Second, is there some other time that would be convenient for you? I was given to understand . . ."

Now even a couple reporters are watching this. Oh Jesus, the last thing Eddie needs is for anybody to write this down. The columnists will make a meal of it. Eddie O'Leary, who hasn't managed a single solitary base hit since getting traded to New York, thinks he's too good to talk to reporters. Alternatively: Eddie O'Leary, who told Kansas City reporters all about how much he didn't want to go to New York and referred to the Robins as a bunch of lazy drunks, is getting cozy with reporters again. There's no way he can win.

"Right," Eddie says. "Right. Okay." He'll say whatever it takes to get this over with. "Tomorrow. Morning."

Bailey hands him a business card, and Eddie—who doesn't have a pocket, who's barely even wearing pants, whose blush is currently extending down to his navel for the entire locker room to see—has no choice but to hold on to it.

"They're just trying to get some good press," Eddie's mom says, her voice crackling over a thousand miles of telephone wire. Usually if he shuts his eyes and pretends he isn't holding the phone receiver, he can imagine he's in his mom's kitchen, but tonight Omaha sounds just as far away as it actually is. "You're one of the biggest names on the team. All you have to do is cooperate, sweetie."

Eddie wants to argue with her, but he really is one of the better-known players on the team, primarily because even on a team as shitty as the Robins, he's a shining beacon of awfulness. If you're talking about the Robins, you can't help but talk about how Eddie O'Leary doesn't know how to hit a baseball anymore. That'll buy you some name recognition, all right.

Last season Eddie had been hailed as a rising star, a serious candidate for rookie of the year. At the beginning of this season, he was playing even better. He was brought here to give the Robins a chance, a future. And instead he's made the team even more of a joke.

Even last year, when things were going well, his roommates would hide the paper and unplug the television after bad games—and Kansas City had no shortage of those. This year he has a patch of hives under his collarbone and a tic in his left eye that are entirely the fault of the seven—*seven*—New York City newspapers that make crucifying him a daily event.

"I don't know," Eddie grumbles. "I don't know why they'd care about what kind of press I'm getting, since there's no way they're going to want to keep me around if I keep playing like this."

"Do I really need to list all the light-hitting shortstops who've had perfectly respectable careers? I hope not, because it's late and I want to go to bed."

"Sorry, Mama," Eddie mumbles. His situation with the Robins is more complicated than his mother is making out. Sure, good short-stops get a little leeway, but not if everyone on the team can't stand them. "I think they're going to make fun of me. This is supposed to be my diary. It'll be easy to make me look like a dumb hick."

His mother sighs. "Edward James O'Leary, why in heaven's name would the team even want that?"

"I don't know." Eddie might feel better if he did know. "Maybe they figure they can fill the stands if people come to boo at me?"

His mother is silent long enough that he knows she's considering whether he's right. The more he thinks about it—Mark Bailey reading that book in the locker room like he was above it all, not even bothering to make conversation with anyone else—the less he likes it. He's probably being paranoid, but after the incident in Kansas City—when a bunch of reporters he had palled around with and played cards with on road trips, whose kids he had signed baseballs for, ambushed him for the sake of good copy—he doesn't think he'll ever not be paranoid about the press. A little bit of paranoia might have kept him from being in this position in the first place.

That night, he stares at the cracked ceiling of his hotel room, unable to fall asleep. He's spent the past two weeks trying to figure out if the problem is the mattress or the dripping faucet or the fact that even in the middle of the goddamn night there are cars honking in this nightmare of a city. Or maybe it's just the knowledge that he's managed to fuck up his career after only one year and one month in the major leagues. That'd make it hard for anyone to sleep.

He's earning just enough to rent a place of his own, but he hasn't unpacked, let alone looked for somewhere to live other than this shitty hotel across the street from the stadium. Mostly that's because he's sure he's going to be sent down any minute now, but also because he doesn't want to hang his six shirts in the empty closet next to his three suits. He doesn't want to deal with the two suitcases that house his entire life.

Objectively, the hotel isn't bad. Sure, it saw its prime sometime around 1928, and the elevators are a bit scary, but it's about twice as nice as the stadium, which has honest-to-God mice romping about without a care in the world and a patch of mushrooms growing in the showers. There are some other players living here, some with their wives, which might be nice if anyone on the team was interested in giving Eddie the time of day.

Really, he ought to be able to fall asleep.

He's averaged maybe six hours of sleep a night since moving to New York. He never had trouble sleeping in Kansas City or in either of the towns where he played in the minors. He's always been the kind of person who puts his head on the pillow and just falls asleep. He figured that was because he was doing something right—fresh air, clear conscience, plenty of exercise, no more than one drink a night—and that people who couldn't sleep were making some obvious mistake.

Now sleep is as elusive as his swing. Maybe if he could remember how to fall asleep, he'd remember how to hit the ball. But things that he's always counted on are completely out of his grasp.

CHAPTER THREE

They hadn't set a time to meet, mainly because Eddie had been an asshole about it: he fled into the showers and then hid in the trainer's room until he was sure the reporters had all cleared out. The entire reason Bailey had given him that business card was for Eddie to call and arrange a time and place to meet, but instead Eddie had procrastinated and delayed, letting the card silently judge him from inside the suit pocket where he ultimately stashed it, until finally it was midnight, far too late to call, and the decision had been taken out of his hands.

When Eddie gets up in the morning, he's greeted immediately by the too-familiar awareness that he's been a dick about something. He dresses as quickly as possible, expecting to find Bailey waiting around at the stadium for him.

Instead, when the elevator doors open onto the hotel lobby, the first thing Eddie sees is Mark Bailey sitting on a shabby velveteen sofa, a cigarette in one hand and in the other the same book he had been reading yesterday. He must have had one eye on the elevators, because he has that book closed and his eyes on Eddie before Eddie has both feet on the worn maroon carpet.

"Mr. O'Leary," Bailey says. He gets to his feet. Today's suit is even softer-looking than yesterday's. Eddie's almost positive that if he really gives it his all, he can manage not to ask what it's made of or whether he can touch it.

Eddie is extremely aware that he ought to apologize for failing to call, but he can't figure out what words to use that won't make him sound like a gibbering fool and also won't be a torrent of chaos. It's been over two weeks now since he's had a conversation with anyone other than his mom. A few days ago, the elevator operator asked him if he thought it was going to rain, and Eddie responded with an enthusiastic diatribe against clouds, and it wasn't until he was really hitting his stride that he realized the poor man was just making small talk, and Eddie was making it impossible for him to do his job. Eddie, mortified, took the stairs for the next two days.

"First names," Eddie says, because that's safe enough, and they had agreed on that last night.

Mark shrugs one shoulder, and in the same movement checks his watch. It's a nice watch—leather band, round face—but inexplicably the band hangs loose on Mark's wrist, like he doesn't know you can poke extra holes in watchbands to make them fit right.

"It's half past ten," Mark says, and Eddie drags his gaze away from the fine bones of the reporter's wrist. "Have you eaten breakfast?" Eddie shakes his head. "Excellent. Neither have I. What time do you need to be at the stadium?"

"Three." And look at that, Eddie's gone thirty whole seconds without saying anything that'll get him sent down to Triple-A or arrested for indecent conduct. The trick is single syllables. He's almost proud of himself for having cracked the code.

"Plenty of time, then." Mark leads the way outside, not checking to see if Eddie's following.

A plain black car is waiting at the curb, its engine running. Mark opens the back door. "After you," he says when Eddie fails to move. Inexplicably embarrassed, Eddie climbs in and slides across the leather seat. Mark gives the driver an address Eddie doesn't recognize—not that he recognizes any New York addresses. The driver is wearing a uniform, which means this is a livery cab or a hired car of some sort.

Bailey answers the question before Eddie can decide whether to ask it.

"I didn't want to leave a cab sitting outside with the meter running all morning," Bailey says, crossing one long leg over the other and leaning back in his seat. "And I wasn't going to put Eddie O'Leary on the subway."

Eddie, unable to come up with a single syllable to get his point across, mumbles something that even he doesn't understand, but apparently the word *cost* is intelligible, because Mark answers.

"Oh, if the *Chronicle* wants to send me traipsing up and down the length of Manhattan, they can foot the bill," he says easily, but something about the way he says it—*traipsing*—makes Eddie think this story wasn't Mark's idea. He remembers that flicker of relief he thought he had seen on Mark's face yesterday when Eddie refused to go out to dinner.

"You don't want to do this story," Eddie blurts out before he can think better of it. God fucking damn it, he was doing so good at not talking.

"Oh, so you do talk. Thank God. I was starting to think I'd have to make this all up from scratch, and fiction really isn't my strength."

Eddie's face heats, because the entire reason anyone knows his name is because he talks too much. "You know I talk," he says, his teeth clenched.

"Mmm," Mark hums. "I know you talk when you're upset, or at least you did that one time. But I've read approximately three hundred articles about you, and there aren't more than six direct quotes. I hardly know what to make of it. It's as if you learned to talk the day you got traded to New York."

The truth is that a sympathetic Kansas City press—overjoyed to have bona fide talent to write about—had kept Eddie's dumber remarks out of newsprint.

"The more I think about it," Mark goes on, "the more I'm inclined to discount how anyone behaves when they've just been told—on national television, no less—that they've been traded across the country, to a new home, a new team, effective immediately."

Either Mark Bailey is a shitty liar, or he thinks Eddie's too dumb to know when he's being humored. But Mark is one of the only people who's bothered making excuses for Eddie. Jack—Eddie's best friend and the Kansas City Athletics' second baseman—had sighed and said that he always knew Eddie's hot temper was going to get the best of him. Eddie's mother had said that there wasn't any use crying over spilled milk, just like she did every other time Eddie got in trouble over the previous twenty-two years. Both of them were kind about it, but neither acted like they might have done the same thing in Eddie's position. Eddie kind of doesn't care if Mark believes what he's saying. He's just stupidly grateful that someone can use their imagination to understand what Eddie had been going through.

"Wasn't national television," Eddie mumbles. "Just Kansas City. And New York." Because, of course, it had happened after a game against the Yankees, which is probably why there had been television cameras in the clubhouse in the first place. "And it happens all the time." This isn't true—usually players learn about trades in the privacy of the manager's office or a quiet corner of the locker room. They don't get told by a bunch of reporters.

"Upheaval is difficult," Mark says.

"Normal for ballplayers. And a lot of other folks, too."

Mark gives a skeptical little sniff, and Eddie has the sense that this sniff is the first time Mark's been sincere all day. "That doesn't make it easy."

"New York is a great city. The Robins have a lot of potential," Eddie says, remembering belatedly that he has a script. He tries to sound like he believes it. It's kind of true, after all: The Robins are an expansion team cobbled together from other teams' spare parts.

Nearly everyone's too old, too young, or not particularly good. Even considering that, their odds of getting anywhere near the pennant at some point in the next five years are better than the A's. Last year, the Kansas City Athletics had been second to last in the league; they had, in fact, spent most of the past decade being awful, even back when they were in Philadelphia.

But Mark isn't writing any of this down. Eddie's memorized lines have gone to waste.

"It's a long season," Eddie says, because you can say that at any point in any baseball conversation and not sound *too* dumb.

"Mmm," Mark says, shrugging noncommittally.

"Who do you root for?" Eddie asks, grasping at a chance to steer the conversation away from his own abysmal playing.

"The Senators, mostly."

Eddie winces. The Senators came dead last in the league last year and the year before that. They've been terrible for Eddie's entire life and probably Mark's entire life, too. "Sorry to hear it."

Mark looks briefly astonished and then lets out a laugh. It's sharp, a whipcrack of a laugh, and it might have sounded mean if not for how pleased he looks. "It's pretty grim. When I moved here, I started going to Giants games, but they were never really *my* team." There's an emphasis on *my*, and the smile drops from his face as suddenly as it appeared.

"At least you're familiar with the stadium," Eddie says, because the Robins are playing at the Polo Grounds, where the Giants played before they moved to California.

"More's the pity," Mark murmurs, and Eddie snorts. He's played in a lot of run-down ballparks, but the Polo Grounds is uniquely decayed. It's held together by rust and pigeon shit. Eddie has yet to find a single light bulb in the place that doesn't flicker.

"And God only knows if we're getting a new stadium," Eddie grumbles before remembering this goes against the script. "I mean, I'm happy to play—"

"It's a hellhole," Mark says, waving a dismissive hand. "It was already a hellhole five years ago. And I will never understand how that old man failed to get the city to give him a new stadium, but now he's dead, and we can't ask him. Anyway, I'm here to talk about you." With that, he produces a faint little smile that for some reason makes Eddie's mouth go dry.

~~

"How do you feel about eggs?" Mark asks as the car pulls to a stop.

Eddie doesn't answer, because he doesn't know how he possibly could. Does he have feelings about eggs? Does anyone? Mark doesn't seem to expect an answer, though, so Eddie just follows him through a glass door into what's obviously a diner. It's the same as any diner Eddie's ever been in, whether in Boston or Omaha or West Palm Beach: vinyl booths, flecked Formica tables, the smell of fried food, aproned waitresses shouting at the cooks in a language that Eddie has been told is Greek.

They sit down and a waitress drops off two worn-looking cardboard menus printed in smudged blue ink.

"We'll need to talk once a week for a few minutes before I write the diary," Mark says after they order. "But since there won't be time for you to approve each week's column, I thought we ought to set some rules about what topics are off-limits."

Eddie narrows his eyes. This feels like a trap.

"Of course," Mark goes on, "you can always change your mind. If there's something you realize later on that you don't want me to write about, you can let me know."

It still feels like a trap. "Why do you want to publish my fake diary when you could pick someone who the fans actually like?"

"That's what makes you interesting," Mark says immediately. "That's what's going to get people to read it. We have a chance to turn their expectations around."

"You think that anything you write is going to make people like me?" Eddie asks like the most pathetic person in the world.

Mark, to his credit, neither laughs in his face nor outright lies. "Maybe. It could happen. But what's more interesting is that you're having a hard time."

Eddie refrains from rolling his eyes at the understatement.

"You had ten votes for rookie of the year," Mark goes on. "A hundred runs batted in, a batting average that never dropped below—"

"Stop," Eddie pleads. It almost physically hurts to be reminded of all that, knowing that it's gone.

Mark pauses with his coffee cup halfway to his mouth. "Not to be too blunt, but either you're going to get your game back, or you aren't, and either way people will want to read about it."

"Jesus Christ, you don't mince words," Eddie says.

"Do you require words to be minced?" Mark asks, an eyebrow arched, exasperation plain in his voice.

Maybe Eddie really is dumb, because only now is it hitting him that Mark Bailey just doesn't like him. He ought to expect it by now. His team can't stand him, and for good reason. The fans boo him when he walks to the plate, for even better reason. What does it matter if one reporter doesn't like him compared to all that?

"No," Eddie says. "I don't. What you said is nothing I don't think to myself a couple times every hour. And while we're not mincing words, I'm not going to talk about the other players' private lives or anything they do off the field."

"Fair. I don't expect you to. I'm not writing a gossip column. Frankly, plenty of people *are* writing gossip columns, and they have that beat covered." He glances at his notebook, then flips back a couple of pages. "A photographer for the paper will come to the stadium tomorrow to get a few shots that look candid. It shouldn't take long." He gestures vaguely across the table. "You photograph well."

Eddie feels his cheeks heat. He knows he—photographs well. He's even used to having it pointed out. Last summer someone at *Sports Illustrated* wrote a paragraph about the wonders of his *biceps* for fuck's sake, and Jack read it out loud to the locker room while Eddie pelted him with dirty socks and the rest of the team catcalled him. He doesn't know why it feels any different for Mark to let on that he's noticed Eddie's objectively not awful-looking.

When he tears his gaze away from the table, he finds Mark looking at him critically. "What color do you call your eyes?"

"Hazel?" he says, as if it isn't perfectly obvious that his eyes are, in fact, hazel.

"They aren't blue," Mark says, sounding bizarrely put out by this. "I'm positive that they're blue on baseball cards and in the *Sports Illustrated* photographs from last year." He leans forward, and Eddie fights the urge to hide behind his hands. "The dimples are real enough. But why did they color your eyes?"

Eddie wants to laugh. Is this guy blaming him for not having the right color eyes? That, at least, isn't Eddie's fault. "I guess they thought blue eyes look better?"

"A travesty. You should sue." He sounds so vicious about it that it takes Eddie a full thirty seconds to realize he's being paid a compliment. A weird compliment, but a compliment.

"Your eyes actually are blue," Eddie supplies helpfully. Also, Mark's lashes are very long. Extravagantly long, really. They nearly brush his cheeks. He's on the verge of saying so when a shadow falls across the table.

"When are you going to start hitting that ball, sonny?" says an old man, one bony hand clutching a cane.

Over the last two weeks, Eddie's gotten a lot of practice answering that question, and this man phrased it much more delicately than the people who heckle him from the stands, so Eddie gives him his best smile. It's a good smile: he's practiced it in front of the mirror to the point that Jack makes gagging noises whenever Eddie so much as grins, and his mother has an entire lecture series called "Vanity Is a Deadly Sin." But honestly his face is one of the only things he has going for him these days, and he's not going to handicap himself.

"I wish I knew, sir," Eddie responds. "I promise I'm trying."

The man points a gnarled finger awfully close to Eddie's face. "See that you do, young man." There's a threat in there, as if Eddie will find him lurking in an alley with a couple of his geriatric buddies and they'll take him out. All he says is "Yes, sir," and then signs a menu for the man's granddaughter.

"You get that a lot?" Mark asks.

But before Eddie can say that no, he only gets it every time he leaves the hotel, someone else approaches the table. This is how it always works: the first person loosens something up in the crowd that lets them convince themselves that normal rules of decent behavior are suspended, and then they start descending on him in droves.

Well, not droves, maybe, but a noticeable trickle. People know his name and his face, and in a city of seven million people, there are a hell of a lot of baseball fans. This is another reason he didn't want to come to New York. There's nobody on the Kansas City Athletics who gets this sort of attention, not at home or on the road. Eddie's skin crawls at the knowledge that he's constantly being watched, that his littlest action might become news. And if that isn't bad enough, here he is—idiot of idiots—deliberately putting himself in front of a reporter.

"Let the man eat his food before it gets cold," Mark says, using the sort of voice that cuts through chatter without actually being loud. It isn't rude so much as it holds the promise of future rudeness. The woman who's closest to the table hesitates. "Please, ma'am, go back to your seat." Mark flicks his hand in a delicate shooing gesture, something that would have Eddie's mother crossing herself and semi-apoplectic if he tried it himself. It works, though, and the people crowding around their booth retreat.

Mark, he realizes, is not a very nice man. It isn't so much a question of whether or not he likes Eddie—he plainly doesn't, but Eddie has the distinct impression that Mark doesn't like much. But he still got rid of the people who were bothering Eddie, and was annoyed with them on Eddie's behalf. That's the closest thing to kindness that Eddie's experienced in weeks.

Eddie flashes the lady his best smile, as if that'll make up for losing out on a chance to complain about him to his face, and when he turns back to the table, he finds it covered in food—an omelet for Mark and three fried eggs with potatoes and sausages for Eddie. "Next time I'll be sure to take you someplace dark," Mark sniffs, apparently more irritated by the fans than Eddie is. "And you can sit with your back to the room."

Something pleased and warm flares up inside Eddie at the *I'll take you* and the *someplace dark* and even the *next time*. He can put those phrases together just a little differently and come up with the image of him and Mark in a bar that's safe, the kind of place he knew how to find back home and can never, ever visit in New York because nothing in this goddamn city will ever be private enough. Eddie takes a huge bite of potato hash so he can't say any of that aloud.

He's homesick, sure, but there has to be a better word for leaving a whole part of yourself behind, just as surely as he left his car and his winter clothes. With nothing he can do about it and nobody he can talk to about it, he feels like that part of himself is barely real. It's not even about the sex—well, it's a little bit about the sex. But he didn't even have that much sex in Kansas City. It was just that he knew where to go and how to be careful. He had to keep that side of him locked up tight and out of view, but at least he knew it was there.

Now that he doesn't even have that much, he feels pitifully aware of how little that was in the first place, and how grateful he had been to have it. He's angry to be without it, and angry that he couldn't expect more, and angry not to have anyone to complain to. It's too much anger, and sometimes it comes out in all the wrong ways, but he can't explain that to anyone, either.

CHAPTER FOUR

Eddie's gotten into the habit of doing laps around the outside of the stadium, because there isn't anybody to bother him—or, worse, *not* bother him. After that, he heads into the stands and runs up and down the stairs, trying not to pay attention to the haunted-house quality of the empty stadium.

All empty stadiums are a bit creepy: too quiet, too vast. But at the Polo Grounds, that silence is sometimes punctuated by a shriek he'd like to think is simply from the feral cat colony that lives under the bleachers, or an ominous creaking sound that might be one of the rafters about to fall down or might be actual, literal ghosts. There's a patch of mud in the outfield that won't go away no matter what the grounds crew tries; Eddie is prepared to believe that it's cursed.

This is the sort of thing he'd usually ask about. *Hey, what's that shrieking sound?* And then his teammates would make fun of him, maybe prank him by dressing up as ghosts. He'd basically have no peace for the rest of the season, possibly the rest of his career. It would be fun, in a very stupid way, and also he probably wouldn't be afraid of the weird noises anymore.

When he's finished running, he wipes his face with the hem of his shirt, summons up some courage, and walks into the clubhouse. Nobody pays him any mind. Price—one of the starting pitchers—is doing a crossword puzzle while the catcher sits on the arm of his chair and says things like "Is that really how you spell antelope?" Rosenthal (the second baseman, who's good by Robins standards and adequate by the standards of any other team) and Varga (the first baseman; the less said about him, the better) are playing a card game that nobody else knows the rules to. Third baseman Luis Serrano is writing a letter. The left and right fielders are asleep in a pair of armchairs that look not only older than Eddie, but older than the stadium. Nobody even turns their head when he walks into the room.

Road trips are a special kind of hell when nobody's talking to you. Usually, the irritation of being away from home is offset by getting to have fun with people who are, sort of, friends.

Eddie's first road trip with the Robins is a solid week of nobody on the team talking to him beyond what's strictly necessary. Well, the batting coach has a whole lot to say, none of it doing either of them a lick of good. Eddie's pretty sure that if he doesn't fix his game in the next week or two, they'll both be out of a job.

"He had the most gorgeous natural swing in professional ball," Eddie overhears the batting coach complaining to the trainer as he's getting changed after a game against the Reds. "Did you see him play last year? Fucking beautiful. And now it's gone. Vanished. How does that even happen?"

"At least he can still field," the trainer says.

"But for how long? You know how it goes."

Eddie knows how it goes, too. A pitcher loses a pitch and, with it, the ability to throw a player out. Someone can't run, and all of a sudden he also can't stop hitting pop flies. Maybe it's physical—a series of injuries having a domino effect. Maybe it's psychological—a lack of confidence spilling over into other areas of the game. All Eddie knows is that he's sitting here, waiting for the other shoe to drop, and so is the rest of the team. The rest of the city. They all know he'll be sent down as soon as he can't field anymore. At this point, Eddie's almost made peace with it. His mother has started mentioning that it isn't too late for Eddie to go to college.

After the last game in Cincinnati, Eddie goes by himself to a hamburger joint and gets some dinner, which he picks at disconsolately and then forces himself to eat, because starving isn't going to help his situation. But, Christ, what he wouldn't give for a home-cooked meal. Or any non-restaurant meal, really. He's seriously considering finding a supermarket and buying a loaf of bread and a jar of peanut butter. Even in New York he only has more restaurant food to look forward to. There's no sense in looking for an apartment with an actual kitchen when he could be sent down any minute.

When he gets back to the hotel lobby, he hears his name. It's the older reporter from the *Chronicle*, George Allen. Eddie's seen him around, obviously, but this is the first time Allen's tried to talk to him. He's sitting on an uncomfortable-looking bench that's stationed between the elevators and the gift shop, which is probably prime territory for staking out ballplayers who run down to the lobby for a pack of cigarettes.

Eddie sits beside him. "Want a cookie?" he asks, because he did stop at a grocery store after all, but he bought a package of chocolate chip cookies instead of sandwich ingredients, thinking he didn't want to find out what would happen to a loaf of bread in his suitcase.

Allen waves the cookies away. "Want to give me a line about what it's like to play for the Robins?"

"I wouldn't know. Not sure you can call what I'm doing out there playing."

It's not a good joke, but Allen laughs anyway and scribbles something down. His hands look arthritic and are covered with age spots, but that pencil moves across the paper with a quickness. Eddie hopes he doesn't sound like too much of an asshole or an idiot in tomorrow's paper. As usual, this occurs to him after the words are out of his mouth. Oh well.

"Do you have kids?" Eddie asks, because that's usually enough to get people going, and what he really wants is to pretend he's having a conversation, pretend he's sharing space with someone who gives a shit. And if this guy's talking about his kids or his grandkids, then there's less of an opportunity for Eddie to say something dumb. Maybe he'll have pictures in his wallet and he'll show them to Eddie.

"No." Allen raises his eyebrows.

"Grandkids?" Eddie asks.

"Don't usually have those without having kids."

Right. Eddie's face heats.

"I used to have a cat," Allen says.

"I wish I had a cat," Eddie says ruefully. "Or a dog." *Or friends*, he doesn't add, because he has some self-respect.

Allen gives him a narrow look. "It'll be all right, kid." Eddie wishes he believed it.

The reporter gets to his feet, struggling even as he ignores Eddie's offered arm, and leaves Eddie alone in the lobby, where he watches his teammates come back in pairs and groups, all pretending not to notice him sitting there alone.

The following afternoon, they leave Cincinnati on a flight for Pittsburgh. And that's another thing Eddie doesn't care for about the Robins: They fly damn near everywhere. They don't even take the train to Boston, and they're hardly even in the air long enough for a drink during that flight. Eddie thinks they could have spent some of that travel budget on hiring a real manager instead of dragging Tony

Ardolino out of retirement to manage the team in between benders, but what does Eddie know.

Halfway through the flight, he finishes his paperback and digs around in his bag for something else to read. He finds a copy of the *Chronicle*, rolled into a tube and shoved into the bottom of his bag. He had bought it at the airport when they were leaving New York, curious about what kind of work appears under Mark Bailey's byline.

He flips to the sports section and scans the articles, looking for Mark's name. It isn't there. What *is* there is the play-by-play for last Thursday's game against the Braves, during which Eddie went 0 for 4. What's also there is the list of league batting averages, and Eddie makes himself slide his finger down the list of names and ever lower numbers until he finds his own plummeting average. And if that's what it was a few days earlier, it's only worse now.

A hand lands on top of the paper.

"Don't," Luis says.

On the plane, he always sits next to Luis Serrano, the third baseman, his road-trip roommate, and one of the few people on the team not to walk in the opposite direction when Eddie approaches, even if that's mostly because he doesn't speak enough English to keep up with clubhouse drama.

Luis taps his temple. "It gets in your head and makes it worse."

"Could I be worse, though? Could I really?"

He's not sure whether Luis understands this, but he's also not sure whether it matters, because Luis simply takes the entire sports section away from him and casually sits on it.

Across the aisle, Ardolino and one of the pitchers, both visibly drunk, are flirting with a stewardess. Eddie grimaces. It's not that he's opposed to the flirting; both men are married, but Eddie had finished being shocked by philandering ballplayers while he was still in the minors. And it isn't that he's opposed to the drinking, even though this likely means that tomorrow there'll be a couple players on the field with hangovers.

Eddie's real problem is that he grew up with Tony Ardolino's rookie baseball card as one of his prized possessions. He can't help but take it almost personally that this guy cheats on his wife, drinks so much that he as good as hands wins to the opposing team, and doesn't seem even slightly interested in tinkering with the batting order or pitching rotation or doing anything else that a manager might do to help a losing team.

When Eddie was eight or nine, his parents took him to see a White Sox game while they were visiting cousins in Chicago. Eddie remembers every hit Ardolino got that day, every catch he made. Ardolino spent the first half of his career on a steady ascent, but then came the bar fights and arrests and a series of trades. Then there were the dirty slides, the bench-clearing brawls, the well-earned reputation as someone better known for violence than talent. He's barely forty now; he could still be playing. Instead he threw his entire career away.

The real problem is that Ardolino sets the example for the whole team. If Tony Ardolino, who played in every All-Star game in the second half of the forties, is drinking and taking pills and staying out all night with strange women, then why shouldn't they all?

At the back of the plane, one of the pitchers is loudly bragging about some woman he went home with last night. Eddie's heard it all before, but today it's hitting him hard. He'd like to think it's because he doesn't want women being talked about that way (and he doesn't, but if he tore himself up about it, he'd literally never get anything done in professional baseball). It's more because he knows that as soon as someone caves in on the silent treatment and starts talking to him, it'll only be a matter of time before everyone notices that Eddie doesn't join in on that kind of conversation. Some married guys don't, but for a single man to sit that out? Unthinkable. In Kansas City, he had Jack to run interference. Here he has nobody.

"Forage grass, six letters," Sam Price says from the seat diagonally in front of Eddie. He's an aging left-handed pitcher who was an ace in the Negro League before spending most of the fifties in the White Sox bullpen. He has a crossword puzzle open in front of him. Every team has at least one guy who's always doing a crossword puzzle, usually with the help of anyone who's in earshot, and on the Robins, it's Price. "First letters *R-E*, last letter maybe *P*."

"*Redtop*," Eddie says, startled to actually know a crossword answer. "It's definitely *redtop*. I grew up in . . ." He realizes his mistake before he finishes the sentence.

Price doesn't turn around to look at Eddie. He doesn't write in the correct letters. Instead he folds the paper up and puts it in his bag, like the puzzle isn't worth doing anymore.

Eddie's face goes hot, and he knows that anyone who's looking—and from the sudden quiet that's fallen over this part of the plane, he's sure everyone who's awake is looking—will see how embarrassed he is. It's his own fault, and now he's made it so Price can't even do his puzzle.

When the plane lands, there's some problem with the bus or the hotel, and Ardolino starts making calls from an airport pay phone. Most of the team disappears into the nearest bar. Eddie, knowing he won't be welcome, waits awkwardly near the bank of telephones. He kind of can't believe he's listening to his childhood idol loudly complain about hotel taxes. As he watches, Ardolino hangs up the phone and fumbles in his pockets, obviously looking for another nickel, swearing loudly enough that a woman walking past covers her kid's ears. Eddie takes pity on him and digs a couple of coins out of his own pocket and hands them over, then goes to the newsstand and changes two dollars into nickels in case Ardolino needs more. It's not like Eddie has anything better to do.

When the team finally gets to the hotel in Pittsburgh, it's late, but Eddie hears doors opening and shutting up and down the hallway. Some guys are going out. Ardolino doesn't pay attention to things like curfews, so nobody'll get fined, no matter how late they stay out. Luis, exhausted by his rookie year, heads straight to bed. Eddie knows that's what he ought to do as well, but he can't face the prospect of another night spent staring at another strange ceiling.

He grabs his wallet and shuts the door quietly behind him so as not to wake Luis. There's a bank of phone booths along one lobby wall, and Eddie slides inside one.

As he drops the coins—so many coins, what is he thinking— through the slot, he knows it's a bad idea. As he reaches into his pocket and then dials the numbers inked along the bottom of the business card, he still knows it's a bad idea. But Eddie O'Leary hasn't ever been deterred by bad ideas, and he isn't going to start tonight. Calling reporters at—he checks his watch and tries to remember which way the time zones go, then gives up—past midnight from public pay phones isn't even the worst idea he's had today.

After four rings, he hears a gravelly "Hello?"

"Mark? This is Eddie O'Leary."

Two beats of silence. "Do you have any idea what time it is?"

"Are you a sportswriter?"

"Because it's half past twelve," Mark goes on, ignoring Eddie. "And you're in Pittsburgh, where it's also half past twelve, so that isn't any kind of excuse."

"Were you asleep?"

A beat. "No. But I could have been."

"Okay, okay. I'm an asshole. Can we just agree about that and move on? Are you a sportswriter? I didn't see your byline in the sports section."

"No. Of course not. Good God, do I seem like a sportswriter?"

Eddie thinks about the nice suits, the too-long hair, the book. "Not really. But what are you, then?"

There's a hesitation. "I write for the arts section."

"Why don't you sound sure about that?"

"I haven't been doing much reporting lately, not that it's any of your business. I write a book review every month or so, that's all."

Every reporter Eddie's ever seen—and, granted, that's only sports reporters and people in the movies—is writing constantly, either scribbling in notepads or clattering away on typewriters or filing stories over the phone. "You're practically unemployed," Eddie says.

"*You're* practically unemployed," Mark retorts.

"Why isn't a sportswriter doing this diary?" Eddie isn't even sure why he cares. It's not like he expects sportswriters to go easy on him. "Are you going to write something about how I'm too dumb to read a menu and I looked down the waitress's blouse? A hick in the Big Apple?"

"Where on earth did you get that idea? I'm not going to write any of those things, for any number of reasons, only one of which is that you *can* read the menu and you *didn't* look down the waitress's blouse." He pauses. "Did you?"

"No!"

"Anyway, that whole premise is boring. I'm already bored. Look. The first diary is in tomorrow's paper. You can see for yourself that I'm not up to anything sinister."

"Okay," Eddie says dubiously. "Sorry I called so late."

"I'm never asleep before two," Mark says after a beat. "My body thinks it's in California. Or maybe it's Alaska. I looked it up once."

Eddie has no idea how or why Alaska enters into it, or whether Mark is up late having fun or just tossing and turning like Eddie does.

"Look," Mark says. "I know you don't trust me, and I can't blame you. But in this instance, you have nothing to worry about." He sounds irritated, like he can't believe what he's been forced to say. "Now go to sleep."

"Good night, Mark." Eddie feels weird about having put himself in a position where he's saying good night to a stranger over the phone, and even weirder about how nice it feels.

"Good night, Eddie."

Eddie listens to his mother talk about the church fundraiser and Mrs. Mulligan cheating at bridge and how the neighbor's dog keeps leaving messes on the lawn. It's an almost completely one-sided conversation, with Eddie only interjecting occasional murmurs of understanding. It's exactly the type of conversation they'd have at dinner if he were home, and as he eats the cold sandwich he bought at the deli near the stadium, he can imagine his mother at the table across from him, and he can pretend that he's eating her potato casserole and that one of the cats is batting a paw against his leg.

"Mama," he says when she starts to wind down. "You know this man from the paper who's doing that diary? Do you think you could find some articles he's written for magazines?"

"You know they have libraries in New York, Eddie."

Eddie knows. Yesterday, after the team got back to New York, Eddie bought a guidebook and spent the afternoon walking around the city, looking at things he's supposed to find interesting. The main branch of the library looks like the kind of building that's printed on the back of money, and Eddie knows he'll never set foot in the place. "I can't. I'll feel like an idiot."

She lets out a sigh. "Fine. What's his name?"

"Mark Bailey."

"Is he a nice man?"

Mark isn't what Eddie's mother would call nice. He probably isn't what anybody would call nice. He's not friendly and warm. But the other night on the phone he was quick to reassure Eddie, even though Eddie had called rudely late. "Yes," Eddie says. "He's nice."

"Then you could ask him for copies of the articles he wrote. I'm sure he has them."

"I can't," Eddie whines.

"Are you worried about what you might find in these articles?"

"No, I'm just curious," Eddie says, and it's at least half true. He bought a copy of the *Chronicle* to read the first of the diary entries, and it wasn't bad. It was mostly about his routine, and Eddie's a bit embarrassed that now everybody knows how much he runs every day and how much time he spends in the weight room, but he's pretty sure he's mostly embarrassed because all that effort isn't getting him anywhere right now. But in the same paper, there was a book review with Mark's byline. It had been a little mean, even if it made Eddie laugh more than once.

"I can't cut out articles from magazines, you know," his mom says. "I'll get fired."

His mother works in the high school library. "I know. Maybe you could read them to me over the phone?"

"Edward James O'Leary, you have got to be losing your mind."

"Mama—"

"What kind of spendthrift degenerates are you spending time with if you think I'm reading entire magazine articles to you on a long-distance phone call?"

He winces. For his mom, *degenerate* is an all-purpose insult that includes everyone from Republican congressmen to the neighbor who won't pick up after her dog, but tonight Eddie feels very aware of the way that word is wielded against men like him. He doesn't usually think about this; when he hears that kind of language in the locker room, he sometimes forgets it even applies to him. And there's no way his mother could guess that Eddie is the way he is. But he's been feeling raw and put-upon, so his mother's words cut him deeper than they ordinarily would, certainly deeper than she intends. "Sorry, Mama."

"I'll see what I can do about the magazines," she says, mollified.

"Are you still smoking?" he asks, a naked attempt to turn the tables.

"Oh, so it's your turn to scold me, is it?"

"The doctor said it's bad for you," he reminds her.

"Listen to you, polishing your halo. It's my own damn fault for raising a caring son," she says, and Eddie has to smile.

At the end of his morning run, Eddie jogs into the clubhouse and tries not to feel anything about how quiet it gets as soon as people notice him. He's about to head into the weight room and kill some time when he hears his name.

"O'Leary!" It's Ardolino, standing in his office door. He's wearing the same shirt he was wearing yesterday, and there's no sign he's slept in the past twenty-four hours, but at least he isn't clutching a bottle, so Eddie's marking it down as a win.

"Yessir?" For a minute, Eddie lets himself hope that maybe the silent treatment is over.

"Newbold's office. Now."

Eddie looks down at himself. He's sweaty. His T-shirt is sticking to his chest. He's wearing sweatpants and a pair of ancient tennis shoes he thinks he accidentally stole from one of his old roommates. "Should I, uh . . ."

"Don't keep her waiting."

Front-office types do this on purpose. They wear three-piece suits

and shiny shoes and then call you into their office when you're dripping in sweat, bleeding from a bad slide, and covered in dirt. It's like
the fact they sign your paychecks isn't enough.

Eddie climbs the flight of stairs to where the Robins brass have
their offices. It's quiet, probably because a bunch of people quit when
they heard Connie Newbold wasn't appointing anyone—meaning a
man—to serve as her proxy on the board of directors. The idea of a
woman making decisions about a baseball team is just a bridge too
far, and Eddie would almost feel bad for her if not for the fact that
you actually do need a front-office staff to run a baseball team, and
also you need a manger more competent than Tony Ardolino, and
it's this lady's fault that the Robins are being run like a Little League
team. *Worse* than a Little League team.

"Mr. O'Leary," Miss Newbold says when she notices him standing in the door to her office. She isn't smiling.

"Yes, ma'am," he says.

"Please sit. What do you need?"

"Excuse me?"

"What do you need from us that you aren't getting? Is there a girl
back home that you need us to bring to New York for a visit? Do you
need help finding an apartment? A psychologist?"

Eddie almost laughs. No, there isn't a girl. No, an apartment
won't do him any good, because he's going to get sent down any day
now, surely. And no thanks, he's not going to say a damn thing to
a psychologist. "Um, no, ma'am. I think I'm just getting adjusted."
He's been in New York for over three weeks, and *getting adjusted* is
wearing thin as an excuse, but it's not like he has a better explanation
for why he's playing the way he is.

Constance Newbold makes a humming sound. "Are you injured?"

"No, ma'am." He can't seriously believe that she thinks he's going
to spill his guts about an injury to *her* if he hasn't told the trainer or
Ardolino. "I'm not injured." And he isn't. He kind of wishes he were,

even slightly, because then his slump would at least make sense. Right now he's as in the dark as everybody else.

He's been trying to figure out who Miss Newbold reminds him of, and he realizes it's every well-meaning teacher who took him aside and asked if something was *wrong*, something at home, poor eyesight, a bad diet. Something, anything, to explain why Eddie was setting off smoke bombs in the lavatories and climbing out of windows and doing everything in his power to be a public nuisance and thorough disgrace. Eddie hadn't had any excuse then, and he doesn't have one now. The fact is that he fucks up, always has, can't seem to help himself. The difference is that he didn't used to fuck up at baseball. It's the one area of his life where he's been able not only to put a leash on his dumber impulses but also to push himself, and it's always worked. He trains harder, he plays better, so he trains even more and plays even better. It's been a steady upward climb until now.

It really ought to be the manager having this conversation with him, not the owner. Maybe she doesn't trust Ardolino to do his job—which is fair, because Eddie doesn't trust Ardolino to do his job, either.

"You let me know if that changes, all right? We want you to be happy. We brought you here because you're young and talented, and we know the circumstances of that trade were . . . less than ideal. But half this team is old, and the other half is—" She breaks off, like she's just realized that she can't call her own ballplayers untalented, however accurate it might be.

It takes him a minute to realize that she's telling him he isn't getting traded anytime soon. Somebody should have told him all this as soon as he arrived in New York instead of letting him fester for nearly a month. He can't say that it would have helped his game, but it sure as hell wouldn't have hurt. And this should have come from

Ardolino, too, not the owner, but Eddie guesses you can't expect a man to pat you on the head and bolster your ego after you've publicly called him a drunken psychopath.

He thanks Miss Newbold and goes to bang things around in the weight room.

CHAPTER FIVE

By the end of a grueling twelve-inning game against the Phillies that the Robins, of course, lose, Eddie is in about as foul a mood as he's ever been in. That afternoon, he'd been looking for some athletic tape, and of fucking course nobody would lend him theirs, so he had to stand around idiotically while everyone pretended he was invisible. During the game, he didn't get a single hit, but he did manage to aggravate that pulled hamstring. What he really wants to do is take a couple aspirin and sink into the whirlpool tub. And then he wants to go home—to Omaha, not across the street to his awful hotel. He wants his mom to make him dinner and listen to him complain.

When he sees Mark in the locker room, propped up against the wall, reading a book and ignoring everyone around him, he probably shouldn't be surprised by the relief. In a room full of players who hate Eddie's guts and reporters ghoulishly waiting for the next time he talks out of turn, of course it's a relief to see literally anybody else.

But that's not all of it. After that phone call—Mark, irritated and kind and sincere all at once, Mark's quiet *Good night, Eddie*—Eddie's been looking forward to seeing him. He's sure that it's just his brain playing tricks on him, making him see friendship when actually Mark is just the only human being other than his mom who's talking to him. Still, there it is, and now Eddie needs to figure out how to wipe this smile off his face. At his stall, he tries to get undressed without sneaking glances at Mark, but he can't resist.

Now that Eddie knows Mark isn't a real sportswriter, he seems even more out of place in a locker room, like he's a different make and model of human being than what Eddie's used to seeing around here. Today he's wearing gray trousers and a blue jacket with brass buttons at the wrists, like he's on a boat in a movie. Eddie's pretty sure nobody's worn anything like that inside a locker room since baseball got invented.

When Mark strolls over, Eddie doesn't know what to say, so he pretends not to notice until a pair of very nice shoes appears in the periphery of his vision. He bends to unlace his cleats and screws up the knot three times before managing to untie it. He can smell—it's not cologne or aftershave, but maybe soap, and not the kind they keep in the showers here. With the room smelling as gross as it usually does after a game, the scent stands out in stark contrast.

"Where do you get your soap?" Eddie asks at the same time Mark asks, "What do you think about Italian?"

Eddie wants to crawl into his stall and die there.

"Um, the drug store," Mark says. "I know a pasta place that's open late and almost certainly doesn't have much of a baseball clientele."

"Pasta's great." Eddie grins, stupidly happy about the prospect of a bowl of spaghetti and someone to talk to. He pulls his shirt over his head. He's dirty and sweaty and the jersey clings to his skin. "Just let me shower first."

Mark is silent for a moment, then slides away and buries his face in his book.

There's no black car waiting at the curb this time, but they get a cab on the Harlem River Speedway. Mark gives the cabbie an intersection that Eddie, of course, doesn't recognize. He'll be traded before he figures out what these names and numbers mean—except he remembers what Miss Newbold said, and maybe he won't get traded. Maybe he'll spend the rest of his career with a team that hates him, in a city that hates him, his game getting worse and worse.

"How do you know a restaurant doesn't have a baseball clientele?" Eddie asks. He's pretty sure he's never heard anyone actually use the word *clientele* in real life. It feels asinine coming out of his mouth, like pronouncing Paris *Par-ee*, but it sounded perfectly normal when Mark said it.

"Well, it attracts a more . . . yachting and polo type of person, if you follow my meaning."

Eddie does not follow his meaning. "They're rich?" Plenty of rich people follow baseball; some of them own the teams.

"They're a particular kind of rich. Even if they recognize you, they'll pretend they don't."

"Well, hell," Mark says when the driver stops in front of a darkened storefront with soaped-up windows. "The place isn't here anymore. I ought to have called ahead."

"I don't mind. We can go someplace else." Eddie's stomach picks that moment to growl and make a liar out of him.

"There's another restaurant just around the corner," Mark says. "It's probably still there." He doesn't sound too pleased about it, but Eddie doesn't have a chance to make sense of this because the next thing he knows, Mark is attempting to pay the fare.

"Let me," Eddie insists. He's making a decent amount. Not a fortune, but he doesn't need to work over the winter like a lot of ballplayers do. He can pay for a cab.

"Expense account," Mark counters, deftly swatting his hand away and putting a folded-up bill into the cabbie's outstretched palm. All Eddie can do is give the cabbie an extra buck and climb out onto the sidewalk.

Eddie only has time to register an Irish name on the door—Mac something-or-other—and then they're inside a restaurant that's dimly lit and paneled in dark wood. It's one of those places that has a bar on one wall and booths all over the rest of the space, but something tells him that this is not the kind of restaurant you go to for cheap steaks and cheaper whiskey. It's too quiet for that, the carpet too soft.

"What can I get you gentlemen to drink?" the waitress asks after they're seated at a booth upholstered in red leather. She has an Irish accent.

"Whiskey and soda, please," Mark answers.

But before Eddie can answer—he wouldn't mind a beer, but has no idea what a place like this has on tap—the waitress is tilting her head to the side and regarding Mark quizzically. "You're—pork chops and applesauce. Where's mister lamb with mint jelly?"

Mark looks—there's no other word for it, he looks stricken. He gets it together quickly, though, and slaps a smile on his face. "It's been ages, Nora. How on earth do you remember me, let alone my order?"

The waitress looks at Mark in a way that Eddie has no trouble interpreting as *I remember people who look like you.* But what she says is, "Mister lamb with mint jelly always left a five-dollar tip. Hard to forget."

She turns her gaze to Eddie. He's pretty sure she's wondering why he's here instead of mister lamb with mint jelly. He just knows that she's going to ask, and then Mark will get that look again. Eddie doesn't want anyone to get that look, not even reporters, so he blurts out, "Whatever you have on tap. Please."

The waitress leaves, and Eddie begins studying the menu with a level of interest he's never before shown any kind of menu, afraid that if he looks up, he'll meet Mark's eye, and then one of them will have to say something. Eddie isn't willing to take any kind of risk that results in him having to say anything sensible right now.

He wonders why Mark hasn't been here in a while. He wonders

what about the waitress's words had hit Mark like a slap. He wonders a lot about mister lamb with mint jelly.

The problem with not talking much is that it frees your brain up to notice things you'd be better off not thinking about. Eddie's mother always says that he'd think better if he kept his mouth closed for an entire minute every once in a while, and maybe she's on to something, because Eddie has never thought so much in his life as he has the last three weeks with nobody to talk to. It's like that thing he read about how people who go blind develop ESP—one sense is gone, so their brains compensate elsewhere. Although that might have been in a comic book, now that he's thinking about it. It's probably for the best that nobody has ESP, because if anyone could look into his thoughts, they'd know what a wreck he is.

When the waitress comes back with their drinks, they order dinner. Eddie, who had been eying the lamb, now can't order it for some reason, so he mumbles something as he points to the menu and hopes for the best. Mark orders chicken, even though the waitress's eyebrows vanish beneath her bangs when he doesn't order the pork chops.

Eddie watches Mark down half his drink in one go. He watches Mark peel bits of paper off his coaster. He watches Mark take tiny, skittish glances around the room like a character in a spy movie who's about to get sniped.

Eddie can't take it anymore. He's still half-convinced it's only a matter of time before Mark makes him look like an ignorant hayseed in that goddamn fake diary, but he just can't let this guy sit there and stew.

"What's your book about?" Eddie asks.

Mark looks up from the wreckage he's making of his coaster, like he's startled to see that Eddie's still there. "A haunted house." He adjusts his glasses.

Eddie could have guessed as much. The title is right there on the dust jacket: *The Haunting of Hill House*, in white capital letters on a black background. Sinister yellowish foliage mostly conceals an even more sinister house in the background.

"You like scary stories?" Eddie asks. This is the kind of conversation he used to make when his old teammates brought their kids to the clubhouse. If Mark doesn't start meeting him halfway, Eddie's going to start asking whether Mark likes spaceships or ponies.

"Not really." Mark adjusts the bridge of his glasses again.

Eddie taps the book cover. "You like this one, though."

"Yes." Mark sounds certain this time, more certain than he has about anything since they walked through the door of this restaurant. "It's not really about a haunted house, though. It's about finding a new home, and maybe finding a new family. Except it's horrifying."

"Because of ghosts?"

"Maybe? I'm not sure. Imagine a woman who's had a terrible life—awful family, no prospects, the whole nine yards. Then she goes to this strange house and makes new friends and falls in love—well, reasonable minds can differ about that last bit—but also either the house is a living nightmare, or she's clinically insane. Neither of those things can undo the fact that she made friends and found a home, though, at least for a little while." He hesitates, bringing his glass to his lips but not drinking. "Do you want to borrow it?" He's clearly just being polite, but Eddie gets the feeling that Mark doesn't do much just for the sake of politeness.

Eddie's about to say something super regrettable, like "I only read books about robots settling Mars," when the food arrives, sparing them both.

Eddie's nearly finished with what turns out to be chopped steak before he notices that Mark is pushing his mashed potatoes around his plate instead of eating them. His hair is falling over his forehead, and he has faint circles under his eyes. Eddie wonders if Mark stares at his ceiling, too, counting the cracks, trying to decide if it's the mattress or the noise or the unsatisfactory contents of his mind that's keeping him awake.

At this point, Eddie's genuinely curious about whether Mark has forgotten they're supposed to be doing an interview. Mark hasn't asked a single baseball-related question. He hasn't asked any questions at all, unless "What do you think about Italian?" counts, which Eddie is pretty sure it does not.

"You ever get furious with yourself for not being able to do something very, very normal?" Mark asks.

Eddie stares for a minute before realizing Mark is serious. "Are you kidding? Have you read the sports pages lately?" Mark cracks a smile, so Eddie keeps going. "You come to me with any questions you have about beating yourself up for not being able to do some pretty basic shit. I'm the industry expert."

"I'll keep that in mind," Mark says, and he looks about a thousand times better than he had five minutes ago. "Excuse me." He gets up, presumably to find the men's room. But when Eddie looks around, he finds Mark talking to the waitress, bending toward her. She reaches out as if to pat his arm, pulling her hand back at the last moment.

The restaurant is quiet, and nobody's come over to bother Eddie, even when he's left alone at the table. "Thank you," Eddie says when Mark returns.

"Hmm?" Mark looks across the table, like he's forgotten Eddie's there.

"For finding somewhere private. It's nice to have a meal without talking to mean strangers about my batting average."

"My pleasure." Mark's smiling now, which is an improvement,

but there's a fragility about it, and Eddie desperately wants to do something to shore it up, to fix it in place.

"Actually, it's nice not to talk about baseball," Eddie says stupidly, because obviously they ought to be talking about baseball. That's why they're here. And now he's gone and put the idea into Mark's head. "But what is there to say, really? I've run out of interesting ways to explain that I just don't know how to hit the ball anymore. My swing is gone, and it's been gone for nearly a month now. I honestly don't remember how I ever did it, and I'm not sure if anyone has ever hit a ball with a bat in the history of the world. A stick less than three inches wide? A ball going nearly a hundred miles an hour? Pull the other one."

Mark laughs, rough and unguarded. His eyes are very blue behind his glasses.

"Anyway," Eddie says, slathering butter over the skin of his baked potato, "thanks for the break. When I'm alone, all I really think about is how badly I'm hitting, and when I'm at bat, that's all I'm thinking about, and when I'm talking to the press—anyway, like I said, thanks for the break."

"Likewise," Mark says, and that brittle smile is back.

When the check comes, Mark drops a ten-dollar bill onto the table, waving away Eddie's money once again.

Eddie slides a couple singles under the check when he thinks Mark isn't looking.

"Did you hurt yourself on that diving catch you made in the ninth inning today?" Mark asks when they're outside. He lights a cigarette and offers one to Eddie, who turns it down, even though he kind of wants to feel the cigarette case in his hands. It's square and gold and looks like it has flowers etched on it.

"I bruised my side a little," Eddie said. "Nothing much."

"Some people might say you shouldn't risk an injury this early in the season."

Eddie snorts. It's easier to talk about this outside, in the dark, than it is with a bunch of people writing down everything he says. "First, I'm going to earn my keep. Second, if the ball is in my reach, I'm going for it. Otherwise somebody's gonna look stupid, and it's probably going to be me." He doesn't mention that the middle of the infield is about the only thing the Robins have going for them, and that if he stops giving it his all, all that's left is total embarrassment.

"I'm only a few blocks uptown," Mark says. "If you walk over to Park"—he points in a direction Eddie thinks is west—"you'll have no trouble getting a cab."

"I'll walk you home. It's late." It's a silly suggestion: Mark apparently lives in this neighborhood, and it isn't even midnight.

Mark opens his mouth like he wants to argue, but then he gives Eddie a little smile. "Have it your way."

The smile makes Eddie bold. "Is that offer to borrow the book still good?"

Mark presses the book into his hand. Eddie already knows he's going to read that book like it's homework.

Eddie's pretty sure he's just letting his imagination get the better of him, but he almost thinks he can smell that soap of Mark's as they walk uptown. The skyscrapers in the distance glow a little more brightly than Eddie thinks they did last night. He holds the book carefully, because it's something special, and it doesn't belong to him.

That night, instead of staring at his ceiling, Eddie reads. It is one weird fucking book. Everyone in it is plain nuts. With a title like that, he's expecting the ghosts of mutilated innocents and bathtubs filled with blood, but instead there are a full fifty pages on architecture and what time the housekeeper sets dinner on the sideboard.

Everything's creepy in a vague way, and that vagueness makes it even creepier. It's not a book he'd pick up on his own; it's probably not a book he'd read beyond the first five pages if it hadn't been from Mark.

He's not sure why it matters that the book is from Mark. Maybe Eddie's just lonely and desperate for conversation, and the book is an opportunity for that. Maybe he just doesn't want Mark to think he's dumb. It can't be because Mark's handsome, because Eddie's been attracted to plenty of men, and never once has it made him want to read a book.

What he does know is that every few pages, he finds something written in the margins in black ink, the handwriting tight and slanted. Eddie's never thought about penmanship for longer than it takes to notice that his own is ugly but readable, at least if you try hard, but Mark's is . . . well, it's *pretty*. It's neat and elegant, and the nib of the pen must be very fine to get a line so narrow. If you look at a *g* on one page, it's identical to a *g* on the other.

Eddie imagines what it must be like to get a letter from Mark, line after line of perfectly curling black ink. He bets Mark always eats his vegetables and that he never runs out of toothpaste. He probably has an accountant, and he probably remembers where he wrote the accountant's phone number, and that it wasn't on the back of a telephone bill. He bets Mark has never had to ask his mom to do his taxes.

But that's all bullshit and he knows it: He remembers the shredded coaster, the hair Mark needs to tuck behind his ears because it's grown too long, the lamb chop–related panic. On the surface, everything about Mark is impeccable, but when you pay attention, you see the cracks. Eddie doesn't know what caused the cracks, and he wishes he did. That's not the kind of thing you can ask, though, so he pays attention to the words on the page.

At first, the notes don't make much sense, partly because Mark uses abbreviations and partly because some of it goes right over Eddie's head. But he notices a pattern pretty quick, especially with the phrases that Mark underlines: he's keeping track of all the evidence pointing to two of the characters falling in love, which might not be so interesting to Eddie except that both the characters are women. Sometimes there are exclamation points in the margins next to something particularly intimate, for lack of a better word, like the women swapping clothes or sharing a bed.

Now, when Mark lent him this book, he didn't say "Here's some morally depraved literature," and he didn't say "Here's a good book, so long as you ignore the lesbians." So Eddie can tentatively conclude that Mark doesn't have anything against lesbians, at least fictional ones. It doesn't follow that Mark has any opinions whatsoever about queer men, or at least Eddie doesn't think it does. It certainly doesn't mean that Mark is queer, does it? In Eddie's experience, men will go out of their way to make sure that you know just how much they aren't queer, but maybe things are different wherever Mark comes from.

Eddie's used to thinking of his queerness as an inconvenience, mostly because he's bad at keeping secrets, and it's a pain in the ass keeping one this big. It forces him to be careful, which is exhausting. He always has to be ready to deflect, to steer conversations away from topics like girlfriends or what he did the previous night. And maybe it's just the past few weeks of loneliness making everything worse, but he currently feels like the only gay man in the world.

Still, this book is something solid that Eddie can hold in his hands, real proof that queer people exist, that *he* exists. Nothing good is coming to the women in this book—honestly, they'll be lucky if the house doesn't eat them or do whatever it is evil houses do in scary books. But they exist, and Mark noticed they exist, and Eddie can look at the words printed on the page and at Mark's perfect penmanship and know that he isn't alone.

Part III
JUNE

CHAPTER SIX

The phone rings at an ungodly hour. Mark's awake, of course, having been rousted from his bed at the crack of dawn by Lula standing on his face and demanding a walk. But that still doesn't make eight o'clock a decent time for a telephone call.

He answers the phone with what he hopes is a bracing lack of warmth.

"What did you *write*?" Eddie demands.

Mark decides to ignore the little thrum of pleasure that goes through him at hearing Eddie's voice over the phone. He sniffs and hopes he sounds properly irritated. "Do you ever call people at normal times?"

There's a pause while Eddie apparently thinks it over. "Not often, honestly. But what the fuck is this?"

Mark's hackles are up. "What on earth are you talking about? That article was basically PR for the Robins in general and you in particular."

"I'm at the stadium. The clubhouse attendant comes up to me and says 'Ha ha, who would've guessed O'Leary is funny,' and he slaps my back."

Mark pinches the bridge of his nose. "Did you read it?"

"No! You can't get a copy of the *Chronicle* at a baseball stadium! You can't even get the *Daily News*. All I know is that they're laughing at me."

As far as Mark can tell, the Robins are retaliating against Eddie's outburst in Kansas City by acting like a pack of junior high school bullies and refusing to talk to him. Anyone who would intentionally be mean to Eddie O'Leary is a disgrace. It's like kicking a dog. "Okay, okay," Mark says. "Hold on."

He gets this morning's *Chronicle* off his coffee table and opens it to the sports section. Holding the phone between his shoulder and ear, he starts to read aloud. "*At this point, the idea of someone hitting a baseball with a piece of ash less than three inches in diameter seems like a figment of my imagination. Has anyone ever hit a ball? Can they prove it?*"

"I didn't realize you were going to write that." Eddie sounds aggrieved. "I sound dumb."

"You do *not*," Mark argues, aghast. Frankly, he's insulted that anyone might misinterpret his writing. "You didn't sound dumb when you said it, and you don't sound dumb in the paper."

Eddie makes an anguished noise.

"Listen," Mark says, scarcely able to believe he's about to go out of his way at eight o'clock in the morning to pat Eddie O'Leary's head. Appalling. This urge to be kind to a relative stranger is unfamiliar and disconcerting, as if he's discovered in himself a hunger for raw meat or an enthusiasm for vaudeville. He doesn't know whether or not to be reassured that this urge seems mainly confined to Eddie. "I truly didn't mean to write anything that embarrassed you. And I didn't mean to write anything that you wanted kept private."

"It's not that. I mean—I was just talking out of my ass. I was making fun of myself. I wouldn't have done that if I had known it would be in the paper."

"You come across as down-to-earth, charmingly self-deprecating, and—" He very nearly says *sweet* and saves himself at the last moment, but not, unfortunately, before he recognizes that word as accurate. The awful truth is that Mark wrote what he did precisely because it makes Eddie seem less a spoiled baby and more a lovable, hapless underdog.

Why he felt so compelled to do this is something he prefers not to think about, but when he sat at his typewriter, he wanted to write about the Eddie who had tried to make him comfortable after the waitress asked about William. It was more than Mark might have done in Eddie's place. "Look," Mark says, "I know all this, because I wrote it, and I'm good at my job."

"Huh," Eddie says after a long moment of silence. "Okay." He sounds satisfied. "Are you coming to the game tomorrow afternoon?" Eddie asks.

Tomorrow is Saturday. Lilian is out of town, so Mark's plans consist of walking Lula, watching television while Lula takes one of her resentful naps, and then going to bed far earlier than his body will let him fall asleep.

"We could have a milkshake after," Eddie goes on, sounding terribly, terribly hopeful.

He thinks about Eddie slipping more money under the check when he thought Mark wasn't looking; he thinks about how painfully ready that smile is even when he's at the absolute rock bottom of his career. He had looked like Christmas morning when Mark loaned him that book. There was a time not so long ago when Mark might have resented it, might have been jealous of someone who could be so easily cheered up. But now, if someone's happiness, however temporary, can be bought with a secluded restaurant and the loan of a book, Mark will pay that price. If Eddie, for whatever reason, wants to have a milkshake, then Mark will buy him a damn milkshake.

"Yes," Mark answers. "I know just the place."

When Mark arrives at the stadium and climbs the stairs to the press box, he's immediately aware that he's made a mistake. The previous two times he came to the Polo Grounds to see Eddie, he arrived toward the end of the game and waited in the locker room. He hadn't set foot in the press box.

But now he has, and Mark's spent enough time around reporters to know that it'll take about forty minutes for every man in this press box to know who he is and have him pegged as an outsider. Mark *is* an outsider, and in more ways than one.

He glances down at his clothing: a cream-colored cotton sweater over a linen shirt and a pair of gray summer-weight wool slacks. When he got dressed that afternoon, on some level he must have known that he was choosing all wrong, because the press box is a sea of badly tailored suits in shiny wool and upsetting plaids. To be fair, there's nothing in his closet that would allow him to blend into this crowd, and he wouldn't have it any other way, but his gray suit would have at least offered some camouflage. Literally any shoes other than loafers—loafers, Christ, he might as well have on a cowboy hat or false eyelashes—would have been more appropriate.

He reminds himself that there's nothing inherently queer about good tailoring, and even if there were, it wouldn't matter. He takes a seat near the exit, adjusts his cuffs, and crosses one leg over the other as if he's not in the least self-conscious. He isn't, really. Not in any of the ways that count. Not anymore.

Caution had become second nature to protect William: a lawyer with political ambitions couldn't have the faintest whisper of queer rumors attached to his name, no matter how rich and well-connected he might have been. No, not just caution—Mark will always be cautious, can count on one hand the reckless things he's done in the whole of his twenty-eight years—but for William, he let ordinary prudence become a full-fledged commitment to a double life.

He kept careful check on his clothes, his hair, his behavior. He was William's perfectly straight roommate, an irrelevant figure on the periphery of William's life. Mark had hated it, and knowing that

William hated it, too, didn't improve things. That said, he'd do it again; he wishes he could have done it for longer. He'd have done more and worse, and he'd have done it for the rest of his life.

Unattached, semi-employed journalists don't need to be straight, though. He's held on to this fact as a small comfort throughout the past bleak year. It isn't that Mark's planning on doing anything to get himself arrested, and he'd rather the co-op board of his building not get it into their heads to make things difficult for him. The circumstances of his life never bring him anywhere near the police, and he'll keep it that way. He's rarely in a situation where someone could physically harm him.

But now he has the freedom to be indifferent to other people's opinions, and this is something he owns as surely as he owns the contents of his bank account; the two, in fact, are inextricably linked, both a sort of inheritance from William. He'd hardly be thinking that he doesn't care whether people know he's queer if it weren't for all that money.

Except—wearing loafers in public is not a life boldly lived. He has all this freedom, and he isn't doing anything with it. Two years ago, he had a job he loved. Now his typewriter is dusty. His *mind* feels dusty. Beneath the layer of grief, something is starting to stir, and he realizes it's the first time since William died that he's wanted anything other than to be left perfectly alone.

In a cursory attempt to blend in with his surroundings, Mark takes out his notebook and tries to become very interested in his grocery list. This might work better if he had an actual grocery list rather than: six bananas, one box of cornflakes, a quart of milk, seven cans of dog food. The same order every week, every month, sixteen months in a row. In a city with more restaurants per capita than anyplace on the planet, and a bank account that never seems to noticeably decrease its bottom line, Mark sure as shit isn't going to learn how to cook for one.

While he's contemplating just how livid William would be if he knew that Mark now considers bananas in soggy cornflakes to be a suitable breakfast, he's rescued from this thought by the sound of his name.

"Junior told me you'd be here."

It's George Allen, one of the *Chronicle*'s baseball reporters. Junior is not Andy but rather Andy's seventy-year-old father, because George is old enough to have worked for Andy's grandfather. He had been on the Yankees beat in the twenties before giving it up in favor of writing a column that eventually became nationally syndicated. But this year, for some reason, he's been traveling with the Robins since spring training.

Mark, though, primarily knows George through years of occasional lunches at which they complained fluently about all manner of things—the weather, crosstown buses, the mysteries of the *Chronicle* building's plumbing—and talked about nothing of any personal significance whatsoever. After William died, Mark avoided George as surely as he'd avoided almost everybody else, and now he doesn't know whether to expect chilliness.

"I hoped I'd run into you," Mark says. "I'm writing—"

"I know, Junior told me. It's one of the infant's bright ideas."

The infant is Andy. Mark bites back a smile.

"That O'Leary kid can't get a hit for love or money," George says.

"His fielding's solid," Mark says.

"It's a hell of a lot more than solid," George says. "He and Rosenthal are carrying the infield."

"People don't like him," Mark says. "They boo him. And his teammates won't even talk to him."

George makes a dismissive noise. "They're giving him the silent treatment. Skipper's orders. It'll be over in a couple more days."

"The silent treatment," Mark repeats. His older sisters used to give him the silent treatment when he snitched on them or played pranks on their boyfriends. The silent treatment? From adults? At *work*?

"They give a guy the cold shoulder. It's an old punishment for loafing, being late, stealing a teammate's girl. Some teams do it to all the rookies, just for kicks. Been doing it since the Civil War, as far as I can tell. A month is a lot, but anything less wouldn't have gotten the point across."

"You're telling me nobody on the team has talked to Eddie O'Leary in a month?"

"Don't look so shocked."

Mark *is* shocked, though. He knows better than to expect his fellow man to be anything other than a complete jackass, but the idea of taking someone like Eddie—and even in the privacy of his mind he refuses to investigate precisely what he means by this—and essentially putting him in solitary confinement makes Mark boiling mad. No wonder the kid can't hit.

The Robins take the field, wearing a uniform that Mark will simply never understand. The word ROBINS is in barely readable red lettering, accompanied by a bird that is absolutely *not* a robin, due to it being bright blue. Whenever Mark thinks about it too much, his head starts to hurt. The road uniform, which he's only seen on his black-and-white television, might make some degree of sense, but he isn't holding out much hope.

Eddie plays miserably, swinging at things he has no business swinging at, fouling all over the place. He screws up a bunt. After that, there's a bad moment where it looks like he might throw the bat, but he catches himself in time.

This is immature behavior, a spoiled, sulky temper tantrum. But there's something awfully vulnerable about it—a man standing there in front of a couple thousand people and a television audience of God only knows how many, all but certain that he'll fail. There's a stiffness in his posture that's absent when Eddie's in the locker room or on the field, and to Mark it looks like the weight of refusing to quit.

Objectively, it doesn't matter whether Eddie O'Leary ever hits a baseball again. Life is awfully hard for an awful lot of people; feeling bad for healthy, decently compensated twenty-two-year-olds is just silly. And Mark *doesn't* feel bad for him, not precisely. He feels—sympathetic, maybe.

The idea of feeling anything at all for someone who isn't Lilian, Maureen, Andy, or Nick feels like sensation coming painfully back to a numb limb. After William died, he closed himself off; he couldn't possibly engage with anyone who didn't *know*. Hiding the fact of William had been bad enough, but explaining the loss of him was somehow even more inaccessible, and so his world shrunk to the people who knew all of him.

Lilian's been telling him for months that he has to get out and meet new people, with the implicit threat that something terrible will happen if he coops himself up in that apartment. It's doubtful that the dire fate she was warning of was Mark developing a fondness for professional shortstops.

It's just—it's been a while since Mark met someone so palpably alone and so eager not to be. The world is filled with people who could happily be alone, their solitude interrupted by occasional conversations with friends. Mark might, in fact, be one of them. But Eddie isn't. You can see the words he isn't saying bubbling away just beneath the surface; you can see every aborted effort to reach out.

Mark mentally slaps himself. The extent of his relationship with Eddie O'Leary consists of two meals, two phone calls, and a couple of conversations in the locker room. It's nothing, and it will stay nothing, and Mark won't let himself forget it.

He sidles up to the edge of the box and takes out his binoculars—well, they aren't binoculars so much as William's old opera glasses. The incongruity of it makes him almost hysterical, but he tamps it down and peers through the lenses into the Robins' dugout. He finds Eddie with no trouble: his cap is off, so it's only a question of finding the head of honey-blond hair. There are six inches on either side of him, as if his teammates are worried about catching some kind of rash off of him. Eddie isn't doing anything to help himself: his body language is awful, stiff and uncomfortable.

He's not talking; he's not chewing tobacco or eating. Open in his lap is—well, Mark nearly drops the opera glasses. In his lap is a book. Mark can't see the cover, but he'd bet that's his copy of *The Haunting of Hill House*.

He hadn't expected Eddie to actually read it and had been fully annoyed with himself for lending the book out. There are eight books sitting on his nightstand, and he's spent a month ignoring each of them in favor of rereading a ghost story. At this point, that book is the equivalent of a child's teddy bear or, perhaps, an adult's psychoanalyst. He's certainly gotten his three dollars' worth.

He has a flare of worry about what Eddie might make of the things Mark wrote in the margins, then reminds himself that he doesn't care what conclusions people draw about him, and Eddie's no exception. Honestly, maybe he'd prefer Eddie figure out that Mark's queer right away, because Mark's in real danger of thinking of Eddie as a friend and he'd like to nip that in the bud if it turns out that Eddie's going to have a problem.

Maybe, subconsciously, that's why he offered to lend Eddie the book. Maybe he just wanted to tell Eddie the truth in the easiest way. Not that a scribbled *lesbian?* and a *literally haunted by the specter of heterosexuality* accompanied by some enthusiastic underlining constitutes a forthright announcement of his own queerness.

He imagines William crossing his arms and looking at Mark over the rim of his glasses: *First you take my opera glasses to a baseball game, then you attempt to declare yourself to a young man via literary criticism. I blame the lack of vitamins in your diet.*

He catches himself smiling—actually smiling, and in *public*—and realizes he's managed to think about William without getting dreary about it. Perhaps Lilian was right about the value of getting out.

Another inning ends without Eddie having an at bat, which means now Mark gets to watch Eddie on the field. On television, the camera usually only cuts to Eddie when he makes one of those impossible-looking catches or fields a double play. In person, Mark can watch Eddie even when nothing's happening; he can see how the awkward stiffness from the dugout has melted away and been replaced with a stance that's loose but ready.

In the bottom of the inning, Eddie gets out on a fly ball. As he's trudging back to the dugout, he looks over his shoulder, up toward the press box. If Mark didn't know better, he might think Eddie is looking for him. Well, maybe he is. Why shouldn't he be? He asked Mark to come. He promised a milkshake after.

There's no way Eddie will be able to pick Mark out, though, so he raises a hand. Eddie catches the movement, pauses, and smiles. Even from this distance, the wattage of that smile stuns Mark. He hopes no cameras are trained on the dugout.

Mark tells himself that he didn't do anything as gauche as wave to a player from the press box. He's just . . . identifying himself. Still, when he turns his head, George Allen is looking at him as disapprovingly as if he'd let out a whoop. And when he glances back at the dugout, the manager is looking up, obviously trying to see who caught Eddie's attention.

"I didn't know they had places like this in New York," Eddie says when they enter the drugstore. "My grandpa used to take me to a soda fountain just like this."

There are soda fountains all over the city; all over the continent, too, as far as Mark can tell. But he knows what Eddie means: there's something distinctly old-fashioned about this place, with its walnut-paneled walls and its glass-fronted cabinets filled with mysterious boxes and bottles. These druggists sold soap to George Washington and tooth powder to the Roosevelts, and they don't want you to forget it.

Still, Mark knows for a fact you can get a tube of perfectly normal toothpaste if you ask the girl behind the counter, and that she'll sell it to you with the same deliberate lack of affect as if you'd asked for a box of condoms.

"Let me guess," Eddie says. "Not a baseball clientele."

They sit on stools at the counter and order milkshakes: chocolate for Eddie and strawberry for Mark.

"That book scared the pants off me," Eddie says. "I nearly called you at four in the morning to blame you for the fact that I couldn't shut my eyes."

If Mark's a little disappointed to have missed out on another inappropriately timed phone call, it isn't a good sign, and he knows it. "I told you it was scary. *Haunting* is right there in the title."

"I still have a few more pages, so don't spoil the ending. Also, I couldn't crack your code."

"My code?"

"Your abbreviations and symbols. I kind of wanted you to decipher some of it for me. That's the other reason I nearly called."

"Oh?" Out of the corner of his eye, Mark sees that Eddie is looking at his milkshake rather than at Mark. This, probably, is where Mark is supposed to say something reassuringly heterosexual, something to dispel any suspicions that Eddie might have gleaned from the margin notes.

Instead Mark takes a sip of his milkshake and says nothing.

"You usually take interview subjects out for milkshakes?" Eddie asks, his face an unflattering red.

After a moment of being a bit too distracted by the blush, Mark registers what Eddie said. And, well. Huh. A part of Mark's mind that's lain dormant for too long whirs into activity, a little rusty but still useful.

Until now, he hadn't considered that Eddie might be queer. But he took the conversation right from queer things Mark wrote to Mark's intentions in spending time with him. If Eddie's queer, then he's being awfully brave in letting Mark know, and he might need some reassurance that he hasn't trusted the wrong person.

If he isn't gay, the worst-case scenario is that he refuses to sit for any more interviews. And that's fine; Andy can find someone else to write these diaries.

There's an easy way out: Mark can smooth this over for Eddie by remarking that the milkshakes were Eddie's idea and that technically it's the *Chronicle*'s treat. Instead Mark makes sure nobody's in earshot, swivels on his stool so he's looking right at Eddie, and says, "Only the handsome ones." He says it lightly; there's about a milligram of plausible deniability in there if anybody needs it.

Eddie goes very, very still. He does not jump off his stool and storm out of the drugstore.

"The last person I interviewed was a ninety-year-old architect who I'm afraid wasn't at all my type," Mark says, idly stirring his milkshake with his straw. "And the one before that was a French composer who probably would have called the embassy if I suggested milkshakes. More important, I *am* a professional, despite all appearances to the contrary. I'm not going to threaten you with bad press if you don't bend to my wicked wiles, or—" He breaks off when Eddie starts laughing, his big shoulders shaking and his eyes bright. "I'm very amusing," Mark agrees.

"Jesus, you are. Yeah, I'm not worried about you taking advantage of me."

"What? I could be dastardly. Don't rule it out. I'm hurt."

"You're something, all right."

"Oh good. Let's talk about your batting average, then."

"So you *are* punishing me for not bending to your wicked wiles," Eddie says, his face assuming an expression he probably thinks looks stricken but actually just looks handsomely peeved.

"You want punishment?" Mark gets out his notebook. "Tell me about your childhood."

Eddie tells Mark about his grandfather driving him to ball games, his mother saving up for new cleats.

He doesn't think it's his imagination that something in Eddie seems to have unwound. If Eddie's queer—which he hasn't exactly said he is, but he also hasn't said he *isn't*, and that counts for something—then it must be a relief to let his guard down, even for the span of forty-five minutes and the duration of a milkshake.

Maybe that's why Mark catches himself whistling—honest-to-God whistling, like a friendly chimney sweep in a musical comedy—after putting Eddie in a cab.

Once a month, Mark gets on the subway and heads to Brooklyn to have dinner with Lilian and Maureen. This time, though, he's done in by the piteous looks Lula sends his way while he's shaving, and so he scoops her up and hails a cab. He tips the cabbie an extra two dollars to pretend none of this is happening.

"You're too young to embrace eccentricity this hard," Lilian says when they arrive at her door, Mark still holding Lula in his arms, a bottle of wine wedged precariously between the dog and his chest.

"Tell that to her ladyship," Mark says. For a moment there in the cab, he thought Lula bestowed an almost approving look upon him. The fact that this is a highlight of 1960 is a secret the dog must never learn.

Lilian crosses her arms. "You're about five minutes away from buying her a diamond collar and getting her nails painted pink."

If Mark had any reason to believe Lula wanted diamonds or manicures, he would have footed the bill months ago. But Lula's tastes are simpler than that: All she really wants is for William to come home. And, well. Of course he'd get her diamonds if it made her feel better.

He's not telling Lilian any of that, though, because she'll start making her sad face and Maureen will probably cry, and then he'll have ruined the evening for all of them by serving as a reminder of the inevitability of unhappy endings.

"That smells delicious," he says instead. Maureen comes out from the kitchen, and he kisses her cheek, hands her the bottle of wine, compliments her blouse, and offers to chop things. He's Maureen's favorite. He smirks at Lilian over Maureen's shoulder, and Lilian gives him the finger.

Lilian's a photographer at the *Chronicle*. Maureen takes photographs of mostly naked men for one of the "fitness" magazines Mark keeps in his nightstand drawer. Their bathroom is perpetually unusable because they insist on treating it as a darkroom.

Mark met Lilian on his first day at the *Chronicle*, when he saw her enter the lunchroom wearing a bespoke three-piece suit that he immediately coveted. He picked up his tray, went to sit beside her, and proceeded to acquire one of those confounding crushes he occasionally develops on queer women.

Last year, when things were at their absolute worst, it was Lilian who got Mark drunk, camped out on his sofa for a few nights, and said soothing things. It was Maureen who made sure Lula was walked and fed and who shoved solid food in Mark's general direction until he caved in and ate a few bites. The memory makes Mark uncomfortable, like he's had an embarrassing accident, but they both let him pretend it never happened.

Their apartment has one bedroom. The boldness of this enchanted Mark the first time he visited. There isn't even the most cursory window dressing of heterosexuality, not even a divan in the corner that one of them could claim was her bed.

Mark coveted this frankness; there was no other word for the bone-deep envy he felt when he saw his friends make no secret of who they were or who they were to one another. Mark always had to be careful, and careful means dishonest; careful means making sure that there's always a lie at hand that he can reach for and use to paper over the truth.

He keeps forgetting that he doesn't have to do that anymore, probably because he's spent the past sixteen months living like a hermit, which affords few opportunities for either deceit or authenticity.

"Wouldn't hurt you to smile," says Lilian, handing him a glass of red wine.

"Wouldn't want your face to freeze that way," agrees Maureen with what she probably thinks is a cheeky wink.

Mark feigns outrage. "If I said that to either of you, you'd slap me, and rightly so."

Maureen throws a wadded-up kitchen towel at his head.

Dinner is coq au vin, and they polish off two bottles of wine among themselves. They don't talk about work; this has always been the rule, because otherwise the women talk about photography, or Lilian and Mark talk about the paper, and the result is somebody getting left out.

"I found the most mysterious thing on my desk this morning," Lilian says. "Three tickets to *A Raisin in the Sun*, playing next Friday. Orchestra seats."

"How mysterious," Mark agrees. "Perhaps you have a secret admirer."

"*And* three tickets to *Sweet Bird of Youth*."

Mark sips his wine and tries to look innocent.

"Why aren't you coming with us?" Lilian demands.

"Baseball," Mark says darkly. "I can't go to the theater and follow night games." He had bought those tickets weeks before being assigned the Eddie O'Leary diaries.

"You could have sold them," Lilian says.

"True," Mark agrees. "You could sell them as well."

Lilian throws her hands up in apparent despair, which is silly, because all three of them know that Mark can afford tickets to however many shows he pleases.

"How's the baseball assignment?" asks Lilian in an obvious bid to change the topic.

"Better than I expected. O'Leary's a talker. The columns write themselves." It's fun, actually, pretending to be Eddie O'Leary for the space of a newspaper column, and it's an unspeakable relief to find that he's interested in work again—interested in anything outside the four walls of his apartment.

"*Bzzt*," says Maureen, making the sound of a quiz show buzzer indicating a wrong answer. "No shoptalk. I want dirt on the Robins."

"How is that not shoptalk?" complains Lilian.

"There's really no dirt," Mark says. "O'Leary's a—" He catches himself before saying that Eddie's a sweetheart. Over the course of his career—if what he currently has can still be referred to as a career—Mark has interviewed many people. Some have been kind. Some have even been flirtatious. But on very few of those interviews has Mark been a person. Instead he's the vehicle by which his subject gets into print. Eddie, though, saw him struggling in that Irish restaurant and had helped. It was a gross lapse of professionalism on Mark's part, and it's pitiful that he's casting that moment as something like friendship, but he doesn't think he's wrong.

He can't tell his friends, partly because he'll sound starstruck, but also because it feels so fragile and nebulous that he's afraid mentioning it will make it disappear. The fact is that despite his best efforts, he does like Eddie, and Eddie seems to like him—no, Eddie definitely likes him. He doesn't think Eddie O'Leary is capable of pretending to like someone. It strikes Mark as further evidence of Eddie's poor judgment: can't he tell that Mark—gloomy and tired, caustic and a little mean even at his best—is unfit for friendship? Eddie—in a strange city with unfriendly teammates—is just lonely. Mark's probably the first remotely friendly person he's met in town.

"He has a short fuse and a loose tongue, but he's all right," Mark adds. "I feel bad for him."

"You feel bad for him?" Lilian repeats, looking a little startled, which Mark supposes is fair. He isn't in the habit of feeling bad for people. Lately, he isn't really in the habit of feeling, come to that.

"Things were going so well for him, and now they aren't."

Maureen and Lilian send one another synchronized glances, and Mark remembers years of exchanging identical glances with William. There's something so comforting in the ability to be wordlessly petty with someone, in knowing that as soon as you have a closed door between the two of you and the rest of the world, you can share all your least attractive thoughts. Although, in fairness to Lilian and Maureen, they're probably just concerned, which is worse.

And William would have understood that, too, would have understood why being the object of other people's kindness is so demoralizing. Mark's tried to explain to Lilian that he simply isn't nice, and she always laughs and pats his arm and calls him lovely. William never needed to be told; he had understood from the beginning that Mark was a sharpened knife, that he had to take extra care not to hurt people.

He knows that if he said this out loud, Maureen and Lilian would immediately take out their Rolodex and begin sending him out to dinner with every eligible homosexual in the five boroughs, and he can't have that.

The problem isn't that he feels guilty, or like he's betraying William. They never talked about it—and why would they have, at their ages—but William was above all practical. There would be no point to Mark never looking at another man. And, more than that, William always wanted Mark to be happy. He would have been annoyed at Mark for doubting that.

The actual problem is incredibly boring, and Mark hates admitting it even to himself. Unless a couple has the good fortune to get hit by the same freight train, their story ends in exactly one way. He can't go through that twice, and he couldn't inflict it on anybody else.

(He imagines telling William this, and can perfectly conjure up the image of William's horrified expression. "How remiss of you not to have noticed mortality until now, darling," followed by a decisive, derisive "you utter *sap*.")

His tongue loosened and his pride drowned by half a pitcher of whiskey sours, he once tried to explain this to Lilian. She listened patiently and then probably tried to remember the appropriate chapter from the book she borrowed from the library on helping one's grieving friends. Plenty of widows and widowers remarry, she pointed out. And, yes, obviously that's true. Good for them, Mark supposes. They're braver than he is. Mark's never claimed to be brave; he's never wanted to be.

"I have ice cream!" Maureen announces, a little too brightly, making Mark suspect he's been sitting there palpably grieving—disgusting behavior—for the last few minutes. "It's that lemon custard stuff you like," she adds. "Like I'd ever give you supermarket vanilla ice cream." She and Lilian laugh, as if not wanting supermarket ice cream is a funny quirk as opposed to the only way to live.

He has no appetite left, but he eats half a bowl before giving the rest to Lula.

CHAPTER SEVEN

Mark is peering inside his oven, attempting to gauge the readiness of a frozen dinner—a new and probably doomed attempt at nutrition—when he hears the apartment buzzer.

It's been a long time since the buzzer sounded. Over the years, he's gotten so used to not inviting people over that he still meets even his close friends at restaurants or their own apartments.

"Yes?" he speaks into the box on the wall.

"A Mr. O'Leary for you downstairs, Mr. Bailey," says the doorman. "Should I send him up?"

They definitely hadn't made plans for Eddie to come here, and the only reason Eddie even has this address is because he walked Mark home that one time. It's brazen and rude for Eddie to turn up out of the blue, but Mark's more curious than he is annoyed, and Eddie's company will at the very least be a reprieve from whatever awaits him inside his oven.

"Yes, I suppose—yes, please do send him up. Thank you."

He has a minute, maybe ninety seconds, before Eddie knocks on the door, and Mark definitely shouldn't use any of that time to duck into the bathroom and check his reflection, but that's what he does anyway. What he sees in the mirror is borderline adequate: He got a haircut earlier that week, and he shaved that morning. He's wearing one of William's old sweaters—and not entirely for sentimental reasons, but because it's comfortable. Hell, Mark bought it in the first place. He takes it off and wrecks his hair in the process. The knock sounds before he can do more than pat his hair back into place.

"I'm sorry," Eddie says as soon as Mark opens the door.

Mark had opened his mouth to ask what on earth Eddie thinks he's doing here, but this takes the wind out of his sails. "Come in?"

"I should have called before coming," Eddie blurts out, still standing in the corridor and making no move to cross the threshold.

"I thought you were in Chicago."

Eddie tries to shove his hair off his face. It must be drizzling, because his hair is damp and sticking to his skin. "I came right from the airport."

They're talking at one another in sentences that don't quite connect; Eddie's obviously anxious, and Mark's hair is messy, and then the dog starts to bark.

"Oh, hey there. What's your name, sweetheart?" asks Eddie, bending to pet Lula. She starts her Little Match Girl routine, acting like nobody's ever pet her in her life. She does this to make Mark feel bad; he's sure of it.

"That's Lula. Just come in. Can I get you something to drink?"

"Um, sure." Eddie finally steps inside and Mark shuts the door.

Mark already knows that Eddie is attractive, that by any sensible measure Eddie O'Leary is a very handsome man. He knows it in the way he knows that the place on Second Avenue has the best bagels in the city and that you can't get a cab at rush hour on Broadway—it's a fact that he doesn't have to think about, and which everybody else knows, too.

But it hadn't *meant* anything to Mark until Eddie stood in his doorway, petting his dog. Mark doesn't know if it's seeing Eddie in Mark's home that does it, or if it's Lula who works some kind of magic, or maybe it's just the knowledge that Eddie is possibly queer that makes things slot into place. The pull of attraction takes him by surprise, like the sand shifting under his feet as the tide finally comes in.

"What can I get you?" Mark hopes he sounds normal.

Eddie doesn't look away from the dog, thank God. "Orange juice?"

"I don't have any." Mark escapes to the kitchen and opens the refrigerator. "I have—let's see—about a half-pint of milk, three bottles of imported beer that have been there since 1958, and—is that ginger ale? I don't entertain much." He shuts the refrigerator and opens the cabinet where he keeps liquor. "There's scotch, gin, bourbon, and—vermouth, I guess?" Mark knows he's babbling, and he knows why he's babbling, which only makes it worse. Still looking into the cabinet, he says, "You know what, I'm going to pour myself a scotch."

"I'll have one, too," Eddie says.

Enormously relieved to have cleared that hurdle, Mark grabs a pair of glasses, then momentarily stutters over the strange familiarity. His hand knows exactly what to do, exactly how the two glasses fit in his palm. He determinedly pushes that feeling aside, reckoning he can take it out later and be as weird about it as he pleases, then sets about pouring their drinks.

When he turns around, Eddie's in the doorway to the kitchen. Logically, Mark knows that while Eddie is large, he isn't as big as a doorway. His shoulders can't actually be that broad.

"Oh. Sorry," Eddie says, stepping aside.

"Want to tell me what's the matter?" Mark asks as he leads the way into the living room.

"I was all set to read you the riot act, but then you're all . . ." He gestures at Mark, as if Mark is supposed to have any idea what Eddie's getting at.

"Read me the riot act? What did I do?"

"It's this week's diary. I sound pathetic again."

"Who told you that?"

"Nobody. I read it for myself. I can read, you know."

"I know you can read! What on earth is this about?"

"You said *slump*."

Eddie's in the middle of what might be a record-breaking batting slump. He's been on the Robins for six weeks with less than a handful of base hits. If anyone's talking about the Robins, they're talking about Eddie's batting slump. "To not mention it seemed strange," Mark says as gently as possible.

"I guess so," Eddie admits. "People don't usually say it, though." He rubs the back of his neck. He looks tired, like he hasn't been sleeping and instead has been spending too much time on airplanes and in locker rooms with people who won't talk to him, and then listening to reporters ask him insulting questions. Mark's been watching Eddie's games, and if they're uncomfortable from this side of the television screen, they must be even worse to live through. If his nerves are frayed, that's no surprise.

"Okay," Mark says. "Why don't we sit down?"

Mark sits on the sofa, and Eddie chooses a wingback chair near the fireplace. Lula settles at Eddie's feet. She hasn't sat at Mark's feet like that once in her life; he swears she's gloating.

Eddie gazes miserably into his drink. "I keep thinking the next at bat will be better."

"We got a letter from a psychologist who had a lot to say about your predicament," Mark says carefully, pretty sure that Eddie won't like this, but feeling a strange pull to offer something like help. "I called her. I wonder if you might want to talk to her or one of her colleagues."

Eddie looks up, panicked. "You talked to a shrink about me?"

"I interviewed a psychologist about what causes a person to have difficulty with a task they used to execute easily."

"Why? There's no way that's going in the diary."

"I'm writing a feature about the Robins' first season for the newspaper's Sunday magazine. It'll run at the beginning of October.

Naturally, your sl—*batting difficulties*—will figure into it." Mark is aware that he phrased this in the way least likely to put Eddie's hackles up, and in doing so may be intentionally obscuring the fact that this article will almost certainly be *about* Eddie. If Eddie is upset over the drivel that Mark's writing in the diaries, then he'll hit the ceiling over the magazine article, even if there isn't anything actually objectionable in it.

Eddie frowns. "You're going to write about my . . ." He twirls a finger around his ear in the universal sign for craziness.

"No," Mark says, treading carefully. "I'm looking for a psychological angle on the phenomenon of . . ."

"Of fucking up?"

"Of having difficulty with something that used to be second nature."

"Okay," Eddie says dubiously. "I guess I can't stop you."

And, well, that's true. Eddie can't stop him. This is the first idea that's interested Mark in over a year, and he's not going to abandon it.

Eddie sighs. "My mom keeps saying that I should see a psychiatrist. She thinks my problem is that I hate New York and subconsciously want to get sent down."

Mark takes a moment to process the information that Eddie O'Leary's mother is the kind of person who uses the word *subconsciously*. "Do you think she's right?"

"Hell, no. I tried to explain to her that I don't want to get sent to Syracuse. I like making money. I liked being good at my job. What I don't like is playing in New York City. She's right about that part."

"Because the other players are unfriendly?"

Eddie shifts in his seat. "That's part of it. I just—I had friends on the team in Kansas City. Omaha's close enough that my mom could drive down to visit. And I had some privacy. I had friends in town, and I had privacy." He's looking directly at Mark.

"You had friends in town, and you had privacy," Mark repeats slowly. If Eddie had meant women, he would have said so. Mark had been prepared to forget their conversation at the soda fountain if that was what Eddie wanted.

That doesn't seem to be what Eddie wants at all. It seems like he wants someone to talk to. The fact that he's choosing a reporter is yet more proof that Eddie O'Leary has dangerously terrible judgment, and he's just lucky that Mark isn't a monster.

"That can't be easy for you," Mark says.

"That's so fucking off-the-record, Mark." Eddie sounds panicked even though they're still practically speaking in code.

"I would never."

"I know!" Eddie says, even though he can't know. He has no reason to trust Mark, and the fact that he's doing it anyway makes Mark want to scream, even though he's embarrassingly pleased by it. "I just—I'm not used to this. Who goes around talking about this kind of thing?"

The answer is that hardly anybody does. Not even Mark. Professional athletes certainly don't. "I'm sorry you don't have privacy."

Eddie makes a dismissive sound and finishes his drink. "Two minutes ago, I was upset that you might write an article making me sound like a headcase, and now I've *told* you that I'm a headcase."

Mark starts to laugh. It's not funny—it's the opposite of funny—but the fact that many psychologists treat homosexuality as an illness is why he never bothered seeing one, even a year ago when he was pretty sure he needed to. He manages to collect himself. "Liking men does *not* make you a headcase. I hope you know that."

Eddie gives him a tiny grin. "I was making a joke."

"You're funny."

Eddie shrugs. "That's another word for it."

Mark starts laughing again. He's making gay jokes with a professional baseball player in his living room. He could not feel more surreal about this if he tried.

"Don't go to the baths," Mark says.

"What?"

"If you want to meet someone. Don't go to the bars or the baths. The bars are owned by the mob, and they use secret cameras to blackmail patrons. The baths are raided too often."

A couple of years ago, he dragged William to the Everard Baths. Mark had wanted, just for a night, to feel less cut off from what felt like every other queer man in the city. It had been a stupid idea, one of the few times in his life he was reckless, but he was at his wits' end, and William must have known, or he'd never have agreed. Mark should have tried to sell William on a book club, not the *baths*, but he had remembered the baths as being fun for reasons besides the obvious. There was a swimming pool and a snack bar, for heaven's sake, and you could have a perfectly normal conversation with someone, just like you would anywhere else, but you'd know they were like you. As soon as they arrived, they ran into someone Mark knew from work—Nick, back before he'd met Andy—and William, panicked, insisted they go home. The next day they heard the place had been raided. Mark hadn't asked for anything like that again.

"Secret cameras," Eddie repeats. "What the *fuck*."

"I mean, they don't bother trying to blackmail regular people, but you're recognizable."

"I figure that's going to be a problem anywhere in this city," Eddie says grimly.

"Your safest bet is to go to parties and meet people that way."

"You go to a lot of these parties?" Eddie asks, his eyebrows raised.

"I'm not talking about—I'm not suggesting you go to an orgy. Just—make gay friends and then, you know. Have sex with them."

"Just have sex with all my new gay friends." Eddie looks very amused.

"It's what people do! I'm trying to be helpful."

"Is that what you do?"

Mark shouldn't answer—it's a personal question, and Mark isn't in the habit of giving out personal information. "No," he says, and is spared from further elaboration by the bone-rattling claxon of the kitchen timer. He nearly jumps out of his skin. It's been so long since he used that timer that he's forgotten it sounds like a nuclear war alert.

"That's my dinner," Mark says.

"Oh, I ought to leave you to it."

"Please don't. I mean, you came all this way to scold me. Might as well get in a few good yells before you head out, or at least help me eat my frozen turkey dinner."

In the kitchen, Mark manages to get the foil tray out of the oven without coming to grief.

"Don't you have a potholder?" Eddie asks.

Mark gives him a look that he hopes communicates how far removed his current mode of survival is from things like potholders.

He peels back the foil from the top of the tray and is greeted with what could charitably be described as turkey in gravy. There's another compartment—Mark can't think of a better word—filled with what had better be mashed potatoes, because any other explanation is too distressing to contemplate. There's an inexplicably triangular compartment containing peas, and a fourth one holding something he cannot and will not try to identify.

He takes a fork and spears a piece of turkey weighing approximately one gram and blows on it. Then, feeling very brave, he eats it.

"Oh, for Christ's sake. It's turkey, not brains," Eddie says. "I ate four of those frozen dinners a day the year I went through my growth spurt. My mom flat out gave up on trying to cook enough to feed me. The beef one is best."

"You can have it," Mark offers magnanimously.

"Eat your supper."

They wind up at the dining room table—Mark shoves aside his

typewriter and notebooks—with two plates, each holding food that somehow looks even sadder outside the context of its space-age foil partitions. Eddie's plate is empty before Mark's reconciled himself to the existence of the peas, and finally Eddie swears and takes Mark's plate, finishing its contents in about four bites. Mark briefly lets himself imagine making Eddie some . . . pot roast, maybe? Something filling.

"What do you usually eat?" Eddie asks.

"I usually eat at restaurants."

Eddie raises his eyebrows. Then he looks around the apartment, as if he hadn't quite taken in his surroundings. "Practically unemployed book reviewers make a better living than I might have guessed."

Mark isn't sure what Eddie's implying or indeed if he's implying anything. He might think Mark comes from money; he might think Mark turns tricks on the side.

"Oh, I didn't come by any of this honestly," Mark assures him. "Book reviewers are paid peanuts."

Eddie shoots him a curious look but doesn't ask any questions.

Mark expects Eddie to leave, but after they put the dishes in the sink, he starts prowling around the apartment, Lula trotting along beside him like she's a museum docent offering a guided tour. He looks at the bookshelves, which is fair game, but then he walks down the hall toward the bedrooms.

Mark nearly stops him, but instead follows along. After all, Mark has been doing some prying of his own, and maybe this is Eddie's attempt to make things even between them. Mark finds that he rather wants things to be even between them.

He leans against the wall, trying to imagine what exactly Eddie is seeing as he pokes about. There's the big bedroom, its mattress conspicuously bare, the smell of dust heavy in the air. There's the little bedroom, with an unmade bed, a chair covered in half-worn clothes, and a nightstand full of books. Eddie even peers into the bathroom. This is the quietest he's been since the day they met.

Mark's stopped paying any real attention to this apartment; it's his home, the backdrop of his life for eight years. Or, rather, it was the backdrop of the life he once had.

When Eddie's done, he comes to stand in front of Mark, close enough that if Mark pushes off the wall he'll be in Eddie's space. Close enough that he has to tilt his chin up a little to meet Eddie's eyes.

"Thanks for dinner," Eddie says. It's the fourth meal they've had together, counting the milkshake, and Eddie's thanked him every time. There's no reason this should be any different.

Mark swallows. "Anytime."

"I think next time needs to be my treat."

"Expense acc—"

"Yeah, yeah. Next time needs to be my treat."

"Okay," Mark says. "Okay."

As soon as Eddie leaves, the apartment is oppressively quiet. Mark doesn't mind quiet; he doesn't mind being alone. But it's too sudden, too abrupt. Eddie's voice filled the apartment, his laughter, too. Except—Mark had been laughing along with him. Mark can't remember the last time he laughed here.

Now it's empty and still, the only sound the Chopin nocturne that the girl upstairs has been practicing, sad and sweet and all wrong.

The apartment's too big for him. It was too big for him and William, an absurd extravagance. A few months ago, he thought about looking for a roommate, but the prospect of sharing space with a stranger—or worse, someone who knows him—isn't any better than rattling around this apartment by himself. Occasionally he thinks about selling it and renting someplace cheaper and more practical. He probably will, at some point, but not yet. Right now he wants to be surrounded by the memories of the life he used to have, evidence that once he was—fuck. Evidence that once he was loved.

Mark blinks past tears as he puts a kettle on the stove. When he reaches for a cup, his fingers automatically close around the handles of two mugs, and he goes still. It had taken him weeks—months, maybe—to break himself of that habit, and now here he goes again. He rests his head against the smooth wood of the cabinet door and tries again. One mug. He drops in the teabag, pours in some water, and calls it a success.

CHAPTER EIGHT

Y ou know," Andy says, "if you were hoping to keep it a secret that
you bring this little lady in to work, maybe keep her in your
office." He's standing in the doorway of Mark's office holding Lula,
who's making an energetic attempt to lick his face. Needless to say,
she's never once attempted to lick Mark's face, preferring to mostly
ignore him the way one ignores light switches and faucets and other
boring necessities.

"Lula, it looks like we've been rumbled," Mark says.

"I found her trying to get into the trash can by the elevators."

When Lula seems especially forlorn, Mark brings her to the
Chronicle. Usually she doesn't leave her bed, but she's been a bit
confused lately—barking at shadows and snapping at invisible flies.
Mark's afraid it's because she's getting older, something he's reso-
lutely not thinking about.

"You haven't been here in days," Andy says.

Mark frowns. "Were you expecting me?"

"Well, as your employer, no. You don't technically even have an
office here. On the floor plan, this is listed as a file storage room. As
a friend, though, I guess I was worried. Everything all right?"

Mark already knows that his friends worry about him, and also
that they know him well enough not to mention it too often. It's
only fair—Mark would worry about a friend who lost their part-
ner, quit their job, and basically stopped talking to everyone they
know. Probably the only thing more disturbing than spending a year

haunting an office that doesn't belong to him is suddenly *not* haunting that office.

"Yes," Mark says, trying to sound reassuring. "I've been spending a lot of time at the stadium."

"You ought to come over for dinner soon, if for no reason other than watching Nick try to act above asking you to get his baseball cards signed. We miss you."

That casual *we* bounces off Mark's consciousness, a pebble against the windshield, but the trick is to keep driving. He's happy for Nick and Andy, just like he's happy for Maureen and Lilian, but every easy *we* they utter makes him think of a *we* he never got the chance to say, and now never will.

"If you try to convince me that Nick actually said that he missed me, I'll call you a liar," Mark says. Nick can usually be relied on not to admit to having either friends or emotions; he's a blessed relief to be around sometimes.

"He said, and I quote, 'How's Mark? You should check on him,'" Andy says, with the air of a man at a card table laying down a winning hand.

"I'm doing well," Mark says, realizing with some horror that the only way he's going to put Andy's—and apparently Nick's—mind at ease is with sincerity. "I hate to admit it, but I'm enjoying writing these diaries. And last night I made myself dinner." He doesn't add that it was a frozen meal, or that he gave most of it to Eddie O'Leary. Andy's notions about journalistic ethics probably preclude getting too cozy with interview subjects. They *definitely* preclude flirting with interview subjects, but Mark is simply not going to think about whether that word is even accurate. "I'm doing better than I was a month ago," he adds, because Andy still doesn't look convinced, and also because it's true. "Anyway," he says briskly, changing the topic, "I'd like to pitch an article for the magazine. Something about O'Leary's slump and slumps in general. I'll send you my ideas."

"I'll look forward to it. Speaking of which." Andy pulls an envelope from his jacket pocket. "This came in the mail the other day. It's from a math professor in Connecticut who specializes in random numbers." He puts three stapled sheets of paper on Mark's desk.

Mark attempts to read the letter. It's mostly typed, but there are handwritten equations. "Nope. That's not making any sense at all."

"I wasn't sure it would. So, the gist is that there's no such thing as a batting slump. At least not as far as O'Leary's record goes. Basically, his stats are consistent with random numbers."

That still makes no sense, but then again Mark's math skills don't go much beyond calculating tips. "He currently holds the league record for consecutive at bats without a hit," Mark says. "That's not random."

"But it could be. You could predict that in a hundred years of tracking these things, someone would have numbers that look like O'Leary's."

"Sure, people are terrible at baseball all the time. And they either quit or get sent down."

"He's as likely to hit a home run tomorrow as he was to hit one last year."

"That's like saying *I'm* as likely to hit a home run tomorrow as he was last year." Mark feels bad talking about Eddie like this, but there's no getting around the truth. "You can't ignore how badly he's doing."

"Nobody's saying to ignore it. Look at it this way. You can treat the past six weeks as a random freak occurrence. There's no meaning to it. There's no reason for it."

"I'm literally asking you to pay me to write something meaningful about it."

"There not necessarily being an external reason doesn't mean it isn't a meaningful experience, or something meaningful to witness. Anyway, the professor's phone number is on there, if you want to call him up and see if you can get a quote. For what it's worth, I don't think he's a crackpot." Andy bends to put Lula in her bed, then shuts the office door on his way out.

Mark spends a few minutes paging through the mathematician's letter. He's pretty sure it's filled with the sort of reasoning that gives statistics a bad name. How can someone discount Eddie's last hundred at bats? At the very least, that string of failures would affect his confidence, which would lead to a lower likelihood of getting a hit during his next at bat, wouldn't it?

By the time he's done reading the letter, his head hurts, and he decides he needs a cup of coffee. Lula is fast asleep, but he shuts the office door behind him so she won't escape and bring more shame upon them.

Over the past month, the fifth floor has lost its abandoned-warehouse aesthetic as the magazine's new employees begin work. The dusty boxes, mismatched desks, and typewriters with missing keys have vanished, all replaced by sleek furniture and equally sleek-looking people. Andy has apparently sunk a tidy sum into this venture, and Mark hopes it pans out.

When he enters the kitchen, he finds four people already crowded into the small space. One is a stranger, doubtless a new hire for the magazine, but he recognizes the other three.

"Coffee maker's broken on the sixth floor again," says Cindy Wertheimer, who mainly covers women's golf, tennis, and college sports. She already has a mug of something in her hands.

"And Cindy didn't make enough for all of us," says Frank Fendall, also from the sports desk. "So now we have to wait."

"Shut the fuck up, Frank," says George Allen.

"There's a lady present," objects the man who Mark assumes works for the magazine.

"*Please* just shut the fuck up, Frank," amends George. "You heading up to the stadium later?" he asks, turning to Mark. "I'll split a cab."

"As long as you don't mind stopping at my place to drop the dog off," Mark says.

"You still writing about that crybaby O'Leary?" Frank asks. It's obviously not a real question, since he knows the answer. "So is he fucking up on purpose, or is he really just that bad?"

Mark ignores him and pointedly checks his watch, partly because that kind of gesture always nicely draws a line under ignoring someone, and partly because he has an ongoing bet with himself regarding how long it will take before someone like Frank moves from generalized insults to ones based on gender, race, or assumed sexual preferences. He keeps an eye on the second hand of his watch, and—

"You know what they say," Frank says before five seconds have passed. "What do O'Leary and a two-dollar whore have in common?"

"Shut the fuck up, Frank," Cindy and George say in unison.

"They both choke when it's time to swallow," Frank announces, looking enormously pleased with himself.

A moment of baffled silence settles over the tiny kitchen.

"That doesn't even make sense," Cindy says, shaking her head. "Honestly, Frank."

"A *lady*," moans the fourth reporter.

"It's because they're both cock—"

"A joke *is* always funniest when you need to explain it," Mark observes. He lets his voice go ever so slightly camp, not that he thinks Frank is smart enough to get it. Everyone else likely will, though, and it gives Mark a sharp, vicious little thrill. This is the first time he's been able to use the truth of his queerness to pierce the comfortable cocoon of homogeneity that bigots like to think they inhabit. He feels like he's throwing a brick through the window of a building he's despised for a long, long time. "Is there anything *you* need me to explain, Frank, dear?" he adds, watching the penny drop and Frank's face go a mottled shade of purple.

"Here's why that joke doesn't work, Frank," Cindy says.

"Is it because Frank's an idiot?" George asks.

"It's also because he's implying a *good* baseball player would swallow," Cindy points out. "And that whores choke, which I don't think they do, not if they're any good at their jobs. The metaphor falls apart."

The fourth reporter looks about two seconds away from apoplexy.

George gives Mark a hard look, but whether it's surprise, exasperation, or disgust, Mark can't tell. The point is that it doesn't matter; it doesn't need to matter to Mark anymore.

When Mark gets to the stadium, Eddie's in the trainer's room. Mark doesn't want to wait around, so he turns toward the maze of hallways that house some offices. Technically, he probably shouldn't be back here, but he's green enough that he can plead ignorance if anyone calls him out on trespassing.

These aren't the executive offices—those are upstairs, far removed from the smell of sweat, far enough to deter players and reporters from dropping by. Given that they're at the Polo Grounds, though, they're probably only a few inches further from entropy than the rest of the stadium. Most of these offices are empty, which makes sense since the Robins seem to be operating on a skeleton crew. He's surprised to hear a voice coming from behind a closed door.

"You and I both know you're looking for a reason to send me packing, and it boils your nuts that you can't." The voice has a bit of Chicago roughness that Mark identifies as belonging to Tony Ardolino, the Robins' manager.

Someone else is talking, but quietly enough that Mark can't make out their words.

"Figurative nuts," Ardolino says. "Metaphorical nuts."

Mark doesn't know whether to be more surprised that Tony Ardolino knows about metaphors or that he's apparently speaking to a
woman. The number of women who can be found around this part
of the Polo Grounds is precisely one: Constance Newbold.

"Nah," Ardolino says. "You can't get rid of me without riling
people up something awful. That's the whole reason you brought me
here, to get a name brand that might draw some crowds." A pause. "I
mean, no, obviously it hasn't worked, Connie, I know that."

A pause, during which Miss Newbold must say something.

Ardolino laughs. "Look, Con, you can't just fire everyone who gets
your panties in a bunch. Ow! Jesus. It took me an hour at a pay phone
in Pittsburgh to find a hotel—and during that time, half my team got
sloshed at the airport bar—because you fired the person whose job
it is to book the fucking hotels, and before that you fired the person
whose job it is to hire people. You can't fire every asshole on the payroll
because there won't anybody left, including you and me."

There's another pause, during which the quieter voice murmurs
something unintelligible.

"Okay, fine, some of them quit. But you're doing the work of half
the front office. I'm doing the work of three people. You can't get rid
of me, because you won't find anyone else dumb enough to take on
all this work."

"Just watch me!" says Constance Newbold, almost a shout.

Mark's just thinking that he ought to make himself scarce when
the door swings open and Miss Newbold steps out. Mark sets about
lighting a cigarette so he looks like he has something to do, but she
ignores him completely. When Ardolino emerges a moment later,
he gives Mark a look that's about six times as shrewd as anything he
expects from Ardolino.

Mark grinds his barely touched cigarette under his foot. He's
heard that the Robins front office is a shambles, and he can make
some guesses as to why Constance Newbold saw fit to fire many of

the men her father had hired, and why others quit. Firing anyone who openly opposed her probably made a lot of sense at the time.

Mark sets off to find George Allen. "Does Newbold really want to fire Ardolino, or was she letting off steam?" he asks, his voice low.

George raises his eyebrows. "Somebody say something?"

Mark repeats as much of the conversation as he can remember. "I'm wondering if Newbold can't find anyone to work for her. Maybe she's being blackballed. Or maybe the organization is being blackballed until she steps down."

"Could be. The other owners don't like her."

"Why would the owners of other teams care whether the Robins are owned by a woman?"

"They can't work with a woman the way they're used to working with one another."

Mark takes this to mean that the other owners don't want to invite a woman to their collusion parties, or however millionaires come up with new ways to hoard their money.

"I'll write about rumors and see what dirt that stirs up," George says. "I'd hate to see Ardolino go, though."

"You like him."

"He's hard not to like. He's a mess, but you get to be as old as me and you realize damn near everyone goes through a time when they're a mess. Problem is that most people who haven't had it happen to them yet think it's virtue and clean living keeping them out of the gutter."

"Isn't that the truth," Mark agrees. "George, how on earth are you keeping up with this? You're covering every game on top of writing two columns a week."

George shrugs. "When you spend a couple decades doing something, it comes easy," he says with the air of someone who's delivered that same pat response any number of times. "Anyway, being around these fellas keeps me young."

"And you don't want to retire?

"I'd rather walk into traffic." He lights a cigarette and turns toward the locker room. "No, I just love this dumb fucking game."

Either the encounter with awful Frank at the *Chronicle* primed Mark to notice unsavory language, or the Robins' locker room is worse than usual, because as soon as Mark walks in, he's hit with a wall of slurs.

He shouldn't be surprised—he's actually surprised that he *is* surprised. It says more about Mark's isolation than it does about anybody else.

Eddie's sitting on the three-legged stool in front of his stall, bending to tie his cleats. He looks up and catches Mark's eye, and Mark doesn't need to wonder whether Eddie just heard the same thing he did. Eddie gives a tiny shake of his head. Mark doesn't know him well enough to understand whether that shake means "Don't come over here, because I'll start crying if anyone's nice to me" or if it just means "Don't be stupid enough to acknowledge what you just heard." So Mark gives him a nod and heads up to the press box. It isn't until he's sitting in one of the creaky wooden chairs that he realizes that the disappointment he's feeling is because he's gotten used to Eddie being happy to see him. And that would be bad enough, but what's worse is that Mark's always happy to see Eddie, too. He's been looking forward to this all day.

Mark doesn't even pretend not to have his opera glasses trained on Eddie the entire game. Eddie's still stiff in the dugout and still walks to the plate like he's on the way to the guillotine. If anything, it's getting worse. It makes Mark physically uncomfortable to watch him, and he knows he isn't the only one. A strange tension settles over the crowd every time Eddie's at the plate, something that might just be plain dejection, but Mark doesn't think so. Whenever Eddie heads back to the dugout, looking utterly defeated, a smattering of applause comes from the upper deck. That's new.

Mark's watched a lot of ball games, and he's watched even more theater. He knows how a crowd acts when they're unhappy: they fidget, they chatter, they get up and leave. This crowd is staying put. They know the Robins will probably lose, they know Eddie probably won't get a hit, but for some reason they care about the game anyway. The crowd is hopeful, but it isn't the kind of hope that comes with a fighting chance. It's a hope that doesn't need success to validate it. It's something like affection, maybe with a bit of loyalty mixed in.

For a moment Mark can't figure out why. Why watch the Robins when a mile away there's a team that wins the World Series more often than it doesn't? Why invest your feelings in a team this bad, a player this out of luck? Every single person here could have avoided rooting for the Robins—nobody inherited team loyalty from their families or their neighborhoods. It would make nearly as much sense to root for the Phillies, today's opposing team.

And then he remembers how he felt when he first watched Eddie on the television, the sense that he was watching something doomed. He recalls what George said a few hours earlier, about everyone going through a period of hellishness at some point. There's something about a run of miserable luck that's near universal. Right now Eddie's living through it on a national stage.

In the sixth inning, Eddie's covering second base when a runner slides directly into him. From the press box, it looks like Eddie's foot was on the bag, and the runner is out. It also looks like the runner deliberately slid feetfirst into Eddie, who's bent over and holding his injured leg. Mark, looking through his opera glasses, reassures himself that there isn't any blood.

The umpire, though, says the runner is safe. The crowd boos in protest, even though the Robins are already three runs behind and it's late in the game. Ardolino jogs out from the dugout, but Eddie is already talking to the umpire. The press box has gone silent as everyone leans forward, trying to hear what Eddie and the umpire are saying. Before Mark can quite figure out what's happening, Eddie is shouting. When he takes off his cap and throws it, it misses the umpire by inches. The umpire's "You're outta here!" is loud enough to reverberate through the huge old bathtub that is the Polo Grounds.

"Can't throw your cap," George Allen says. Mark hadn't even noticed when George took the seat next to his. "Also can't call an umpire a motherfucker."

"I didn't hear that," Mark says.

"Fifty years and I can lip-read most profanities at a hundred yards."

Mark knows, logically, that Eddie has a temper. That outburst Eddie had after learning of his trade was proof enough. But Mark has never seen that temper in action until now. He watches as Eddie heads off the field in the direction of the tunnel that will take him to the locker room.

He wonders if Eddie hears the crowd cheering for him.

~~

"You shouldn't be here," Eddie says, his words too loud in the empty locker room. He's sitting on his stool, his head in his hands.

"Says who?"

Eddie looks up. "Press comes in *after* the game."

"I'm not here as press." Mark's here as an *idiot*, a fool of a grown man who sees a friend—not a friend, barely even an acquaintance—having a bad day and wants to help. "Did you get hurt?"

"If you're not here as press, you shouldn't be here at all."

Mark knows Eddie's right; you can't just wander into a locker room. "Want me to take off?"

Eddie sighs and visibly deflates. "In a minute."

"How's your leg?"

"Just bruised." He lifts an ice bag and shows Mark his calf. "He didn't get me with his spikes. I don't think he meant to hit me at all."

Mark is much less sure of that. He wants to touch Eddie's calf, checking for broken skin. He wants to demand an X-ray, a tetanus shot, a splint. He wants a doctor—a team of doctors—to come in here and prove that Eddie's perfectly fine.

"I'm more pissed about that shitty call," Eddie says.

"It happens, right? That's not the first bad call you've ever seen." He's pretty sure it is the first time Eddie's mouthed off at an umpire, though.

"Did you see how good Luis's throw was?"

"The crowd was really with you," Mark says.

Eddie looks at him like he's nuts. "When I struck out three times and got thrown out of the game?"

"Well, yes." Mark feels foolish trying to put into words the feeling he had watching the crowd earlier, and he knows Eddie won't believe him anyway.

"Get out of here before people talk," Eddie says. Mark knows he just means that people will notice that Mark's in a part of the stadium where he shouldn't be, but it still rubs him the wrong way. It's an echo of all the other times he's kept to the shadows because otherwise people might talk.

Mark should go. He shouldn't have come in the first place. But he also isn't going to leave Eddie sitting here alone and miserable. He looks rough, all nerves and tension with some fatigue layered over the top. He looks worse than when he showed up at Mark's apartment a few nights ago; he's been looking progressively more ragged all season. He needs a decent meal and someone to tuck him in, and the fact that for one deranged moment Mark wants to be the one to do it is truly not a good sign.

He puts a hand on Eddie's shoulder. He means to say something comforting, but he's startled by the strangeness of touching someone. No, not that—people do touch him. Lilian and Andy shake his hand. Maureen hugs him. Nick's perfected this back slap that's about as close to a hug as a fairly paranoid queer man can get. It takes Mark a moment to realize what's different: this is Mark reaching out, Mark using touch to communicate something that he can't—and shouldn't—put into words.

"I'm sorry this is happening," Mark finally says.

Eddie puts his own hand over Mark's and squeezes. It means nothing; Mark knows this. He's seen Eddie's teammates touch one another in all kinds of ways. But Eddie doesn't let go. He looks up, his eyes tired and bloodshot.

"I was exhausted the first year I was in New York," Mark says, and he doesn't quite realize this is the story he's going tell until he's already telling it. "I came here under—less than ideal circumstances. I managed to enroll in college despite not having a high school diploma, and then had to work two jobs to pay for everything. The sane and normal thing would have been night school. But no—I had to take the same number of classes a semester as people who weren't even working one job. I had to get all As. I was trying to prove something, and I still don't know if I was trying to prove it to myself or to my—to the people who thought I was worthless. And I kept on going, even after I graduated and got a good job."

He's eliding over years of his life here. The truth is that he kept pushing himself even when he didn't have to worry about rent, even when he was in a position where he could write his own ticket at the *Chronicle* and turn down work for *The New Yorker* and *Esquire* as often as he accepted it, but the urgency—the sense that his own failure was chasing him—only let up when he started sharing a bed and a breakfast table with a man whose implicit faith in Mark's worth was unshakable, bedrock-solid.

"I'm sure that I'm supposed to tell you that you shouldn't do that," Mark continues, "that you should believe in yourself without needing proof, but I'm not like that, and maybe you aren't, either. What I can tell you is that whatever calamity you're imagining? There's a day after that."

Mark should have known better than to try his hand at pep talks, because that was a pretty bad one by any standard. There's a day after calamity? Uttered by a man who's spent sixteen months *reeling* from calamity? Did he seriously just offer "there's always tomorrow" in dead, embarrassing earnest as an attempt at comfort? He's about to apologize and back out of the locker room when Eddie's expression shifts into something that might be the distant relation of a smile.

"Mark," he says. His eyes are hazy and a little surprised.

A moment passes and the atmosphere palpably shifts, rapidly closing the distance between warm and scorching. Mark's entire consciousness compresses to the overheated space between Eddie O'Leary's palm and shoulder. That heat had been there when they said goodbye a few nights earlier. He can't deny that there's a spark, and he doesn't want to. It looks like Eddie doesn't want to, either.

After the game, Eddie's never alone in the locker room long enough for Mark to say a single word to him. First, he's surrounded by reporters. Then there always seems to be a teammate nearby, and it takes Mark a minute to realize that the Robins are shielding Eddie from the press.

Mark watches as Eddie heads out with Ardolino and a few players. Eddie isn't a good enough actor to look anything other than both baffled and delighted as his teammates pay attention to him. He beams at the second baseman, and it's the first time Mark's seen this smile, Eddie's real smile, turned on anyone but himself. Good. Eddie deserves this—he deserves to have teammates who talk to him and want to spend time with him. It's silly that Mark thought they might go out and grab something to eat.

"You taking a cab back downtown?" George asks when the locker room is mostly cleared out.

They had shared a cab from the *Chronicle* to the stadium, only stopping in front of Mark's building long enough for Mark to take Lula upstairs.

"Sure," Mark says. "Where do you live?"

"Twenty-Ninth and Third."

"We're practically neighbors," Mark says, surprised. He's known this man for years. But he shouldn't be surprised. Mark remembers deflecting conversations away from neighborhoods, knowing that any reference to where he lived would invite questions about how he afforded it, whether he had a roommate. "I'd have thought you'd live in the suburbs," he tells George when they're in the cab. "Queens or something." He doesn't mean anything by it, only that married, middle-class white people seem to take any opportunity to move to a house with a lawn.

"We always figured we'd move when we had kids. And that never happened, so we stayed put. Lived in the same apartment since the twenties."

George's wife died two years earlier—there had been an awkward lunch at which Mark couldn't imagine what to say, until George saved the day with a litany of complaints about the Knicks. Mark supposes he was aware that George didn't have any children, because you can always count on parents to mention that fact at least once an hour. He doesn't know why it feels important—why the existence of children or grandchildren should change the complexion of a person's grief, or even whether it does. He thinks of George alone in his apartment, no children visiting to make sure he's taking care of himself. But that isn't George's life at all—he's spent the past few months with the Robins, bouncing from stadium to hotel room to airplane to train. Every time Mark sees him at the Polo Grounds, George runs into some old friend. At the *Chronicle*, he's treated like a minor celebrity. He's about as far from alone as a man can be.

Still, Mark balks at the idea of sending George home alone. "Do you want to come up for a drink?" He has the fleeting, hysterical thought that it sounds like a come-on. "The doorman will make sure you get a cab home."

Mark's sure George will say no, and is even a bit preemptively disappointed. But then George shrugs. "Sure. Why not."

Lula greets George like her oldest, dearest friend despite having never laid eyes on him until a few hours earlier in the cab.

"I think she just hates me," Mark says.

"Most people's dogs don't hate them. Dogs just don't have it in them."

"Yeah, but she wasn't—she isn't—" He stumbles over how to end the sentence. It isn't complicated: *She wasn't mine. I inherited her.* He doesn't know why he can't get the words out. Instead he says, "She was really William's dog," as if George will even know who William was.

"Ruth's cat spent fifteen years pretending I wasn't there," George says. "And when Ruth died, he kept up the act."

Mark goes still. He knows he's staring. But Ruth was George's wife, which means George made the comparison right there, out loud, plain as day. It's one thing for Mark to do that, or for Lilian or some other queer person. An elderly sportswriter, though? Mark thinks he's within his rights to be taken by surprise.

"Can I get you something to drink?" he manages. "I have the usual things." Remembering how little he had to offer Eddie the other night, Mark picked up a couple bottles of tonic and soda, and now he has a pitcher of orange juice in the refrigerator, too.

"Whiskey, neat, thanks."

When Mark returns to the living room with a pair of whiskeys, Lula is sitting next to George on the sofa, despite having never once been allowed on that piece of furniture. She looks so pleased with herself that Mark doesn't have the heart to shoo her off.

"Be careful with O'Leary," George says.

"Everything I'm writing is practically a PR piece," Mark says, thinking that George is worried about the Robins making life difficult for *Chronicle* reporters.

George grunts out a laugh. "Kid, I don't know what you're doing with O'Leary, but it isn't public relations."

"I beg your pardon," Mark says weakly. He knows he's been . . . flirting, maybe, with Eddie, but only in private.

"Anyway, I'm not talking about the damn diaries. I'm talking about spending time alone with him. He's not married. You're a smart kid."

Mark realizes this is why George agreed to come up for a drink. He couldn't say this at the *Chronicle* or at the stadium, or even in the cab with the driver there to overhear.

"You know what locker rooms are like," George says. "Shit, you know what the world is like. I guess you don't make any secret of what you are?"

Mark, who had been standing, sinks into a chair. There's no venom in George's voice; there's not a trace of disgust or accusation, but Mark can't quite bring himself to look at the older man, not wanting to see what's on his face. "I'm trying—" he starts. "For a long time, I—" No, that won't work, either. "Not anymore," is what he settles on. "Not since . . ."

"Who the hell's idea was it to send you into the locker room anyway? The littlest Fleming? I guess he doesn't know about . . ." He makes a vague gesture in Mark's direction.

Andy *does* know, of course, but he's rich and idealistic, and that sometimes makes him blind to hard truths. Or maybe he figures it isn't an issue, since it's not like Mark's the first gay man to enter a locker room. Baseball's been around since the Civil War, for heaven's sake. "I have every right to be in that locker room," Mark says.

"I'm not talking about rights. I'm talking about how this is going to blow up in your face, and my face, and especially O'Leary's face. This afternoon at the *Chronicle*, you as good as told four reporters, and even a shithead like Frank is capable of taking a clue. It's only a matter of time before someone tells someone else and then the Robins are asking why we sent a—a—"

Mark can almost hear the ugly words George considers and dismisses. "Homosexual?" he suggests.

"—a homosexual into their locker room. People will ask whether O'Leary, having spent so much time with you, knew."

Mark wants to say that it *is* about rights, that they wouldn't be having this conversation if he had the same rights as that idiot Frank. But he knows that isn't what George is getting at: the point is that this is dangerous for Eddie.

He recoils at the idea of having to act like he's exposed Eddie to gay radiation just by having shared a few meals that were maybe a shade too friendly to be written off as strictly professional. Mark hasn't crossed a single line with Eddie; he's done nothing that wouldn't pass muster if he were straight, or at least pretending to be straight.

George gets to his feet, one hand braced on the small of his back. He coughs, and it's the kind of cough that sounds like a thousand identical coughs have come before it, and it's only a matter of time before his rib cage simply gives up. Mark wants to ask if George is okay, but George sends him a quelling look that plainly communicates one, he is not okay, and two, Mark is not going to change the subject. "I think you should talk to Fleming and hand this assignment off to somebody else," George says.

"I'll think about it," Mark says, even though he won't.

George looks around. "How long has it been?"

Mark doesn't need to ask what he's getting at. "Sixteen months. Well, closer to seventeen now."

George frowns, probably counting back, remembering that February 1959 is when Mark stopped being available for lunch, stopped doing practically everything. "Only two things in the world people count by months. How old a baby is, and how long since something awful happened."

Lula tries to bite George's shoe on his way out the door.

"I think she blames me," Mark blurts out. "For William not being here anymore."

He hasn't told anyone that. Lilian would say he was giving the dog too much credit. Maureen would cry.

George puts on his hat. "Could be. Ruth's cat ran away a month after the funeral."

CHAPTER NINE

Two days later, Mark and George are sharing another cab home from the *Chronicle* when they hit a patch of traffic crossing Canal Street.

"Connie Newbold herself called the *Chronicle*, demanding to know who my source was for that column about Ardolino being fired," George says.

"Did they tell her?"

"No. But you should know that your name came up."

"I didn't have anything to do with that story except for pointing you in the right direction."

"We work at the same paper. They know you're ghostwriting that diary for O'Leary, and everybody in the league knows by now that O'Leary's a talker."

"He's never said anything about Ardolino. He's a good kid," Mark adds, as if that phrase could possibly encompass precisely what Eddie is—hot-tempered but fundamentally kind, sweet but far too trusting.

"You're not planning to take my advice, are you?" George says.

"No," Mark says slowly. "I'm not going to act like I'm a danger for decent people to associate with."

"I didn't mean—"

"I know," Mark says, although it's pretty clear that George meant exactly that. Mark can't exactly fault him. Maybe Mark *is* a danger, but he shouldn't have to act like it, and if that's a contradiction, then he doesn't really care.

When the cab pulls up in front of George's building, George thanks him for the ride. "I'm sorry," George says as he gets out. Mark doesn't know if he's apologizing for what he said, for how Mark interpreted it, or just for the world being what it is. "You're not bothering anybody," he adds before shutting the car door, and Mark supposes that *you* could mean Mark in particular or queer people in general. Or maybe it means Mark and Eddie.

It doesn't matter exactly what George means by any of it. He's making an effort, and it's more than Mark expects from straight people—especially older ones. George is old enough to be Mark's father—his grandfather, even—and the contrast between "You're not bothering anybody" and "Get out of my house and never come back" is pretty stark. George is a decent man, full of what he probably considers the right principles, and he's trying to make those principles encompass people like Mark.

It's really the minimum Mark ought to ask from the universe, but it's a hell of a lot more than he expects, so he finds that he's in a tolerably good mood as he pays the cabbie and walks the rest of the way home. It's the end of June, and nice enough for him to take off his jacket even at night.

Maybe it's the warm breeze that makes him feel unguarded enough to acknowledge how much his—it takes him a moment to identify this not as simply a good mood but as something like *contentment*—owes to looking forward to the next time he gets to talk to Eddie. It's just a little flirtation—it's not like Mark's going to do anything about it—but it still feels nice.

"You're making it a problem," William would say. "Over a year without so much as kissing someone, for pity's sake. You're turning it into a milestone, and you know where that leads. It leads to you crying at the Rockefeller Center Christmas tree."

Mark tells imaginary William to fuck off. Last December had been unspeakable—how could it have been anything else, when every goddamn Christmas song is about missing people—even though William hadn't even cared about Christmas. Neither does Mark, for that matter. But Mark had been gloomily obsessing over how he'd get through it, which of course had made everything that much worse.

He thinks of Eddie's hand on his in the locker room, remembers the look in his eye, and it's like he's caught an English phrase in a foreign bazaar, a bar from a half-forgotten song, and he lets himself remember what it is to *want*.

"Well then, there's your answer," imaginary William says, smug as all hell, and for some reason it's that remembered smugness, the way William would flick the newspaper up over his face to end a conversation, the way he was stubborn and righteous and entitled—that's what makes Mark's eyes prickle, right in the middle of Lexington Avenue.

He might never stop missing William, but these moments of being *accosted* by missing him are happening further and further apart. He has no idea if this is normal. It occurs to him that he could probably ask George.

He takes a lap around the block to compose himself, but when he's upstairs in the privacy of his apartment, there's nothing to stop him from wallowing to his heart's content. Instead he pets a grudging Lula, then picks her up to let her look out the window. He doesn't suppose she really appreciates the view, but she always looks so attentively at the treetops of Gramercy Park, at the lights of the buildings surrounding the park and the taillights of the cars on the streets below. "It's your inheritance," William used to tell her. "Think of all the dogs who don't have any kind of view at all."

Now it makes Mark laugh, and he thinks that even if he never goes back to the way he used to be, he might still be all right.

Mark kneels in front of the television, adjusting the dial. A television that might have been state of the art in 1952 is just not cutting it in 1960. He can make out the number on the back of Eddie's away jersey and knows that what he's seeing is Eddie throwing a runner out, but the picture is too grainy to get any detail.

His face is maybe two inches from the glass, close enough for static electricity to tug at his hair. He remembers sitting in this exact position six weeks earlier, watching Eddie strike out. He had known he was watching a disaster, the shipwreck of a career. He's still pretty sure that's what he's watching. The only difference is how badly he wants to be wrong.

He gets to his feet and adjusts the antennae, and the picture on the screen suddenly shifts into focus long enough to see a Cardinal at the plate.

Abruptly, the screen returns to static. Swearing, Mark smacks the side of the television, but it doesn't help. He looks around the room, as if he's going to find a solution somewhere among the Wedgwood and Hepplewhite. He puts on some shoes, ignores Lula's pointed glance toward the leash, and before the inning is over, he's in a bar he always walks past on the way to the subway.

It's a weekday evening, and the bar is filled with people stopping in on the way home from work. Mark's never set foot in the place—there was never any point to drinking here when he could have a drink with William at home. But there's a television hanging over the bar, and that's all he really cares about right now. He slides onto a stool and orders a scotch and soda without taking his eyes off the screen.

Buddy Rosenthal gets a triple, the next batter strikes out, and then Eddie's in the on-deck circle.

A few seats over, someone grumbles, "Ardolino's gotta be drunk or asleep not to send in a pinch hitter for O'Leary. It'll be a waste of Rosenthal's triple."

Mark manages not to glare at the stranger, but honestly, he had the same thought. So, no doubt, did Eddie.

"That poor kid is trying," says the bartender. "Grit."

A few people grunt their assent. Nobody's really talking to one another, but they're all talking about the same thing with the bartender as a sort of intermediary, in the way that strangers at a bar do when they have no real interest in a conversation but still want to hear someone else's voice.

He doesn't want this to be the end for Eddie. He desperately, desperately doesn't want this to be the end for a man who's reckless and short-tempered but *kind*. Bad things shouldn't happen to people like Eddie O'Leary. Mark knows what it feels like to have the rug pulled out from under you, for the things you count on to disappear in the blink of an eye, and he wants something else for Eddie. He wants proof that something else exists on the other side of what looks for all the world like an ending.

Mark leans forward on his stool. This game is the next thing to meaningless, but he's watching it like it's the seventh game of the World Series and he has money on one side.

Eddie walks up to the plate. The first pitch is a ball. The second would have been a ball, at least according to the announcer, but Eddie swings at it anyway. And the third pitch—Mark thinks his heart stops at the sound of wood connecting with leather. The bar goes silent for long enough to hear ice bumping against glass.

"Well, will you look at that," says a man a few stools over.

"Attaboy," says a man close to George Allen's age.

The camera shows Eddie safely reaching first before abruptly switching to Rosenthal being thrown out at home. The inning's over, and Eddie's hit didn't amount to anything.

The commentators immediately start talking about how Eddie's hit was meaningless, that his batting average is terrible, that even with a hit he's *cursed*. He's a waste of money, a waste of a roster spot. Eddie's bad luck, they're saying, extends beyond his batting slump, beyond things he can control.

Mark's heart is racing with indignation. The commentators are being ridiculous. He knows that. This kind of bloviating is just how they fill the dead air.

"What a pack of ghouls," says the man two seats over.

"They won't let the kid alone," agrees the bartender.

"Cursed, my hat," says someone else. "He's had a bad slump. Show me the man who hasn't."

Two men clink their mostly empty glasses, toasting bad luck. Toasting the fact that bad luck is both inevitable and impermanent. Even terrible things come to an end.

"To slumps," Mark hears himself saying, and buys a round of drinks.

When the game is over—the Robins lose by a single run—he goes home. After the noise of the bar and the racing of his heart, the apartment is heavy with quiet. He grabs the nearest notebook and transcribes as much of the conversation at the bar as he can remember, along with his thoughts, knowing that it's all going to make it into the piece he's pitching for the magazine. Knowing, too, that Eddie won't like it. But Mark has gone so long without caring about anything that he has to chase this flicker of interest.

He reaches for Lula's leash. She looks at him like she's torn between scolding him for not knowing that this isn't an official walk time, and not looking a gift horse in the mouth. If she had a pocket watch, she'd take it out and check it. But he has to get out of here before the emptiness gets to him, before he starts seeing all the spaces that shouldn't be empty.

Except, what he thinks of isn't William in his favorite chair, his arm extended toward an ashtray that isn't there anymore, but

George Allen sitting with Lula on the couch. And then Eddie taking up all the space in the kitchen doorway. And Lilian unpacking Chinese takeout in the dining room while Maureen slips Lula half a fortune cookie.

Those are empty spaces he can fix. They're hardly even empty, just an ellipsis. He could have Lilian here in an hour if he needed to. And who cares if Mark has a silly crush on Eddie; who cares if Eddie is just paying attention to him because he's lonely. Mark's lonely, too. There's a good chance that his phone will ring at an ungodly hour that night, and Mark is looking forward to it. He's looking forward, period, and that's new, too.

Part IV

JULY

CHAPTER TEN

Thanks to thunderstorms in Chicago, today's game against the Cubs gets canceled, and half the team takes it as a sign to hit the bars early, which means half the team will be playing hungover tomorrow.

Eddie says as much to Luis in the cab back to the hotel.

"It will not matter," Luis says. "Drunk, not drunk, we play the same."

Luis goes to bed, because he, at least, is responsible, and Eddie tries to find a spot in the lobby to finally finish Mark's book. He's been putting it off, not wanting to know what awful fate awaits the characters. But before he can find a comfortable place to sit, he hears his name. Turning, he sees Sam Price on a stool at the hotel bar.

Eddie's been on the team for two months, and Price has never said a word to him before now. Honestly, Eddie's not sure he'd even expect Price to talk to him under normal circumstances, silent treatment or no. First, he's a pitcher, and second, other than Ardolino, he's mostly friendly with the other Black players and cordial to everybody else. It had been like that in Kansas City, too; Eddie's always figured that nobody wants to waste their time sifting through the bigots to figure out who the non-bigots are, so they play it safe.

"Take a seat," Price says, gesturing at the empty stool beside him. He has an empty glass and a filled-out crossword puzzle on the bar in front of him.

"Good evening," Eddie says, then tacks on "sir" like a prize fucking idiot.

Price seems to agree, because he blinks slowly and shakes his head a little. "Have a drink." He waves the bartender over.

"I don't—"

"Have a goddamned seltzer, I don't care. I don't know how they do things in Nebraska, but in civilized places you can't sit there and take up space at a bar without ordering something."

Eddie is vaguely surprised that Price knows where he's from. He orders an orange juice.

"You don't drink," Price says.

"Sure I do. Just not—" Eddie doesn't know how to finish that sentence. Just not enough to get blind drunk five nights a week? Just not enough so that he's hungover during a game? "Just not always," he finishes. "My dad drank too much," he adds before he can think better of it.

"I'd like to know whose old man didn't," Price grumbles. "Doesn't stop anybody else. Look, I know you think Ardolino is a useless old drunk—"

"I don't—"

"You said it on television. Have the courage of your convictions."

Eddie tries to fight back the urge to defend himself, or, better yet, to get up and storm out. "What I said was in the heat of the moment. And I regret it. I don't think he's useless. I don't really care how much he drinks, but I think he sets a bad example. He's the manager, for chrissakes. He's supposed to stop guys from staying out too late or getting blind drunk, and instead he's doing it right alongside them."

"A bad example," Price repeats. "Whoever said a bunch of grown men need an example. You're one of the youngest on the team, and you're twenty-two. An example," he scoffs. "Set your own goddamn example."

Eddie turns his attention to his orange juice so he doesn't say that he can think of three players who are throwing away their careers—not to mention their marriages, the respect of their kids, and probably their health—in exchange for some New York nightlife.

"He's not all bad," Price says. "Give him a chance."

"I wouldn't know."

"What?"

"It's not like I've had a chance to get to know anyone on the team."

"Oh, don't pout. Better men than you have put up with worse than the silent treatment. You earned it. Did you even think about apologizing for what you said? I mean, yelling at the umpire and getting thrown out of the game counts as an apology for most of these clowns, but you could consider being an adult about it."

Eddie almost laughs, because it's true—after Eddie cursed out the umpire, most of the team thawed. Sometimes he'll get invited out, mostly as an afterthought, but it still counts. And if he asks for a roll of tape or some oil of wintergreen, someone will lend him theirs. Nobody's warm, but they're treating him like a teammate, because when Eddie got thrown out of the game, he was treating *them* like teammates.

"And if you want someone to be an example," Price goes on, "you know how Tony and I played together for a couple years?"

Eddie doesn't point out that, given the number of times Tony Ardolino was traded late in his career, he played with practically everyone in both leagues. "Yeah," he says. "What about it?"

"That was '51, '52, right? Not every team was integrated. Anyway, he started spiking players who tried to start shit."

As far as Eddie's aware, Tony Ardolino never needed an excuse to spike anybody. In one of George Allen's columns, syndicated in the *Omaha World-Herald* and stuck between the pages of Eddie's algebra textbook to read on the sly, he wrote that Tony Ardolino regarded the spikes of his cleats as having a special affinity with the flesh of second basemen. However, if some of those incidents were retaliation for bad behavior, Eddie is reluctantly intrigued.

"What about that catcher?" Eddie asks. A few years ago, Ardolino had barreled straight into a catcher and broke the guy's collarbone. That's around the time everyone agreed Ardolino might be a psychopath.

"He had it coming," Price says darkly.

"Okay, so he's a jerk for a good cause," Eddie says, although he's a little surprised to learn that Ardolino cares about anything but alcohol and women. "Good for him."

"And you may have noticed what people *don't* say in the Robins locker room."

"Yeah, I have," Eddie admits. There are very few racial slurs, even of the "I'm only joking" variety. Plenty of nasty language about women, though, and queer men—but Eddie doesn't let himself think about that, so he doesn't. "You're gonna tell me that's Ardolino's doing?"

"You see somebody else in charge here?"

Eddie wants to say that he's waiting for some evidence that anyone at all is in charge, but it's true that if he had been paying attention to anything other than his own misery, he might have wondered what exactly happened to get the team to behave itself.

"Okay," Eddie says. "So he did something good."

"Hell, no, it isn't good. It's right. And he does it. He knows people are paying attention to this team, and he's making sure it stands for the right things. He's doing it for the players, and also for the fans. Tony Ardolino knows how to set a goddamn example."

"I didn't know," Eddie says stupidly.

"I know you didn't know," Price says, a little mockingly. "There's a whole wide world beyond Eddie O'Leary's batting slump."

"Hey," Eddie says in the Cubs' visitors' locker room, just before the game is due to start. A few of his teammates glance over. "Hey," Eddie repeats, a little louder. "Can I say something?"

"I don't know, can you?" mutters one of the outfielders, two stalls over.

"I want to apologize," Eddie says, before he runs out of nerve. "I'm sorry for what I said when I learned I was being traded here. I was really upset and taken by surprise, and I think I would have run my mouth about any team I was getting traded to. I don't want to make excuses, but I wish I hadn't said any of it."

He glances around, and nobody seems angry with him. The guys playing gin rummy are looking up from their cards with only mild curiosity. Rosenthal looks like he'd like to get back to lacing his cleats. Varga's having trouble getting his shirt over his head, and it's kind of nice to see evidence that it isn't only playing first base that Varga can't manage with any finesse. He owes these guys an apology, and maybe he should have done it weeks ago, but he's not sure he could have done it then, when he was still so cut up about being traded.

"And none of what I said is true anyway," he says, which is more or less honest. He had called them talentless layabouts, and they definitely aren't layabouts—they might have better chances if that's all they were. What they are is just a bunch of people who were thrown together, half of them playing just because it's another year to put off retiring or getting sent down, some brought up too soon from the minors, and a whole bunch of them playing positions they've never played before, because that's what the team needs.

"That's enough of that," Ardolino says. "Apology accepted, O'Leary. Can we go play some baseball now?"

And damn it if the apology doesn't work, because after the game he gets dragged out to a bar. He has a beer and listens to an outfielder and the bullpen catcher have an argument about the Democratic National Convention in which they're both wrong. Then he has another beer and admires some wrinkled, wallet-sized photographs of the apparently limitless number of babies his teammates have fathered. It's all incredibly normal and a little boring, and Eddie will never take it for granted again.

When it's nearly midnight, he throws some money on the table to cover his drinks and says he's heading back to the hotel. Really, that's what they all should do, but Eddie has the sense to keep his mouth shut about it. Enforcing curfew is Ardolino's job, and he won't do it because he's two tables over with his arm around a lady. Eddie has never in his life heard of a manager who drinks with his team, but—he takes a deep breath and reminds himself that getting irritated won't win them any games—Ardolino clearly has other priorities.

When he gets back to the hotel, he doesn't even go to bed, though, so he's basically a hypocrite. Instead he digs some coins out of his pocket and heads to the nearest phone booth.

"It's midnight," Mark says instead of answering the phone in a normal way.

"Were you asleep?" Eddie asks.

"That's not the point."

"Are you ever asleep at midnight?"

A pause. "No, but that's not the—"

"Do you even *want* to be asleep at midnight."

"Oh my *God*."

"I rest my case."

"I'll rest your case," Mark grumbles, but Eddie thinks he can hear the smile in his voice.

"So, this book," Eddie says. "You've read it more than once." The dust jacket is worn, and the binding is broken; it's as battered as Eddie's own copy of *The Martian Chronicles*, which he must have read eight times in high school. But according to the copyright page, *The Haunting of Hill House* only came out last fall, which means Mark must have read it a bunch of times in a row.

"So what?"

Eddie can't imagine wanting to reread this book. He finished it late last night, and now has it hidden at the bottom of his suitcase, face-down, so it doesn't accidentally scare him. "What do you like about it?" he asks, hoping it doesn't sound like *What is wrong with you?*

Mark is silent, and Eddie isn't sure if the line's gone dead or if he's just put his foot in his mouth.

"It has all the ingredients of a happy life, but put together wrong. Someone who understands you, a house to live in, food on the table," Mark begins.

Eddie doesn't say that most people probably wouldn't consider that enough. But apparently Mark does, and Eddie files that away, adding it to the tiny stockpile of facts about Mark that he's amassed.

"There's another version of the story, in some other universe," Mark goes on, "where two eccentric women live together in a weird old house and share sweaters and read in bed. I mean, that's what happens in this book. It's temporary, and it ends—not so well. But it happens anyway."

Eddie thinks about how he had felt at the soda fountain. Logically, Eddie already knew there were other queer people in New York. But hearing Mark say so made him feel like he was in a strange new place and heard someone calling his name.

"And so it *can* happen," Eddie says.

"It's just—I don't know. I like seeing it in black-and-white. There are other books with queer characters, obviously. I mean, I have a shelf full of them—"

"You do?" Eddie's never come across a character he can even imagine might be queer. But maybe that's because he always expects everyone to be straight. Maybe it's because he's been so careful not to think about that sort of thing. He wants to borrow a book from that shelf, one that Mark's written all over.

"They're on the second bookcase over from the fireplace. I'll point it out the next time you come over. But anyway, it's not like I'm just charmed by the novelty of seeing lesbians in a book. This is so . . . domestic. It's about a house."

"But Hill House is not so great at being a house."

Mark laughs, bright and loud, and Eddie can picture his face. "No, it's terrible at being a house. The walls are the wrong dimensions, and the rooms won't stay put. But maybe that's the only kind of house poor Eleanor deserves."

"No," Eddie says, and it comes out firmer than he means. He's not sure why he feels so strongly about this, except that he suspects Mark hasn't been reading this book just because he likes seeing queer people live, however briefly, under the same awful roof. "Eleanor deserves someone to share sweaters with. But without the ghosts or demons or whatever."

Mark goes quiet again. Eddie wonders what would happen if he asked about the empty bedroom, about the missing boyfriend, about any of the things Mark talks around.

The operator's voice sounds over the line, tinny and bored, requesting another dime. Eddie's already fed a shameful number of coins into the slot, but he has no intention of stopping. A long-distance call of this length would cost a serious amount of money from a house phone; from a pay phone, it's criminal—and Eddie's never telling his mother about it. He's never telling anyone about it.

"Hold on," Eddie says, digging in his pocket. "I know I have another couple of nickels."

"Wait, don't put any more money in," Mark says. Eddie can

imagine him looking at his too-big wristwatch and realizing how long they've been on the phone. He gets ready for Mark to say that it's too late, or to scold Eddie for spending too much on a phone call. "Give me the number of your pay phone and I'll call you right back."

"Really?"

"Not if you're going to be boring about it. Now hurry up before we get disconnected."

Eddie tries not to sound too giddy as he reads Mark the phone number, and tries not to bounce on his toes as he waits for the phone to ring.

They talk for a while longer, conversation drifting from the book to some mischief Lula got up to, to how Eddie thinks he'll never get used to spending so much time on airplanes. They aren't talking about anything in particular; it's just talking for the sake of talking.

They only hang up when they're both yawning. Eddie stays in the phone booth for a minute longer, his hand still on the receiver. Then he hears someone calling his name, far too loud for—Eddie checks his watch—half past one in the morning. When he turns, he sees Ardolino and Price crossing the lobby. They're clearly only just getting in, Price notably steadier on his feet than Ardolino.

"Who were you on the phone with?" Ardolino asks. "You got a girl?"

Eddie freezes. "Uh."

"Don't tease him, Tony," says Price. "Let the kid be."

"Is she pretty?" asks Ardolino. "Because that could be the problem."

Eddie grits his teeth, knowing what's coming. One of baseball's grosser superstitions is that you can break a batting slump by having sex with an ugly woman. He can't help but think about how those girls would feel if they found out. But this is such a universal locker room superstition that it's as common as someone telling you to drink soup to ward off a cold.

"Fuck off, Ardolino," Eddie says, his voice low and tight. His hands are balled into fists, his fingers digging into the flesh of his palms.

"Definitely not pretty, then. Sorry, pal." Ardolino grins and slaps Eddie's shoulder.

"Ardolino," Eddie says warningly, furious that he's hearing this shit from the team's manager, and remembering that baseball card in his old bedroom. He barely notices when Price shoves him toward the elevator.

"You fools are in public," Price hisses. "Keep your stupid mouths shut for sixty seconds."

"Sam," Ardolino whines.

"Fifty-nine, fifty-eight," Price counts. The elevator doors open, and Price has a hand on each of their backs as he maneuvers them into the elevator. "Fourth floor," he tells the elevator operator, giving him a dollar.

"But I'm on the third floor," Eddie points out.

"Forty-five, forty-four," Price goes on.

Eddie rolls his eyes and figures he ought to go along with whatever Price has in mind. Approximately forty-three seconds later, he's in what has to be Sam Price's room.

"You need to stop talking about people's girls," Price says as soon as the door is shut, a finger hard against Ardolino's chest. "And you," he says, turning to Eddie, "need to stop being such a pill."

"I'm not a—"

"I agree with you," Price says. "These guys drink too much. They're pigs when it comes to women. But you can't just say so. Well, I can't, because—" He makes a circular gesture around his face, and, right: Sam Price can't put his neck on the line, because he already gets treated like shit in too many ways. "And you can't, because . . ."

For a minute Eddie thinks Price is going to say that Eddie can't speak up because he's queer. He's never been confronted, never been—accused, he supposes. As far as he knows, nobody's even suspected. His mouth goes dry, and for once he's at a total loss for words.

"Because team matters," Price says, looking at him thoughtfully. "Calm down, O'Leary."

"Okay," Eddie says, when really he ought to deny that he has anything to be calm about. He's getting this all wrong, and Price is still looking at him as if he's a crossword puzzle that's nearly solved.

"Team matters," Price repeats. "And anyway, Tony is good in most of the ways that count."

"It's true," agrees Ardolino, pleased with himself.

"Put a sock in it," says Price.

"Sorry," Eddie mumbles. "Sorry, Ardolino," he adds, remembering his manners.

To his surprise, Ardolino wraps him in a hug. Eddie is not a small person, not by any measure, but he's pretty sure Ardolino could crush him like a bug. He smells like Eddie's father—bourbon and drugstore cologne. When Ardolino lets him go, Eddie steps back and finds Price giving him a meaningful look, a clear *I told you so*. "Yeah, yeah," Eddie mumbles. "Have a good night."

Ardolino's cheerful answering "Good night!" is still ringing in his ears as Eddie reaches the empty hallway.

When Eddie gets back to New York, there's an envelope waiting for him at the front desk of his hotel. He doesn't get much mail, so it's no surprise when he recognizes his mother's handwriting. On the elevator, he tears it open. Inside is a collection of magazine clippings. The accompanying letter says this is just a fraction of the articles she could find—"Does your Mr. Bailey ever walk away from his typewriter?"—telling him never to ask where these clippings came from, like she thinks she's in trouble with organized crime or the CIA.

He had planned on showering and going to sleep, but instead he drops his suitcase and flings himself onto the bed to read the articles.

The first is dated 1956 and is a profile of an art dealer who engaged in some kind of shady business practices. It's brutal. Mark eviscerates this man and leaves him for dead, but Eddie can't tell exactly how he accomplishes it. Everything he recounts is an observed fact, a quote, a detail: the expensive cut of the man's suit, his secretary's whispered apologies, a sloppily framed painting. Eddie's left with the sense that a murder's been committed, but the weapon is missing. As Eddie reads, he hears the words in Mark's voice.

The next article, which is about a handful of architects, is different. These architects haven't done anything wrong; Mark isn't exposing their crimes. Except—he's definitely exposing them. Mark has held them upside down and shaken them so everything falls out of their pockets. Eddie can see their flaws and their gifts. He can see them as clearly as if they're sitting in front of him—clearer, even, because who has that kind of insight into someone they happen to meet?

Eddie doesn't want this—this talent, or whatever it is—turned on him. If Mark's writing a magazine article about the team, then it's going to be like this, all of him laid bare for the world to see, and Eddie doesn't want any part of it.

He's not going to think about that, though. Partly because there isn't anything he can do about it, but mostly because he *likes* these articles. He reads them all, finding himself smiling at a particularly vicious observation or unvarnished fact. This is even better than reading Mark's margin notes. It's like thousands of words of margin notes. It's Mark, but highly distilled, two-hundred-proof. When Eddie carefully smooths out the clippings and stows them in his bedside table, it probably ought to be a sign that he's in trouble, but he thinks he's already known that for a while.

CHAPTER ELEVEN

This time, Eddie remembers to call before showing up at Mark's apartment. Well, he sort of remembers—he just had a couple drinks with Rosenthal and Varga, and his brain might not be at its best. He gets as far as the front door of Mark's building, then doubles back toward the last pay phone he saw.

"Sure," Mark says when Eddie asks if it would be all right if he dropped by. "When?"

"Now?"

"Eddie. Are you calling from the lobby of my building?"

"No," Eddie says, offended. "Of course not. If I were in the lobby of your building, I'd be able to see a pair of actual, literal suits of armor and some scary marble babies—"

"It's neo-Gothic!" Mark argues, whatever that means. "And those babies are *cherubim*, you heathen. The building has style!"

"It has something, all right. What it has is a bunch of rich people who like living in buildings with suits of armor standing around like a couple of bouncers."

Mark slams the phone down, but not before Eddie hears him laugh.

When Eddie gets upstairs, Mark opens the door before Eddie knocks. It has to be eighty degrees outside, but he's wearing a cream-colored sweater that's too big on him. He doesn't have on any shoes. His hair is—well, it isn't messy, it probably isn't capable of that—but it looks soft, like there isn't any stuff in it. He's rumpled, like some of the starch has been rinsed out of him, and Eddie wants to burn this image onto his retinas.

Mark takes a second too long to step away from the door. Eddie wants, he realizes, to take Mark into his arms. Maybe he's known that for a while, because it doesn't come as much of a surprise. And, sure, he's wanted Mark ever since meeting him, at least in a physical sense, at least in all the ways he's used to ignoring. But this, this is different, and not just because he's starting to wonder if Mark wants the same thing.

Eddie tries not to be too obvious about looking, but it's been almost two weeks since he's seen Mark, and it'll be over a week before he sees him again, because the team leaves tomorrow on another road trip.

"You'd get fined by the team if you were caught leaving the stadium like this," Mark finally says, eying Eddie's rolled-up sleeves and loosened tie. He might be right if anyone on the Robins got fined for anything at all.

"You haven't been to a game," Eddie says. The team's been back in New York for a week. He knows he sounds too eager, but his tongue has been loosened by alcohol, and besides, he'd swear Mark's looking at him like he might feel just as eager. The last time they were together, it was in the locker room after Eddie got kicked out of the game, and Mark's hand had been cool and steady, his voice disconcertingly earnest as he tried to calm Eddie down.

"Did you want me to come?"

Eddie refuses to believe this is a serious question. He called Mark almost every night during their road trip and once after they got back. It ought to be blindingly obvious that Eddie wants to see him. He shuffles forward, nearly closing the small distance between them, and settles his hands on Mark's hips. Mark goes very still but doesn't step away or even look away.

"I missed you," Eddie says. He circles his thumbs over Mark's hips, the wool of his sweater rough but soft. He's kind of impressed with himself for being so bold, and he supposes he has scotch and soda to thank for that.

"You've been drinking," Mark says, apparently coming to the same conclusion. He takes a step backward, and Eddie's hands drop to his sides. "I didn't think you drank."

"You've seen me drink. I've had a drink right here." Eddie points helpfully at the sofa.

"A beer here, two sips of whiskey there." Mark waves a dismissive hand.

"I was out with the team. Had three drinks. Turns out I'm a cheap date."

Mark laughs. He has such a good laugh. It's too loud and a little rusty, and it makes Eddie want to laugh with him. "I'm pretty sure *Lula* could have three drinks before showing it. You're getting along okay with the team now?"

"Yeah," Eddie says, aware he's grinning like a fool.

"I'm glad. Sit down. I have orange juice."

Eddie sits on the sofa, joined immediately by Lula.

"That dog is staging a full-on mutiny with regard to furniture," Mark calls from the kitchen.

Eddie's never seen a less mutinous-looking dog in his life. She wags her tail, and Eddie scratches behind her ears. Her muzzle is mostly gray, and she moves like her joints are stiff, but also like that isn't going to stop her. She moves like half the Robins' roster.

Mark returns with two glasses of juice and sits on the other end of the sofa, tucking one leg underneath him and turning sideways. "I kept away from the stadium, because I realized I had to tell you something, and I wasn't looking forward to it."

Eddie feels himself tense, sure he's about to get let down gently. "Okay, go ahead, then." He attempts a smile to show Mark that it's okay.

"You know I'm queer."

Eddie raises his eyebrows. "Yeah, we established that. So am I, in case you forgot."

"I don't make much of a secret of it."

"What, you just tell people?" That seems impossible, not to mention dangerous.

"Not in so many words, but I don't keep it a secret." Mark frowns into his orange juice. "Some people don't, you know."

"Aren't they worried about being fired? Or . . ." Eddie doesn't want to say out loud any of the other consequences he can think of. Anyway, Mark already knows.

"Sometimes they have jobs in industries that are basically run by other queer people—theater, literature, art—or they have enough money not to worry about getting fired. Sometimes it's just people with nothing to lose."

"And which category are you in?"

Mark straightens his glasses. "A little bit of all three. But listen, Eddie. Some people at the paper know about me. Other reporters covering the team might know. You probably shouldn't be seen acting friendly with me."

Eddie doesn't say anything, just scratches Lula behind the ears and looks at Mark.

"I should have thought of it myself," Mark goes on. "But George Allen mentioned that I ought to stay away from you. Aren't you going to say something?"

What Eddie wants to say is that it's mighty interesting that George told Mark to stay away from Eddie, but instead Mark is letting Eddie have the choice. "Is there something I'm supposed to say?"

"How about, 'Okay, Mark, I'll only meet you in well-lit public places or, for preference, not at all, because I care about my reputation.'"

"Right. I probably also ought to mention that I'm going to be seen with lots of women."

"Are you?"

Eddie isn't sure whether he's imagining that Mark sounds disappointed. "No, I'm fucking not. I'm not stringing women along. I don't know what you think of me, but I'm not dragging other people into my own personal mess."

"Mess?" Mark repeats weakly.

"I don't know what else you'd call it when I really want to kiss this reporter who's just told me he thinks I ought to stay away from him."

For once, Eddie actually means to say the stupid thing that comes out of his mouth. He wants Mark to know. No, that isn't right—Mark already knows, at least if he's been paying even the slightest bit of attention, and Eddie just wants to say it. He wants it out in the open, something they can't pretend isn't there. Even if nothing ever comes of it, he wants Mark to know.

"I can't do that," Mark says.

"I mean, neither can I, but that doesn't usually stop me."

Mark chokes out a laugh.

"I know we're going to stay professional," Eddie goes on. And he does know it. He may not be great at resisting his worst impulses, but he's not starting something with anyone, least of all a reporter. He hasn't worked his ass off for the past ten years to throw it all away. "But I *want* to kiss you, and I thought you ought to know."

"You thought I ought to know."

Eddie shrugs. "I'm an honest guy."

Mark brings the empty glasses to the kitchen, and Eddie slouches against the back of the sofa. Unlike the rest of the furniture in this apartment, the sofa is comfortable, worn in, the way furniture only gets when it's been battered into submission over the course of years.

He's dimly aware of Lula's chin on his thigh, and he absently puts his palm on her head.

When he opens his eyes, Mark's standing in front of him, an odd expression on his face.

"Didn't mean to fall asleep," Eddie mumbles.

"It's been a long time since I've seen Lula sleep anywhere besides the spot by the door," Mark says, but he wasn't looking at the dog. He was looking at Eddie, and they both know it.

"I can put you in a cab," Mark says, "or, if you really aren't safe to go home, you can spend the night on the sofa."

"But my virtue," Eddie mutters darkly.

"Okay, get up. Time to go home."

Lula snuffles and burrows between Eddie's thigh and the sofa cushion.

"Lula votes that I stay," Eddie says, but he's already getting to his feet, scooping up the dog in the process. "Lend me another book? One that you've written all over. From your secret queer shelf."

Mark's mouth opens a little, like he's about to argue, but then his cheeks go pink and he pulls a book from the bookcase. Eddie takes it without looking at the title.

"It's a thriller, and everyone in it is gay," Mark says. "And awful. The author is apparently gay as well. And awful." He pauses and shrugs. "One relates."

Eddie starts laughing, and he doesn't know what his face is doing, so he buries it in Lula's fur. "Thanks for keeping me company," Eddie tells the dog, kissing her on the head before returning her to the sofa. "And thank you, too," he tells Mark.

They stand at the doorway for a minute, too close, Eddie stealing glances at Mark's mouth and Mark doing the same thing, and the fact that they aren't kissing is taking up more space than any kiss possibly could. But Eddie just said that he wouldn't, so he won't. Instead he lifts a hand and brushes a piece of hair away from

Mark's forehead, then skims his palm over Mark's shoulder on the way down.

"Good night," Eddie says quietly.

Eddie hates Los Angeles. He hates everything about it, from its stupid stadium to its umpires' demented strike zones to the meatballs he had at lunch that are giving him indigestion. He especially hates that the Dodgers are drawing crowds approximately five times larger than the Robins can expect on any given day.

Yesterday he got a double, and today he got a single. Getting two hits in two games feels like a miracle, but then he remembers that he can count on one hand the number of games last season when he *didn't* get a base hit. He shouldn't be celebrating something so minimal, something so ordinary. That thought robs him of all the relief he should have at—theoretically—breaking his slump. Instead he decides that yesterday and today are aberrations, and tomorrow he'll go back to striking out, flying out, fouling out.

It's been over two months of this. For the hundredth time, the thousandth time, he imagines how this slump would feel if it were happening in Kansas City, where he had friends to buy him drinks, to make him feel better. Where he'd be able to forget his problems in someone's bed, even just for a little while.

But this slump probably wouldn't have happened on the Athletics, and even if it had, it wouldn't have mattered. On the A's, he'd been an outstanding player on a perpetually godawful team. On the Robins, he's a godawful player on a godawful team that has . . . potential. It sounds like a line you feed to the press, but he can see it. For all that they drink too much and lack discipline, he can see what they could be, what they might be in a year or two with the right development and the right leadership, a few retirements, and a couple of trades. Eddie could have bat a thousand last season, and the Athletics still would have been, at best, mediocre. Here, Eddie matters in a way he never did; his success matters and his failure matters. And if the team hasn't traded him or sent him down yet, they're probably not going to. Whatever the future holds for the Robins, it holds for Eddie, too.

The Robins won today's game, mostly because the Dodgers had a bad day, so the team is going out. They wind up at some bar that Ardolino likes, and Eddie stays just as long as it takes to finish a beer. That, he figures, is enough not to look like a killjoy.

Back at the hotel, he glances around the lobby to make sure nobody's watching him, even though there's nothing wrong with making a damn phone call, then ducks into a phone booth. It's the third night in a row that he's called Mark, and maybe Mark's expecting it, because he picks up on the second ring and doesn't go through the motions of asking Eddie whether he thinks this a decent time for telephone calls.

"You got another hit." Mark sounds genuinely pleased, which only makes it worse, because how pathetic is it for people to be happy for you when you do the absolute bare minimum?

"I thought that when I started getting hits again, I'd start playing the way I used to. I know that's dumb. But I guess I thought it was like a light switch. It's either on or it's off. And, shit, what if this is what *on* looks like now? What if this is how I play now?"

He thinks about telling Mark this is off-the-record, that the last thing in the world he needs is for this conversation to appear as a diary entry, but he's afraid that saying so will turn this into an interview, when Eddie wants to feel like he's calling a friend. He's almost positive he *is* calling a friend, but he isn't sure enough to put it to the test. And so he needs to trust that Mark won't write anything that hurts him.

"It's not stupid," Mark says, his voice taking on that tinge of fussy arrogance that always makes Eddie believe him. "That's how everyone experiences setbacks. At least, I do. The awful part is over, so why can't I feel normal again? Why can't I eat at my favorite restaurant? Why can't I set foot inside my favorite bakery?"

Absently, Eddie sweeps a finger into the coin return, checking for a nickel that someone forgot to collect, but only finding smooth cold metal. "What kind of setbacks?" he asks, greedy for more information, more clues about Mark's life. He can make a guess at a bad beginning—the cool straightforwardness with which he'd said *people who thought I was worthless* had made Eddie want to call his mother immediately. As to what came later, he can make a hazy sketch—a long relationship followed by a nasty breakup—based on what Mark's told him, and even more from what Mark hasn't told him. But he wants to hear it from Mark.

"Just, you know. Personal things."

Eddie supposes that puts him in his place. Of course he shouldn't expect Mark to share personal details with someone he's interviewing for work, maybe flirting with a bit just for fun. "Sorry, I didn't mean to overstep," he says, making sure he doesn't sound too put out.

"No, no, I didn't mean it like that. I'm not trying to be cagey. I spent years having to protect my—the person I was with. I had to be careful not to mention him. And the easiest way to avoid mentioning one key detail of your private life is to never mention any details of your private life."

Eddie already guessed about the boyfriend, but it still feels like a victory that Mark told him. But Mark sounded sad, so Eddie isn't going to push it. "So what about these fucking idiots planning murders with strangers?" he asks, because that book Mark loaned him is full of lunatics. He read the whole thing on the flight to California.

"But Edward, the repressed gay longing," Mark says, audibly perking up, and Eddie feels a shiver at the use of his full name, at the phrase *gay longing* coming from Mark's mouth, and at the fact that Mark just said that, out loud, on a telephone where operators could be listening in.

Eddie wants to say that these characters could have just fucked like sensible people instead of doing any murders at all, and that while train lavatories aren't known for their atmosphere, Eddie can attest that two determined people can get the job done. He can't though—he doesn't dare.

"Want to hear about the awful book I bought at the airport newsstand?" Eddie asks instead. "I feel really petty about it."

"Yes, please," Mark says, sounding like a kid who's been offered a second scoop of ice cream.

Before ten minutes have passed, Mark has committed to buying this book first thing in the morning and reading it immediately so they can be petty about it together tomorrow night.

CHAPTER TWELVE

The first home game after the road trip, the Robins lose and Eddie goes 0 for 3. His body is almost vibrating with nerves, with the certainty that the past few games of mediocrity were the best he'll ever manage.

Eddie keeps glancing up at the press box, even though he probably won't be able to pick Mark out. He doubts Mark will be there anyway. It's just that it was a long road trip, and he hasn't seen Mark in over a week. They talked nearly every night. Eddie changed a five-dollar bill into nickels and dimes at the front desk of every hotel, long-suffering concierges counting out coin after coin so Eddie could slide them into the slot of the pay phone, every coin confirmation that whatever this is—good idea or bad—it's not stopping. He'd like to actually *see* Mark, though.

Eddie knows it's best that Mark not spend too much time at the stadium. Not because of what he said about being notoriously queer and destroying Eddie's reputation or whatever he thinks is going to happen, but because Eddie saw Mark's face that time the guys were making rude jokes in the locker room. Eddie's used to it; he doesn't think about it having anything to do with himself anymore. At least not most of the time. Kind of. He can shut it out, is the point, and pretend he's somebody else. Usually. Mark obviously can't, and he shouldn't have to.

"Solid fielding," Ardolino says after the game, voice gruff, eyes not meeting Eddie's. Even though the team's being friendlier, they give him a wide berth after a bad game, like his luck might be contagious.

Eddie should go home. He should take one of the sleeping pills the team doctor prescribed after Eddie mentioned that he can't sleep. But they make Eddie feel slow and hungover, and he can't play like that, so he doesn't take them. Also, the team doctor hands out pills the way Eddie's grandpa handed out hard candies. Eddie doesn't think the doctor even writes down who's taking what, which Eddie feels is really the least a doctor ought to do.

Instead he gets into one of the cabs lined up outside the stadium and takes it downtown. He waves to Mark's doorman. Any doubt Eddie had about whether the doorman recognizes him is put to rest when the doorman shyly asks him to sign something for his kid. Eddie signs it, of course. He waits while the doorman calls up, then gets into the elevator.

According to his watch, it's nearly eleven. He knows he's fucking up by dropping by this late, dropping by at all. But everything he does lately is some variety of fucking up, and this feels like the least dangerous mistake he can make. He isn't starting bar fights, at least, or drinking alone in his hotel room. He isn't trying to pick anyone up. He isn't further alienating his teammates or pissing off the coaches.

"Sorry," he says when Mark answers the door. "I know I shouldn't have come. I'm being unprofessional. You have to put up with me for work, and I'm taking advantage of that. And for all I know you might have had someone here."

Mark steps aside so Eddie can walk through the door and get accosted by the dog.

"That's not a real apology," Mark says. "It's just a clumsy way of asking for reassurance that I'm not upset with you."

"Probably," Eddie mumbles as he scratches Lula's head.

Mark pinches the bridge of his nose. "For the record, I like you coming by, regardless of the hour. I'd like it even more if you called ahead. I'm not putting up with you for professional reasons, and I'm furious with both of us that I'm playing along with this blatant compliment fishing." He hesitates. "And you really don't need to worry about bumping into any guests at this hour."

"Is there any time when I should be worried about guests?" Eddie asks before he can decide not to.

Mark gives him a level look. "No, more's the pity. What's the matter?"

"You aren't mad at me?"

"No."

For a minute, Eddie's awash in relief that there's someone who isn't mad at him, someone in this city who doesn't wish he had stayed in Kansas City, or in Omaha for that matter. Everyone, including Eddie for the most part, wishes he had never picked up a baseball bat.

"Did you watch today's game?"

Mark looks away. "Yes," he says, like he's embarrassed. As well he should be—Eddie played disgustingly. "I've been watching all your games."

"Everyone in this town hates me."

"You know," Mark says, "the whole world doesn't revolve around baseball."

"Easy for you to say."

"No, I'm serious. I'm afraid this is going to sound harsh, but most of the world—even most of this city, if you can believe it—truly does not give a shit about baseball. Do you realize there's a presidential election going on? And that it matters? It matters a hell of a lot more than baseball. Practically everyone I know is biting their nails to the quick *except you*."

"I'm not *dumb*."

"That makes it worse! I'm not saying you shouldn't care about how well you're playing. Of course you should care. It's your job. But it isn't who you are. Your batting average isn't who you are."

"That's a relief, because my batting average is—"

"Eddie!" Mark snaps. "It's not who you are! Also—*listen to the crowd*. They're cheering for you."

"Not all of them," Eddie mumbles. He definitely heard booing today.

"In that same stadium, people booed *Willie Mays*. Some jerks pay their two dollars just to boo. In New York, it's an insult if nobody bothers to boo."

Eddie's never seen Mark lose his temper. Mark is always quiet and calm, even when he's rude, like he's above having a temper. "Sorry," Eddie says automatically. He pets the dog so he doesn't have to come up with anything intelligent to say. Lula looks at him like she knows what he's up to but will tolerate it in exchange for scratches.

"Now go sit down." Mark disappears into the kitchen and comes back a moment later with a glass of water. "Drink," he orders.

"I shouldn't read the sports page."

Mark smacks him lightly on the side of the head, then comes to sit next to him on the sofa. "More people are rooting for you than you think. You should see some of the mail we get at the paper."

Eddie figures that if people are writing to the paper, it probably has more to do with what Mark's writing than it actually does with Eddie.

"George was telling me that there's been a line for the ladies' rooms at the Polo Grounds for the first time he can remember," Mark continues. "Rumor has it that women are going just to see you."

Eddie knows Mark's trying to cheer him up, and he suspects Mark doesn't go out of his way to coddle people, so that's nice. Still, he's doing a pretty bad job of it. "I'll always have my looks to fall back on."

"I wish this wasn't happening to you."

It's hard for Eddie to think of this as something that's happening to him. He's the one who picks up the bat and then doesn't do anything useful with it. During one of their phone calls, Mark told him about some crackpot math professor whose theory, apparently, amounts to the idea that statistics aren't happening at all—honestly, he can't make heads or tails of it. All he knows is that at the end of the day, he's the one who can't do his job. All the nasty things that people are saying and writing about him are nothing more or less than the truth.

"I know there's a world beyond baseball," Eddie says. He's thinking of what Sam Price told him at the hotel bar. There's a whole world that doesn't care whether he's playing lousy baseball. There are things that matter more. There are things that should probably matter more *to Eddie*. "But it's been ten years. I've spent ten years hardly thinking about anything other than this game and how to get better at it. And this is the first time there hasn't been an answer."

Mark is giving him a weird look, one that it takes Eddie a second to decipher. "It's okay, you can write that down," Eddie says, and Mark darts off.

"There are things you can do," Eddie says when Mark returns with a pen and notebook, "to get faster, more agile, stronger. You can study opposing pitchers, practice fielding plays, and play smarter baseball. If you have an injury, you can treat it. You can get glasses, or new spikes, or a better pair of batting gloves. But I'm—okay, I don't think this is bragging, but I could not be in better shape. I run every morning, and I'm lifting more than I ever have. There's nothing left to do, nothing I can fix. I'm going to fuck up—shit, you can't write that. I'm going to fail. I'm going to lose, and I'm going to do it in front of a lot of people, and the only thing left for me is to figure out whether I can stand to keep on losing, or whether I ought to throw in the towel." Mark's pen scratches across the paper, so fast that Eddie can hardly believe he's forming letters. He tries not to think about the fact that his little rant is probably going to appear in the newspaper later this week.

"What would throwing in the towel look like?" Mark asks.

"My mother keeps sending pamphlets about college."

"What would you study?"

"Beats the hell out of me."

"Did you eat dinner?"

Eddie's momentarily confused, because that's not an interview question. "Don't worry about that. It's late. I should go."

Mark puts down his notebook. "That's not what I asked."

Eddie follows Mark into the kitchen. He watches, his heart inexplicably in his throat, as Mark pours Eddie a bowl of cornflakes and carefully slices a banana into it.

~

"Your doorman recognizes me," Eddie says when he finishes his cereal. Mark's probably wrong that anyone will care or even notice that Eddie's spending time with a gay reporter, but he should still have the full picture about what's going on.

"Ah." Mark presses his lips together. "I should have guessed."

"You do have two bedrooms."

"Three, actually," Mark says, looking confused. "At least, if you count that little room off the kitchen. Sometimes I forget it's even there." He sighs. "I suppose if anyone was looking for a sign that their apartment is too big, they couldn't ask for a better one than forgetting the number of bedrooms. What's your point?"

"It wouldn't be strange if I spent the night here. Not that I'm going to, calm down. What I mean is, this seems like a quiet building.

No starlets or politicians. No gossip columnists or photographers lurking in the bushes."

"I already told you that you shouldn't spend time with me," Mark says.

And that is not at all the same thing as Mark insisting that he won't spend time with Eddie. "Right, but I am spending time with you," Eddie points out. "People do stay over at friends' houses. It's not a suspicious thing to do. That's why people have guest rooms in the first place."

The skepticism is etched on Mark's face. Eddie hates whatever made it so easy for Mark to believe that his existence is a danger.

"You're an adult," Mark says finally. "And an intelligent one."

Eddie tries not to preen. "If you say so."

"Well. I think you're naive, but I'm not in the business of making other people's decisions. And I suppose you're only naive once. It's a pity to have cynics rob you of the chance to be foolish. But I—" Mark stops talking and suddenly looks very, very tired.

"Yeah?" Eddie prompts.

"I suspect you only learn things the hard way. And I don't want to be that lesson."

Eddie frowns. "I don't follow."

"It's so easy for things to go to hell. And even easier for you, for someone people are already watching."

"If you're trying to tell me it's hard to be queer and in the public eye, I might have already figured that out," Eddie says, more than a little insulted.

"There's knowing, and there's having it proved to you. I just—it happened to me, and nobody needed the enticement of selling a story to a paper. They just did it for the sheer delight of ruining a queer kid's life."

"I'm sorry," Eddie says.

"It was a long time ago, and it worked out fine in the end," Mark says, calm and decisive, slamming the door shut on that topic. "I just don't want to be that for someone else."

"Then kick me out. Ask me to leave."

Mark doesn't say anything. Eddie's heart speeds up.

"Go ahead, Mark. I can get a cab," Eddie says. "No hard feelings."

"Hmph." Mark blows the hair off his forehead.

Eddie feels stupidly triumphant. He bites his lip so he doesn't grin. Nobody should be this pleased about not being kicked out of someone's home. "Show me this little room off the kitchen," he says, mostly to change the topic.

Mark rolls his eyes but leads the way to the kitchen, where indeed there's a little door in the corner, leading to the smallest bedroom Eddie's ever seen. When Mark flicks the light switch, Eddie can see a bed frame with no mattress, a stack of suitcases and boxes piled into a corner.

"It's meant to be the maid's room," Mark says, and Eddie starts to laugh.

"No, I'm sorry, but this building was designed to answer the question 'Where should we store the maids?' and the answer is 'In a shoebox behind the kitchen.'"

"I never stored a maid in there!" Mark protests. "I've never stored a maid anywhere. We mainly used it for our skis." He's laughing, though—giggling, really—and it's infectious, graceless, and a little rough, like he never figured out how to make his laughter as polished as the rest of him. Eddie doubts he even realizes that he mentioned a *we*, an *our*.

"If you think having a separate room for your skis makes you a man of the people, that's even worse," Eddie says, even though it's not like he has a leg to stand on, with his two-dollar long-distance phone calls and his cabs all over the city. He can't pretend that a maid's bedroom is any more extravagant than his utter reliance on hotel maids and clubhouse attendants. "My dad was a Communist Party organizer in the thirties. He's got to be rolling over in his grave when he sees the way I live."

"They had communists in Nebraska?"

Eddie is momentarily outraged. "Yes, there were communists in Nebraska. Haven't you ever heard of Mother Bloor—you know what, never mind. Easterners." He shakes his head.

"My father was in the army. Probably still is, for all I know. Not exactly a leftist agitator."

Eddie's never heard Mark mention his family. Mark rarely mentions anyone. "Not on good terms?"

He suspects that Mark doesn't go around sharing any bit of his life story with anyone, and that sharing even this much with Eddie is a kind of offering, a show of trust.

They're standing awfully close, the two of them crammed into the doorway of this bizarre little bedroom, neither of them making any move to step either inside the room or back into the kitchen.

"Not on any terms," Mark says, but there isn't any bitterness there; it's just a statement of fact. He adjusts his glasses. The way they sit, they usually conceal a bump from what looks like a long-ago broken nose, and whenever they slip, he's quick to push them up. "They aren't in my life, thank God." He takes a deep breath, shoots an annoyed look at Eddie, like Eddie's making him do this, and goes on. "They kicked me out when I was seventeen. Someone caught me kissing another boy and told them."

"Jesus." He's pretty sure that if he attempts sympathy, Mark will claw his eyes out. But Eddie can't not say something. He just can't. "You didn't deserve that," he says, and watches Mark visibly, predictably bristle.

"It turned out fine," Mark says quickly. "For a lot of people, it doesn't. So don't waste your pity on me. And honestly, they were pretty awful to begin with." Eddie's about to say that this doesn't do anything to change the fact that his parents kicked him out when he was still a kid, but Mark adjusts his glasses again, concealing that bump, and Eddie, in a rush of fury, understands.

"It's not pity," Eddie says. "And I don't think I could have a single feeling about you that's wasted." He worries this might be too much, but when he leans in even closer, Mark mirrors his posture. "Look at that, I was sincere, you didn't die—good work, team."

Mark laughs and still doesn't move away. Everything about this feels fragile. They're flirting and telling secrets and standing too close. Eddie knows it, and he bets Mark knows it, too. Eddie's fingers find Mark's, and he twines them loosely together.

"I'd like to stay the night," Eddie says, and watches Mark's eyes widen. "On the sofa. Or on the floor of the shoebox. But I'm going to go home."

Mark swallows. "Thank you for coming to see me." When he speaks, he's as calm as ever, but his fingers briefly tighten around Eddie's.

CHAPTER THIRTEEN

Hoping to get in some extra batting practice, Eddie arrives at the stadium early. He's surprised to find Tony Ardolino already in the clubhouse. Ardolino usually staggers in an hour before game time. Today, he's wearing dark sunglasses and holding the biggest paper cup of coffee that Eddie's ever seen. Eddie doesn't even know where you get a coffee that size. Ardolino grunts something like *Good morning* when he sees Eddie.

Eddie gets changed out of his street clothes and is ready to head off to the batting cage when Ardolino reaches out and grabs the hem of his shirt.

"Wait for me," Ardolino rasps. He goes into his office, rummages through a drawer, pulls out a jar, and drops three green pills into his palm. They're greenies—an upper that's ubiquitous in locker rooms. The one time Eddie tried them, they made his heart race, took away his appetite, made him talk nonstop for three hours, and inflected all his thoughts with paranoia. It was like all the things he finds most intolerable about himself were quadrupled. At this point, if he really thought they'd do anything for his swing, he might—just might—give them another try, but he's already strung tight enough, thanks.

Ardolino holds out his palm and offers the pills to Eddie, who shakes his head. Then he drops all three into his mouth and washes them down with coffee.

"Clean living?" Ardolino asks, inexplicably following Eddie out to the field. "Religion? Heart condition?"

"Huh?" Eddie's following none of this.

"I'm looking for a reason why you don't drink or do anything fun. It can't be that you're boring."

"I mean, it might be. You don't know that I'm not boring." Eddie doesn't point out that Ardolino has seen him drink; he had a few drinks with Ardolino and three other ballplayers just the night before. Eddie had been the one to make sure Ardolino got home in one piece. It's probably not a great sign that he can't remember this.

"You swear at umpires. You're a bit of an asshole. I don't think you're boring," Ardolino says in a way that Eddie couldn't possibly confuse with an insult—or a compliment, for that matter. It's more like a doctor puzzling over an X-ray.

"Plenty of boring assholes in the world," Eddie points out. "You've played the Red Sox."

"See, that's not something a boring person would say."

When they reach the field, Sam Price is already in the dugout.

"Price!" Ardolino hollers as he leads Eddie toward home plate. "Get over here!" He turns to Eddie. "Price's pitching to you this morning."

"Okay," Eddie says tentatively. "What's going on here?"

"We're trying to unfuck your swing."

"*Ardolino* is trying to unfuck your swing," Price says, coming to stand on the pitcher's mound. "*I* lost a bet."

"Go fuck yourself," Ardolino says. He shoves a bat into Eddie's hands. "Show me your stance."

"I can just use the pitching machine, you know."

"It's an order."

"We probably shouldn't use the field. Grounds crew won't like it."

"Ardolino paid them twenty bucks," Price calls out. "So hustle."

"Are you kidding me right now?" Eddie feels slightly hysterical at the idea that Tony fucking Ardolino is going to tell him how to adjust his grip or his stance. This is pretty much his twelve-year-old self's dream come true, but right now he just wants to run in the other direction.

"Fucking hold the bat, O'Leary," Ardolino says. "I have things to do."

"Okay, okay." Eddie puts the bat over his shoulder like he's posing for his baseball card picture. He feels like a total jerkoff.

"Take a practice swing," Ardolino says.

Eddie does.

"You look like shit," Ardolino says.

"I don't care what anyone says, you're one hell of a coach, Ardolino," Price calls from the mound. Ardolino gives him the finger without turning away from Eddie.

"You're all stiff," Ardolino says. "There's no way that's how you swung last year."

Eddie has no idea how he did anything last year or any year before it. "I used to go on instinct, but that's gone."

"You mean you never thought about it, because what you were doing worked?" Ardolino asks.

"Yeah."

"That's how I did it, too. Nothing to think about. What we need is a shitty hitter over here. Hold on."

A minute later, he returns with Harry Varga, having apparently dragged the first baseman out of the weight room.

"Show us how you hit the ball," Ardolino orders.

"I show you that four times a game," Varga complains.

"Four times a game, my ass. Show O'Leary. Make him hit the ball the way you do."

Varga sighs and comes around behind Eddie. "Move your left foot. Other direction. No, not like—oh for fuck's—" He gives up trying to explain and just starts shoving Eddie around, pushing one of his hips forward and tugging an elbow back. This might be vaguely sexy if it weren't a teammate doing it.

The trainer comes out, probably to make sure his players aren't killing one another.

"That look like Varga's stance and grip?" Ardolino asks the trainer.

"Yeah, not bad."

"Okay, let's go!"

Somebody puts a batting helmet on Eddie's head and pushes him toward the plate.

"Remember, hit the ball like Varga, not like yourself," Ardolino says.

Price's first pitch is low and outside, but Eddie swings at it anyway. He misses.

"Again," Ardolino says.

They do it five more times. On the sixth pitch, Eddie hits the ball. A neat line drive, a double if he were lucky.

"Why'd you teach him to bat like Varga?" someone calls from the dugout. Buddy Rosenthal, the second baseman, is leaning against the rail, along with the catcher. Eddie's sure they hadn't been there earlier. "Have him hit like someone who's actually good."

"Then get your lazy ass over here, and put your money where your mouth is," Ardolino says.

Rosenthal climbs out of the dugout and spits a wad of tobacco into the dirt. Swearing the entire time, he shoves Eddie into place the same way Varga did. It feels deeply unnatural. The bat is wrong in his hands, and his feet are wrong on the ground. Everything is in the wrong place. His head is even at the wrong height. When Price pitches to him, he feels like he's playing some sport he'd never heard of before this afternoon, like he's trying to hit a football with a golf club.

This time, he hits the second pitch deep into left field. Might have been an out, but it might have been a triple, depending on how bad the opposing team is.

"Do it again," Ardolino orders.

It continues to feel so weird it's almost unsettling. He remembers Hill House, its walls and floors not connecting at right angles, and that's how he feels now: so many off angles it's almost spooky. Beneath this stance he's adopted, he can feel the remnants of his old stance wanting to come out, and it's an effort to ignore them.

"We should stop," Eddie says. "Don't want to tire Price's arm out." He hasn't been counting, but he'd bet Price has thrown the equivalent of four innings.

Price tells him to shut the fuck up.

A few more players have trickled onto the field. "He needs to angle his wrists," says one of them. "No, tell him to break at the wrists after contact," says another.

It feels insane. Like someone teaching him how to breathe or blink or swallow. But he does it anyway, following instructions when he can and letting himself be moved around like a rag doll the rest of the time. He stops thinking about it as baseball and starts imagining that he's learning something brand-new.

For some reason, Ardolino has gotten into the habit of sitting next to Eddie in the dugout, explaining his decisions in a way that might be directed to Eddie or might just be thinking out loud. But today he starts to ask for Eddie's opinion. Well, he says what he's going to do, and then barks, "You got a problem with that, kid?" Eddie then either says, "No, why should I, goddammit?" or voices an objection along the lines of "It doesn't matter what you tell him to do, Varga's going to try and steal third."

It's making him think about the game in a way he doesn't usually try to put into thoughts, let alone words. The past few days have been a mindfuck. Whatever the guys did to him at batting practice the other day stripped away Eddie's last connection to his old swing. He's not sure if that's what they meant to do, or if it's even a good thing. When he picks up a bat, he has to think about what to do with it, something he hasn't really done since seventh grade.

"Luis should have spent another two years in the minors," Eddie says after Luis hits a neat line drive that is, unfortunately, snapped up by the opposing team's center fielder. "He'll be something to look out for in a couple years."

"Varga belongs in right field," Eddie hisses a few innings later, when they're back in the dugout after Rosenthal nearly concussed himself trying to cover for Varga. "The right fielder belongs in the old folks' home. The entire bullpen belongs—"

"In the Harlem River?" Ardolino whispers back, and Eddie laughs, even though it's mean.

"Move Luis to center field," Eddie says after the game in Ardolino's office. "Bring a third baseman up from the minors, someone who can actually throw left. Trade—"

"No trades," Ardolino says, settling in his chair, his feet on his desk.

"Why in hell not?" Eddie asks.

"You know, Connie's been on my case about this for months, and she's a hell of a lot more persuasive than you, let me tell you."

There's so much happening in that sentence that Eddie immediately writes it off as the sort of drunken confession that you need to forget about, before realizing that Ardolino is, if not actually sober, then mostly sober. The blockade of empty bottles disappeared at some point in the last month, and Eddie—too focused on his own troubles to pick up on anything else—hadn't noticed.

That night on the way to Milwaukee, Ardolino beckons Eddie to the back of the plane and deals him into a poker game. Eddie doesn't particularly enjoy poker. He also doesn't enjoy the kind of conversation the three other men are having—details of the previous night's conquests, only interrupted by attempts to flirt with the stewardess so brazen that they're almost comical. In fact, Eddie's pretty sure they are comical—nobody's taking them seriously, including the stewardess.

But he recognizes something almost formal about all of it: These guys have had basically this same conversation and played this same poker game and taken this same flight dozens of times before. It's just how they pass time together. Eddie can ignore it the same way he ignores his mother nagging him about enrolling at the community college during the off-season. He doesn't have to like it. He doesn't have to look at Ardolino and compare him to the man on that faded old baseball card in his drawer back home; Ardolino is just a guy doing his job.

And if Ardolino is just someone doing his job, then maybe so is Eddie. A job he's useless at, but still. Everyone's being decent to him. People sit next to him. He gets asked to come out for a drink after games. He feels like he could belong.

This should make him happy, right? He isn't sure why it doesn't. This is almost how things were in Kansas City, and that was always enough. He has people to talk to and joke around with, people to have dinner with when they're on the road. When he walks into the clubhouse, people say hi to him. The jokes and slurs and assumptions aren't any different from any locker room he's ever been in. If it's bothering him now, it's his own fault for being sensitive. If he feels like he doesn't belong, it isn't the Robins' problem.

CHAPTER FOURTEEN

Eddie's drying off after his shower when he sees Mark leaning against the wall just like he was the first time they met. This is the first home game they've played after their road trip. It's only been a week since they've seen one another, so it's not like he forgot what Mark looks like. He doesn't think he could. He doesn't think anyone could. It's just that he isn't expecting the relief.

Maybe *relief* isn't the word; Eddie isn't sure there even *is* a word. It's a tug and a *yes* and a *there he is*. He needs to look away so he can get dressed without staring, and there's no way he can talk to Mark right now while only wearing a towel. All he manages to put on are his underwear and a pair of pants before he breaks.

"You came!" he says. He sounds too happy. Nobody's ever been this happy to see a reporter.

"I did." It's steamy and hot in the locker room—even steamier and hotter than it is everywhere else in the city this summer—and Mark has his jacket thrown over an arm. His sleeves are rolled up. And still he doesn't look like he's spent three hours in a sweaty press box. "Nice play in the fifth."

Eddie shrugs. That play wasn't bad, but in nine innings, all he managed was two singles and a walk, and the Robins lost. Still, this is four games in a row where he's consistently gotten on base. He's trying not to hope this means his slump is over, for real this time. He's trying not to think about it at all, or he's going to start getting superstitious about shoelaces or some shit. He played decent baseball tonight; it's just something that happened.

"Just say thank you," Mark says, his voice low. His eyes drift to Eddie's bare chest before snapping away.

"Thanks," Eddie says. He's smiling. There's no reason for him to be smiling like this, and he absolutely cannot stop. His face muscles have gone rogue.

Mark gives him a mildly exasperated look and walks away, heading toward where George Allen is talking to the catcher. Eddie gets dressed and then answers some reporters' questions about whether he thinks his slump is over. He's really perfected his talking-to-the-press bullshit face this season, if nothing else.

Eddie gets dressed the rest of the way and then whips Rosenthal with a wet towel, because he's trying to act normal and nothing's more normal than a friendly little locker room attack. Rosenthal vows his revenge, and Eddie's probably going to wind up with shoes filled with shaving cream or plastic spiders at some point in the near future.

Mark disappears around a corner. Eddie tries to look casual as he slopes off in the same direction. All he finds is an empty hallway, and he's about to turn around when from one of the offices he hears Tony Ardolino talking to a woman who could only be Constance Newbold.

"You could *consider* changing the lineup when the team has lost *five games in a row*," Miss Newbold says. "It being your job and all."

"We've been through this."

"We have! And you've been stubborn and ignorant."

Ardolino laughs. "Ignorant! You're one to—"

"You put that lineup together when O'Leary was still in a slump. If you look at only the past ten games, he has the third-highest batting average on the team. You're wasting him. Here's how it should go. Serrano, O'Leary, Rosenthal, Varga—"

"Changing the lineup every time someone has a good week or a bad week just messes with their heads. Same thing with trades."

"It's their job to cope with those things!"

"It's really not, Con."

"I do not recall giving you permission to call me—"

Her last words trail off for some reason, which gives Eddie time to wonder why the team's owner thinks she can tell the manager what to do about the batting order—or, for that matter, why Ardolino thinks he can call the owner by her first name. He vaguely remembers hearing—back when he was still in Kansas City, and the sports pages of every paper in the country were reporting gossip about New York's luckless new expansion team—that Miss Newbold wasn't totally ignorant about the game. She was apparently a "baseball enthusiast," in her own words, and had played in college. But that also describes Eddie's mom, for fuck's sake. Although his mom could probably rustle up a better lineup than Ardolino.

Before he can decide how he feels about it, the office doorknob starts to move and he hurries down the hallway, around the corner, and straight into Mark.

"Hi," Mark says. He looks pleased to see Eddie, almost goofy about it. Eddie had not been aware that Mark's face could even arrive in the ballpark of goofy.

"Want to get dinner?" Eddie asks quietly, because suddenly his only priority is getting Mark alone.

"I drove George Allen up here, so I'll have to drive him back."

"So you *don't* just take cabs all over the city."

"I absolutely do take cabs all over the city," Mark protests. "But I have to run the car every couple of weeks so the battery doesn't drain. Also, George was looking peaked this morning, and I didn't think he ought to go up and down the subway stairs. It's easier to convince him to let me give him a ride than it is to orchestrate things so we happen to be splitting a cab."

There's a steady note of irritation in Mark's voice, as if he isn't confessing to doing a good deed. "So you only came tonight as a chauffeur?"

"Not just that."

Eddie doesn't know if that means Mark came to see him or if he has someone else to talk to. Over the past month they've established a routine of Eddie calling with a few observations that Mark turns into a diary entry. He doubts that Mark actually needs to talk to him in person.

"Have dinner with me after you bring George home."

"I heard someone ask you to go out for drinks."

Eddie doesn't think that's a no. He's pretty sure a no from Mark is literally just a no. He knows that Mark doesn't want to start anything with him, and he respects that. But he also respects the way Mark is leaning slightly toward him, the way his lower lip is a little bit wet. Respect, on second thought, is probably not what this is at all.

He knows, logically, that Mark is right. Nobody gossips the way ballplayers gossip, and even something as bland as "Eddie O'Leary's friendly with a queer reporter" could make its way through the league in a matter of months. If, in the context of that gossip, Eddie did anything even remotely queer, people could jump to some accurate conclusions. But a lifetime of not allowing himself to want or be wanted is not a price he's willing to pay to avoid that risk. Maybe it took briefly becoming a shitty baseball player to reassess his priorities; maybe it took meeting Mark. All he's sure of is that he *is* sure.

He probably ought to be more shocked by this than he actually is. But when he looks at Mark, he just thinks: *Of course I'd take that risk.*

"Come with us," Eddie says.

"What a terrible idea." Mark looks almost amused.

"I want to see you."

"Eddie."

"I think you want to see me."

"*Eddie.*"

"I bet Lula misses me."

Something stricken momentarily crosses Mark's face. It's there and gone in the blink of an eye, and Eddie's not sure he'd have even noticed if he weren't paying such close attention.

"I'm kidding," Eddie says quickly. He isn't sure what he said wrong, but he wants to fix it. "Your dog doesn't give a shit about me."

"I swear to God, if I'm developing a neurosis about my dog on top of everything else," Mark mutters. He reaches into his pocket and pulls out a gold rectangle about the size of his little finger. "There's a key in there. Let yourself in tomorrow morning before eight o'clock, and walk the dog. I'll still be asleep."

Eddie doesn't know what this means. Is it a challenge—Eddie can see Mark, but only if he wakes up really early? Is it a way for Mark to discharge whatever dog-related guilt is bothering him without having to actually see Eddie? Or does Mark just want a chance to sleep in?

The little gold box is surprisingly heavy and warm from being in Mark's pocket. Eddie turns it over in his palm. Embedded on one side is a minuscule clock, along with an even more minuscule knob to wind the clock. There's a mechanism of some sort on the side, and when Eddie touches it, the rectangle swings open, revealing a key and a blade, hinged together like the world's fanciest Swiss army knife. A tiny gold pencil slots inside the whole affair. The knife and key aren't gold, at least; they're made of whatever metal keys and knives are supposed to be made of. Barely legible, in small and worn-down letters, MFB is engraved.

"Careful," Mark says. "I know it looks delicate, but the blade is sharp."

"This is beautiful." Eddie's never seen anything like it. He's never even heard of anything like it. If given all day and a bottomless budget, he wouldn't even know where to find something like it. He closes the box, secreting away the knife and key, then slides the pencil in. "How will you get in tonight?"

"The doorman has a spare key."

Eddie wants to say that Mark shouldn't trust him with this thing, whatever it's called. He's sure it's valuable. It's probably irreplaceable. "What's your middle name?"

"Francis."

"Mark Francis Bailey," Eddie says, the monogram a barely noticeable change in texture under his callused thumb. "I'll see you tomorrow."

The nightclub is hot and crowded, and the music is about twice as loud as it needs to be. Eddie slouches in the corner of a booth and watches Tony Ardolino dance with some woman who isn't his wife. He's never met Ardolino's wife, isn't even sure if she's in New York. Come to think of it, he's not sure whether they're still together. If there had been a divorce, Eddie would have read about it—just like he read about Ardolino's previous divorces—but that doesn't necessarily mean one isn't in the works.

A couple of other women have materialized at their booth, and he isn't sure whether Ardolino summoned them from wherever he manages to produce women at a moment's notice, or whether they've arrived under their own steam.

Eddie keeps sliding his hand into his pocket to check that the key holder is still where it belongs. It would be so easy to walk out of here and catch a cab and see Mark right away. He's done it before. But Mark said tomorrow at stupid o'clock in the morning, so that's when Eddie's going to show up. The more he thinks about it, the surer he is that Mark picked the time of day that's least likely to lead to anything interesting. And that, Eddie figures, is proof enough that Mark wants something to happen.

Sam Price and his wife slide into the booth, a little out of breath from dancing. This club is in Harlem, and about half the people here are Black, which means, according to Price, that he can "sit down and have a goddamn drink and not worry about who's bailing Tony out of jail."

"Your pal got poor Connie pretty hot under the collar," Ardolino says, squeezing into the booth next to Price.

"Huh?"

"The reporter. The one who looks like William Holden. Connie Newbold's pissed off at him."

"Mark? He doesn't look anything like William Holden," Eddie says, offended on Mark's behalf. "Pick a different movie star."

"That's not the—"

"Isn't William Holden blond? And old?"

"O'Leary," Price says. "Focus."

"Actually, he looks kind of like Clark Kent," Ardolino says.

"Clark Kent is a drawing," Price says. "Or is that just the only white man in glasses that you can think of?"

"Wait, what does Mark have to do with Miss Newbold anyway?" Eddie asks.

Ardolino raises his eyebrows. "Don't you read the paper?"

"Luis yells at me in Spanish if I even look at the paper," Eddie says.

"A month ago, there was a column in the *Chronicle* about how Connie wants to fire me."

"Mark Bailey wrote a column about that?" Eddie asks. Out of the corner of his eye he sees Price deftly switching his half-empty glass with Ardolino's full one.

"Nah, George Allen wrote it, but the tip came from Bailey."

"I didn't say anything to Mark about trade rumors," Eddie says.

"Maybe not," Ardolino says, not sounding particularly convinced. "But he overheard me and Con fighting. Anyway, good for him for giving Connie a scare. But watch what you say around him."

"I don't say anything around him!"

"The pair of you's as thick as thieves."

Eddie opens his mouth to defend himself, but there really isn't anything to say. Ardolino is right. This is why—well, one of the reasons why—Eddie knows it's a bad idea to get friendly with a reporter. Not because he really suspects that Mark is mining him for information, but because his teammates will always be suspicious. And Eddie really needs his teammates not to go back to hating him.

"Okay, fine," Eddie says. "We're friends. Maybe I got lonely when the team spent an entire fucking month not talking to me, who knows. I don't talk to him about you assholes, though, and he knows it."

Price gives him a look that Eddie bets is exactly what Sam Price Junior sees when he brings home a bad report card. "Be careful."

"I already told you," Eddie says. "I'm being careful." He knows Price and Ardolino are just talking about Mark being a reporter. They don't know about Mark being queer. Or maybe they do—Mark said people might. Maybe Mark was right about Eddie only learning things the hard way, because he hadn't thought until now about how it would feel to have a teammate look at him and really wonder.

Price is still looking at him, and Eddie's worried that all his thoughts are playing out on his face, so he quickly takes a sip of his drink. Ardolino gets back up, heading toward the dance floor, but Price and Mrs. Price remain, their heads bent together, their voices low.

Eddie's been nursing the same whiskey and soda all night, but it looks like Price and his wife are at the bottom of their glasses. The club is too busy for there to be any hope of flagging down a waitress, so Eddie offers to go to the bar and get a round.

"Ask the bartender to use a light hand on Tony's," Price says.

Mrs. Price sighs. "I thought he quit."

"He did. He's quit three, maybe four times. It never sticks for more than a year or two."

"Poor Tony." Mrs. Price frowns at her husband.

Eddie levers himself out of the booth. *Poor Tony.* He knows from overheard whispers that his own father used to try to quit drinking. He doesn't know why it took hearing about it from the Prices to think of Tony Ardolino as someone who doesn't want to drink, someone who might even be ashamed of his drinking habit. Eddie winces, remembering what he said to the television cameras in Kansas City.

The space around the bar is just as crowded as the rest of the club, so Eddie has to squeeze through a throng of people.

"Hey," says a woman on a barstool.

"I'm sorry, ma'am," Eddie says automatically, assuming he's accidentally elbowed her.

"For what? You're Eddie O'Leary, aren't you?" She's about his age, with light brown skin, a dark pink dress, and cat-eye glasses.

"Guilty as charged." Eddie breaks out his best smile.

The woman turns to her companion—probably her sister—and the two of them start doing that whisper-shriek thing that Eddie's only seen very tipsy women even attempt.

"She just got dumped," the woman in glasses says, pointing to her companion. "And I just got fired, so we're having a night out to drown our sorrows."

"How's that working out so far?"

"Like a charm. But listen, listen." She leans in. "We were just saying we're in the Eddie O'Leary Club. And then, boom! You show up out of nowhere."

Eddie is a little horrified to learn that he not only has a fan club but has run into two of its members.

"The Losing Streak Club," the woman clarifies.

"The Hell to 1960 Club," says the second woman.

"Oh." Eddie's not particularly thrilled about being a symbol of losers, the mascot of bad luck. "The season's barely half over. And the past two weeks haven't been half bad," he argues, a little depressed that he's in a place where "not half bad" is a huge relief.

"But spring 1960 was one for the record books," she says.

"Happens to the best of us," the other woman agrees, and they clink glasses. "At least that's what everyone keeps telling me."

That, Eddie supposes, isn't so different from what the math professor told Mark, or from what Mark's been telling Eddie himself. Sometimes when bad things happen to you, it's just because the dice get rolled a certain way. He finds that almost impossible to believe about himself, but would fight anyone who even suggested that these pretty strangers were anything but blameless.

Eddie finally gets the bartender's attention and orders drinks for his table, then motions for another round of whatever the two women are having.

"You're sweet," the woman in glasses says.

"I get that a lot," Eddie says. "That, and 'You're a jerk.' Not much middle ground."

"Poor thing. You just could not hit the ball at all in May, could you."

"Or June," Eddie says. "Don't forget June."

"It was incredible to watch."

"Painful."

"Uh, thanks?" Eddie says.

"I mean, I didn't get fired on television. I have that going for me at least."

"The cameras aren't even the bad part," Eddie says. "Not even the crowds."

"What is?"

Eddie opens his mouth to say it was letting his teammates down, just like he's told every reporter who's asked, but what he says is, "Being alone. When you're the only one fucking up, you're all alone. Oh, shit, sorry about the language."

But the women aren't paying any attention to his language, because one of them is crying now, and the other one is hugging her. The one with the glasses says something in Spanish, her words muffled by the taffeta of her friend's dress. Then she turns to Eddie and says the same thing before hugging him. The other woman joins in the hug, and Eddie can't do anything but pat their backs, get them some autographs from Ardolino and Price, and put them safely into a cab.

CHAPTER FIFTEEN

There are three newspapers waiting on the doormat outside Mark's apartment. Eddie unlocks the door as silently as possible and puts them on a little table that seems designed to do nothing but hold newspapers and mail.

Lula's already by the door, so he holds his finger up to his lips, as if the dog's going to understand the signal to be quiet. She does stay quiet, though, just wags her tail and walks in a happy little circle when he reaches for the leash.

"Don't wake Mark up," he whispers. But maybe the dog calls Mark something else? Not that dogs call anyone anything, but when Eddie's mother is talking to her cats, she refers to herself as Mama. *You don't want to tear up Mama's nice curtains*, and that sort of thing. He doesn't think he can have Lula call Mark *Dad*, though, not even in his head.

He snaps the leash on Lula's collar and heads back out. The dog clearly has an agenda and simply hauls Eddie along on what must be her usual route. She tugs left when they leave the lobby, then right to cross a street, at which point she leads him around the perimeter of this weird gated and locked park that just sits in the middle of the neighborhood, as if a park behind lock and key makes any sense at all. Some perverse part of Eddie wants to climb the fence or force the lock, just on principle, but he's not going to make Lula an accessory to crime. Lula continues to pull him along until she arrives in front of a bakery and stares at him pointedly. He takes the hint, tying her leash on a fence that surrounds one of those mysterious cellar areas where New Yorkers keep their trash cans.

Inside the bakery, Eddie looks in the glass cases. He's never seen any sign of cake or pastry in Mark's apartment. He'd like a few minutes to think, but there are already two people waiting behind him, shuffling their feet, and he doesn't know how long he has before Lula runs out of patience. "Two cherry Danishes and a loaf of that bread," he says, pointing at a dark brown loaf that looks like it might have vitamins or something. "And two coffees. Wait. Do you have coffee?"

The white-aproned woman behind the counter looks at him patiently. "We have coffee," she says in an accent he thinks might be German.

He manages to get his hand around both cardboard coffee cups and tuck the paper bag under his arm, and then lets Lula lead the way back.

Mark's still asleep, so Eddie sets the food and one of the coffees on the counter and drinks the other one on the couch while reading the newspaper. The *Chronicle*, annoyingly, doesn't have funny pages. He manages to avoid the temptation to read the sports page and instead flips through the rest of the paper. It's filled with a lot of the same stories he's been hearing about in the locker room, on subways, in bars: a presidential election picking up steam, Russians shooting down an American spy plane, a Nazi caught in Argentina and ready to be tried. He feels like he's tuning in to a show when it's nearly over, and he'll never catch up.

After a while, he hears footsteps and the sound of a door opening.

"It's ten o'clock." Mark's voice is scratchy. On one side, his hair is sticking up all helter-skelter. His pajamas are wrinkled. Eddie's charmed that Mark has pajamas. He's never seen pajamas on an adult under the age of forty. "You're still here."

Eddie has a moment of doubt. Had Mark meant for him to go home after walking the dog?

"I picked up some breakfast." Eddie gets off the couch and, in the kitchen, hands Mark the coffee and the bag of pastry.

Mark goes completely still.

"Lula seemed to think I ought to go to that bakery," Eddie says, mostly to fill the silence.

"Of course she did. Of course. Thank you." Mark slides the pastries out of the bag and onto a couple of plates. "How much do I owe you?"

"Oh, for fuck's sake," Eddie says, throwing up his hands.

Mark's mouth twitches up in the general direction of a smile. "I didn't think you'd actually show up." He hands Eddie a plate. The cherry filling is unnaturally bright, and the pastry itself is huge.

"I figured if you didn't want me to come, you wouldn't have asked."

"You were right," Mark says, as if it's nothing, as if that isn't the best thing Eddie's heard in *weeks*. "God, I needed the sleep." He yawns. "I forgot what it's like to wake up on my own."

Mark waves Eddie in the direction of the dining room table, where he shoves aside some papers and a mint green typewriter. He still seems half asleep, so Eddie starts telling him the story of the girls he met in the bar last night. "I can't stop thinking about it, you know? A pair of total strangers came up to me and pretty much said that I'm a symbol of failure. But in a good way?"

"Did you mind?" Mark has a flake of pastry on his upper lip. Eddie tries not to stare at it.

"I would have, a month ago. Two weeks ago, even. But what they were really saying is that I screwed up, and I'm still here. I get that now."

"You didn't screw up. You aren't screwing up. You're playing your best."

It's kind of sweet that Mark doesn't realize that this is so much worse than if the problem was that he wasn't giving it his all. "The part of me that used to swing a bat is broken. The hits I've been getting lately feel totally different. They come from a different place." He feels weird saying it, like it's too oddball to say out loud to a non-baseball person.

"Your stance is different."

"My grip and my swing, too."

"You're better about not swinging at pitches that are low and inside."

"What?"

"George says that you've dropped the habit of swinging at them. You're drawing more walks now."

"Huh." Eddie hadn't even realized. "None of it's the same. I'm not the same player I was a few months ago. And I know that sounds dumb—it was only a batting slump, not a tornado or whatever. But something broke, and I got put together different, and I think that's maybe what those girls are talking about. You get jilted, you get fired—maybe those things change you."

"Maybe that job was awful. Maybe that woman's boyfriend was rotten."

It's so rare that Mark attempts anything like optimism that Eddie's distracted for a moment. "Maybe," Eddie says, trying to figure out how to word this in a way that doesn't make him sound either stoned or like a beatnik. "But maybe it was just a bad thing that happened. Maybe that was her dream job. Maybe that was the only man she'll ever love. Maybe something awful happened, and those girls are going to be changed by it, but they're still people, and good things can still happen to them. It's like you said—even after a disaster, there's still tomorrow."

Mark stares at him. Eddie's not sure what he said wrong, or if maybe there's something off about the pastry, even though his tastes fine. The cherry filling is a bit too sweet, but—

"Don't move," Mark says, riffling through the pile of papers next to him. "Don't say a word." He finds a notebook and pencil and starts writing. "Say all that again," he says, his pencil already scratching across the page.

Eddie does as he's told, repeating his words as best as he can. They sound even less impressive the second time around, but he supposes Mark can make them into something decent if that's what he wants.

When he's done, he waits for Mark to finish writing.

"Is that going in the paper?"

"No idea," Mark says. "None." He looks a bit wild-eyed. He's still wearing rumpled pajamas, and his hair is still mussed. Eddie can make out the faintest trace of stubble along Mark's jaw. He has the sense that he's seeing something rare—Mark unpolished and plain, without whatever armor he gets from his beautiful clothes and his sweet-smelling soap and his perfect hair. It's not necessarily that this is a truer picture of Mark, or something more real—it's just private, and the fact that Eddie gets to see it is driving him crazy.

"I was also thinking," Eddie says, because running his mouth is the only thing that's going to stop him from doing something even stupider with it. "Who gets to decide what losing even is? I mean, I know that who wins and who loses is pretty cut-and-dried in baseball. But this is a game where hitting the ball a third of the time is a job well done, and hitting it half the time is practically unheard of. With everything else, it's even more confusing. I mean, I'm never going to get married and have kids. Some people will look at that and feel bad for me, right? But if I did get married, it would mean something went wrong. So the fact that I'm not married with a family of my own is a good thing, you know? It's a win. It means that I'm still able to be myself."

Mark passes a hand over his mouth. "Yeah. I—wow. Okay."

"Sorry, I know I'm rambling. I know some things are just bad. I'm not saying things happen for a reason—I hate that. I'm saying that things *happen*. And it doesn't have to mean anything except what it means to you. Nobody else gets to decide."

Mark gets to his feet, and Eddie's afraid he's going to walk away to wash the dishes or make a phone call or do anything to get away from Eddie's talking. But he leans forward, one hand braced on the table between them.

"Let me know if this isn't a good idea," Mark says, and leans in.

Eddie has just enough time to anticipate it, just enough time to shut his eyes and register that Mark's lips are soft and cool and maybe a little sticky from the pastry. And then Mark's leaning back, looking at him like he's waiting for the other shoe to drop.

Eddie wants to say that it's not a bad idea, that it's a *great* idea, but he's never been a good liar. It's a terrible idea. Hell, it's been a terrible idea since Eddie started showing up at Mark's place.

But Eddie's never paid much mind to whether an idea is good or bad and he's not starting now. He wants this. Mark wants this. That's good enough.

He crosses to Mark's side of the table and takes hold of his collar, reeling him back in for another kiss. This time he can taste the overly sweet cherries on Mark's lips. He has the skin-warm crumpled cotton of Mark's pajamas in his hand. Mark's fingers, tentative and slow, cup the edge of his jaw. And this is just the beginning—their mouths are still shut, and they're barely touching, their hands still firmly in respectable places.

Eddie gets his free hand on the back of Mark's neck, threading his fingers through his hair. It's straight and silky and nothing like Eddie's own. Mark makes a soft noise, something between a sigh and a hum, and his lips part just a little.

When Eddie feels the tip of Mark's tongue on his lower lip, it's like some kind of internal safety mechanism inside Eddie gets unlatched. He's all bad ideas now, so he gets his hands on Mark's hips and pushes him back until he's sitting on the table, then steps between his legs. Eddie's already a bit taller than Mark, and this position just makes the difference that much more. Mark tilts his head back as Eddie leans over him.

It's too fast; it's too much. He's not taking Mark to bed right now, and if they keep this up, that's where they'll wind up. He decides not to think too much about why he doesn't want to peel Mark's pajamas off and lay him out on this table, because of course that's *exactly* what he wants to do. But his instinct is that if they do that now, it'll be too easy to dismiss everything else—the milkshakes, the phone calls, the gold key holder in Eddie's pocket—as nothing but the warm up for fucking rather than the beginning of something else.

He pulls back a little and presses a final kiss to the corner of Mark's mouth. "I need to head back uptown," Eddie says, his lips moving against Mark's cheek.

"You're . . . what?" Mark sounds dazed, his voice rough and slow, and Eddie's taking it as a personal compliment.

"Want me to come walk Lula tomorrow?"

Mark slides off the table to stand in front of Eddie, and they're back to being almost the same height. "What are you playing at?"

Eddie shakes his head. "Nothing. I promise."

"Eddie—"

"See you tomorrow, bright and early." He expects Mark to stop him, to ask for his key back, and for a minute Eddie thinks maybe he's overstepped. But when he glances back over his shoulder, Mark is still standing by the table, his fingers over his mouth.

The damnedest thing is that waking up at six in the morning helps Eddie fall asleep early enough to wake up at six the next morning. It's the first time since moving to New York that Eddie doesn't lie awake staring at the ceiling, cataloging his worries.

This time he stops at the bakery on the way to Mark's, so that later he won't have to juggle two coffees, a bakery bag, and a dog leash. He picks up the newspapers in front of Mark's door, lets himself in, grabs the leash, and scoots Lula out the door.

"What if we take a different route?" he asks the dog when they get outside. He tries to turn right. Lula keeps going left. Eddie, recognizing a hill not worth dying on, goes left, too. Apparently there are particular stop signs and fire hydrants and trash cans that have to be visited and assessed in the same order. Eddie obediently follows behind. Honestly, his presence is purely for show. Show, and the ability to open doors. Lula doesn't need anyone to walk her; she only needs a human around to keep up appearances.

When they wind up back at the deranged suits of armor flanking the door of Mark's building, Eddie doesn't stop. "Come on, you already had your walk. Now I can have mine." She looks at him like he's unreliable and very dumb and is lucky to have a dog like her to keep him in check, but she trots along ahead of him anyway.

He noticed a second key in the fancy key holder, and on a whim, he tries it in the lock that bars the park gate. There's a sign on the seven-foot-high wrought iron fence saying that dogs aren't allowed, but when Eddie turns the key in the lock and the gate swings open, Lula walks in like she owns the place, so he figures Mark's brought her here before. Eddie finds a bench in the shade. He cannot for the life of him figure out why this park has to be locked, but he has to admit that the fact of the lock makes him feel like he's someplace secret and special.

"Oh, deal with it," he tells Lula, who would probably be tapping her foot impatiently if dogs knew how to do that. Resigned, she finds something interesting to smell and proceeds to ignore him.

Eddie gets the distinct impression that this is a good neighborhood by New York standards: plenty of cabs at all hours, a profusion of older women wearing hats and pearls, a discreet sign for a tennis club. He could have guessed from the interior of Mark's apartment alone that Mark is well-to-do—that place is twice as big as Tony Ardolino's, and Eddie knows the kind of money Ardolino made during his playing career.

A while ago Mark said something about not coming by any of his money honestly, and Eddie figures that means he inherited it from someone in his awful family or that he got a lot of presents from the missing boyfriend. Or, hell, maybe he got lucky at the racetrack—Eddie doesn't know, and he's sure he shouldn't care. He's not in any kind of position to be thinking of a future with Mark, but that isn't going to stop his brain from spinning out all kinds of dumb ideas, and he'd like to have a clear path for those ideas to run along. Even in his fantasies, that apartment, with its memories and its uncomfortable furniture that long predate Eddie, is Mark's home. Mark has a past that Eddie can't ignore even in his daydreams, because that past is part of who Mark is.

Mark's already awake when Eddie opens the door. He's showered and dressed and drinking one of the paper cups of coffee at the dining room table.

"Did Lula abduct you?" Mark asks, not even bothering to conceal his impatience. Eddie grins.

"I made her take me to the park." Eddie grabs his own coffee and pastry—a slice of date nut bread this time—and sits across from Mark.

"And she let you? My poor darling," he says to the dog. "You've been kidnapped."

"She was pretty rude about it, if that makes you feel any better."

"I would have ransomed you," Mark tells the dog, fully ignoring Eddie. Lula looks between the two humans like they've both lost their minds and proceeds to go to sleep by the front door.

The phone rings, and Mark frowns at his coffee for a moment before finally getting out of his chair and answering it.

Eddie tries not to listen, but it's not like he can stop his ears from working.

"Yes," Mark says. "That's right. The furniture and art were appraised in '56, and that's reflected in the taxes I paid. I thought you had the documentation from the appraisers." A pause, during which Eddie can hear Mark pacing back and forth as far as the telephone cord will allow him. "I have copies. Yes, of course I do." There's another pause. "All right, you too."

After the click of the receiver being replaced in the cradle, a moment passes before Mark returns to the dining room.

"My accountant," Mark says. "Some problem with insurance."

"I knew you had an accountant!" Eddie exclaims, slapping his palm on the table.

Mark raises his eyebrows. "You seem very excited about my accountant."

"When I met you, I thought to myself: That's a man who has an accountant."

Mark stares at him and then lets out one of those whipcracks of stunned laughter. "Oh my God, I've been *leveled*. Has anyone ever been so insulted?" He sinks into the chair across from Eddie's. "A man who has an accountant. That puts me in my place."

"I only meant that you looked like you had your life together," Eddie protests.

"That looks like a man who flosses his teeth."

"It was a compliment!"

"That man sure does pay his bills on time," Mark says, the back of his hand against his forehead.

"How is that a bad thing?" Eddie cannot even imagine the steps it takes to pay a bill on time.

"Do I dare to eat a peach?" Mark says, even though Eddie can't see how peaches enter into it.

"My mom did my taxes this year." And last year, and the year before that, and also every year, but Eddie isn't going to mention that.

Mark gives him a withering look. "You're making this so much worse."

"I thought you were beautiful! I couldn't believe how beautiful you were." Beautiful and smart and a little mean, like he was made in a lab to lure Eddie to his doom. But instead of doom, it's this: coffee and breakfast, a dog snoring on the carpet, the near certainty they'll do this again.

Mark goes still, his eyes very wide, like he's never seen his reflection, like he doesn't look this way on purpose.

"Everything about you was lovely. It always is. I wanted to touch your suit. I kept thinking you couldn't possibly be as much of a wreck as I am, except—" Eddie skids to a stop, afraid he's gone too far.

"Except?" Mark's voice is strangled.

"Your hair was too long. Your watch is too big. That waitress. Sometimes when you laugh, it sounds like you're surprised by the sound." He reaches across the table for Mark's hand and slides two fingers beneath the loose watchband, along the soft underside of his wrist. He can feel Mark's pulse, fluttering and fast. "It wasn't until you laughed that I really knew I was in for it."

"My laugh is awful," Mark says.

"I can't stop thinking about you."

"You're lonely."

"So are you," Eddie says, watching Mark wince at the truth of it. "Doesn't change anything."

"Like hell it doesn't. You need to go make friends with your team, and then go out and have fun."

"I've been out with my teammates three nights in a row."

"You need to figure out some way to meet men your own age," Mark says, ignoring Eddie. "I'm the only queer man you've met in New York."

"My own age. You're what, five years older than me?"

"Six."

"Oh, well in *that* case." Eddie isn't going to point out that he can't exactly go strolling around Greenwich Village until he gets picked up. "Clearly, the only solution is for me to go fuck as many twenty-two-year-olds as possible and then do, like, a double-blind study to see if I still want to kiss you."

Mark swallows. "I'd question the methodology of that study."

"I bet you would," Eddie says nonsensically. "You know I'm not new at this, right? I didn't have some kind of big homosexual epiphany when I met you. Your allure isn't that powerful, jeez." He watches, delighted, as Mark cracks out a giggle and then tries and fails to wipe the smile off his face. "I was thinking of going home when I have a few days off next month, so if you need references, I can probably get them," he adds, as deadpan as he can make it.

Mark gives him a scowl that has no heat in it, then takes a bite of his date bread in a way that seems to indicate that he thinks the discussion is closed. The bite is precise and tidy and exactly the kind of bite a man with an accountant would take, but Eddie exercises a lot of maturity in not pointing this out.

Instead he pulls Mark out of his chair. Really, he doesn't need to pull at all—Mark's on his feet, his arms around Eddie, almost as soon as Eddie touches him. Mark collapses into the kiss, like it was taking all his effort *not* to kiss Eddie, and he's finally giving up.

Eddie kisses him, trusting in the warmth of their lips, the spark that rises between them, to say what it's too soon to put into words. He can feel every place where their bodies touch, their chests pressed against one another, and he tries to memorize how they fit.

It's not any kind of surprise when Mark bites Eddie's lip, and even less of a surprise that Eddie likes it. Eddie hears himself groan, but he isn't going to appear on television with bite marks, so he moves his mouth out of biting range and kisses beneath Mark's jaw, hard. *Mark* isn't going to be on television. Then again, under his ear. The top button of Mark's shirt is already open, so Eddie flicks open the next one and kisses the place where Mark's neck meets his shoulder.

It would be so easy to undo the rest of the buttons on Mark's shirt and then his trouser buttons, too. He'd bet that's what Mark wants, pressing up against him like that.

Instead he brushes his lips across Mark's, steadies himself, straightens up. "I ought to go," he says, his hands still on Mark's ribs.

"You ought to stay." There's something careful and strained about Mark's voice. He sounds—not uncertain, but almost upset, like he knows perfectly well what Eddie's up to with this.

Eddie sticks his hand in his pocket to feel the gold key holder. "See you tomorrow."

"This is insane, you know," Mark says, but as he says it, he's leaning toward Eddie. "You coming all the way down here to walk my dog. It's nuts."

Eddie bites his lip to hold back a grin. "Okay, I guess I shouldn't come back tomorrow. Do you want your key back?"

Mark narrows his eyes. "See you tomorrow." He says it like a dare, which is so nonsensical that Eddie just has to lean in and kiss the corner of his mouth.

CHAPTER SIXTEEN

The signs take Eddie by surprise.

It's not the first time he's seen his name on a fan's homemade poster. It is, however, the first time the sign is right behind the dugout, the first time the women holding it call out his name during batting practice. Eddie manages a polite wave, then pulls down the brim of his cap as if it'll shield him from view.

"For fuck's sake, go over and ask them to go out after the game," Ardolino says.

"I'm not—"

"Yeah, yeah, we all know you're a Boy Scout, O'Leary. Invite them out so the rest of the guys don't spend the entire game hitting on them and trying to look up their skirts. Jesus, kid."

"If I call dibs then nobody else will bother them," Eddie says, trying to make sense of Ardolino's apparent new interest in making his team act like gentlemen.

"I don't give even half a shit what the rest of the team says to girls in the stands or where they point their binoculars, but I do care about the fact that if you notice any of that happening, you're going to spend the entire fucking game thinking about it instead of playing baseball, and I'd really like to win a game today."

Eddie goes over to the girls. He takes his cap off and introduces himself like a complete idiot, but the girls just giggle, and only then does he realize they're the same girls from the nightclub. He apologizes, but they seem happy that he remembers them at all; they must think his life is a whirlwind of strange women, and he probably shouldn't correct them.

One of them shoves the sign at him along with a ballpoint pen. The sign reads YOU CAN DO IT, EDDIE! He's kind of touched and a little insulted, but he'll take cheerful condescension over heckling any day. He signs it in his neatest handwriting. One of these days he's going to come up with a decent autograph that doesn't look like a fourth-grader's penmanship assignment, but today is not that day.

"I don't know if you ladies like dancing," he says, putting the cap back on the pen, "but some of the team is going to—"

"Jeez, O'Leary," Ardolino says, throwing an arm around Eddie and grinning up at the girls. "It's like you don't know how to ask out a pair of beautiful women." He proceeds to give the name and address of a nightclub that Eddie completely fucking hates, the kind of place where scantily clad showgirls have plumes on their heads. "Give them my name at the door." And then he drags Eddie away.

"Thanks," Eddie mumbles.

"You will never be smooth," Ardolino says.

They eke out a win against the Cubs. Eddie manages to get on base three times, and only one of those is a walk, so he's flying pretty high when he returns to the locker room. He's almost managed to forget that he's going to have to go out tonight.

"Good game," he hears Mark say as he's returning from the showers.

Eddie nearly drops his towel. "You're here." It suddenly occurs to him that he's *kissed* this man. Twice. And now he's in the locker room, and Eddie's *naked*.

This seems to occur to Mark at exactly the same time, because he focuses on a spot over Eddie's shoulder. "Um. I'm going to go do a thing over there for a minute."

Eddie gets dressed, or at least he tries to.

"Gotta put your pants on before your shoes, big guy," Rosenthal says from the stall next to his.

"Ah, fuck." Eddie looks at his naked leg, ending in one black oxford.

"You'll get it right one of these days," Rosenthal says brightly, clapping him on the shoulder. Eddie resists the urge to pinch him.

He manages to get his pants on, though, and then he even talks to the asshole from the *Post* for a little while before going off in search of Mark.

Eddie finds Mark around the corner. "I was just about to ask if you wanted to go grab dinner," Eddie says, "but I'm going out with some of the guys. And these women who had a sign. Did you see them?"

"The entire television audience saw them, including me. That's why I'm here."

"To talk to those girls?"

"Yep."

"About me?" He's not sure if Mark wanted to talk to those women for the diary or for this magazine story he's writing, and he's not sure if he wants to ask.

"No, about war in Southeast Asia—yes, about you, Eddie. But they must have left before the end of the game, because they were gone by the time I got here. Somebody did get photographs, though, so at least I have that."

"They probably went home to get ready. I—or Ardolino, really—asked them to go out with us after the game. Hey, do you want to come along? You could talk to those girls."

Mark shakes his head but he looks tempted. "That's probably not a great idea."

"Please, Mark. It's going to be one of those awful nightclubs. The waitresses wear all these feathers and look like sexy birds."

Mark looks amused. "I never could resist feathers."

"It's going to be terrible," Eddie laments.

"You're really selling it."

"You'll come, though, right?"

"You'd better run it by your teammates."

"Don't move."

Eddie finds Ardolino. "Can I bring Mark to the nightclub?"

"Who the fuck is Mark?"

"He's ghostwriting those diaries for the *Chronicle*."

"You mean Bailey? The one who wrote about me getting fired."

"He didn't actually write—"

"The one who's writing those diaries about how you're terrible at baseball?"

"I mean, that's not really what they're about."

"That's definitely what they're about. And you want to bring him to a nightclub."

"He wants to talk to those girls who brought the signs."

Ardolino gives him a narrow look. "You know the team *just* came around to tolerating you. If a single thing that happens tonight winds up in the paper, everyone's going to blame you."

"He's not that kind of reporter," Eddie assures him.

"He'd better not be. Tell him the whole night's off-the-record. And he buys his own drinks."

Eddie practically skips over to where Mark's leaning against the wall, reading a book.

"He says it's fine. Anything anyone on the team does is off-the-record, though."

"Naturally."

Eddie's about to ask whether Mark wants to get a hamburger or something before heading to the nightclub when Mark checks his watch. "I'd better head home, then."

"Why?" Eddie protests. He was looking forward to sharing a cab.

"Well, first of all, I double-parked. I'd better leave before I get towed."

"A life of crime," Eddie says. "Wow." But really, everyone who arrives at the Polo Grounds after the first inning has to either double-park or just go home. There's basically no parking, because this stadium was built before Henry Ford had his bright idea.

"Second," Mark says, looking down at what he's wearing, "you can't possibly expect me to show up at a nightclub wearing khaki slacks and a cardigan. This is what I was wearing to vacuum. I ran out of the house like this when I saw the signs." He sounds scandalized. He looks wonderful, and Eddie nearly says so. "I mean, I hear the waitresses look like sexy birds. I need to step up my game. Besides, I have to walk Lula."

Eddie, of course, isn't going to argue with that.

The collar of Mark's shirt is open, and Eddie can see the edge of a red mark that he put there that morning. His mouth goes dry.

Mark follows Eddie's gaze and brings his hand up to his collar, his fingers brushing the edge of the bruise.

They are very much in public, so Eddie looks away, anywhere, the cigarette butts littering the floor, the flickering light bulb, the water-stained ceiling. "I'll see you later, then," Eddie manages, not daring to so much as glance at Mark as he says it. When he returns to the locker room, he finds Ardolino giving him a very curious stare.

People can say what they will about Tony Ardolino, but he sure has an eye for beautiful women. Eddie hadn't really noticed when he saw them at the bar or in the stands—possibly because women are not exactly his specialty, possibly because his attention was taken up with being mortified—but in cocktail dresses and makeup, the Iglesias sisters are stunners.

"Varga's the only one of them who isn't married," Eddie tells them in a low whisper after they get drinks.

"Oh, honey," one of them says. "You're just a baby, aren't you."

He must look scandalized, because the other woman pats his hand. "Don't worry. We're just dancing."

"And getting our pictures in the paper." They both giggle.

This is the kind of place with enormous semicircular booths and waitresses who make sure the glasses of famous patrons are never empty. Eddie tries to station himself on the edge of the booth so he'll have a view of the door and can flag Mark down as soon as he comes in, but he quickly finds himself in the center of the booth to make room for people coming and going from the dance floor. And that means pretty much everyone other than him. Ardolino, Varga, and Rosenthal are already dancing.

When, out of the corner of his eye, he sees someone slide into the booth, he perks up, thinking it might be Mark. But it's the Prices. Mrs. Price has on a red sequined cocktail gown and a little matching hat-type-thing. Eddie manages to wave over one of the scary bird waitresses and get them some drinks, so he isn't paying attention when someone else approaches the table.

"Sorry," Mark says. "Traffic was a nightmare."

Eddie's had an entire scotch and soda, and he's sure that whatever he's feeling is written all over his face. He watches Mark lean over and introduce himself to the Prices, shaking their hands.

"I can go get those girls for you," Eddie offers. "Their names are Carmen and Bobbie Iglesias." He looks over at the dance floor, where one sister is dancing with Ardolino and the other with Varga.

"I don't think they'll thank you for that," Mark observes. "I'll talk to them when they come back to the table."

Eddie nods as if he has any idea what Mark's talking about, as if his head isn't empty of thoughts and filled with the scent of Mark's cologne. He's built up a resistance to the fancy soap, so the cologne takes him by surprise. He wants to press his face into Mark's neck, and somebody ought to give him a prize for resisting.

When the song ends and people start piling back into the booth,

Eddie remembers his manners and makes introductions. Most of Eddie's teammates already know Mark from the locker room, but Mark shakes everyone's hands before turning his attention to the Iglesias sisters. Eddie gets the waitress's attention and orders another round of drinks.

He doesn't know why he's surprised when Mark winds up dancing with one of the sisters. For a horrified moment, he thinks he's going to need to dance with the other one, but Varga steps in and saves his life.

"I can't dance!" Eddie protests when Ardolino begins to mock him, only letting up when Mrs. Price steers Ardolino toward the dance floor. Sam Price stays behind long enough to pour out half of Ardolino's drink into Eddie's glass.

"He's been nursing that drink since we got here," Eddie says. He thinks Price will look happy about that, but instead he only looks tired. Then Price follows his wife, and Eddie's alone at the table with nothing to do but watch the dance floor. Or, specifically, he watches Mark.

Eddie is momentarily outraged that Mark is standing too close to that girl. Carmen, he thinks. He's going to give her the wrong idea, leaning in like that. Mark shouldn't lean into anyone but *him*. They're talking and laughing, and Eddie just finds the whole thing objectionable.

And his *suit*. All of Mark's clothes are lovely, and Eddie is slowly becoming obsessed with Italian wool, but tonight Mark is wearing a narrow black suit that's been tailored to within an inch of its life. He looks—well. Nobody else on the dance floor looks half as good as him. Not even Tony Ardolino, and it's only because Eddie is nearly done with his third drink that he's able to admit that Tony Ardolino looks really good in a suit.

The band plays about a million songs before anyone returns to the table, and then it's only Rosenthal who comes back in order to bully

Eddie into dancing with someone. "I can't dance!" Eddie insists. "In my contract it says I'm not supposed to do anything that'll result in injury!"

"I'll show you injury," Rosenthal says, hauling Eddie off by the sleeve.

Eddie finds himself being rescued by the shorter sister. Bobbie, probably. He's about to thank her when, instead of taking him away from this terrible place, she starts dancing with him. "Betrayal," he whimpers. "Mark, I've been betrayed," he says, because Mark is there, dancing with Mrs. Price.

Mark laughs in his face and twirls Mrs. Price away.

"They're all mean," Eddie says.

"You're sloshed," Bobbie says. "Wow."

"I had three drinks," Eddie confides.

Bobbie starts laughing. "You're a sweetheart. I want to fold you up and put you in my pocket. I hope you get your swing back, baby. I've never rooted for anyone as hard as I'm rooting for you."

"That's nice of you," Eddie says, because he really isn't sure what else he can possibly say, and also all his attention is currently devoted to not stepping on this nice lady's feet. "But why? There are tons of ballplayers who are having bad seasons, if that's what gets you going."

She's quiet for a few beats. "I guess you were so good last year and so bad this spring. To be on top of the world and then have to struggle like that? It'd be hard for anybody."

Eddie's horrified to realize that he has tears in his eyes. He tries not to think about how good he felt last year, how it felt like all the hard work he'd put in was paying off in exactly the way it was supposed to, how it felt like he had earned something, like his success was complete, finalized, done. And then—it just slipped away. He doesn't know what went wrong, and at this point the only thing he's sure of is that it could happen again.

"Aw, honey, it's okay," Bobbie says, and kisses the corner of his mouth. "I knew you were a sweetheart." She steers him off the dance floor, leading him toward the restrooms instead of back to the booth, probably understanding that he'd rather not explain his fit of the weepies to his teammates. She pats his shoulder, and he guesses that he's supposed to splash water on his face, so he ducks into the men's room.

He probably shouldn't be surprised when Mark appears a minute later.

"You all right?" Mark asks. This is the kind of place where the bathroom has an attendant who stands there with towels, so it's not like they have any privacy. Eddie tries to keep this in mind, even though it's honestly pretty hard to keep anything in mind right now between the scotch and Mark's cologne.

"I've had too much to drink, and now I'm going to cry if anyone looks at me the wrong way, but I don't think I can leave until I've made sure those girls get home okay," Eddie explains.

"Carmen just said they're about to get a cab and head home. So why don't we go make sure that happens, and then we can take off?"

Eddie's too tipsy to remember exactly how they get back to the booth, but he's dimly aware that Mark is making excuses for him. "I'm going to pour him into a cab," Mark tells Mrs. Price before kissing her on both cheeks and shaking somebody's hand.

At the curb, it's Mark who hails a cab for the girls and pays the cabbie. Eddie should object, but he doesn't think he could successfully get his wallet out of his pocket at this point. The next thing he knows, Mark's hand is on his elbow, and he's being put into a cab himself. "You're coming, too, right?" Eddie asks.

"You'd better believe I am." Mark climbs in next to him. "I hate to think where you'd wind up if I left you up to your own devices."

"My devices are terrible," Eddie agrees. "I had three drinks."

Mark laughs, bright and sudden and a little silly.

"You're a good dancer," Eddie says. "And your suit is pretty."

Mark flicks a meaningful little glance in the direction of the cabbie.

"I know," Eddie whispers. "All night, I've been reminding myself. Get those girls home, and don't be . . . you know. It was hard to remember after that last drink, but I did it."

"You did a good job," Mark says, but he sounds sad.

"And now I'm exhausted." Eddie slumps against the back of his seat.

The cab stops in front of Mark's building. "Oh," Eddie says happily. "It's your place."

"I hope you don't mind, but I didn't want to figure out how to get home after tucking you in. Not a lot of cabs in Washington Heights at two in the morning."

Eddie spends a happy moment contemplating Mark tucking him in before he's jolted to awareness by being tugged out of the cab and into the lobby.

"Hi, Pete!" he says to the doorman.

"Good evening, Mr. O'Leary," Pete says. He and Mark exchange a look. The look is probably about Eddie being very drunk.

"Is it too late for me to call my mom?" Eddie asks when they get off the elevator on Mark's floor.

"She's in Omaha?" Mark checks his watch. "It's past midnight there."

"That's too late," Eddie says sadly.

"Was she expecting a call from you?"

"No, I just wanted to tell her how much I miss her."

"You know, most people don't get like this when they're drunk," Mark says, fumbling with his key. It's not the fancy key, because that one's safe in Eddie's pocket. He pats it, like he does a couple dozen times a day.

"You mean dumb."

"No, Eddie. I mean sweet."

"That's what the nice lady said. She said I'm a sweetheart, and she wants to fold me up and put me in her pocket."

Mark laughs. "A woman of excellent taste."

Eddie's delighted with the implication that Mark, too, wants to fold him up and put him in his pocket, even though he can't see how that would work or why anyone would want to do it in the first place.

Lula dances in a circle when they get inside, and Mark grumbles something about how he never gets this treatment. Eddie picks Lula up so she can lick his face more efficiently and without the risk of Eddie falling over and never getting up again.

"We're having a sleepover," he tells the dog.

"You sure are, but first you're getting undressed," Mark says. "I don't have anything for you to sleep in, but there's no way I'm sending you home in a wrinkled suit."

"You're so smart," Eddie says, marveling over this wisdom. He tries to loosen his tie and pull it over his head, but gets it stuck on one of his ears, and he can't get it off without putting the dog down. He feels like an idiot, but Mark's laughing, and he'd be okay with feeling like an idiot all the time as long as it made Mark laugh like that.

"Let me," Mark says, taking the dog. A minute later he's helping Eddie with his top button. His lips are very red, and his hair is falling in his face.

Eddie leans in. He's telegraphing his moves, giving Mark a second to step back. But Mark just shifts his hands from Eddie's buttons to his shoulders, and when Eddie steps in, brushing his lips across Mark's, Mark kisses him back. Eddie already knows it's not going to go anywhere tonight, but it doesn't need to. It's just the taste of lemon and tonic on Mark's lips, the feel of Mark's thumb stroking his neck. It's a good-night kiss, and it only ends when Eddie's smiling too broadly to keep going.

CHAPTER SEVENTEEN

The first time Eddie wakes up, it's because Lula's standing on his face.

"You're a menace," he hears Mark whisper. "Leave him be." Then he hears what's probably Mark putting on his shoes, followed by the leash clipping on to Lula's collar, and then the door being shut so quietly that Eddie smiles into the couch cushion.

The next time he wakes up, the curtains have been opened, and Eddie moans as he squeezes his eyes shut.

"It's nine o'clock," Mark says, shoving a cup of coffee under Eddie's nose.

"Thank you," Eddie croaks, taking the mug and wincing as he opens his eyes. "I'm dead."

"You have half an hour before my friend Lilian gets here."

Eddie gets to his feet a little too quickly, like he's going to run out into the street in his underwear. Something inside his head knocks against his skull. It's probably his brain, or what's left of it.

"Hush. It's okay. She doesn't care about men in their underwear, or about men in their underwear in other men's apartments, for that matter. She's safe. But I thought I'd give you a chance to escape if you wanted."

Eddie manages to shower and dress before the doorman calls up. Lilian, it turns out, is about Mark's age, with short dark hair and horn-rimmed glasses. She's wearing what looks like a man's suit.

"Maureen's going to die of jealousy," she says after shaking Eddie's hand. "Simply die." She doesn't ask what Eddie's doing at Mark's apartment, but she does give Mark a long look that he answers by swatting her shoulder and disappearing into the kitchen.

"I have pound cake," Mark calls.

"Did you make it?" Lilian asks, looking hopeful, and Eddie takes a moment to decide whether to slot Mark into the category of human being who might *make* a *pound cake*. Lilian must be confused.

"No, picked it up yesterday," Mark calls back.

"Who's Maureen?" Eddie asks.

"My lover," she says, scrunching her face up. "There isn't a better word, sorry, but I do like to be clear."

"Oh," Eddie says, understanding dawning. That's what Mark meant by Lilian not caring about whether men spend the night with other men. He shoots a look toward the kitchen, not really thinking about why he does it, and notices Lilian regarding him quizzically.

"*Girlfriend*," Mark says, carrying three plates and a pound cake. "That's the better word."

"*Girlfriend* sounds like we work together. 'I'm going to the Automat with one of my *girlfriends*.'"

Mark hums thoughtfully as he cuts huge slabs of cake for each of them. "*Boyfriend* really doesn't pose that problem. The real alternative, of course, is not to say anything at all." He and Lilian share a look that Eddie can't understand.

Eddie stuffs his mouth full of cake so he can't talk, because nothing he says is going to be safe. Anything he says is going to make him look queer or make him look like an asshole, and a mouthful of cake is the only sane option left to him.

"Enjoying the cake, Eddie?" Mark asks, shedding the grim look from a moment earlier and giving him an indulgent smile.

Eddie gives him a thumbs-up.

"Lilian's a photographer at the *Chronicle*," Mark says.

"Not on the baseball beat, alas." She gives him a professional once-over. "I bet you take a nice photograph."

"That's what Mark says." And shit, that's why Eddie isn't supposed to be talking. Lilian raises an eyebrow at Mark. Mark takes a prim sip of coffee. Eddie crams some more cake into his mouth.

"We're going to do some shopping and see a matinée," Mark says when Eddie gets to his feet. Eddie wants to make a break for it before he can say anything disastrous. "You're welcome to join us."

"I have a doubleheader. Have fun, though." He doesn't do anything stupid like kiss Mark goodbye. He does bend down to give Lula several kisses, though, and tries to telepathically communicate to her that some of them are for Mark.

In the cab, he thinks about what Mark said about Lilian being safe. He's almost positive that he trusts Mark's judgment about this, and that nothing that happened this morning will cause him trouble in the future.

When Mark first told Eddie that he didn't make much of a secret about his queerness, Eddie hadn't really understood what that meant—does Mark go around with men? Openly go to gay bars? But he thinks he gets it now. Mark and Lilian had talked about Lilian's girlfriend as if it hadn't mattered. That, he guesses, is what Mark wants—but not only in the safety of his apartment.

It seems wildly implausible from where Eddie's standing. His mom once told him about people in India who only eat fruit that has fallen from trees. Eddie doesn't know if this is true or just one of those things his mom gets backward, but if there are people only eating things that fall out of trees, then good for them, but he doesn't see how you can do that and expect to have a normal life. You can't go to a restaurant or get whatever vitamins you're supposed to. He figures your teeth probably fall out.

That's what it feels like when Mark says he doesn't keep being queer a secret: a truly bizarre and possibly dangerous choice. If there were even rumors about Eddie being queer, he doesn't know what he'd do. He couldn't get a job—any job—in baseball, and God only knows what his mom would think. He wouldn't be able to look anyone in the eye. It's enough to make his heart race, even in the safe anonymity of the back of this cab.

Obviously, he knows things are different for some people—artists or eccentric millionaires or whatever. But Eddie isn't one of those people, and he never will be, and so he has to play by the same rules as everybody else.

He feels unaccountably angry about it, knowing there's this tiny slice of relative freedom that he never even thought about until this morning, but which he's now furious he'll never have for himself. It's ridiculous; he doesn't even want people to know he's queer. He's being silly, and he knows it.

There are plenty of things he ought to be worrying about, and this isn't one of them. The Robins have a doubleheader against the Cubs this afternoon, and Eddie needs to get on the board. He needs to do his job.

At the hotel he shaves and gets changed and buys an apple to eat on the way to the stadium. When he walks into the locker room, three of the guys say hi to him at once. Two months ago, he would have given half his teeth for that. And he's still pretty thrilled. The smile he gives them is genuine. He's so relieved to have a team, to feel like he belongs—

Except that the extent to which he doesn't belong somehow hadn't occurred to him until now. His mother's always on him to use the sense God gave him, but the problem is that he tries to think of one thing at a time, to put things into neat little boxes, and sometimes that keeps him from seeing the big picture. He simply did not think of himself as a homosexual baseball player until today. In the world of baseball, he's *normal*, he's *regular*. The fact that he likes men is something he keeps in a tiny, cordoned-off part of his brain, a part he doesn't even think about when he's being a baseball player.

He can't do that anymore, though. The box in which he keeps his queerness got swept away at some point in the past few months, and he's only noticing now. Everything that used to be safely stowed in that box is all over the place, and Eddie's never going to be able to put it back. He's going to have to think about how he's different and how it's *not fair*, and he's going to be upset about it.

He wants to talk to someone, but, as usual, he can't. He can't even talk to Mark, because Mark is the reason that safe little box got ruined. Mark is the problem here. Mark thinks the danger he poses is that people will notice that Eddie's queer, but the real danger is that *Eddie* finally noticed he's queer—or at least noticed the implications. He's outside, alone—just as outside and alone as he was when nobody was talking to him, when he was in a strange city and on a strange team. That strangeness is something he'll have to carry with him and something he'll have to carry alone.

Part V
AUGUST

CHAPTER EIGHTEEN

Eddie stops by on the way to the airport for the sole purpose of kissing Mark goodbye. It's another of his bafflingly chaste kisses: one hand someplace decent, like Mark's hip or shoulder, the other hand unacceptably gentle on Mark's jaw, and the kiss itself little more than a lingering brush of lips. Mark ought to have put an end to those kisses as soon as they started, because he knows perfectly well that they're Eddie's line in the sand, a declaration that whatever happens between them won't be written off as mere sex. The fact that he's going along with it is proof that his judgment is hopelessly compromised where Eddie O'Leary is concerned.

"I'm late," he says against Mark's lips. "Cab's waiting."

Mark should ask why he bothered stopping by in the first place but instead presses in for another kiss, then pulls back, out of breath, and all but shoves Eddie into the hallway. Mark leans against the closed door, his fingers on his lips.

Mark tells himself that there can't be any harm in a couple of kisses. People kiss one another all the time. They're both adults; they're both unattached. Maybe there's something to be said about the ethics of kissing the person he's writing about, but Mark can't even pretend to be the kind of person with active scruples about journalistic ethics.

Besides, this is nothing. It's kissing. It's kissing that's probably going to lead to sex, and that's it. It's physical. It's physical, but with someone he likes, which he's certain is still just physical. Eddie's surely in the same boat; he doesn't have the time or freedom for anything more.

He gets dressed and heads to work after apologizing to Lula for leaving her behind. On the subway, a pair of teenage girls are sitting close together, one rapidly whispering into the other's ear, her mouth shielded by a cupped hand. Occasionally, the one who's being whispered to opens her eyes wide and says something along the lines of "Meredith! You *didn't*!" They're both giggling. It's something Mark's seen a thousand times, probably: a secret urgently spilled into the ear of a confidante, someone's excitement doubled by virtue of sharing it. Mark's been the person whispered to, often enough; he's rarely been the whisperer.

And yet—this morning he wants to whisper his own secret into someone's ear. At the core, his secret is probably no different from what those girls are whispering to one another. He feels like he's at the beginning of something good, or maybe the end of something bad, and he wants to tell someone.

Surely, keeping secrets should be second nature by now. He spent seven years organizing his life so the faintest rumor of queerness never touched William. Secrecy is part of being queer, something he's known for as long as he's known that word. He thought he could forcibly cast aside the secrecy, just as he did the shame, but maybe he knew all along that it would only work if he exclusively associated with other openly queer people—which is probably exactly what he ought to have done to begin with.

It isn't too late to walk away from Eddie. But he isn't going to. When he thinks of Eddie's hand on his jaw, careful and sweet, Mark knows that he's going to come back for more.

Mark has barely settled in at his desk at the *Chronicle* when there's a knock at the door. "Come in," he calls.

"So, I have bad news," Andy says, and Mark's ready to hear about the newspaper folding. Or worse. Has something happened to Lilian? Or—Christ—Eddie's plane? People need to stop saying that there's bad news and then *pausing*. He's already braced for the worst—his hands in fists, his teeth digging into his lip—when he registers Andy's next words. "It's George Allen. Last night he had a heart attack."

It's not like he and George are particularly close, but Mark *likes* him. It wasn't that long ago that George was in his car, in his apartment. And the phrase *heart attack* is always going to be a gut punch. "Did he survive?" Mark asks as levelly as possible.

"God, yes. I'm so sorry. I should have opened with that. He's at St. Vincent's. I don't know the details. Look, I know it's a lot to ask, but can you fly out to Pittsburgh to join the Robins for the rest of this road trip?"

Mark's ready to say that no, of course he can't. He has a dog to look after; furthermore, he has no interest whatsoever in traveling to Pittsburgh or anywhere else right now.

"It would only be for this road trip. There's a kid on the sports desk who can take over next week. It's all right if you can't," Andy says, looking defeated. "We can always get something off one of the wire services."

And that, for some reason, is what makes up his mind. The *Chronicle*'s been good to him. George Allen's been kind to him. And he feels a surprising loyalty not to the Robins, but to their fans, to the people who open the paper every morning hoping to read some good news about their ill-fated team; he feels like they and he are in this together.

"Okay," Mark says. "Why not."

"Oh, thank God," Andy says.

"It's been a while since I've done any actual reporting," Mark cautions. "You might wind up needing to use the Associated Press coverage anyway."

"We'll cross that bridge when we come to it. There's a flight out of Idlewild at three that'll get you there before the game. Oh, and before I forget, can you turn in a draft of the magazine article by the beginning of September?"

Mark hasn't written a single word.

The article Mark pitched is about the phenomenon of slumps, looked at through the lens of what happened to Eddie. He knows he can make it good: he feels a spark of interest that he hasn't felt in ages, a sure sign that he's on to something. He thinks it'll resonate for a city that seems to have been looking for an underdog to root for. But if it's good—if it's as good as Mark thinks it might be—it'll be one step further toward immortalizing Eddie as someone who spent half a season playing some of the worst baseball anyone's ever seen.

Eddie will hate it. He's sensitive about the fluff Mark writes about him; a full ten thousand words about his slump will be enough to make him forget Mark's number forever.

Well, something has to end this thing between them. Mark supposes it'll have to be this article. He finds that he very much doesn't want it to be.

"Sure," Mark says. "No problem."

~~

Lula regards Mark suspiciously as he pulls a pair of dusty suitcases out of the tiny third bedroom. The last time anyone used them was the winter of 1957, when he and William spent a week in Acapulco. But he can't think about that right now. Instead he packs the minimum he'll need for a week: two suits that don't wrinkle too badly, six shirts, a handful of sweaters, a sport coat, five ties, underwear. He sweeps the contents of his medicine cabinet and bathroom sink into a shaving kit. He manages to squeeze everything into two suitcases. Then he remembers that he needs to pack the portable typewriter, and there's no way he can carry two suitcases and a typewriter.

He stares at his luggage and decides he'll pay people to help carry it all. There was a time when he could have got by with the clothes on his back, a paperback novel, and maybe a toothbrush. He had been adept at simply surviving, at not thinking about, let alone wanting, more than the bare minimum. The gap between who he is now and the man he was then is deep enough to bring him up short, stumbling at the edge.

The difference is—well, it's money, no way around that, but it's also nearly a decade of being looked after, and treated as someone worth looking after. When William bought this apartment and filled it with nice things, Mark had been torn between worry that he'd fallen in love with a shameless prodigal and the faintly hilarious idea that his name on the deed might be some kind of compensation. Now, though, he can imagine how clear it must have been to William that, after being thrown away, Mark needed tangible proof of his value.

He's in the cab by two o'clock, in Brooklyn handing Lula off to Maureen at two thirty, and then finally climbing the stairs to a Pan Am jetliner a full fifteen minutes before takeoff.

He has a moment of disorientation as the plane takes off, but it's not until they've reached the top of the clouds that he realizes what it is—he's never flown in an airplane without William.

He drinks the glass of wine the stewardess offers him and looks out the window. Maybe being so far off the ground demands some perspective, or maybe he's simply had a glass of wine on an empty stomach, but his time with William seems so brief: he lived twenty years before, he'll probably live forty or fifty years after, and William was only seven years in between. The extent of time in front of him feels vast—not in the miserable way he had thought of it last year, but as something with sunny blue horizons he hasn't yet reached.

He's besieged by one of those babyish fits of aggrieved injustice that he's had for the past year and a half. He never could have guessed the extent to which grief feels like an accounting error—he died at thirty-*four*? That can't be right! Double-check your math. But now he's thinking that what's just as unfair as Mark losing William is William losing *this*: an overpacked suitcase, the giddy thrill of someone waiting for him, something good about to happen.

CHAPTER NINETEEN

Thanks to the evident death wish of a Pittsburgh cab driver, Mark arrives at the stadium before the first pitch. He goes directly to the press box, where he gets a few curious looks and some questions asking after George.

As a childhood fan of a perennial underdog team—and honestly calling the Senators underdogs is doing a disservice to underdogs—Mark always feels a vicious little thrum of nasty pleasure when another team is struggling. He's surprised that he doesn't feel that way about the Robins. He actually wants this team to do well, or at least to acquit themselves non-embarrassingly. And, sure, part of it is that Mark wants things to work out well for Eddie, but there's more to it. He remembers those girls who brought the signs to the ballpark. He wants to believe that this team can turn it around. He wants to believe in the possibility of a second act.

When he checks the scorecard, he sees that, wonder of wonders, Ardolino has changed the batting lineup, and Eddie's batting second.

During Eddie's first at bat, Mark realizes he's holding his breath, and when the bat connects with the ball, his fingers grip the edges of his typewriter so tightly he feels the plastic creak. But Eddie gets on base. It's a strange feeling, having a personal connection, however minor, to someone who's being watched by thousands—hundreds of thousands, if you count the television. It ought to be a reminder of the gulf between them, but it just makes Mark want to protect

Eddie. It's foolish, but Mark's making peace with the fact that everything he feels about Eddie is a little foolish.

Eddie gets on base again in the fifth inning, and his fielding is as impeccable as ever, but the Robins still lose.

Mark heads first to the Pirates' locker room to get a line from the winning pitcher to round out the article he still needs to write, then goes to the visitors' locker room. When he walks in, he doesn't even mean to seek Eddie out, but he does it anyway, automatically, so he sees it when Eddie notices him.

Eddie's still in his uniform pants, threatening one of the relief pitchers with his sweaty undershirt or something equally disgusting, but he's doing it silently because locker rooms are usually quiet after a loss. He looks right past Mark, but then his brain seems to catch up with his eyes, and his gaze snaps back. Mark doesn't know if Eddie just isn't making any effort to put on a normal expression, or if he doesn't know how, or if, somehow, this is the best he can do. But whatever the case, for a minute he looks plain overjoyed. It's just written there on his face for the entire Robins roster and the press to see. Nobody else in this room is smiling, and Eddie's bright grin is a neon sign.

Mark thinks fast and turns to Ardolino, who's answering questions about his decision to pull the pitcher at the end of the sixth inning. His heart's racing. Does Eddie have no sense of self-preservation? He mechanically writes down whatever Ardolino is saying and tries to decide whether there's a believable heterosexual explanation for the way Eddie looked at him. And, sure, of course there is. Anyone might be happy to see a friend—but not a reporter, not right after a loss. At least, he doesn't think so. Best-case scenario, people assume Eddie's an oddball; that explanation might hold up even if they know Mark is queer.

"I heard about George," Eddie says as Mark slides his notebook into his shirt pocket. He's showered and dressed now, but he looks like he threw on his clothes as quickly as possible, and his hair is dripping onto his collar. "Any word on how he's doing? I guess you got sent in to pinch hit for him."

"All I know is that he's in the hospital." A droplet of water is working its way down Eddie's temple, and Mark wants to swipe it away, preferably with his tongue.

"I bet you haven't had dinner."

"You'd win that bet, and I won't get any dinner until I have this story filed."

With any luck, that will be enough to keep Eddie from making an explicit dinner offer in full hearing of half the team. Mark gives what he hopes is a normal-looking wave, and goes off to write his story.

When he finishes, he heads in the direction he hopes leads out of the stadium. But before he can even turn out of the corridor, he finds Eddie sitting on a bench, reading a paperback.

"What are you doing here?" Mark asks.

"Thought I'd walk you back to the hotel, maybe get some dinner."

"You've got to be less obvious," Mark hisses, even though the hallway is empty. "You've just got to."

"Nothing wrong with friends getting dinner," Eddie whispers back.

"When I—" Mark doesn't know how to explain that the real problem is that when he walked in the locker room, Eddie looked like a cartoon princess who'd just run into her fairy godmother. "You can't look at me like that in public."

"Like what?"

"When I walked into the locker room, you smiled."

"It's well-known that only homosexuals smile," Eddie agrees.

Mark sighs in despair.

"You worry about me," Eddie says. "It's sweet. So, dinner?"

"Sure," Mark says. "Why not. While we're at it, let's hit up the finest gay bars Pittsburgh has to offer."

"I was kind of thinking more along the lines of spaghetti, if that's okay?"

Mark looks at Eddie, at the open, hopeful expression on his face. Surely, somewhere in the vicinity of Forbes Field, they can find a suitably non-romantic restaurant, someplace brightly lit and with plastic tablecloths. Mark is certain that whatever is clutching at his heart can't possibly survive fluorescent light and plastic tablecloths. "First I want to drop off this typewriter at the hotel."

He manages to persuade Eddie that he can carry his own type-writer, at least.

They wind up at the kind of Italian restaurant that offers a trough-size bowl of spaghetti and meatballs and a giant basket of bread for a grand total of a dollar fifty.

"Meals come with either a glass of red wine of unspecified variety," Mark says, studying the menu, "or a bowl of ice cream. Wine or ice cream. In what universe is that a reasonable choice? It's like—football or a haircut. Trombones or a spoon."

"You could get both for an extra seventy-five cents," Eddie suggests.

"That's not the point. I don't want either. It's that the binary of wine and ice cream shouldn't exist."

Eddie raises his eyebrows in a way that clearly communicates that he thinks Mark is in a mood. It's both annoyingly presumptuous and completely correct. Mark is so used to not being known that it's a strange feeling, and he realizes he wants it to happen again.

"You don't want ice cream?" Eddie asks.

"Maybe I don't like ice cream."

"Don't you?" Eddie asks, like he hasn't watched Mark drink a milkshake.

"You should see your face. I do like ice cream. I'm just fussy about it."

"Imagine that," Eddie murmurs, eyes on his menu. "Mark Bailey, fussy. Were you always like this? Did you demand—I don't know—butterscotch pistachio ice cream on a silver platter for your fifth birthday party?"

"If you're asking whether my family had money, no. My father was in the army—enlisted."

"And you didn't want to join?"

Mark actually laughs. "4-F," he says, tapping his glasses. "Thank God." This is probably where he ought to give some more biography, but the waitress arrives just in time to spare him. "What about your parents?" Mark asks after the waitress takes their order. He already knows the answer, having researched those basic facts before meeting Eddie that first time.

"My mom's a librarian, and my dad sold tractors," Eddie says. "He died when I was twelve, though, and my stepdad teaches science at the high school."

"You get along with him? Your stepdad?"

"Yeah. He's the most boring man to ever live, but he loves my mom. He likes to grill," Eddie adds, as if this grilling is a salient fact.

Again, Mark knows he ought to say something about himself. The truth is that Mark's every instinct is to hold bits and pieces of himself back. Whenever conversation drifts close to anything important, Mark decides that there's no reason in the world why he ought to tell Eddie about it. They're not settling down together. They're not even fucking. Mark could nip this in the bud; he could make it clear—to Eddie, maybe even just to himself—that this is where Mark has to draw the line.

But he also wants that feeling he had earlier, that feeling of being seen for who he is, and of being liked anyway.

"My family was rotten," Mark says. Well, if he was looking for a way to ruin the romantic mood of their dinner, this sure ought to do it.

"You've mentioned," Eddie says.

"I mean, they were rotten before they threw me out. My older sisters were okay, but they got the hell out as soon as they could."

"Do you keep in touch with your sisters?"

"One moved to California. We exchange Christmas cards."

Eddie's foot nudges his under the table. "We don't have to do this, you know."

"Do what?"

"I like knowing things about you, but it's okay that you don't like talking about it. I don't think I'd like talking about it, either, from the sounds of it."

"It's not—look, I don't *care* about them. I actually don't mind talking about them, because it's like talking about the situation in Vietnam or Berlin or whatever. Dismal, but it doesn't have any bearing on my life. I don't know why I brought it up."

"Okay," Eddie says, but he sounds doubtful.

Mark does know why he brought it up, though, and it's precisely because it has no bearing on his life. Even when he tries to be candid, he does it in the cagiest possible way. Truly, he has no idea why Eddie can't see that Mark is utterly unfit for—for whatever this is. Friendship, Mark reminds himself. Friendship with kissing. That's all.

But even friendship requires some level of honesty. If he wants to keep Eddie around for a bit—which is a shitty way to put it, like Eddie's a stray cat—then he needs to stop being cagey about the things that matter.

He needs to tell Eddie about William. At this point, it's strange not to. Part of Mark's reluctance is that he doesn't want to see Eddie's face do sad, sympathetic things. And yes, he's a private person. The people he's closest to—Lilian and Maureen—were in his life when it happened. He hardly had to tell them anything after that first horrible phone call. Last summer he told Andy for, he told himself, work reasons. It had been excruciating, filled with "I'm so sorry" and "How awful" and the ever-present fact that there's no word in the language that Mark feels comfortable using to describe exactly what William was to him. You can't even begin to tell the story without having a word.

But overlaying all those perfectly good reasons is something nebulous. He doesn't want to cast what he's doing with Eddie—which is, however short-lived, something fundamentally *happy*—in the context of . . . grief, he supposes. He doesn't want to make himself into a tragic figure. When Eddie talks about his life, he tends to share good things, and here Mark is talking about his awful parents and estranged sisters, trying to figure out how to mention his dead lover. He doesn't know how to explain that the fact of William is *good*, even now. He's sure that if he says all that, he'll sound like he's still in love with a dead man, haunted by something he should have made peace with, rather than glad to have had what they did.

The food arrives, and Mark is spared having to say anything. Instead he fusses over his pasta for a few minutes, cutting his meatballs into increasingly tiny pieces, then shaking Parmesan cheese all over everything, taking two bites, and putting his fork down. Eddie doesn't press for an explanation, because he never does.

"Sorry," Mark says quietly. "I'm terrible company."

"Nothing to be sorry about." Eddie nudges Mark under the table, the toe of his shoe sliding against Mark's.

A few minutes pass during which Mark shreds a piece of bread and doesn't accomplish much of anything else. "You know, I thought you were such an asshole when I first read about you."

"I sort of am," Eddie says.

"You are not," Mark says, glaring. Eddie looks pleased.

"I have a short fuse and piss people off at least once a day. Ardolino is going to throw me off a bridge if I tell him one more time that we need a real first baseman. Just this morning, I filled Rosenthal's suitcase with three dollars' worth of rubber snakes, and I don't even feel bad about it. I bought up all the snakes from three Woolworth's. Next time we play the Phillies, I might need to slide into that fucker who hurt my leg. I'm a bit of an asshole, Mark, there's no point in denying it."

"My point," Mark says, his voice pitched to maximum sniffiness, "is that you're being awfully patient with me. You're a sweetheart."

Eddie grins. "You've mentioned that."

Mark takes a fastidious little sip of wine so he doesn't reach across the table and put his finger in Eddie's dimple. "I apologize for being tedious."

"You couldn't be tedious if you tried," Eddie says, voice low and a little rough.

The look Eddie sends him has Mark flagging down the waitress for a check so they can get out of there before he crawls across the table and gets them both arrested.

CHAPTER TWENTY

When they get off the hotel elevator, they're standing too close. There's nobody in the hallway, which is good, because Mark can't honestly say that he'd act differently even if the entire Robins' roster and a newsroom's worth of reporters were standing around.

The ten seconds it takes for Mark to fumble his key out of his pocket and unlock the door last an eternity. Mark can hear his own pulse. As soon as the door shuts behind them, they reach for one another.

Mark isn't expecting the instantaneous heat of this kiss. He isn't expecting Eddie's hand on his jaw, holding him still so Eddie can slide his tongue alongside Mark's. He isn't expecting Eddie to back him against the wall. Their previous kisses have mostly been slow, almost careful, and this is neither of those things.

"This is a terrible idea," Mark says against Eddie's mouth.

Eddie pulls back. "Get the fine print out all at once."

"What?"

"All the disclaimers. All the warnings." He glances down at his watch. "You have thirty seconds."

Mark tries to summon up some irritation, but instead he's standing just inside the doorway to a hotel room, feeling an impossible mixture of exasperation and heat and something else, something softer and fonder and that he doesn't want to give a name to, but which he sees reflected back at him when he looks at Eddie.

"One-time-only offer," Eddie says. "Complain as much as you—"

Mark leans in and kisses him again. This time, though, he slips his hands lower, palming Eddie's ass and pressing even closer. Mark can feel him, hard in his suit pants, and knows Eddie can feel him, too.

Mark is rusty at this. He can't quite remember how you go about figuring out what someone likes and then giving it to them. He can't remember how you get from kissing to sex when the path between isn't paved with experience. A younger Mark knew, or maybe was too brash and selfish to give it much thought.

The hand on his jaw shifts, Eddie's thumb moving to Mark's lower lip. Mark draws the tip into his mouth while glancing up at Eddie. And so he's watching when something gives way in Eddie's expression, the last traces of restraint slipping away and being replaced by something dark and urgent. Only then does Mark really understand that Eddie's been holding back. Not just now, but for weeks. Eddie, who can't even look at food without eating it. Eddie, who seldom has a thought without speaking it aloud. He's been trying to behave. He's been trying to be good. All those kisses, those times he left just as things were beginning to get heated—that was Eddie trying his best, and now he's at the end of his rope.

"Please," Eddie says, a little desperately, like he isn't quite sure what he's asking for.

"I have you." Mark kisses Eddie hard, then, making it filthy enough that Eddie can't possibly miss his intent. He presses the length of his body flush against Eddie's.

"Mark, please," Eddie whines against Mark's mouth.

"Shh. We have time."

"I—I know, but I—Mark."

It's possible, Mark realizes, that Eddie's never had time before. He remembers what it was like, never having the luxury of a locked door and the guarantee of privacy. Sometimes the safest thing in the world is to get out of there fast.

"I'm not going anywhere until you come or tell me to stop," Mark promises, and Eddie lets out a desperate sound. "Is there anything you want in particular? Or do you just want me to take the edge off, and then we can—"

"Yes," Eddie begs. "Please."

"I know," Mark says, unbuttoning Eddie's pants and giving him a firm, slow stroke, "you've been waiting."

"*Mark*."

Mark kisses his neck and turns them both around so Eddie's back is against the wall. He can do it this way, turning his attention on Eddie, not thinking about anything else. "You've been so good."

"Oh, fuck." Eddie's voice sounds broken. Ragged. He's trembling a little. Mark takes mercy on him and drops to his knees. He has a brief, hysterical fit of worry that he might not remember how to do this, or that his technique has, over the years, become so specific to the desires of one person that it won't translate to another. Then again, he's pretty sure he could do this terribly, and Eddie wouldn't care. The state he's in, he might not even notice.

Mark presses a kiss to Eddie's hipbone. "Shh," he says. "That's it." Mark's surprised by the soothing, gentle note in his own voice. Then he gives Eddie what he wants.

He forgot how much he likes it, forgot how much he relishes having this kind of—the word, unfortunately, is probably *power*. How petty of him. But Eddie's hand is in Mark's hair, and he keeps making these ragged, pleased, grateful sounds, and how could Mark not love it?

Eddie doesn't last very long after that. His fingers tangled in Mark's hair, his body goes tense.

When Mark gets to his feet, Eddie has an arm thrown over his eyes, but his other arm snakes around Mark's back and pulls him close.

"You okay?" Mark asks.

"Embarrassed," Eddie mumbles, pulling Mark in for a kiss. "Too quick."

"You were lovely," Mark says, meaning it.

"Gimme a minute." Eddie's still slumped against the wall. Framed against oatmeal-colored hotel wallpaper, nobody ought to be beautiful. His hair's a wreck, even though Mark doesn't remember messing it up. But his buttons are all still done up, his tie still tied.

"I want your clothing off," Mark says. "I want you in that bed."

Eddie has all his clothes off before Mark's managed to undo half his own shirt buttons, and then he bats Mark's hands away and undresses Mark himself. All the while, Eddie's murmuring things like *God, look at you* while he pauses to kiss whatever skin he's just exposed. It's a shambles, Mark's shirt caught on his wrist, one shoelace hopelessly tangled, and Mark just bites back a smile and quietly extracts himself from the wreckage.

Finally, Mark pushes Eddie onto the bed and crawls over him, kissing him. Eddie's hands are light on Mark's ribs, like he doesn't quite know where or how he's allowed to touch.

"You can, you know," Mark says.

"I can what?"

"Whatever you like. I'll stop you if I don't like it."

"You too," Eddie says. He's hard again, pressing against Mark's thigh, and whenever Mark gives him a little friction, his kisses get more frantic.

Mark can't get over the feeling of all that muscle underneath his fingertips. For months, he's been trying not to ogle Eddie in the locker room. Now that he's allowed to not only look but also touch, he's a little overwhelmed. He catches himself petting Eddie's biceps, and then Eddie rolls onto his side, and Mark can't do anything but stare a little.

"Come on," Eddie says. "Tell me what you like."

"I—" Mark starts, but he isn't sure how to finish. The unfortunate truth is that what Mark likes at the moment is just how into this Eddie is. He wants to put his mouth on every part of Eddie and to pay attention to the sounds he makes. Maybe he wants to take his time, to make sure that Eddie knows what it feels like to be lingered over.

He's very aware of Eddie's eyes on him, Eddie's callused fingers tracing a circle on his hip. "Anything," Mark says, which is true, if not exactly the practical direction that Eddie's looking for. He'd be lying if he said he hadn't thought about it, but his daydreams have been all over the place. He doesn't know what will please him most, at this moment, with this man, but he's willing to bet that they can make it good together. He's liked everything they've done, from kissing to talking on the phone to eating breakfast. Whatever they do is going to be worth the wait, and he's so sure of it that his mouth goes a little dry.

Mark takes Eddie's hand, measures it against his own, and hums in satisfaction. Then he guides Eddie's hand between them. "Do you think you can—"

Eddie grabs them both, and Mark gasps. It's almost perfect, it just needs—

"Do you have any slick?" Eddie asks.

"In my suitcase. The smaller suitcase," Mark says, surprised to find that he's already out of breath. "There's a tin in the shaving kit."

"A tin," Eddie repeats, getting off the bed. He fumbles the suitcase, its contents hitting the floor in a clatter. He looks over his shoulder, apologetic, but his gaze seems to get caught on Mark's body. Mark feels himself flush.

"In the shaving kit," Mark repeats, his voice rough.

"This?" Eddie asks, holding up the slick.

"Mm-hmm."

Maybe Mark should have just gotten it himself, but he has the sense that Eddie likes to make himself useful—in bed, as well as in general. And besides, he's enjoying lying here, naked and ready and waiting to be pleased. It's an odd sensation, something new, like he's trying on a different style of suit that he's surprised to find he likes.

"Come here," Mark says, pushing a pillow behind his head. "Just come here and kiss me and finish what you started." And then Eddie's there, on top of him, his mouth soft and his hand just right. "That's right, sweetheart," Mark says, and Eddie gasps. "That feels so good."

Mark isn't sure exactly what he's doing, or why the words leaving his mouth seem to work for Eddie, and it doesn't matter, because it's working for Mark, too. He'd worried that this would be strange, that there would be too many ghosts in the room, but every time he tells Eddie how good he's doing, he can't forget who he's with. Eddie's presence, the Eddie-ness of him, is loud enough to drown out everything else, and after a while Mark isn't thinking much of anything at all.

Eddie passes out afterward, sprawled naked and gorgeous across the lumpy hotel mattress, because of course he does. Mark lights himself a cigarette. All he can think is that he ought to have picked someone up a year ago and fucked them, because maybe then this would feel less significant. Right now he feels shaken, and he has nobody to blame but himself. It's his own fault that he's currently combing his fingers through Eddie's tangled curls and arranging a blanket over him so he doesn't get cold. It's his own fault they're going to do this again tomorrow.

Eddie rolls over, and Mark watches as he begins to wake, realizes where he is, and opens his eyes. He looks happy, which makes Mark feel worse about everything. He takes his hand away from Eddie's hair.

"Hey, Mark," Eddie says, sounding a little groggy. The bedspread is tucked under his chin. He's adorable, and Mark's heart is doing awful things about it. "Can I ask you something?"

"Sure."

"Did you have anything to do with that story George Allen wrote about the rumors about Ardolino getting fired? The guys all think you did."

Mark doesn't know what he was expecting Eddie to say, but it isn't that. That column ran over a month ago, and this is the first time Eddie's even mentioned it. "That's your idea of pillow talk?"

"It was just on my mind. But if you don't want to—"

"I overheard Ardolino and the owner arguing. It sounded to me like she was threatening to fire him. I told George, who went and found his own sources." Mark doesn't have his glasses on, so Eddie's face is unreadable—the only time it's ever been unreadable. Mark grabs his glasses off the nightstand.

"So the guys are right," Eddie says. "I told them they were wrong. You could have told me, given me a heads-up."

"It didn't even occur to me."

Eddie looks like he's been slapped. He rolls a little to the side, putting just enough space between them that Mark feels like a shitheel.

"I don't mean it that way," Mark says, reaching out and resting a hand on Eddie's hip. "All I mean is that I didn't think about how it would connect to you."

"I don't want the team to think I'm feeding you stories. And that column made Ardolino look awful—like, how bad must he be if the team that dragged him out of retirement wants to get rid of him halfway through the season?"

Mark considers pointing out that the story was George's, that the Robins front office comes off much worse than Ardolino does, or that anyone could have overheard that argument. But that isn't what Eddie's getting at, and Mark knows it.

"I *am* writing about the team," Mark points out, as gently as possible. He cannot believe how gentle he's being, how gentle he nearly always is when Eddie's being impossible about this one topic. He's been more patient with Eddie than he has with anyone, except possibly Lula. "If they're upset about an article I didn't write, they're going to be livid when the magazine piece comes out."

"Is there anything in this magazine article that's going to be a problem?"

"You seem to think that anything I write is a problem. I'm a writer, and I'm writing about your team. And you don't like it, which is fair. But what I write isn't your business."

Mark believes every word he says, but hearing them out loud makes him realize how far they are from the whole truth. Eddie doesn't have any say about what Mark writes—that much is true—but *Mark* does, and right now Mark simply can't imagine sitting down at a typewriter and producing an entire article that he knows Eddie won't like.

Mark could write *something*, but it would be watered-down, lukewarm, unseasoned. His main talent—such as it is—is a certain causticity that he is in no way prepared to turn on Eddie, or even Eddie's teammates. Anything he writes about Eddie will be something between a mash note and advertising copy. It doesn't bear thinking of.

He feels a burst of irrational anger toward Eddie. It was such a relief to have something he wanted to write about, and now it's gone, and instead he has a pile of feelings that aren't going to do him any good at all.

He can't tell Eddie any of that. He half suspects that if he did, Eddie would insist that he write the article anyway.

"Sorry," Mark says. "Almost all my friends are reporters. Except you. Sometimes I forget that not everyone puts the story first."

"I'm your friend?" Eddie asks, a little teasing, but he looks pleased. He grabs Mark's hand.

Mark rolls his eyes. "I assure you that I wouldn't be here if you weren't." He means for it to be a little snide, only then realizing just how much he's admitted.

Eddie shifts his grip on Mark's hand and tugs him close, and Mark goes without protest. He's half on Eddie's lap. They shouldn't be kissing—they should never be kissing, but especially not now, not when it couldn't possibly be clearer why this is only going to end in Eddie feeling betrayed.

"You have a lot of friends?" Eddie asks, because he could not possibly be more transparent.

Mark sighs, despising himself for going along with this. "No, Eddie. I have five friends, and you're the only one I've . . ." He gestures at the bed, scowling. "Christ. Are you happy now?"

"Yeah," Eddie says, beaming. "You bet I am. You don't do this with, uh, non-friends?"

Mark can't believe he isn't going to be spared any of his dignity, that he's cooperating in this dismantling of his defenses. "I haven't done this with anyone at all in a long time."

"I have."

"Do you want a medal?"

Eddie laughs, loud enough that Mark puts a hand over his mouth so nobody in the hallway will hear. "But I'm not doing it with anyone else right now, and I'm not going to."

Mark realizes that he's been maneuvered into exclusivity. This is either a level of strategy that he didn't know Eddie was capable of or a sign of how far gone Mark is. He thinks about protesting, but Eddie's hand is squeezing his at the same time his lips reach Mark's neck. Mark feels the rough, warm press of Eddie's palm against his lower back at the same time he opens his mouth on a gasp.

"I'm taking a shower," Mark announces, and it's absolutely not an invitation, but Eddie winds up in there with him anyway.

"I'll be more careful about what I tell other reporters," Mark says as Eddie's hogging all the hot water. "I mean, George is the only sports reporter I talk to and he's in the hospital, so that's an easy promise to keep, but there you have it." He's fully disgusted with himself, and it must show, because Eddie looks amused and concerned and terribly, terribly smug.

"I trust you." It sounds like a confession, like Eddie would prefer to keep his back to the wall and his mouth shut when reporters are around, but instead here he is naked in Mark's hotel bathroom, Mark's fingers working shampoo through his hair. "It's not a bad idea," Eddie says, and Mark doesn't know which one of them he's trying to convince. "And you haven't acted like it's a bad idea, not once. You just keep letting me closer. You secretly think it's a great idea."

"I take it back," Mark says. "We're not friends." Eddie's laughter bounces off the tiles.

CHAPTER TWENTY-ONE

On the plane from Pittsburgh to Cincinnati, Mark plants himself next to the reporter from the *Daily News* in order to prevent Eddie from sitting next to him.

"I'll take the window seat if you like," Mark offers.

"Uh, sure?" the reporter says, then introduces himself, but Mark doesn't catch his name because he's busy watching Eddie out of the corner of his eye. Sure enough, when Eddie boards the plane and spots Mark already sitting next to somebody, he frowns. Mark pretends to be engrossed in his book.

"This your first time traveling with the team?" the *Daily News* reporter asks.

"Yes," Mark answers, not looking up from his book.

"The hotels usually aren't this bad. I don't know why this team needs to book hotels a goddamn hour away from the ballpark."

Mark realizes two things at once: He knows the answer to that question, and not everybody does. Ardolino is booking the hotels himself. Some dormant journalistic instinct has kicked in during the past few days, and he's piecing together stories even when he doesn't want to be.

Mark spends the rest of the flight effectively trapped between the fuselage of the airplane and a monologue about hotels. So much for his hope of a nap.

When they disembark onto a revoltingly hot tarmac in Cincinnati, there are buses waiting to take everyone to the hotel. But Mark's had enough of being in close quarters with strangers, so he strides off in a direction that he hopes will bring him to a taxi. He can almost feel Eddie's gaze on his back, but he refuses to turn around.

Later, when he's unpacking in the hotel room, there's a knock on his door.

"Was it something I said?" Eddie asks.

"You have to be careful," Mark says after Eddie's safely inside.

"It's so silly to pretend we aren't friends. People are allowed to be friends, Mark."

Mark isn't going to waste both their time explaining things Eddie already knows.

"Come out to dinner," Eddie says. "It's Ardolino and Price and some guy from *Sports Illustrated*, so you won't be the only reporter, and everyone is going to be on company manners anyway."

Mark's been trying and failing to reconcile himself to his fate of a soggy room service club sandwich.

"Come on," Eddie wheedles. "Look, everybody already knows we're friendly. You write really nice things about me."

"I write *what*?" Mark sputters. "I *beg* your pardon."

"You always make me sound smart and funny."

"You've sure changed your tune since you accused me of making you sound dumb. And if people know we're friends, it's not because of my writing. It's because you aren't capable of keeping a secret."

"I'm not, am I?" Eddie asks, eyebrows raised about as high as a pair of eyebrows can go.

"Frankly, I'm amazed you've kept your private life secret for as long as you have. I'm telling you, Eddie, when you look at me, it's obvious."

"You only think so because you know how I feel."

Mark has to look away. He can't listen to Eddie talk like that with any kind of equanimity. He wants to argue. He wants to tell Eddie that his feelings are incorrect, which is an absurd line of argument, or that his feelings are dangerous, which is much less absurd, but it's not like Eddie will listen to that, either.

"Change your shirt, and come on out," Eddie says. "We're meeting in the lobby in half an hour."

"I need to take a shower," Mark says, but Eddie must see that Mark's being worn down, because his face lights up.

Eddie shows no signs of leaving, so Mark showers and shaves, and when he returns to the bedroom, he finds Eddie on his bed, reading the book Mark brought with him.

Mark takes a minute to look. Eddie manages to fill the entire bed, one big arm tucked behind his head. He must sense Mark watching him, because he drops the book onto the mattress. "This is a change. It's usually you in a suit and me in a towel, dripping all over the place. You know, you're a lot hairier than I thought you'd be."

"Sorry to disappoint," Mark says acidly.

"If you think anything about you is disappointing to me, then I'm doing a better job than you think of hiding my feelings."

And then Mark's furious with himself, because he as good as set Eddie up for that. Ugh.

He gets dressed, or at least he tries to, because before he has his pants buttoned, Eddie's behind him, kissing his neck.

"We don't have time," Mark protests. Eddie's lips are warm and soft, and they're sending shivers down Mark's spine. His hands are rough against Mark's stomach and chest, his fingertips playing, embarrassingly, with Mark's chest hair.

"I know," Eddie says against Mark's neck. "Later." He doesn't make any move to step away, though, just wraps his arms tighter until Mark can feel Eddie's heart beating against his back. He can also feel that Eddie's starting to get hard.

"Are you trying to get yourself worked up when you know there's nothing you can do about it?" Mark asks, trying to sound peeved and probably failing. He extricates himself from Eddie's grip and turns to face him.

"Not really," Eddie says, looking bashful. "Not exactly. Well, maybe a little? It's just nice, you know?"

"What is?"

"Knowing that later we can . . ." He glances at the bed. "I like knowing that."

"Me too," Mark says before he can think better of it, then looks away when Eddie beams at him.

They wind up at a steak restaurant. Mark wonders if ballplayers have a list of functionally identical steak restaurants in every city that has a Major League Baseball team. This one—like all the others—has deep-red leather booths, dark walnut paneled walls, and a pervasive smell of cigar smoke. The only difference seems to be whether the walls are adorned with paintings of dogs and horses or photographs of boxing matches. Tonight's restaurant seems to have split the difference with photographs of horse races.

The reporter from *Sports Illustrated* seems annoyed that Mark is there, encroaching on what he probably thought was going to be an exclusive.

"Nobody's working," Ardolino says. "We're eating, then we're going out."

"On the Athletics, nobody really had dinner with reporters," Eddie says, and then "Ow!" He shoots a hurt look across the table at Price. "What was that for?"

"Oh my God," Price mutters. Price looks at Mark, who only shrugs. Mark proceeds to order the steak least likely to weigh as much as one of his suitcases. He briefly considers ordering the fillet of sole, but can't decide if that's too . . . well. He figures he ought to order something incontrovertibly masculine, so steak it is.

There's a harrowing moment at the end of the meal when Eddie looks like he's about to cover Mark's portion of the bill, but Mark manages to get a ten-dollar bill out of his wallet and onto the check before anyone else notices.

After that, they wind up at some nightclub and are joined by women who, Mark knows logically, cannot possibly have materialized out of thin air, but certainly seem to have done so. Tony Ardolino is the type of man who seems to be able to effect that sort of magic.

"I had a huge crush on him when I was a kid," Eddie whispers when he notices Mark watching Ardolino. "Actually, it lasted pretty much until the minute I met him."

Mark snorts, but then feels bad about it. "He's not bad."

"No, he isn't. He's—well, it's not my business to talk about it, but I like him."

Mark realizes that Eddie is one, keeping a secret, which is possibly a first; and two, being discreet about Ardolino because Mark is a reporter. He probably ought to be annoyed by the second thing, but mostly he's relieved that Eddie's capable of discretion.

"I think you're going to need to dance for at least a few songs before we can get out of here," Mark says.

Eddie's eyes darken, because apparently he picked up on the *I'm getting you into my bed at the first available opportunity* subtext. "And what're you going to be doing while I'm dancing? Seems unfair."

"I don't particularly enjoy dancing, and these women didn't get dressed up to dance with reporters."

"You danced with those girls last week."

"That was for work. Now quit complaining, and go cut a rug."

Eddie drains his drink and goes off to dance. He's truly a rotten dancer, and Mark's heart goes out to the poor woman who's been saddled with him, not that she seems to mind. No, she doesn't seem to mind at all. She's looking up at Eddie with precisely the sort of look Mark might himself employ under the same circumstances.

He isn't jealous. He isn't even envious: He doesn't particularly want to be dancing with Eddie O'Leary or with anyone else. Nor does he begrudge anyone the dubious pleasure of dancing with Eddie.

It's the deceit of it that rankles. Not that Eddie's actively deceiving anyone by dancing with a woman. It's more that the entire pantomime of heterosexuality is a bit too close for comfort. He's spared any further unwanted insight into his own psyche by the *Sports Illustrated* reporter sliding closer to him in the booth.

"You're friendly with these guys," he says.

"I'm not really a sports reporter," Mark says. "After this season, they'll never have to see me again. So they can afford to be generous without worrying I'll overstay my welcome."

"But you know O'Leary."

Probably the reporter is just making conversation, and there's no reason for Mark to worry. Or, more likely still, Mark and Eddie seem like friends, because they are, which is *fine*—except for how it isn't. "I'm doing a story on him. He's a good kid." As he speaks, he's aware that he's scrubbing his voice of any potentially campy inflection, any trace of softness or slyness. He's been doing that throughout the evening. He's being cautious for Eddie's sake, and cautious means faking straightness as hard as possible.

He finishes his drink and turns the conversation to the upcoming football season.

After exactly three songs, Eddie comes back to the table, yawns extravagantly, and announces that he's heading out. "Either of you want to split a cab?" he asks, looking between Mark and the other reporter. Mark supposes he has to give Eddie credit for not just telling Mark that it was time to leave.

Unsurprisingly, the other reporter decides to stay. Eddie and Mark don't bother getting a cab. It's a ten-minute walk to the hotel, and the weather's fine.

"Did you have a good time?" Mark asks. He means the question sincerely, but it comes out nasty, and of course Eddie notices.

"Did something happen?"

"No, I'm being—ugh—just ignore me."

"Fat chance. Tell me what happened."

Mark figures he can either tell the truth, come up with a plausible lie, or submit to an evening's worth of worried interrogation. He's had enough deceit for the night, so he discreetly makes sure there isn't anyone in earshot. "I hate pretending to be straight."

Eddie's quiet for a moment. "I didn't think you bothered pretending."

"What do you think would have happened if I sat down at that table like my flaming self?"

"You aren't flaming. Jesus, Mark."

"Fine. My usual, discernibly queer self. What would have happened? I'll tell you what. Your teammates would have wondered, and that *Sports Illustrated* reporter would have asked around, and I don't even like to think about what might have happened next. Anyway, it isn't your fault. You asked me to come, I said yes, and now I'm pissy about it for no good reason."

"It seems like a good enough reason to me. I don't much care for pretending myself. It's just, you know, I don't have a choice."

Déjà vu hits Mark like a baseball to the cranium. He's had this conversation. Christ, he's had versions of this conversation dozens of times, and they always went precisely like this. It's like driving a car around and around the same block.

If he keeps this up with Eddie—something he shouldn't even be contemplating—he's settling in for more of the same. It's not anyone's fault—Mark understood as much when he was William's secret, and he still understands now that he's Eddie's secret. It's not their fault. Mark doesn't expect anyone to turn their lives upside down and open themselves to violence and persecution.

But that doesn't mean he has to like it. It doesn't even mean he has to stand for it. If he had any sense, he'd call it quits with Eddie and find some nice art dealer or poet with whom he could live somewhat openly—someone with whom he could have a life.

Back in Mark's room—and of course they go to Mark's room without even the slightest pretense of this being something that has to be discussed in advance—Eddie flops onto Mark's bed and grins up at him.

"What," Mark says, a hand on his hip. "Am I expected to do all the work tonight?"

"Wow, you are in *such* a mood," Eddie observes, not sounding particularly annoyed about it. He tucks a hand behind his head and grins some more.

Mark loosens his tie and tries to look above it all. "I don't know what you're talking about."

"Sure you don't. Come here. For fuck's sake, Mark."

Mark hesitates, his hand still on the knot of his tie.

"I'll make you feel better," Eddie coaxes.

And apparently now Mark is easy—not that he's ever been anything else, honestly, but now he's shameless, because he climbs onto the bed, one knee on either side of Eddie's hips.

"And how, exactly, are you going to do that?"

"You tell me."

"I couldn't care less," Mark says, and is horrified to discover it's the truth. Eddie gets the message and tugs him down by his tie, then rolls him over as if he's nothing more substantial than a pillow.

"You're telling the truth, aren't you?" Eddie asks after fumbling so atrociously with the buttons on Mark's pants that Mark has no choice but to do the job himself. "You really don't care."

"I do have a vested interest in both the process and the outcome," Mark says like a total asshole, a futile attempt to recover at least some of his dignity. "I just happen to enjoy a lot of things."

Eddie braces himself on a forearm, his free hand on Mark's jaw. "I expected you to be, you know. Fussy."

Mark is torn between preening—why, yes, he *is* incredibly fussy— and defending himself. "I feel certain I ought to be offended."

"You're picky about everything. About food. About clothing. I figured you'd be picky about this, too."

This brings Mark up short. Is that how Eddie sees him? Demanding? Mark's afraid it's true: he hasn't made it easy for Eddie, asking him to walk Lula at ungodly hours, generally giving him trouble for no reason. But Eddie only looks amused—no, he looks very much like he does not mind when Mark is difficult, and also wouldn't mind the slightest bit if Mark carried that attitude into bed. Something goes hot in Mark's belly.

"I'm not picky. I'm *particular*. I care about quality. I like nice things. And it's been perfectly clear to me for weeks that whatever happened between us was not going to lack for quality."

"Has it, now?"

"Yes," Mark says, poking Eddie in his chest. It's like poking a wall. "And you don't need to look so smug about it."

"Oh, I beg to differ. I need to look exactly this smug about it. My dick just got called *quality*."

This is too much for Mark, who has to roll to the side and bury his face in the pillow so the people next door can't hear him laughing.

"And by a connoisseur, no less," Eddie continues.

"I'm not a connoisseur of dick," Mark says into the pillow.

"Come on. It's not every day your dick gets that kind of compliment. Let me enjoy it," Eddie says. He's still mostly on top of Mark.

Mark decides they've had enough giddiness for the evening, so he slips a hand inside Eddie's pants. He does, at one point, murmur something about quality dick that has both of them giggling like a pair of fools, but Eddie gets them back on track, dispatching their clothes and sliding down the mattress.

"Let me?" Eddie says, kissing the inside of Mark's thigh. Mark can feel the scratch of invisible stubble against his skin.

"Be my guest." Mark gestures expansively. "You're good at this," he says a few moments later, his mind empty of everything except the wet, soft heat of Eddie's mouth.

Eddie looks up. "Lots of practice."

"Yeah?" Mark, an idiot, hadn't thought about it, but of course Eddie would enjoy being on his knees, pleasing someone. "Anything else you like to practice?"

"Can I, uh. God, I want to be inside you. Can I? Do you like that?"

Mark's mind goes blank, unable to stop himself from imagining it, from wanting it. "I do. But not tonight."

"You know you can say no, right? We don't have to do anything you don't want. We don't have to do anything at all." Eddie sounds so sincere that Mark doesn't know what to do. He's perfectly aware, thank you very much, that he doesn't have to do anything he doesn't want. But the idea that this might be new information to Eddie, information that he wants to make sure to pass on, is oddly touching.

Mark palms Eddie's face and tries to pull him up for a kiss. "I do want that. But not tonight. Do you have any idea how awful the seats in the Crosley Field press box are? You can fuck me as much as you please when I have access to comfortable chairs."

Mark wouldn't have thought this an especially erotic speech but Eddie visibly disagrees. "Me too, okay?"

"Hmm?"

"You can fuck me anytime," he says bluntly.

Mark doesn't know why he's surprised. He really needs to stop being surprised by Eddie. "Duly noted. For now, you can keep doing what you're doing," Mark offers magnanimously, and Eddie does as he's told. But the idea has made Mark want more.

Mark fumbles on the bedside table and finds the little tin of slick. "You can—would you—"

Eddie looks up, mouth wet, eyes a little dazed. "I thought you said you didn't want—"

"I don't." This is an unanticipated complication of sleeping with someone new. He can't rely on Eddie to simply know what Mark likes, and he can't speak in the kind of shorthand that couples use to communicate needs in the heat of the moment. "I just want—something." He bends a knee to get the point across, feeling stupid and exposed and inarticulate, three things he rarely feels at all, let alone at once.

But Eddie doesn't seem bothered. "God, look at you." He traces a finger between Mark's legs, and Mark guesses he hadn't been that inarticulate after all. "This is the fanciest slick I've ever seen. Flowers on the lid. And it's *pink*," he says, scooping some out. "I guess Vaseline's not good enough for Mr. Quality."

Smiling despite himself, Mark pushes Eddie's head back down, and Eddie laughs into the skin of Mark's inner thigh.

"You want to tell me what that was all about earlier?" Eddie asks later on, after they've cleaned up, when they're lying on the ruined sheets, a blanket pulled carelessly over their legs.

Mark starts to bristle, because he already told Eddie. He explained, and in small, understandable words, that he just doesn't like pretending. He doesn't like keeping who he is a secret any more than strictly necessary.

"I don't like being a secret. I've been a secret. A roommate. A friend. Nobody important. And then—well. That made it really difficult, after. I mean, during, too."

Eddie looks like he isn't quite following, and God knows there's no reason he ought to be, what with the shambles Mark's making of things.

"Hold on," Mark says. His chest is tight, and there are beads of sweat at his hairline. He gets out of bed and steps into his pants, thinking this is the kind of conversation that requires at least a little clothing. He takes his wallet from his pocket and pulls out a strip of photographs. Climbing back into bed, he hands it to Eddie.

Eddie handles the photographs carefully, as if he knows without being told that they're irreplaceable.

Mark imagines seeing these photos through Eddie's eyes. A younger Mark—Christ, much younger, he can hardly stand to look at himself—sitting almost on the lap of another man. Both of them are grinning at the camera. God, William looks young, too. These photos were only taken a couple years ago, so there's no reason for him to look so egregiously young, infinitely too young to simply not exist anymore.

"His name was William. He died a year and a half ago." *A year and a half*, Mark repeats to himself. Not months anymore.

Mark can almost hear the questions cycling through Eddie's brain and braces himself for a minor, gentle interrogation. "You look happy," Eddie says. "And so does he."

"We were on vacation," Mark says, as if explaining away the short-sleeved shirts is the first order of business here. You can't see it in the photos, but Mark knows there's a faint sunburn across their noses and cheekbones. "And we ran into one of those photo booths. You know, the kind where you sit inside and a minute later it prints the pictures. There's nobody who develops it," he adds, in case Eddie needs it spelled out for him why they could be so open. "William didn't want to, but he humored me." With the distance of time and maybe a little age and wisdom, Mark wonders if William was so obliging in the small things because there was no way he could ever be with the one big thing.

"We have other photographs." Mark swallows. "*I* have other photographs." There's one Lilian took that Mark has framed in his bedside drawer, William mid-laugh and Mark trying to smack his shoulder. Mark can't remember anymore what was so funny. There are dozens of William and Lula, or just William, but not so many of Mark and William together. "These are my favorites, though."

"What happened? It's okay if you don't—"

"It's okay. He was thirty-four. He had a heart attack. It was sudden."

"That must have been awful. I'm so sorry."

Eddie is being *tactful*, which is not something Mark knew Eddie was capable of being. Or, rather, it's something he knows perfectly well takes Eddie an enormous effort.

By now, Mark shouldn't be surprised when Eddie is generous and big-hearted, but it's still a little startling to be the object of that generosity. It makes Mark feel like an error's been made, like someone got him too nice a present for his birthday and he can't possibly hope to reciprocate. Mark isn't big-hearted or generous, and he never will be; he doesn't particularly want to be. He likes to hoard up his kindness and distribute it carefully to those he's deemed worth it, which is probably a selfish and shitty attitude, but Mark doesn't have goodness to spare, and he isn't wasting any of it.

Eddie's body is warm against Mark's side. He can hear the beating of Eddie's heart, smell his aftershave.

"How did you meet?" Eddie asks.

Mark doesn't know why he isn't expecting it. It's one of the first things you ask about a couple. In this context—mostly naked, in bed together—the question ought to be jarring, but instead it's an outstretched hand. It's so easy to remember that winter, and how eagerly he would look up every time the bell on the shop door chimed. "I worked at a bookstore around the corner from his office."

"What did you sell him?"

"The latest Rex Stout. Then he came back two days later, and two days after that. Nobody with a full-time job reads *that* fast." William must have bought fifty dollars' worth of merchandise before Mark could bring himself to believe that the man in the dark blue suit was coming to see *him*. It had unfolded so delicately: drinks, dinner, an invitation upstairs, both of them wary for entirely different reasons, coaxing one another along like a barn cat being offered a saucer of milk.

"So anyway, he left me his money, because—" Mark doesn't know how to finish the sentence. Because William wanted to make sure Mark was looked after? Because the money would have gone to Mark if they had actually been married? Because he wanted to annoy his parents from beyond the grave? Because he felt guilty? Mark usually tells himself that William did it because it was the only declaration he could ever make, even though it came too late. He gives that sentence up as a bad job and sighs. "I'm never going backward. I'm never—" Hell, another sentence he can't finish. He's never going to go back to erasing himself from someone else's existence, to confining the truth of himself to an apartment full of heavily insured art and antiques. "Do you understand what I'm saying?"

"Loud and clear," Eddie says, and Mark doesn't believe him, doesn't even come close to believing him, because if Eddie really understood, he'd leave.

CHAPTER TWENTY-TWO

Paying attention to every play in every game has Mark in a state of abject weariness, and after a doubleheader against the Reds, he thinks he might actually collapse if anyone so much as speaks to him. He hopes that whatever reporter winds up taking over George's beat is made of stronger stuff than Mark. The one bright spot is that the press boxes at every stadium they visit are far superior to the one at the Polo Grounds, a sweltering death trap separated from home plate by nothing more than a flimsy length of rusty chicken wire that probably dates to the Hoover administration.

Well, no, the actual bright spot is that all week, Eddie has been playing decent baseball. Mark would find the process of describing games with any level of accuracy or interest completely unbearable if Eddie was still in his slump. His fielding remains excellent, and he's hitting well enough. He isn't at the level where he was last year, and Mark knows that Eddie doesn't believe he'll ever get there again, but he's playing like he belongs in the major leagues.

Whatever the reason for his improved game, Eddie's relief is palpable. The tension in his shoulders and the furrow between his eyebrows have all but vanished.

The team is playing . . . respectably. To say they're playing *well* would be an exaggeration, but for a brand-new team with dubious leadership, they're doing about as well as anyone could expect, which means that now, with seven weeks left in the season, they're fighting with the Phillies for second-to-last place in the league.

Maybe more important than any of that—to Eddie, at least—is that Eddie's teammates like him. Eddie is, unsurprisingly, the loudest person in the locker room. Some of the older players are visibly exhausted by him, but in the way people get exhausted by puppies. Buddy Rosenthal, the second baseman, has started to plant himself between Eddie and reporters whenever Eddie's a bit too talkative.

Mark's a little surprised to find himself on the receiving end of this treatment.

"Has your stance changed again?" Mark asks Eddie. "It looks different than it did a few weeks ago."

"Yeah," Eddie says. "I had to turn everything upside down in order to—"

"Heyyyyy," says Rosenthal, inserting himself between Eddie and Mark. "Don't you want to talk about my double play?"

"That was my double play, too," Eddie says, but Rosenthal drags him away with a hand over his mouth.

Over by Price's stall, Ardolino is howling with laughter.

"What," Rosenthal protests with his hand still over Eddie's mouth. "What's so funny, old man?"

"Never mind," Ardolino says, ducking a pair of balled-up socks that Price lobbed at his head. "Oh God. Yeah. Definitely don't let O'Leary talk to Bailey. God forbid."

Now Price has his hand over Ardolino's laughing mouth. "Did you just *lick* me? You nasty motherfucker." Price wipes his hand on the back of Ardolino's jersey. "Who raised you?"

The next day, an article appears in the *Herald Tribune* about Tony Ardolino and Sam Price, pioneers of racial harmony in the locker room.

"This is the first good press I've gotten since 1951," Ardolino says, clutching the copy of the paper he bought at the airport newsstand. "I'm framing it."

"I'm just grateful they didn't say Ardolino's licking me was the latest in his string of violent assaults," Price says, standing in the aisle next to Mark's seat on the airplane to St. Louis. "Off-the-record," he adds, narrowing his eyes.

"Bailey's good at keeping things off-the-record," Ardolino says, climbing over Mark into the window seat. "At least when he wants to."

"Don't we all fucking know it," Price mutters. "Don't let him drink or feel up any stewardesses," he tells Mark.

"I'm not a babysitter," Mark complains.

When Eddie boards the plane, he shoots a dejected look at Mark, then at the occupied seat next to him. And—surely Mark's imagining things—but did Ardolino sit there to prevent Eddie from doing so?

"Get back here, O'Leary," Varga bellows from the rear of the plane. "We need to deal you into this game."

"But I always lose," Eddie says.

"Like I said, we need to deal you in."

Eddie trudges off to the rear of the plane.

"My girlfriend got me one of those sleep masks," Ardolino says, producing the item from his pocket. "She thinks she's hilarious." He puts it on. The eye mask has enormous, terrifying, mascaraed eyes embroidered on it. "But the joke's on her, because I wear it every flight."

Mark's about to ask since when does Ardolino have a girlfriend. Last he heard, Ardolino had a wife, but there have been whispers about a divorce petition.

Ardolino lowers his voice enough that Mark has to lean in. "What're the odds on O'Leary learning to keep a poker face."

"Zero," Mark says immediately. "They're going to clean him out of all his cash."

"Huh?" Ardolino shoves the mask up onto his forehead, and the effect of four eyes on one face is enough to make Mark recoil. "What are you talking about?"

"Varga and Rosenthal and whoever else is playing poker," Mark says, concerned that Ardolino might have gotten a head start on drinking despite Price's best intentions. "They're going to clean him out."

Ardolino lets out a sigh and gives Mark a very tired look. "I'm going to sleep."

"Okay? Good for you."

But apparently the nap doesn't take, because after the plane is in the air, Ardolino pulls off his mask. When the stewardess comes by for their drink orders, he asks for a ginger ale.

"I'm avoiding reporters," Ardolino says, explaining his presence next to Mark. "Well, not you, only real reporters. The asshole from the *Times* wants to talk about platoon batting orders or some shit. Why don't I change the batting order to adjust for hitters' strengths? Why don't I look at what some jerkoff in Boston is doing?"

"Why don't you?" Mark asks.

"Because those strategies are for teams with a chance," Ardolino says, voice low. "They help you eke out a win against the team that you're fighting for the pennant. They aren't for teams like us."

"I know you aren't telling me that the Robins are a bad team and so you're fine with losing."

Ardolino shrugs, and Mark raises his eyebrows. "The point of this year is to take a grab bag of men and make them into a team. And the way you do that is to let them be a team. Having them worry about who's batting fourth only makes them look at their teammates as competition. They need to mess around together off the field. On the field, they need to learn how they work as a unit."

When Mark doesn't say anything, Ardolino points at him. "You can write that down."

"I thought I wasn't a real reporter," Mark says, but he gets out his notebook and copies down what Ardolino said. He has no idea what he'll do with it. It wouldn't make sense in one of Eddie's diary entries, and it doesn't fit in with the magazine feature.

And yet, maybe it does fit there. In a story about how close one career came to ending, maybe there's another story about a career that came back from the dead. He can almost see it—a story that's more about the team than it is about Eddie. The relief hits him like a slap.

"So you're not enforcing curfew, because you want your players to have fun together," Mark says.

Ardolino grins. "Let's go with that."

Tony Ardolino is painfully handsome when he smiles. No wonder Eddie had a crush on him. Darkly handsome men with darkly captivating pasts aren't Mark's type, but he sees the appeal. "I have to say, in none of the interactions I've had with you do you seem like the kind of man who puts innocent people in the hospital."

Ardolino's expression shutters, which was pretty much Mark's intent. "I'm not going to talk about—"

"No, of course you aren't, and I'm not asking." He deliberately puts his pencil away. This is not the first interview he's done, regardless of what Ardolino thinks. "I'm pointing out that I don't think it's just the drinking." According to George, Ardolino's drinking problem has been an open secret for years. Mark doesn't know exactly when the drinking started, but rumors of violent bar fights started circulating maybe five years ago. There had been an arrest in spring training, and suspicions that his former team pulled strings to get him out of trouble with the cops on a few other occasions.

"Oh, it's definitely the drinking," Ardolino says grimly.

"Well, it's not only that, because Eddie willingly goes out with you when you drink, and I'm positive he wouldn't if he thought he was going to watch you hurt someone. For that matter, I don't think he'd like you if he thought you were prone to senseless violence. And he definitely thought you were dangerously violent when he got traded."

"He didn't exactly make that a secret."

"That's my point. But he likes you now." No, that wasn't accurate. "He admires you," Mark says, a little surprised to realize it's true.

"Well, that's because he has rotten judgment."

Mark wants to tell him that he doesn't know the half of it. "My point is that a few years ago anyone would have written you off, but now you're managing a team. Doing the work of three people, no less," he adds, referencing the conversation they both know he overheard.

Ardolino levels a hard look at him, and Mark thinks he's getting a glimpse of the man who knocked people off barstools on a semi-regular basis. "I'm going to meetings," he finally says, quiet and rushed. "No idea if they'll work. Can't say I'm optimistic, but I like my liver the way it is, and my girlfriend isn't the type to bail me out of jail, so here we are."

"Off-the-record?"

"Nah," Ardolino says, as if his attending meetings for his drinking problem—hell, even acknowledging that he has a drinking problem in the first place—wouldn't be front-page news in New York, wouldn't infuriate the entirety of professional baseball.

"When we get back to New York," Mark says, "I'm going to call you up and schedule an interview. Maybe you'll say no. Maybe you'll say yes, and we'll just talk about boring things, and I'll pick up the check. Or—" And this is a gamble, but he remembers that fight that he overheard between Ardolino and Connie Newbold. He'd paid attention to the firing angle—for the very good reason that Ardolino being fired would have been a scoop. But what he missed was the obvious subtext of Ardolino not being the least bit worried about being fired. That was not a quarrel between employer and employee. That was a quarrel between two people who were going to forgive one another. Or maybe not—maybe his emotions are getting in the way, and he's seeing romance, or at least sex, everywhere he looks.

Mark gives Ardolino his mildest expression. "Or you can bring your girlfriend, and we can have a very interesting interview indeed. Completely up to you. I won't be running any stories that make the Robins upset," he adds, because obviously he can't come right out and admit that he won't be writing anything that upsets Eddie, but Ardolino knows they're friends. Ardolino might know even more, but Mark can't think about that, or he'll wind up spending the rest of the flight hiding in the men's room.

Ardolino looks at him for a long moment. "I'll run it by her."

Mark settles back in his seat and tries to read his book, but he keeps getting distracted every time he hears Eddie plaintively wailing, "You guys, not again!" or "Oh man, I really thought I had a good hand that time!" and then, bizarrely, "You can't tell me that patch of mud in right field *isn't* ghosts."

Mark makes sure to keep the smile off his face.

"My mom drove in!" Eddie is plainly, obviously, alarmingly delighted by this. Mark isn't sure he's ever met anyone over the age of eight this pleased to see their mother. Mark wishes he weren't so charmed.

They're in St. Louis. Mark's grasp on the geography of the central part of the country might be vague, but even he knows that Omaha isn't anywhere near St. Louis. "How far is that?"

"She says six hours, but she's lying. It's probably seven. That, or she's racked up a pile of speeding tickets. Come out to dinner with us."

"She drove seven hours to see you. She doesn't want to have dinner with a stranger."

"She likes to meet my friends," Eddie says sunnily, and Mark has to bite his lip to avoid shushing him. They're having this conversation at top volume in a crowded locker room, surrounded by the team and press. Mark's pretty sure the only thing that's keeping this conversation from being the most homosexual thing to ever happen in the Cardinals' visitors' locker room is that Eddie seems totally oblivious to there being any reason it ought to be kept a secret.

And so, Mark responds in kind. "Sure. I'd love to meet her."

Eddie's mother turns out to be an older, female version of Eddie: large and blond and loud. When Eddie said his mother was a librarian, Mark had unconsciously pictured a small, meek, mousy woman, probably with glasses and a cardigan. This woman is . . . well, Mark can see where Eddie gets it from.

"I can't believe you drove seven hours," Eddie says, hugging his mother.

"It was six. I told you it was six, Edward."

"Then you were speeding."

"Aren't you going to introduce me to your friend?" She beams at Mark.

"Mom, this is Mark Bailey. Mark, this is my mother, Kathleen Brodowski."

Mark puts out his hand, and Mrs. Brodowski takes it, but doesn't let go.

"I know exactly who you are," she says, her voice going dangerous. "You're the one who's writing those shameful articles about my Eddie—"

"Mama, don't," Eddie pleads.

"Filled with lies and falsehoods," she intones, squeezing his hand even harder.

"I'm sure I don't—I wouldn't," Mark stammers. "I beg your pardon, ma'am."

"Don't tease him, Mom. It's mean."

"Of all the things to say, writing that I'd have preferred Eddie take up the drums." She shakes her head sadly.

Mark tries to figure out where drums enter into it. Two weeks earlier he wrote something about how Eddie's sure that driving him home from late-night practices made his mom wish he'd taken up the drums instead. Or maybe it had been the tuba. The point of the diary entry had been the sacrifices Eddie's family made for him and how he wants them to have been worth it. But he hadn't written anything mean, not about Eddie or about his mother.

Then he recognizes the twinkle in Mrs. Brodowski's eyes. It's a familiar twinkle, one he's gotten to know well over the past three months.

"Ma'am, I believe it was the tuba," Mark says solemnly, and she erupts into laughter.

"She didn't mean any of that." Eddie looks worried. "You know she was kidding, right?"

"So I gathered," Mark says. Eddie's mother is still holding Mark's hand and uses it to reel him into a hug. He winds up with a face full of curly blond hair.

They go to a steak restaurant. Eddie and his mother talk constantly. They talk over one another. They finish one another's sentences. Mark isn't quite sure how either of them find the time to actually eat. And it's not like they're ignoring Mark. Mrs. Brodowski is forever turning to him and telling him a story about Eddie's childhood.

"That's off-the-record," she says after one such interlude, wagging her finger at Mark.

"No, ma'am, I'm afraid the history of Eddie and the neighbor's cow is going on the front page of tomorrow's *Chronicle*," he says gravely.

She cackles loudly enough for half the restaurant to hear, then launches into a story about Eddie's father falling into a fishing hole. Eddie's grinning into his beer.

"That man had no business using sharp objects," says Mrs. Brodowski. "Not knives, not fishhooks, not so much as a staple remover. Especially not after a few drinks, but not ever, if I'm being honest. Eddie definitely didn't get his coordination from that side of the family. Not sure where he got it, come to think."

"Not sure *if* I got it," Eddie grumbles.

"Pfft," say Mark and Mrs. Brodowski in unison, and she flashes him a pleased, conspiratorial grin before launching into another story about Eddie's father.

Mark starts to do the math. Eddie's father died when he was twelve, so ten years ago. And Mrs. Brodowski can't be older than forty-five. She remarried, and long enough ago for Eddie to casually refer to her husband as his stepdad. He wonders how long it took for her to be able to talk about Eddie's father without it being sad. Maybe it helped that she probably had to talk about him to Eddie. Maybe being able to talk about him at all helped.

Mark imagines sitting down to dinner with a new acquaintance and telling the story of how, on a trip to France, William miscalculated the exchange rate, wound up spending the equivalent of thirty dollars on a dog bowl for Lula, and then insisted that this was precisely what he had meant to do all along. For months, Mark would get a little giddy every time he saw that stupid bowl. "The most expensive bowl on the Eastern seaboard," he used to say. "The finest porcelain in the land." William would argue that, amortized, the bowl would pay for itself by 1975, which Mark is almost positive isn't how amortization works. All Mark knows is that he's never throwing that bowl out.

He could tell that story. Not now, of course. But . . . to Eddie, maybe? To George? But a yearslong habit of secrecy—a secret he built his life around—is hard to break.

He skipped lunch, and the wine is going to his head, so he sits back and enjoys watching Eddie and his mother. Eddie is—well, he's basking in his mother's affection. It's probably a little immature.

Mark's certain he ought to think so, at least. But instead he's happy that Eddie has a parent who loves him. Mark really shouldn't be here; Eddie ought to know better than to do anything to jeopardize his mother's fondness for him. Or maybe she'd love him anyway. It can happen like that, obviously, although Mark's not in the habit of anticipating good outcomes for that sort of thing.

After dinner, Eddie insists on checking the pressure in his mother's tires, then tries and fails to give her money for a hotel room.

"Then call me as soon as you get home," Eddie insists.

"It'll be three in the morning," his mother says. "The phone will wake up poor Luis. He already suffers enough with you as his roommate."

Mark is mentally congratulating Mrs. Brodowski on landing on the only argument that might deter Eddie from insisting on a phone call anyway, when Eddie speaks up again. "Then call Mark's room. Room 602. He never sleeps. You wouldn't mind, would you, Mark?"

"No," Mark chokes out. "Of course, please do call me, ma'am."

There's a beat of dead silence, the first quiet moment all afternoon. Mark doesn't have a single particle of doubt that she just came to some very accurate conclusions, and he's just as sure that Eddie doesn't realize it.

But Mrs. Brodowski recovers quickly. "What good would that do you? You still won't know whether I'm alive or dead until you see Mark in the morning. So I'll leave a message at the front desk for you like a normal person. For heaven's sake, Edward, you don't have the sense God gave you." She sounds genuinely exasperated. She hugs her son, and over his shoulder shoots Mark a look that he thinks might be one of commiseration, as if they're together in the hopeless business of protecting Eddie O'Leary.

As soon as they're alone in Mark's hotel room, Mark turns on Eddie. "You may not have realized it," he says, seething, "but you told your mother that you're aware of my sleeping habits."

"I only know because you've told me," Eddie says blithely. "We've never even spent the night together." This is only true because every night Mark makes Eddie sneak back to his own hotel room.

"You've made it perfectly clear to her that you and I don't have a professional relationship." Mark paces the length of the room.

"We don't."

"Clearly," Mark says, letting the scorn drip from his voice.

"We're friends. Friends who talk about things like having trouble sleeping. And I know you'd do me the favor of taking a call from my mother."

"Do you now," Mark says acidly.

"Was I wrong?"

"That's not the point. You didn't see her face when you said that."

Eddie's leaning against the wall, his hands in his pockets, looking like he doesn't have a care in the world. "Sure I did."

"What?"

"I'm easing her into it."

"Into what?"

"The idea that I might be, you know—"

"Oh, I certainly do."

"—with you."

Mark pinches the bridge of his nose. "I—Eddie—you can't do that. She loves you."

Eddie is quiet, an expression on his face that Mark might call pity if that made any sense at all. "Which is why she'll be fine with it. Eventually. It's like when I told her I was playing baseball instead of going to college. I had to tell her bit by bit, get her feet wet."

"It really isn't! It's not like that in the least."

"No offense, but you don't know my mom very well."

"I know how badly these things can go!"

"Are you under the impression that I don't know that, too? That somehow, you're going to explain it all to me right now?" Eddie rolls his eyes like some kind of teenager.

"Besides, you aren't."

"I'm not, am I?"

"With me," Mark clarifies. "You're not with me."

Obviously, he's trying to hurt Eddie, and he knows that makes him a complete bastard, but he only gets the satisfaction of a fraction of a flinch before Eddie shrugs. "Fine, we aren't together. But it's not like I can tell her anything more accurate. I'm not going to tell my mom that we're fucking. God, Mark."

"I'm not—ugh!" Mark is exasperated to the point where he doesn't even have any words. "You don't have to tell her anything!"

"Sure I do. You said you don't want to be a secret. Well, there you go. Not a secret."

"What point do you think you're making? Do you think you're proving that it's a bad idea for me to stop hiding?" Mark asks, incredulous.

"No, dummy. I mean literally, exactly what I said. It's not in code. I don't have any ulterior motives. Why is this so hard for you to get?"

For a minute Mark just opens and closes his mouth like the biggest fool in the world. "She's your mother" is all he can say.

"Look, I get that your parents are assholes. And I get that William had to keep you a secret. And I get that both those things fucked you up something awful—I mean—" He breaks off, evidently deciding a bit belatedly that he's gone too far. Mark might laugh any other time, but right now, for some reason, he's on the verge of tears. "I'm not going to do anything to make it worse for you. That's all."

It is utterly disgusting and intolerable that in addition to Eddie being sweet and—well, the entire biceps and pectorals problem—he has to be perceptive, too. Mark hates it. He sniffs, and it comes out a sniffle. "It's not your job to worry about that."

"Oh, right, because we're not 'together.'" There are audible quotation marks around *together*, and Eddie sounds unacceptably amused about it.

"Ugh. You're insufferable."

"I get that a lot." Eddie pushes off the wall and comes to Mark.

"I doubt that," Mark says. He tries to continue pacing but Eddie's blocking his path. "I doubt ballplayers say *insufferable*."

"It's completely adorable how you get like this." One of Eddie's arms has snaked around Mark's waist. "My mom has this cat who likes to be pet, but he hisses on the way to my mom's lap every goddamn time. It's fucking hilarious."

"I take it back. People probably learn the word *insufferable* in order to talk about you accurately."

Appallingly, Eddie starts in on Mark's shirt buttons, and only then does Mark realize his tie is already off.

"Do you want to fight some more?" Eddie asks, tossing Mark's shirt onto the floor.

Mark shakes his head, and Eddie goes to unfasten Mark's watch. He pauses, his eyes darting to Mark's. Mark's face heats. That morning, he stopped at the cobbler in the hotel lobby to get another hole punched in the watchband, because it's *his* watch now—it holds some memories, sure, but it's also the thing he wears to tell time, and he might as well make it fit. It's *nothing*, and it isn't nothing at all, and Mark can tell that Eddie knows all this without being told. Eddie doesn't say a thing, just puts the watch carefully—so, so carefully—on the nightstand, and goes back to undressing Mark.

It's not until later, after Eddie's gotten dressed and kissed Mark good night, after Mark's checked the hallway to make sure it's empty, and Eddie already has one foot out the door, that Mark works up the courage to ask. "Can I, um."

"Yes," Eddie says.

"You don't know what I was going to ask."

Eddie closes the door and steps back into the room. "Try me."

"Can I tell Lilian?"

"Yeah." Eddie doesn't hesitate, which doesn't do anything to make Mark more confident about his answer.

"Are you sure?"

"Yes, Mark. Tell any friends you like. I already know you're going to be careful."

Mark wants to ask how Eddie could possibly know this when Mark has said that he doesn't want to be careful. But of course he's right, so Mark can't even argue with him.

Eddie looks like he's calculated the precise distance between *We aren't together* and *Can I tell people?* and noticed how Mark covered that distance in about an hour. For a minute it looks like he's going to say something about it, but he decides to be merciful and instead leans in and kisses Mark. Then Mark again goes through the steps of making sure it's safe for Eddie to leave.

"He introduced me to his *mother*," Mark hisses into the phone when Lilian answers. As soon as he was sure Eddie had gotten on the elevator to his own room, Mark crept down to the lobby like a criminal, not even sure who he was trying to hide from.

"Hi, Lilian, how are you? How's Maureen? How's my neurotic little dog?" Lilian answers.

"Ugh. I'm calling long-distance. I don't have time for this. Wait. Lula's all right, isn't she?"

"We're *all* fine, Mark. Okay, when you say that he introduced you to his mother, I assume we're talking about—"

"Yes," Mark says, cutting her off. "We don't need to use names." He thinks he can hear her sigh, but he can't be sure.

"I take it that things have—".

"Yes."

"—progressed."

"That isn't the point."

"It sort of is, though."

"He introduced me to his mother. He all but told her *why* he was introducing us."

Lilian's quiet for a moment. "Sometimes people take calculated risks," she says eventually. "Is it hard for you because it makes you think about William? I mean, is Eddie's openness hard because you have to reconcile it with William doing the opposite?"

Taken aback, Mark stares at the telephone receiver for a moment. "First of all, this has nothing to do with William. Second—it wasn't William's fault."

"I know that, darling."

They've had this conversation dozens—possibly hundreds—of times in the past, but not since William died. The familiarity of it is making Mark feel dangerously close to losing it. "How could William have acted otherwise? With the world as it was in 1952, and with me sitting there as a cautionary tale about what happens when your family finds out."

"I *know*. But it still had an effect. It still happened to you."

Mark winces, remembering the holidays and weekends that William visited his family and Mark was left alone in their apartment, half convinced that this would be the time William didn't come back. This time, surely, William would realize that a future in Congress or even at City Hall meant leaving Mark.

It would have been so easy for William not to come back, to leave Mark behind as surely as he'd leave the furniture and the silver, the framed art. There would have been none of the public messiness of divorce, none of the awkward explanations, just a packed suitcase, a change of address, and Mark would learn about William's marriage from the newspaper just like everybody else.

Mark knew these worries weren't fair to William, but the entire situation wasn't fair to *him*. It still isn't. He'll never know what William would have done—whether he'd eventually have given up his dreams of a future that couldn't have included Mark—and even that uncertainty is unfair.

The worst part is that—despite everything—Mark thinks William was right. He was right to protect himself from a cruel and backward world. If William had asked Mark whether he wanted to meet William's parents, Mark is almost certain he would have said no. And he doesn't know whether that's rational on his part or completely fucking nuts. He has no idea whether his ability to think about this sort of risk has been compromised—not by William, but by living in a world where any of this is a consideration.

CHAPTER TWENTY-THREE

When, finally, they get back to New York, Mark is ready to lie down on the tarmac and never get up.

"Most of the guys drove," Eddie says, picking up Mark's larger suitcase.

"Bully for them," Mark says. "I'm getting a cab and rescuing my dog. She's probably gained ten pounds in the past week and won't want to come home with me. Just what I need is for that dog to hate me even more." He knows he's babbling and is beyond caring.

"My point is that I'll split a cab with you."

"It'll take you out of your way. The dog's in Park Slope."

"Good. I want to see Lula, too."

This strikes Mark as a perfectly sensible desire; everyone ought to want to see Lula. Besides, Eddie needs to carry Mark's suitcases; Mark certainly can't do it alone.

"I miss my bed," Mark says once they're in the cab. "I miss my dog. I'm sleeping for twelve hours, and I'm calling the police on anyone who tries to stop me."

Eddie glances at his watch. "You might get in eight hours before Lula wakes you up."

"Don't be ridiculous. You'll walk Lula and let me sleep."

Eddie's face lights up at this. It really shouldn't.

"What apartment should I buzz?" Eddie asks when the cab pulls to a stop in front of Lilian and Maureen's building.

"2F," Mark says, and only then realizes that Eddie has left him in the car, which is very sweet, but Mark gets a second wind at the prospect of seeing Maureen's reaction to Eddie O'Leary on her stoop.

It turns out to be entirely worth the effort of hauling his tired body out of the cab.

"Holy mother and all the saints," Maureen says, crossing herself.

Lilian appears behind Maureen. "Lula, darling, what a charmed life you lead, if you have celebrities escorting you home."

Lilian shakes Eddie's hand and introduces him to Maureen, so Mark can concentrate his attention on wondering if it would be too conspicuous to fall asleep on the sidewalk. Lula tugs at her leash hard enough that it escapes from Maureen's grip, and she darts up and down the sidewalk, the leash trailing behind her like a streamer. She spins in a circle at Mark's feet and then gets on her hind legs.

"Why, it's nice to see you, too," Mark says, scratching her head. "I'm not accustomed to this kind of welcome from you. Or any kind of welcome, to be honest. Or even a silent recognition that I'm alive, if it comes to that."

Eddie bends down to pick her up, and she licks his face, so maybe Lula is just happy to rescued from the terrible fate of being overfed home-cooked meals by indulgent lesbians.

"Do you want to come up for a drink?" Maureen offers.

"I will kill anyone who stands between me and my bed," Mark says.

Lilian raises an eyebrow at Eddie, who raises both his eyebrows back at her, and they both laugh. Mark hates everyone except Lula, the best dog in the world, and the cab driver, the hero who will bring him home.

Mark must nod off in the cab, because when he opens his eyes, they're in front of his building. Before he can fish his wallet out of his pocket, Eddie is opening the cab door and gently shoving him out. "I already paid," Eddie says.

Mark ought to protest, as he and Lula comprised two-thirds of the taxi's passengers, but instead he only yawns. The doorman appears equally delighted to see Lula and Eddie. And Lula, amazingly, acts pleased to see the doorman. Things must have been dire indeed if Lula's this happy to be home. He wonders what kind of canine torture chamber Lilian and Maureen are running over there.

Upstairs, Lula lets out a yap that Mark translates as "You haven't fed me in a week," which he supposes is accurate in a way, so he gives her what is undoubtedly a second, if not third, dinner.

"You want a bath?" Eddie asks.

"Oh God, yes." A week of grimy ballparks, shared transportation, and hotels has left Mark feeling positively diseased. He wants to scrub himself thoroughly, preferably while immersed in scalding water.

Only when he hears the water running does he realize that Eddie is drawing him a bath. Mark doesn't deserve any of this, and Eddie has to be smart enough to know it, but Mark is too tired and selfish to point it out. So he just takes off his clothing, letting it fall to the floor in the living room, then the hallway, then the bathroom, and settles into the tub.

He shuts his eyes. The room smells good. It also smells like his shampoo, which means Eddie probably dumped half a bottle of the stuff into the tub as the world's most expensive bubble bath, but that's fine. He hears the toilet lid close, and when he opens his eyes, Eddie is sitting there.

"You could get in," Mark offers. He means it, in a way. Kind of.

"I don't think I'd fit in that tub even if you weren't in it," Eddie says, sounding amused. "But I'm going to go shower in the other bathroom. The maid storage bathroom."

Mark snorts. "There's no soap in there. Nobody's ever used that shower. Take my stuff."

He shuts his eyes again, and he must drift off, because when he opens them, Eddie's standing over him, his hair wet and a towel wrapped around his waist.

"Okay, you can't sleep in there, and I don't think I can lift you out, so you ought to get out now on your own steam while you still have any."

"You could try," Mark says, more intrigued by this possibility than he might have thought.

"Maybe in the off-season." He reaches out a hand. "Come on, lazybones."

Mark lets himself be tugged to his feet and wrapped in a towel. He lets Eddie roughly dry him off. *Lets* is not the correct word, and he knows it.

"You're staying, right?" Mark asks.

Eddie's smile is terribly broad.

Mark probably should have guessed that waking up with a heavy arm thrown over him would be, to put it mildly, disorienting. You can't, he supposes, share a bed for seven years and then *not* share a bed for a year and a half and then expect yourself to react like a sane person to what is apparently a ghost sharing your mattress.

"Hey," Eddie mumbles, pulling Mark closer. Mark isn't sure what he did to wake Eddie up. He thought he was just lying there, his confusion quietly self-contained.

"Hey yourself." Mark rolls over and burrows into Eddie's chest. Eddie smells reassuringly Eddie-like, even with the strange overlay of Mark's soap and shampoo.

Mark peers over Eddie's shoulder and squints at the alarm clock. Even though he's been sleeping in this room for over a year, he still hasn't bought decent curtains, which means there's enough light coming in from the streetlights below that Mark can just make out the small hand pointing to four. He's disgusted with himself for waking up.

There's a rustling at the foot of the bed, and Mark nearly gives himself a heart attack.

"It's just Lula," Eddie mumbles.

Now Mark is fully awake. "Is she having some kind of episode? What's she doing in here?"

"Is she not allowed? She jumped on the bed after you fell asleep, and I figured it was okay."

She's very much not allowed, not on the bed or any other furniture, but that's not the point. "She always sleeps against the door," Mark says.

"That seems uncomfortable."

"She likes to make me watch her suffer."

"Why doesn't she sleep in her dog bed? It's made of honest-to-God velvet. It has *tassels*," Eddie adds, as if the tassels ought to settle the matter.

"William got her when she was a puppy. I think she's too old to understand that he isn't coming back."

"She's waiting for—Oh my God," Eddie says, his voice a whisper. "Sorry," he mumbles, "I'm a fucking weirdo when it comes to dogs."

"Are you—" Mark doesn't need to finish the question, because it's manifestly obvious that Eddie is indeed crying about Lula. "You really are a sweetheart."

Mark's eyes have adjusted enough to the dark that he can see Eddie roughly scrub away tears using the back of his hand. "Don't," Mark says, and hands him a tissue from the nightstand.

"I'm fine, I'm fine."

Mark, at a loss, strokes Eddie's hair and attempts a hushing sound. "You love my dog," he says, unaccountably satisfied by this.

"Yeah, Mark, I love *your dog*."

Lula then stands up, makes a noise of acute frustration, and jumps off the bed.

"I think we woke her up," Eddie whispers.

Then comes the sound of paws landing on the sofa.

Mark couldn't possibly say why this strikes him as funny—why the dog being annoyed with him but not sulking at the door has him in stitches. Lula's airs and graces were always a bit hilarious before they started seeming tragic. Before he manages to collect himself, Eddie's started laughing, too.

"Who'd have thought you were capable of cracking a smile at four in the morning," Eddie says, sounding unbearably fond.

"How disgusting of me," Mark says, but before he can finish speaking, Eddie's mouth is on his. Or, to be more accurate, his own mouth is on Eddie's, because Mark's very much afraid he's the one who's initiating this kiss. Not that Eddie seems to mind. Eddie rolls them over so Mark is on top, leaning down and brushing the messy hair out of Eddie's face and kissing him and kissing him.

Some internal warning system alerts Mark that he's being far too affectionate, but that warning system is weeks too late, and Mark would have ignored it anyway. Eddie's gotten past any defenses Mark might have had in place, and Mark can't bring himself to regret it, even though he knows—even as he kisses Eddie, even as Eddie's hands are big and firm on Mark's sides—that this can't last.

"Come on," Mark says, and he isn't quite sure what he means, but Eddie seems to get it anyway, his hands slipping low, eager, exploring. He rolls Mark onto his back, trailing kisses along his jaw, down his neck.

"Can I?" Eddie mumbles against his throat.

"The stuff is still in my suitcase."

"I, uh, unpacked for you. It's—" One of his hands disappears for a moment, and there comes the sound of him fumbling around on the nightstand. "It's right here. Your five-dollar slick."

"It's not five dollars! It's twenty-five cents." For heaven's sake, it says so on the lid. And it's not slick. Technically, it's a salve that Mark puts to a higher purpose, not that he's ever admitting as much.

"Well, it's going to cost you an entire quarter to get fucked, because this tin is tiny."

Something in Mark goes hot and liquid at *get fucked*, and maybe even at the notion that it's costing him money, but he's not going to examine that particular nuance anytime soon. "I suppose I can afford it, if you make it worth my while," he says lazily.

Eddie slides down the bed and braces himself on one arm, meaning that Mark has the perfect view as Eddie touches him, as his biceps bunch and flex, as the yellow streetlight catches his hair. Eddie's fingers are steady and sweet, and when he bends his head to take Mark into his mouth, that's sweet, too.

And Mark is at home. He has no idea why that matters so much, why this feels fundamentally different from sex in a hotel room. He wants to say that it feels real, but the hotel room sex felt plenty real. It's just—this apartment has always been safe, protected. *His.* And this, what they're doing, deserves that sort of safety. He wants to wrap them both up and tuck them away and not let anything outside these four walls get to them. Impossible and foolish, but he wants it anyway.

"Get a move on," Mark says, prodding Eddie's shoulder with his foot. Eddie pulls off and laughs, low and rough and utterly obscene, before kissing the inside of Mark's ankle.

He watches, greedy and fascinated, as Eddie braces over him, as he takes his goddamn time getting down to business because *of course* he does. Of course he's careful and kind, and Mark could put an end to this by demanding to get on top, but instead he lets it happen at Eddie's pace, lets himself be—taken care of? More than that, probably, but that idea's going to have to join all the other things he isn't going to think about.

And, okay, maybe Eddie has a point with all this dawdling, because it's been a while and Eddie is—well. This is a lot. He steadies himself, focuses on Eddie's ragged breathing, the sight of Eddie's broad chest rising and falling, the idea that Eddie is doing this *for him*. Eddie's jaw is set, his expression serious and almost stern, not something Mark's ever seen there before.

"You all right?" Eddie asks. He sounds ruined. He sounds desperate. Mark is still surprised by how much he gets off on Eddie's shameless desperation.

"Yeah. You can—please."

Mark can feel Eddie paying attention to him, to how he reacts to every shift in angle or tempo. He wants to shut his eyes. He wants to get his glasses off the nightstand and turn on every light in the apartment. He doesn't know what he wants, but Eddie seems to, and gives it to him.

Mark's always loved this, loved being at his body's mercy, and he's tempted to ask for more, for harder, because maybe that would do something to shake off the intimacy. He suspects that Eddie would know what he was up to, and that it wouldn't work anyway.

"Just like that," Mark says, remembering how Eddie likes hearing that he's doing a good job. "It's so good, Eddie."

Eddie breathes out a laugh and takes Mark's face in his hand, his palm warm against Mark's jaw. "Oh, is it?" Mark makes himself look back, even though Eddie's just a blurry shadow. He lets Eddie see whatever there is to see in his face.

Mark knows that what he's going to be thinking about, the sensation that will last in his mind far longer than he'll want it to, is the feeling of Eddie's face buried in his neck when it's all over, when they're lying there in cooling sweat, trying to muster up the strength to move. He feels like every part of him is wrapped around Eddie, like they're tangled up in something dangerous and lovely and terribly, terribly precious.

CHAPTER TWENTY-FOUR

Mark considers flowers, he really does. That's the normal thing to bring hospital patients, but he can't imagine George Allen doing anything with a floral arrangement other than throwing it in the trash. So he buys a bagel with lox and a book of crossword puzzles and brings them to the hospital, along with two paperback mysteries from his own shelves.

He was wise to avoid the flowers, because when he gets to George's private room in St. Vincent's, it's already half filled with gladiolus.

"Smells like a funeral home," George complains after snatching the bagel from Mark's hand.

"Let me guess. Andy and his father."

"Ha. Yes. The carnations are from the sports desk. The one by the window is from the Robins," he says, pointing to an arrangement that's about ten times as tasteful as anything Mark expects from a baseball team. "Ruth's nieces are responsible for the rest." George takes a bite of his bagel and looks around the room. "Ruth died in her sleep. No hospital, no flowers."

William died at work. Mark found out when, after a frantic night, he called William's office and was told the truth by a stunned, tearful secretary. William's parents arranged the funeral, and it was only by reading the obituary in the newspaper that Mark knew where to go. He might not have gone if Lilian hadn't put him in a suit and taken him herself. His memories of that week have a hazy quality, like he's only seeing them in a foggy mirror, but what he remembers clearest of all is that Lilian never let him out of her sight.

"When are they letting you out of here?" Mark asks.

"Another week, but that's only if I stay with one of Ruth's nieces or go to a convalescent home. Fat chance of that happening."

"Why not?"

"The nieces are nice enough. But they'd fuss over me and expect me to like it. No thanks."

Mark shudders in sympathy. He thinks, inanely, of the empty room in his apartment. It's a silly idea, though, so he doesn't say anything.

"And they wouldn't let me work," George adds.

"You're not retiring, are you? You'd better not be. I stopped in at the *Chronicle* this morning, and the kid they're going to have covering the Robins looks about twelve."

"What, you don't want to take it on full-time? You weren't terrible." George gestures at the stack of *Chronicles* on his bedside table.

"George, it was like a week at a penal colony. You really have no choice but to get better." Mark knows as soon as he's spoken that he's made an error.

He forces himself to notice that George is—not well. He's pale. Gray might be more accurate. And somehow he seems shrunken, although he can't possibly be much smaller now than he was two weeks earlier.

"This is my second heart attack," George says. "It looks like *better* isn't on the table."

Mark fights the uncharacteristic urge to say something cheery, like about how President Eisenhower bounced back after his heart attack, or that doctors are often wrong. But those platitudes would only be for himself. He keeps thinking about the matter-of-fact way George treated him like a fellow widower, an unlooked-for kindness. It's been a long time since Mark's devoted any energy to actively resenting his parents, but George's kindness makes him feel sad and a little angry in a way he hasn't in years. The idea of George being *gone* leaves him more raw than he should be at the idea of losing a colleague.

"I'm really sorry to hear that," Mark says.

George shrugs. "This bagel is good. The place on Second Avenue?"

"Where else?"

Mark looks around the small room, casting about for something to say that doesn't involve either mortality or bagels. His gaze catches George's medical chart and the name written on the top in neat nurse's handwriting: JACOB APFELBAUM. He knew that was George's name—it had come up in conversation years ago that in the middle of World War I, *Chronicle* readers might have balked at a byline that sounded German, let alone one that sounded Jewish. There had been dozens of writers and actors who had made the same choice.

It's not the same thing, but it occurs to Mark that he isn't the only one in the room who knows about the tug-of-war between being yourself and being *palatable*.

George notices him looking at the chart. "All the cards say George Allen. Even the ones from Ruth's nieces."

"Does it bother you?"

George makes a wavering motion with the hand that isn't holding the bagel. "Ruth was the last one to call me Jacob. Her nieces call me Uncle George. I mean, I *am* George Allen. I wouldn't want anyone to call me Jacob who hadn't known me in short pants." He has another bite, chews thoughtfully. "You know, I lied to you."

"About what?"

"You asked why I went back to beat reporting. I told you it keeps me young. The truth is that the older you get, the more things you lose, and baseball is something I have left."

All Mark's experience with loss has been people being wrenched away from him. His discomfort must be visible because George shakes his head.

"It isn't all bad. You get older, and things change. That's the price of admission. You lose the people who knew you first, and then you start to lose everyone else. You lose your work. You lose the place where you grew up. You get things in return—new people, new hobbies, a chance to see everything new that the world has to throw at you. But you lose the things you've had the longest, the things that went into making you."

Mark can't quite get past the idea of losing people being *not all bad*. "Where did you grow up?"

"Orchard Street."

Mark raises his eyebrows. "It's still there, last time I checked."

"Sure, the street still is, and some of the buildings, too. But it's all new people, and fuck me if I don't sound like a Republican, but it's not my old neighborhood anymore. That's not because I don't like immigrants, or because I wish there were still pickle carts on the street, but because my neighborhood exists in 1915. Hell, the people who live there now will be having this same conversation in forty years. We all lose the places and the people who made us. That's my point."

"But you said baseball was something you hadn't lost. It's pretty different now than it was in 1915, too."

"It's still the same neighborhood, though," George says, cracking a smile. His eyes are a little unfocused, and Mark realizes that this uncharacteristic garrulousness is perhaps the result of morphine. "There's one other reason I went back to reporting," George goes on. "This generation of reporters? Even the ones I can't stand—the ones who think they're psychoanalysts or gossip columnists. Half of them were taught by reporters who were copying me. Hell of a thing for the ego. You think I'm exaggerating—"

"Not at all," Mark protests.

"Go back and look at what I was writing in the thirties, and tell me I'm wrong."

Somewhere in the bowels of the *Chronicle* building there must be clippings of everything George Allen wrote over the past forty or fifty years. How many words would that be? Mark can't do that kind of math in his head, but it has to be five million words, maybe ten. You could take one percent of that and have a respectable book. And, sure, some of those articles are going to be ephemeral—play-by-play accounts of games nobody needs to remember, reports of trades that everyone's forgotten. But there will be other pieces, too.

"The things you have left, and the things you leave behind," Mark says, mostly thinking aloud. He's getting ahead of himself, reaching for a notebook and pencil that aren't there.

"In any event," George goes on, "the doctors told me no more stairs, and that means no more baseball stadiums."

The Polo Grounds doesn't have elevators. Neither do subways, airplanes, or even some hotels. George certainly couldn't travel with the team. Hell, Mark's healthy and twenty-eight, and he barely managed it for a week. "Are you going to keep writing your column?"

"We'll see how much I can do from a hospital room." George lets out a laugh. "Who am I kidding. I'll walk out of here on my own if I need to. I'm not dying in a hospital bed, and I'm not retiring." He coughs, and it sounds painful. "It's a beautiful game, sometimes." There's a sense of loss in the old man's voice: He'll probably never see another game in person. This game that he's devoted his life to writing about, this game that he decided he'd like to spend his last years around, has been taken from him. That's what George just told him, though. This is what time does.

"How's O'Leary?" George asks.

"Playing decently. Getting on base every game, doesn't look like he's on the way to the electric chair when he's in the on-deck circle."

"I know that already." He gestures again to the stack of newspapers. Mark notices a transistor radio on the bedside table; George has probably been listening to games. "I mean, how is he?"

Mark isn't sure what exactly George is asking. Does he want to know whether Mark is following his advice and keeping his distance from Eddie? "I met his mother," Mark finally says, figuring that at least will let on that Mark is still ignoring George's advice. "Picture Mae West cast as a librarian from Nebraska, and you'll have a pretty good idea."

He thinks of Eddie all but telling his mom. He's been taking that memory out and turning it over in his hand like a smooth, polished stone. Mark's best efforts at keeping himself a secret—and that's what he did during the entire road trip, however much he hated it—won't do Eddie any good at all if Eddie insists on acting like that. In fact, Eddie seems dead set on making it so Mark *can't* keep their friendship—if not the whole truth of who they are to one another—a secret from anyone at all. He's making it impossible for Mark to follow what he knows to be the most prudent course of action. And yet, when Mark remembers how it felt when Eddie basically told his mother *This is the man I spend my nights with*, he feels so warm and—loved. He feels loved.

He shakes his head, because he can't think about that now. He can't think about it at all.

"Eddie's going on the *Tonight* show when the team's in Los Angeles next week," Mark says. "And he has a couple of local television appearances coming up, too."

"Figures," George says. "He's all anyone asks about—the nurses, the orderlies, my nieces. 'How's that nice kid Eddie O'Leary?'"

"I wonder when he went from being a disgrace to baseball to being a nice kid," Mark muses.

"I'd say it was right around your second diary entry," George says.

"Oh," Mark says, surprised.

"*Oh*," George repeats, a little mocking. "You knew what you were doing."

Mark feels his cheeks heat, and it's definitely time to leave.

"How do you feel about rugelach? I'll bring some on Friday."

When the phone rings at eight o'clock that night, Mark stares at it in bewilderment. He saw Lilian at work a few hours earlier. He just saw Eddie on the television five minutes ago. Nobody else really calls him.

"Hello?"

"Jesus, Mark. Why does it always take you so long to get to the phone?" Eddie's voice is just above a whisper. "It's three inches away from the sofa."

"Why aren't you on the field?"

"Seventh-inning stretch. I'm calling from Ardolino's office."

"Are you all right?" Mark asks, but he supposes he would have seen it with his own eyes if Eddie had been injured during the game.

"Yeah, yeah. Ardolino and I are picking you up at ten. Wear tennis shoes."

"What—"

"Just do it."

"What makes you think I even own tennis shoes?"

"You have a pair of rackets in the maid storage room. Don't be ridiculous. Bring your notebook."

There comes the clatter of a receiver being dropped carelessly into the cradle, followed by the dial tone.

Well. Tennis shoes mean it certainly isn't a nightclub, which means the slacks and cotton sweater he's already wearing are probably good enough.

At a quarter past ten, the doorman buzzes, and Mark heads down to find Eddie in the lobby, leaning against the doorman's desk and chatting with him.

Mark can tell when Eddie notices him: he doesn't stop speaking, he doesn't move his body, but his eyes drift over to Mark and his mouth curves in the sort of smile that can't be faked—and, if you're Eddie O'Leary, can't be suppressed, either.

"Where am I being abducted to this evening?"

"That's for me to know and you to find out."

The car is an immaculately polished pale blue Lincoln Continental with Buddy Rosenthal behind the wheel, Tony Ardolino in the passenger seat, and first baseman Harry Varga in the back. "Am I going in the trunk, or are you strapping me to the roof?" Mark asks from the curb.

"You can sit on my lap," Ardolino says through the rolled-down window. He pats his thigh. Mark sighs and climbs into the back seat, resigned to being crushed between two oversized athletes.

"Where's Price?" Mark asks, realizing that he rarely sees Ardolino without Price.

"He says getting arrested isn't as fun for him as it is for the rest of us," Ardolino says. "He's sitting this one out."

"I knew he was the only sensible one of you," Mark observes weakly. He really doesn't want to get arrested, either, but doubts Eddie would have brought him along if they were doing anything actually dangerous.

"Wait, who's pitching, then?" Varga asks, leaning forward in a way that sends Mark into Eddie's side.

"Jim Schmidt is meeting us there," Rosenthal says. "He lives in Hackensack or Paramus or one of those places."

Mark has been to New Jersey maybe half a dozen times, and one of those was when he and William got lost on the way home from an antique store in the Hudson Valley. William refused to ask for directions until Mark got out of the car and threatened to hitchhike back to Manhattan. He watches in some curiosity as the car emerges from the Holland Tunnel.

"You're gawping," Eddie says as they pass a factory, smoke billowing out even at this hour.

"You take me to the loveliest places," Mark murmurs, pitching his voice low enough that only Eddie can hear.

Eddie grins. Mark's terribly aware of all the places where his side presses against Eddie's: thighs and hips, arms and shoulders. He's familiar by now with Eddie's body, can shut his eyes and imagine the bulk of quadriceps, the surprisingly pointy elbows. Being pressed up against that body in public is doing something to his mind. They're touching, but Mark isn't allowed to reach over and smooth his hand down Eddie's bicep, can't rest his palm on Eddie's thigh. He's almost in Eddie's lap, but the one thing he can't do is touch Eddie with his hand.

The drive can't be more than half an hour, but it feels interminable. When the car finally pulls to a stop, Mark elbows Eddie until he gets out.

Only then does Mark realize where they are. It's the suburbs. There are trees—elm and maple and oak and all the usual suspects—and some patchy grass. Beyond that is a baseball diamond. It's barely visible in the dark; this is not the kind of field that has lights. It's probably where the church beer league plays.

Rosenthal gets back in the car and turns on the headlights, illuminating the field enough that Mark can see that the infield is scruffy, the base path weedy, the foul line invisible. Mark is hit with a visceral memory of playing baseball on an almost identical field when he was a kid, of mosquitoes and sunburns, dandelions in right field.

Another car pulls up and two people get out. The older of the two is Jim Schmidt, one of the Robins' starting pitchers. The other is a kid, all skinny arms and legs. He's fourteen, maybe fifteen.

"I brought Johnny, so watch your fucking mouths," Schmidt says.

Varga appears with a bag of gear that must have been in Rosenthal's trunk. He drops it by Eddie's feet. A minute later he comes back with a case of beer, which he shoves into Mark's arms. Mark tries not to visibly stagger under the weight.

"It worked last month," Ardolino says. "I figure it can't hurt to try again."

"I don't know why it has to be in the middle of the night in the middle of nowhere," Eddie complains.

"Because this is not a public event," Ardolino says. "And we don't want an audience."

Several sets of eyes turn to Mark.

"Bailey's invited because he's writing about O'Leary and seems to know how not to make him look like a doorknob," Ardolino says. "And he isn't going to make any of us look bad. Right, Bailey?"

"Right," Mark agrees. He sets the beer on the nearby bleachers and feels for his notebook and pencil in his pocket. He's starting to get a sense of what's happening tonight, but wants to let it unfold on its own rather than draw attention to himself with questions.

Eddie grabs a bat and heads over to home plate while Schmidt waits on the pitcher's mound. Varga puts on catcher's gear. "What, I played catcher until I fucked my knees up in Korea," he says when Eddie eyes him dubiously. Mark hadn't known that. He takes out his notebook and writes it down.

"I don't get it," Rosenthal says to Ardolino, his voice low. They're sitting in the bleachers now. "O'Leary's hitting fine."

"Fine," Ardolino scoffs. "Did you ever play against the Athletics last year? No, you wouldn't have, you were on a National League team. If he settles in at fine, if he stays *fine* for the rest of his career, it's a goddamn waste. It's a sin and a crying shame."

"I still think he's injured and lying about it."

"He's not injured. Is he injured, Bailey?"

"No," Mark says before registering that he probably shouldn't sound so confident about this. "You really think he could keep a secret for months? He'd have told ten reporters within ten minutes of getting hurt."

Rosenthal laughs. "True."

Ardolino catches Mark's eye as if to say, *We both know he can keep secrets.* Mark doesn't react.

Varga is adjusting Eddie's stance, shoving him around and smacking him when he does something wrong. Next to Mark, Schmidt's teenage kid is leaning forward, his hands braced on his knees, his eyes wide. Even if your dad plays professional baseball, it probably isn't every day you see Eddie O'Leary being taught how to hold a bat. Eddie must not like something Varga is doing, because he swats Varga's hand away. Varga swats him back, and the situation in the batter's box devolves into a slap fight.

"Jesus Christ. Children," Ardolino mutters.

Mark is surprised by the note of weariness in Ardolino's voice. Ardolino is different tonight, in some way, and it's only when Ardolino waves away Rosenthal's proffered bottle of beer that Mark realizes what's changed: Ardolino is sober. Granted, Mark's seen him sober before, namely on the airplane last week. But it's nearly midnight, and Ardolino is devoting his free time to illicit, suburban batting practice rather than hitting a nightclub.

Maybe that's why Mark is here, to document Ardolino's sobriety, his qualities as a leader. But that could have been done in broad daylight and with photographers present. Moreover, Mark suspects that Ardolino would have made sure to orchestrate things so that Sam Price got in on the good press. No, they've brought Mark here to watch whatever Eddie's doing.

What Eddie's doing at the moment is hitting the kind of pop-ups and fly balls that basically hand an out to the other team. Rosenthal groans and gets to his feet, then proceeds to do the same thing that Varga had done a few moments earlier. He pushes Eddie this way and that, says incomprehensible things about wrists and breaks, swears at Varga, then gets out of the way.

"He's smart," Ardolino says. "He pays attention."

There's a defensive edge to Ardolino's voice, as if he's waiting for Mark to laugh at him. "He is," Mark agrees.

"Maybe not book smart," Ardolino goes on, as if Mark hasn't said anything. "But he knows the game as well as some guys who've been playing for twice as long."

Actually, Mark's pretty sure that Eddie *is* book smart, at least regarding anything he's interested in. He reads whatever Mark hands him, and while Mark suspects this has more to do with Eddie's interest in Mark than in, say, Patricia Highsmith, he's perfectly equal to having an intelligent conversation about anything he's read.

"I hope I don't see anything in that paper about him being dumb," Ardolino says. "He's sensitive about it."

Mark abruptly realizes that he's being warned. He can't very well assure Ardolino that he'd gut himself before insulting Eddie O'Leary in public or in private. "I promise you'll see nothing of the sort."

Ardolino grunts, apparently satisfied. "He reminds me of myself at that age."

Mark knows Ardolino's history. Even if he hadn't researched it for this story, he already knows most of it through some kind of cultural osmosis. No kid who paid attention to baseball in the forties could have avoided knowing all about Tony Ardolino.

"You didn't have a slump your second year," Mark says.

"He has a hot temper, and he's hard on himself."

"I think you've just described half the league. Half the men I know, for that matter."

"Maybe. Maybe I'm just flattering myself when I look at him and think that was me in '42. But I don't want him to waste this."

Mark knows this isn't about Eddie. It's at least half about Tony Ardolino and his regrets, and probably even more about what it feels like to live with your regrets when you don't have a bottle of Maker's Mark to soften the blow.

"I've been thinking a lot about second chances," Mark says. He needs to write that article, and he can't write about slumps without disappointing Eddie, but maybe he can write about what's on the other side of a slump, if you're lucky. "Although *second chance* makes it sound like you're out on parole. What I really mean is a rally. When you think something's over, done, last nail in the coffin, and then it turns around. That's what's happening to Eddie, and I think it's what's happening to you. If this team goes anywhere—anywhere at all, Tony—that's at least partly your doing."

Ardolino snorts. "If this is your soft sell to get me to sit for an interview, fine. I'll do it."

"You're already sitting for an interview," Mark says, holding up his notepad. "What I need is a third angle—there's you and Eddie, but I need a third to make it work. Right now I'm thinking of the return of baseball to the Polo Grounds, but that's not good enough, not without a person behind it. I want Constance Newbold."

Before Ardolino can answer, Eddie connects with the next pitch. The sound of a good hit might be uniquely satisfying at a stadium and even noticeable over the television, but in the emptiness of a grassy park, with nothing but trees and a handful of men as witnesses, it sounds almost elemental.

"We're never seeing that ball again," Ardolino says.

"What's he throwing?" Mark asks, gesturing at the pitcher. With the field only lit by the headlights of Rosenthal's car, it's too dark to tell a fastball from a changeup. Mark has no idea how Eddie's even hitting these pitches, whatever they are.

"Fuck if I know. Shh."

Eddie hits the next pitch, too.

He remembers what George said: it can be a beautiful game. And maybe Mark's seen some of that, maybe when the sun is shining and the stadium smells like freshly cut grass, maybe when every play seems like a coalescence of talent and luck. The thing about baseball is that it's slow, and that each game is, essentially, meaningless. That's enough to make plenty of people stay away from it. But the glacial pace and the low stakes give you time to look at each individual component of the game and properly appreciate it.

A few years back, a popular, if slightly maudlin, book came out about a dying ballplayer. Mark had complained to William that it was a novel-length metaphor in which baseball stood in for life. William had retorted that nobody has ever written about baseball without it being a metaphor of some kind or another. William had been something Mark isn't: a baseball fan. Mark only followed the game first for his father's sake and then for William's, a sort of secondhand enthusiasm.

Now, though, he thinks that the game may have earned those metaphors. It's slow and often seems pointless. It's beautiful, when it isn't a mess. There's a vast ocean of mercy for mistakes: getting hits half the time is nothing short of a miracle, and even the best fielders are expected to have errors. The inevitability of failure is built into the game.

Eddie hits the ball again, and Mark can't see where it goes. "That's a left-field home run in the Polo Grounds," Ardolino says.

Schmidt's son is so still he may not even be breathing. When Eddie hits the next pitch—another crack, another ball they'll never find—a sound leaves the kid's mouth that's like air leaking out of a tire.

"Is this what his swing looked like last year?" Mark asks Ardolino.

"Not even close. That was ballet. This is—I don't know, Greek wrestling or something."

Mark knows a good line when he hears it, so he writes that down.

When he watches Eddie's next swing, he can see it. Eddie's fighting to get that bat to do what he wants. It looks fierce and a little brutal, but still, somehow, beautiful.

"I wish Sam could see this," Ardolino says.

"He'll see it at the next game."

"Wouldn't have taken you for an optimist, Bailey."

Maybe Mark is wrong. Maybe this swing will slip away from Eddie, or maybe it will settle into something just above marginal, something good enough but never great. He knows better than to count on good things lasting. But when he watches Eddie—when he sees that stern set of his jaw, and when Eddie flashes a grin toward the bleachers—Mark thinks he's seeing something that's for keeps.

"I need your help," Eddie says the next morning. Mark's still under his blankets, mostly asleep. He's not entirely sure how it came to pass that Eddie is standing over his bed, holding a cup of coffee out to him.

"This kid got called up from Syracuse," Eddie says. "He has one suit, and it's—Mark, it's so bad. I told him I'd meet him at Rosenthal's tailor in Williamsburg, and I need you to come to help me set him up with what he needs. Also, I don't know where Williamsburg is."

Mark drinks half his coffee while trying to come up with an answer.

"And before you start saying that it'll look weird for you to come with me," Eddie says, "all anyone has to do is look at you, and they'll know why I thought you'd be helpful in picking out clothes."

Mark can't really argue with that, now, can he? "How much time do we have?"

They wind up getting out of the cab in front of a Williamsburg storefront only ten minutes late. The rookie is already there, looking lost and so young that Mark's surprised the police haven't stopped to ask him where his mother is.

Inside, Mark has an exceptionally satisfying conversation with the tailor about various Italian worsteds, then deliberates with the tailor's wife over how they can outfit this poor rural baby in adequate clothing without either bankrupting him or bringing shame upon the team, and finally bullies Eddie into buying a new suit for himself. Before leaving, Mark winds up ordering a tweed jacket, because, as the tailor said, that tweed was never going to be so cheap again. He even lets himself get talked into suede elbow patches.

It's been years since Mark bought a stitch of clothing anywhere other than the Upper East Side of Manhattan, and he feels faintly revolutionary about it. What's next, denim and patchwork? Argyle pants and bolo ties? The vista of sartorial possibility has never been so broad. Mark is scandalized with himself for letting his sights drift beyond the safe shores of Brooks Brothers and Bergdorf Goodman.

"You gonna be okay?" Eddie asks on the way back into the city, the rookie safely stowed in the front seat of the cab, his face pressed against the glass like a toddler at the zoo. "Do we need to stop at Bloomingdale's for you to get in touch with your roots?"

"I don't like you very much," Mark sniffs, and Eddie laughs all the way across the bridge. Mark decides to be proud of himself that Eddie even knows what Bloomingdale's is, because two months ago he certainly knew nothing of the sort.

After they drop the kid off at the hotel near the ballpark, Eddie firmly telling him to stay in his room until it's time to go to the stadium for the game, they head back downtown to Mark's apartment.

"Thank you," Eddie says.

"Nothing to thank me for. Can't have your teammates going around looking like foundlings. And since that child is seven years old, an off-the-rack suit is only going to make him look like he's on his way to his first communion."

"He's my age, you know."

"Driver, let me out of this vehicle at once."

The driver, fortunately, does not take Mark seriously.

Inside Mark's apartment, Eddie scoops Lula up in the same movement as he wraps an arm around Mark's waist, drawing him close.

Mark doesn't mean to sink into Eddie's embrace, he really doesn't, but he does it anyway. He puts his chin on Eddie's shoulder, presses his face into the crook of Eddie's neck, and breathes in.

"You ought to go home and take a nap before the game," Mark says.

"I'll nap here." Eddie pulls Mark in for a kiss.

Mark extricates himself and begins to take off his jacket. The apartment, even with the air conditioner humming in the window, is warm.

"Stop," Eddie says. "I—if you don't mind." His face is going red, even as he's crowding Mark against the foyer wall. "Leave it on." He drops to his knees, and Mark remembers what Eddie said about wanting to touch his suit.

"You like my clothes," Mark says, probably unnecessarily.

"I think I have a full-fledged thing about your clothes," Eddie mumbles into the fine wool of Mark's trousers.

"Do you and my pants need a moment alone?"

"It only works if you're in them." Eddie glances up, his expression both sheepish and smug. "I'm trying to figure out how much clothing I can leave on you while still doing what I want."

"Nearly all of it, I'd think," Mark manages. "I'm on excellent terms with my dry cleaner."

Mark winds up with his cheek pressed against cool plaster, his hands scrabbling at the wall and finding no purchase, his trousers lowered the bare minimum, only enough to trap him in place.

Later, after they manage to reach the bed, Eddie falls asleep and Mark rolls over to set his alarm clock so Eddie won't oversleep and miss his game. When he turns back to face Eddie, he's hit with a memory. Maybe it's something about the angle of the light coming through the window, or maybe it's just the shared midday nap, but Mark remembers lying in a bed in William's old apartment as the truth of what was happening slowly dawned on him. Bruised and jaded and not used to being loved, he hadn't been expecting it. He hadn't expected to realize that the fondness he felt for the man next to him was love, and even less had he expected to be loved in return. It had felt so real it was nearly tangible, taking up actual space in his chest. He hadn't known then that it would grow, that it would put down roots and fill up all the spaces inside him, fusing with flesh and bone until there wasn't any way to separate it from the rest of him. He hadn't realized what it would be like to have it taken away.

He puts a hand to his chest, as if he'll be able to feel the familiar, alarming warmth growing there, and with it, an equally familiar fear. All those warnings he's been flinging at Eddie about safety, about staying away from Mark for his own good—they were meant to make Eddie understand the danger, but now he suspects he was just giving voice to his own fears. Maybe he doesn't know how to untangle caring for someone with worrying that it will be their un- doing. The bitter irony is that William's self-preservation made it so Mark rarely had to worry. If Eddie is hurt, and it's Mark's fault, he doesn't know how he'll live with it.

CHAPTER TWENTY-FIVE

N o, no," Mark says, straining to be heard over the noise of the bar. The Yankees game is on one television, and the Robins are on the other. He's been trying to keep from looking at either screen, but the crowd hollers whenever the Robins do anything resembling professional baseball, and so he keeps glancing up out of reflex. He's seen both of Eddie's at bats (a double and a walk; the bar lost its collective mind over a *walk*).

"Okay," Nick says. "Explain it to me again." They're crammed together at a too-small table, and the temperature in this room is about twenty degrees hotter than Mark wants it to be. But he came here with a mission. He needs advice, or maybe just a stern talking-to, and there's nobody else in his life he can rely on to be sensible in this situation.

"There's a man," Mark starts. He isn't sure how to finish, though. "He thinks we're together."

Nick looks amused. "Is he wrong?"

"He should be."

"Why?"

Eddie gave Mark blanket permission to tell whoever he trusted, but the fact that Eddie does things like that is the entire problem. Still, the best way to get across the scope of this problem is by telling Nick directly who they're talking about. He leans across the table and whispers, "It's Eddie O'Leary." Just as when he told Lilian, he gets a messy little rush from the fact that he's allowed to do this.

Mark watches as the meaning sinks in for Nick—his eyes widen, but he recovers quickly and takes a sip of his drink. He doesn't even flick a telling glance at the television screen. Nick is not a man who needs to be told about the need for discretion.

"Okay, fair."

Mark feels a wash of relief. "You understand, right?"

"Sure. Ballplayers gossip, reporters gossip, so the first time this guy does something remotely queer, it's an open secret kept by six hundred or so people. People stop talking to him. Maybe he gets traded, sent down, released. Or, you know. Worse. Christ, it would keep me up at night."

It's good to know that Mark was right that he could count on Nick not to sugarcoat things.

"You can't stand the thought of that," Nick goes on, "and you also can't stand the idea that it would be your fault. Well, that part's easy. It's not your fault, because he can make his own choices."

Mark sighs and drains his drink. "I think his judgment is clouded by his feelings."

"Buddy, I'd like to know whose isn't."

"He's young—well, twenty-two—and kind of sheltered," Mark says, even though *sheltered* isn't the word. Eddie just isn't jaded. "I don't think he realizes what it means to make a decision now that can create dead ends later on."

Mark goes silent long enough for the Orioles pitcher to strike out two Yankees.

"Mark. How old were you when you met William?"

Nick's the only person Mark knows who can say William's name without wrapping it up carefully in cotton wool. "I was twenty."

"And do you ever regret it? I don't mean all the time, but some-times. Do you ever think about what kind of life you might have had if you met someone else?"

That's a brutal question to ask someone in Mark's position. For a minute he just stares at Nick.

Nick lights a cigarette. "I'm asking because I wonder about Andy sometimes. If, when I realized the direction things were heading with us, I quit my job and moved away, he'd have met some nice woman. They'd be married now, a kid on the way, jointly filed taxes, the whole package. Safer than he is now. That's a fact. He doesn't think of it that way, probably because his brain works right, but I do, so I thought I'd ask."

"When he was alive, I thought about it," Mark admits.

"And that doesn't mean you wished you never met him. Doesn't mean you wanted to leave. It just means that thinking about awful things is a little hobby you have. Me too. Shitty hobby."

"I want him to be safe."

"Sometimes when Andy's late, I convince myself that somebody realized about us and decided to take it out on him."

"Oh my God, Nick. This isn't helping. This is the opposite of helping."

"Oh, was I supposed to lie to you? You already know all this."

"So, what, I should just accept that being with me could ruin everything for him?"

"Fuck no, you should be furious about it. But what do you expect this guy to do? What do you expect any of us to do? We have to live our fucking lives."

This conversation is going completely off the rails, and Mark tries to get it back on track. "I don't think he understands the risk. Or rather, I don't think he understands that whatever he's feeling for me isn't worth the risk."

"You don't think that maybe he's the best judge of that?"

"No!"

Nick is quiet. He regards Mark, tapping his cigarette rhythmically against the ashtray. "Why not, though? Why don't you believe him?"

"Because—"

"That's what we in the business call a rhetorical question, pal. Now be quiet so I can watch the Yankees lose."

The next morning, Mark wakes Eddie a minute before the alarm is set to go off. Eddie grins lazily up at him, and the look on his face is so fond that Mark has to shut his eyes. It's tempting to get back into bed and just let Eddie . . . adore him.

Mark pulls back. "You have to go."

Eddie gets up agreeably enough and throws on some clothes. In the doorway, he stoops to fuss over Lula, picking her up and letting her lick his face.

"We can't keep doing this," Mark says.

"So you keep telling me."

"I know. That's the problem. I'm going to tear myself apart with worry. I want to be the kind of person who lets you take your own risks and then lives with the consequences, but I'm not."

Eddie puts the dog down. "Okay. What do we do about that?"

"I don't know. All I know is that I can't be the person you lose it all for. I really can't, Eddie, you see that, right?"

He spent all night thinking about what Nick said: *Why don't you believe him?* There's something inside Mark that won't let him accept that being with him is a rational choice for Eddie to make. He could pretend otherwise, but that doubt will still be there—not doubt in Eddie, but in himself, or the world, or something else he hasn't even figured out yet.

"The person I lose it all for," Eddie repeats. "That's how you see yourself, isn't it? Mark, you're not going to ruin my life. You're the person I want to build my life around."

Mark lets himself imagine it for a minute. It's a mistake, because in that minute he sees it: a life, a future. He forces himself to come back to reality. "You have a road trip coming up."

"Ten days in California, then a few days off."

"Spend that time thinking about it." Two weeks of having fun, and Eddie might realize that whatever he thought he felt for Mark doesn't amount to much. They met when Eddie was lonely and angry; now he's neither of those things and, given a little space, might realize he doesn't need Mark. "Don't call me."

Eddie ought to look upset; at the very least, he ought to look like the message has finally gotten through. Instead he looks sad—no, he looks *pitying*, which is just so wrong that Mark wants to kick him.

Then, even worse, he leans in and kisses Mark, lovely and slow. And Mark, idiotically, kisses him back. Eddie's lips are soft and warm, the fingers of one hand interlaced with Mark's and the other cupping Mark's jaw. They fit together so well, and they're just familiar enough with one another's bodies for an embrace to feel like belonging.

"Do you want your key back?" Eddie asks.

Mark should have expected that, but it takes him by surprise—both the question and how badly he wants Eddie to keep that key.

That absurd gold trinket was one of the first things he bought himself for the sheer sake of its loveliness. Nobody needs a gold key holder and impractically tiny pencil with an even more impractically tiny knife and clock. But it's exquisitely made and a miniature marvel of engineering, and it always pleases Mark to hold it. It pleases him even more to think of it in Eddie's pocket. There are so very few perfect things in the world that it feels only right to share them.

He should ask for it back, but he doesn't, and something like understanding is dawning on Eddie's face.

"Sweetheart," Eddie says.

Nobody has ever called Mark that—nobody *should*. "Don't." Mark shakes his head. He can't. "You need to leave."

Eddie kisses him once more before walking out the door.

Mark is afraid that if he stays in one place, he'll start having a full range of emotions that he isn't interested in experiencing, so he puts Lula's leash on and heads to the bakery. Half an hour later, he's smuggling both a dog and a box of rugelach into the cardiac care ward of St. Vincent's.

George is scowling at the newspaper when Mark enters his room.

"Rugelach, as promised," Mark announces, slapping the box down on the table next to George's radio.

"I'm pretty sure visiting hours are over," George says. "And visiting hours for dogs probably don't exist."

"Yes, well, I thought I probably ought to figure out whether you like dogs before I make my proposal."

"Sure, I like dogs." He proves his point by feeding Lula an entire rugelach. "What proposal?"

"I'm tired of living alone, so if you're still looking for somewhere to stay, you can have my spare bedroom. Actually, not my spare room, because that's where I'm sleeping. You can have the big bedroom."

"You're tired of living alone," George repeats.

There's probably a better, more honest way for Mark to explain it. He doesn't want to live alone, that much is true, but it's because living alone in that apartment will always feel wrong. It had been a home, a safe haven, a refuge, and maybe that's what George needs right now. Mark has been living in such a closed-off, locked-up way—for the past year and a half, but also before that. He might not be able to have exactly what he wants, but he refuses to live in the emotional equivalent of a safety deposit box.

"We both know that if you're left to your own devices, it'll be delicatessen sandwiches and ballpark hot dogs, and you'll just be back in this hospital bed in a month," Mark says.

George narrows his eyes speculatively. "You can cook?"

Mark swallows. "I can cook." That's not quite accurate, so he amends it. "I'm a very good cook, and I've had enough meals with you that I know what you eat."

"Huh."

"Look. I have too much time on my hands. You'd be doing me a favor. But if you'd rather stay somewhere else, I won't have any hard feelings. I realize I'm being presumptuous by even asking." He lowers his voice. "I'm not going to bring strange men home, if that's what you're worried about."

George blinks. "I hadn't even considered that."

"Once you're on your feet, I could drive you to the ballpark. You might not be able to climb up to the press box, but I can see to it that you have a chair brought to you on the lower level."

"Do you have a telephone in the bedroom?"

"I can have the phone company put one in."

"You mind me monopolizing the phone line?"

"Not in the slightest."

"What about a television? I'll need a television in the bedroom."

"Consider it done." Mark's been meaning to buy a new set anyway. He can get one of those remote panels installed next to the bed so George can change the channel without getting up.

"Money's no object, huh?"

"Hasn't been for a while," Mark agrees.

George taps his fingers on the bedsheet. "You don't put any of that new music on the phonograph, do you?"

Mark suppresses a smile at the phrasing, but the truth is that he hardly listens to any music at all these days, barring whatever violin solo the girl upstairs is practicing that week. "I promise that won't be a problem."

"All right."

"All right?"

"I get out of here in a week. You can come pick me up. You have an extra typewriter?"

"I do. Anything else you need? No? Excellent." He helps himself to a rugelach. "George," Mark says. "Why do you think Constance Newbold didn't appoint someone else to be president of the organization?"

"Spite," George says promptly. "Everyone wanted her to go, so she stayed. She couldn't leave without letting them win."

Mark can respect that. It's like refusing to speed up when you're being tailgated. For some reason, it reminds him of what Nick said the other day, but he doesn't want to think about that.

When Mark gets outside, after giving his name and phone number to the nurse on duty (who looks at Lula like she might be seeing things), he has the sudden urge to tell Eddie—about George, about the nurse's double take at Lula, about the new television he's about to splash out on. It's familiar, this reflex to turn to a person, to *the* person, to *his* person, and he recognizes it as someone might a troubling new symptom, a sign that the disease has progressed further than anticipated.

He hails a cab and goes home to his empty apartment, but he knows it won't empty for long.

Part VI
SEPTEMBER

CHAPTER TWENTY-SIX

While the team is in Los Angeles, Eddie goes on the *Tonight* show and manages not to make a fool of himself, but the whole time he's wondering whether Mark is watching.

He's trying to avoid thinking about statistics, since it would take a miracle for his batting average to recover from a slump that lasted nearly half the season, but he can't help but be aware that he's been batting over three hundred for the past month. His teammates like him, nobody's booing him, and he's playing decent baseball. This is everything he wanted in those first horrible weeks after getting traded, but now that he has it, all he wants to do is use an entire roll of nickels to call Mark and complain about the horrible detective story he read on the airplane.

After a ten-inning game against the Dodgers, which the Robins win by a single run, Eddie gets on a plane for Omaha. Or, rather, he gets on a jet to Chicago and then two separate propeller planes to Omaha. It takes fifteen hours. He could probably have gotten to the South Pole faster. By the time he makes his way down the stairs to the landing strip, he's ready to punch the next airplane he sees.

"I think you're crazy," his mother says when she picks him up at the airfield. "Traveling all this way and then having to do it again the day after tomorrow. Not that I'm not glad to see you, honey."

Eddie doesn't point out that she's the hypocrite who drove seven hours in a 1952 Plymouth station wagon to have dinner with him just a few weeks earlier. But he wanted to see his mom, and he didn't want to spend his time off in the same city as Mark while he's still under Mark's weird telephone call ban. If he thinks too hard about it, he starts to feel insulted that Mark apparently thinks two weeks apart will be all it takes for Eddie to forget about him.

He has a decent time, though. His stepdad grills too many steaks and makes a pitcher of whiskey sours, Jack drives in from Kansas City, and the cats go into hiding, their presence only occasionally making itself known as pairs of spooky eyeballs barely visible in cabinets and closets. The whiskey's gone to his head: He already knew this wasn't his home anymore, but if the cats don't even recognize him, then he's really out of luck. There's no coming back from that. The trouble is that if this isn't his home, then what is? It's sure as shit not his hotel in New York.

"I wish I were on an American League team so I'd see you at least a couple times a season," Eddie tells Jack. This is mighty sappy of him. He would never have admitted such a thing last year, but now that he's accumulated a wealth of other things he shouldn't say, this particular truth doesn't seem so bad.

Jack grins at him. "Doesn't look like you're hurting for company."

Eddie frowns, not sure what Jack's getting at.

"I've seen pictures of you out and about with Tony Ardolino," Jack says. "Good for you. I'm glad you have girlfriends. You were always so shy."

Eddie knows he's drunk, but it takes him a few tries to parse what Jack's saying. Back in Kansas City, Jack worked so hard to keep the other guys from teasing Eddie that Eddie sometimes wondered if maybe Jack knew about him, or at least suspected. Now he searches Jack's face for any sign the other man is speaking in euphemisms or reciting the story that they're all supposed to pretend is true. But no, Jack seems genuinely happy for him. Eddie probably ought to be relieved. Maybe he's better at keeping secrets than he thought.

"Don't believe everything you see."

"Okay," Jack says, still grinning at him. "The next time I open up a magazine and see a picture of you with a beautiful woman hanging off your arm, I'll assume it's an optical illusion. Or Robins propaganda."

Eddie doesn't know why he's so disoriented to learn that Jack had no idea. Or maybe Jack did suspect, and now he's reassured to have his suspicions put to rest. Either way, the man Eddie's considered his closest friend since they were in the minors doesn't know that Eddie likes men, and Eddie will never tell him.

Last year it hadn't even occurred to Eddie that he wanted Jack to know. No, that isn't even true—if given a choice, Eddie would have begged for Jack never to find out. But that's because the extent of what he was keeping from Jack was that he wasn't interested in women and occasionally had sex with men. That hadn't seemed like a big secret to keep from a friend. But if he has someone like Mark—a person to share his life with, a person he cares about—then keeping that person a secret might be a barrier to friendship.

He thinks of Mark having to keep his own private life a secret for years. It's the kind of secret that seals a person off from everyone around them. Eddie's heart breaks a little for him.

Right now Mark is all Eddie wants to talk about. Mark is the most important thing that's happening in Eddie's life, even if Mark is being ridiculous and insulting about it. Maybe there are some facts that are essential to who he is, and keeping them back means a person can't really know him.

And maybe it would be like that even without a Mark in his life. Maybe the fact of his liking men is itself important enough that you can't know him without knowing that. Until now, he thought of being queer as something both dangerous and trivial, something that he kept to one corner of life, safely contained, like an embarrassing health condition. But now that truth seems to have seeped out into everything else, and he doesn't see how he can possibly be known without that essential fact.

He understands why Mark doesn't want to hide. It's not just the burden of continually lying, it's keeping your existence a secret. When the world has decided that people are supposed to be a certain way, but you're living proof to the contrary, then hiding your differences is just helping everybody else erase who you are.

And that's exactly what Eddie's going to do for as long as he's playing baseball. He's going to let himself be erased—and Mark along with him, if Mark lets Eddie stick around. Eddie feels queasy with shame at asking Mark to do that again. But that isn't what Mark seemed worried about when announcing his stupid two-week phone call ban—he'd seemed mostly worried about Eddie. The difference matters—it gives Eddie space to come up with a solution, if he can think of one.

Jack leaves early in the morning, and while Eddie's watching the truck disappear down the road, his mother comes up behind him. "You don't seem all right," she says. It's not a question; there's no room in her voice for argument.

And, well, he has his hands shoved in his pockets, and he's frowning off into the sunrise, so yeah, Eddie's pretty much telegraphing his not-all-rightness. Maybe he wanted his mom to ask. Maybe he just needs someone to know.

"You remember Mark Bailey?" he asks, still looking out the screen door.

"How could I forget?"

"I think he doesn't want to see me anymore."

She hugs him, just like he knew she would. She's still in her nightgown and fluffy bathrobe, and he clings to the softness for a minute.

"I'm sorry, baby," she says.

He pulls back to look at her. If she's uncomfortable about this, he wants to know. He knows, he *knows* that she'll love him no matter what, but she might only love him *despite* this—she might love him but in a way where her affection skips over this thing that she doesn't care for. She might ask him never to talk about this again, might ask him to erase that part of him for her, and he knows he'd do it.

She looks like she's steeling herself for something and his heart starts to break. He gets ready to be disappointed.

"Is he not, well. What's the word we're going to use? Interested in . . ." She gestures pointedly at him.

It takes a few seconds for him to understand that she's asking if the problem is that Mark is straight. He almost laughs with relief. "He's afraid it'll ruin my career if it gets out."

"He's got a point."

"I know he does."

"He cares about you." She's seen them together, after all.

"Yeah." Eddie's pretty sure it's pushing the envelope to actually ask his mom for advice, but he's going to do it anyway. "He told me not to call him for two weeks. He's hoping I come to my senses."

"Why in heaven's name can't you just keep things behind closed doors?" she blurts out. "What on *earth* do you want to do in public with this man?"

"A lot of people know about him, so he's worried that just going out to dinner will be enough to get rumors going."

"Now hold on," his mother says. "He gets to be as honest as he pleases, bless him, but he expects you to live a double life? Or does he expect you to just be lonely? What exactly does this man want you to do, honey?"

"It's more that he doesn't want to be the one to make trouble for me. I can't really blame him for that."

"I'm sure we can blame him for something if we really put our minds to it," his mom offers, but instead Eddie spends the morning telling her about Lula, about Mark helping the rookie buy suits, about the dumbest shit that could not possibly interest anyone but a mother, and she doesn't falter, not once.

There are storms over Illinois, so Eddie winds up spending the night in a hard-backed chair at an airfield in Cedar Rapids. In the morning, stiff and bleary-eyed, he gets on the first flight to Chicago, and from there takes a jet to New York. It's two o'clock before he lands, and he barely manages to get to the ballpark for the first pitch. He's pretty sure he could have driven back from Omaha in less time and with a hell of a lot less lower-back pain.

Even as he's scrambling into his uniform, he knows this game is going to be rotten. He's already forgiven himself for inevitably striking out and, maybe, for yelling a little at the umpire. There will definitely be ill-advised cursing today. Even under the best conditions, Eddie doesn't always make the most prudent decisions. On effectively zero hours of sleep, he's a wad of bad ideas rolled into the approximate shape and size of a professional baseball player.

Ardolino looks at him and recoils. "Do you have the flu? You're not playing if you have the flu. Go home and don't breathe on me."

"No sleep," Eddie says. "Airplanes."

Ardolino apparently knows how to make sense of this, because he nods knowingly and claps Eddie on the shoulder.

When Eddie manages to hit a triple in the fourth inning, he's a little annoyed—partly because running is about the last thing he wants to do with his poor, weary body, and partly because a man feeling this decrepit simply should not be able to hit a triple. In the month of June, he could not have gotten a base hit if the fate of the free world depended on it, and he was in fighting form that whole time. Now his bones are held together by spit and rubber bands, he's about two seconds away from falling asleep in the dugout, and he hits a goddamn triple? The illogic of it is killing him.

He was already annoyed by the utter lack of reason for his batting slump, and now he's annoyed by the lack of reason for this triple. When, later in the game, he hits a stand-up double, he's even more pissed off.

"Baseball is not a game that makes sense, my friend," Ardolino says after the game, clapping him on the shoulder. "It has never made sense, and it never will."

"It fucking should."

"Is this baby's first time experiencing things that don't make sense?" Price asks, his face a mask of faux sympathy even as he hands Eddie a beer. "Baby's first injustice?"

Eddie showers, and when reporters start talking to him, he says maybe a little more than he should about Midwestern airports and propeller planes and the shameful lack of sense in this game.

He collects the rookie before Varga and Rosenthal get any bright ideas about letting him tag along on their nightly debaucheries and drags him back to the hotel. Eddie sleeps for twelve hours, and when he wakes up, he's still in a shitty mood, cranky before he even opens his eyes. Technically, he could call Mark; the two-week phone ban expires today. But if he does that, he's going to say a lot of things that don't need saying, and there's every chance that Mark will repeat the same infuriating nonsense he said the last time they talked, and then Eddie might cry.

The hotel room smells of mildew. Spending so much time in hotel rooms, he more or less stopped noticing, but now, after some time away, he's smelling it again. He's got to get out of here. This is really no way to live. He wants—he wants not to have to be one person in all the hotels and stadiums he bounces between, and some other marginally realer person only in islands of dark and quiet. That's not possible, but having a place to hang up his clothes might be a start.

In the morning, he goes to the stadium, warms up, and hits a single and a double off the Pirates. The Robins win by three runs.

After the game, one of the reporters—not Mark, of course not Mark—asks him if he thinks he's got his swing back.

"No," Eddie says. "But I think I have somebody else's swing, and it's working out fine. I just hope they don't want it back." He's only half joking—the swing he's using doesn't feel natural; it feels like a car he hot-wired and sped away in, the tires peeling on the pavement—but everyone laughs and writes it down. Every time he swings the bat, he's fighting something. It feels like when he yells at umpires, or when someone slams a door in the middle of a fight. It's satisfying in a visceral, kind of nasty way, and he likes it. This is probably how boxers feel.

Last year—and all the years before it, ever since Little League— batting felt almost peaceful. Not effortless—God knows it wasn't effortless—but natural. But there's nothing natural or peaceful about hitting a projectile that's coming at you at nearly a hundred miles an hour. There's a violence that baseball, at its best, disguises in a way that other sports leave out in the open. Baseball has a way of looking like fun even when it's grueling. Eddie thinks that he had to get to the root of the ugliness in order to play the game again. He had to see it for what it is. Maybe he had to find something to fight.

He has the sense not to tell this to the press, but he wishes he could tell Mark.

When he's dressed, he finds Ardolino at Price's stall.

"If a person wanted to go to Greenwich Village, why might they want to do that?"

"Want to repeat that in English, slugger?" Ardolino asks.

What Eddie wants is an excuse to go to the Village. Last month, Varga and one of the relief pitchers asked Eddie if he wanted to come along and listen to someone play the trombone at a Village night-club. Eddie made an excuse, because he had mentally cordoned off that whole neighborhood as out-of-bounds, even if it couldn't *only* be a place for queer people if Varga was going. But now he wants to see for himself. It's stupid—he shouldn't need visual proof that there are people like him. And it isn't like he's going to pick anyone up. He just wants to look, that's all. He can't very well tell Ardolino that he wants to reassure himself that queer people exist. "What's there to do in Greenwich Village?" he tries.

Ardolino blinks at him.

"Jesus wept," Price mutters.

"Hey, Rosenthal," Ardolino shouts across the locker room. "What's the name of that place where you made me listen to men with beards playing jazz?"

Ardolino writes down whatever Rosenthal says, then conducts a silent conversation with Price. Finally Ardolino sighs. "I'll go as your chaperone."

Eddie's alarmed. "I don't need a—"

"Like hell you don't."

~

They take a cab, because Ardolino's knees can't handle subway stairs and his budget covers cab rides even with an ever-increasing number of ex-wives receiving alimony checks. The driver lets them out on what looks like a pretty unremarkable city block. It's not that different from the part of the city where the stadium is. Hell, it's not that different from some of downtown Omaha, not that he's dumb enough to tell that to Ardolino or anybody else. The streets are mostly lined with low buildings. At street level are barber shops, laundries, restaurants, and all the usual storefronts.

After a few minutes, Eddie starts to pick out differences. There are more people out than he might expect in Washington Heights—or Omaha, for that matter—even though it's past ten o'clock. He can hear live music coming from a nearby basement, and that's absolutely grass he's smelling. There's nothing overtly queer, but it doesn't take a lot of imagination for Eddie to believe that one of the bars or restaurants might be the sort of place with a bartender who doesn't ask questions, a place with a shadowy back room, a place of the sort he had relied on back home.

He isn't looking for that kind of place tonight. First, he just doesn't have enough privacy as a halfway famous person in this city, and second, he really doesn't want anyone to touch him but Mark. He doesn't see either of those facts changing anytime soon.

"Keep moving," Ardolino mutters, elbowing him in the ribs. "Don't gawk like some kind of hayseed." Eddie doesn't point out that he's pretty sure he is some kind of hayseed.

The jazz club is closed, but there's a restaurant across the street, one with a few tables on the sidewalk.

"I'm sitting there and getting a coffee," Ardolino says. "Do you want to take a walk around the block, and come meet me back here in twenty minutes?" He sounds like Eddie's mom letting him go off on his own in Woolworth's when Eddie was seven years old.

"Thanks, Dad," Eddie says.

"The blocks aren't rectangles in this part of the city. You have to pay attention. This is Seventh Avenue." He points in one direction. "That's Greenwich Avenue." And then he points in the opposite direction. "And that's West Fourth Street. Do you need me to write that down?"

Eddie gives him the finger and walks off.

"Twenty minutes!" Ardolino calls after him.

Eddie may not have any kind of grasp on Manhattan geography, but what he does have is eyes in his head, and he can tell right away that the streets aren't meeting at right angles, and not a single one of them seems to be running parallel to the rest of the grid he's halfway memorized. Still, Greenwich Avenue is clearly the main thoroughfare, so that's where he turns.

There are bars and restaurants, as well as more coffee shops than he would have thought any neighborhood could possibly need. He tries not to look at anyone too closely—he's just a tourist, taking in the sights. But he knows what he's looking for, and soon enough he finds it: a woman lights another woman's cigarette, a man in a snug white T-shirt looks over his shoulder at another man, and when a bar door opens, letting out a burst of music, there's the briefest glimpse of a man wearing what might be lipstick.

There are other people, too—little old ladies with scarves tied under their chins, a man pacing up and down the street carrying a fussy baby, a couple of old men playing dominoes on a stoop, their game lit by streetlight. It's not that different from Mark's neighborhood, only busier, louder, and with a lower percentage of millionaires.

Eddie keeps getting turned around by the crooked streets, but he can find his way back to Greenwich Avenue just by looking for the people. On one of his trips up the side streets, he sees a tiny, nearly invisible street leading off it. If there's a sign, he can't see it in the dark. It may not be a street at all, since it's too narrow for any but the smallest car. The mouth of the lane is bracketed by a bookstore that's closed for the night and a sleepy restaurant. There's a gate across the opening, but it's slightly ajar, and Eddie's never been much of a rule follower, so he slips in.

Immediately, Eddie notices the quiet. The murmur of traffic, music, and conversation drops away. It's a dead end, nothing more than a narrow lane ending with a brick wall and lined with two-story buildings. Across the street is a big, weird gingerbread castle, its windows dark, the place clearly a municipal building that's long been abandoned. Next to it is the hulking mass of what he thinks is a prison, with hardly any windows on this side. This is probably a great place to get mugged—there wouldn't be any witnesses.

Or—someone who's halfway famous could come and go from this place without too many people noticing him or who he's with. When he sees a handwritten FOR RENT sign pasted in a window, he takes out a scrap of paper and the tiny gold pencil from Mark's key holder and scribbles down the phone number.

When he gets back to the café, he finds Ardolino talking to an aproned waiter. Eddie hangs back. The waiter is smiling, and so is Ardolino. Generally speaking, smiling is not something Tony Ardolino's face does. It used to—he was smiling broadly on that rookie baseball card that's still at Eddie's mother's house. On special occasions, Ardolino will allow his mouth to curve in a somewhat upward direction at something Price says.

The waiter must be a fan. Ardolino is still one of the most recognizable people in baseball. And, in fact, the waiter hands a piece of paper to Ardolino, probably looking for an autograph. But Ardolino doesn't sign it. He grins again, then shakes his head and hands the paper back without even reading whatever's on it.

Eddie approaches, and the waiter slips away.

"Did you get kidnapped?" Ardolino asks, the smile disappearing back to wherever he keeps it.

"I got here on time. I just didn't want to interrupt you and the waiter," Eddie says, the words out of his mouth before he can think twice.

"Look, I'm not going to complain if someone thinks I'm handsome," Ardolino says, as if that's a good enough explanation, as if men haven't literally been killed for less. "Can't blame a man for having good taste. Price, too."

"Price has good taste?" Eddie asks, taken aback.

Ardolino gets to his feet and smacks Eddie on the side of the head. "He doesn't mind about that sort of thing. We've both played with guys like that. It happens."

Eddie doesn't dare turn his head to look at Ardolino. He doesn't want to know if that was pointed information being sent his way or just an offhand remark, or even advice for Eddie not to be a bigot. He doesn't know what he wants it to have meant.

CHAPTER TWENTY-SEVEN

The next morning Eddie wakes up at the godawful hour of six o'clock, as if his subconscious wants him to walk Lula. That's only fair, since the rest of his brain also wants to walk Lula—he really misses that dog. But now he has half a day to kill before he needs to be at the stadium, a full six hours to fill up with bad choices.

Maybe it isn't a bad choice so much as a half-assed one. He keeps thinking that when he talks to Mark, he ought to have a plan, a solution, something to put Mark's mind at ease. He doesn't know how it would work, with both of them feeling guilty—Mark about putting Eddie at risk; Eddie about asking Mark to be more of a secret than he wants to be. All he has is the knowledge that he loves Mark and the near certainty that Mark feels the same way. He puts his token in the slot and takes the subway downtown.

When he passes a pay phone, he remembers to call Mark, but the line is busy. When he gets to Mark's building, he walks around the block and tries again, but it's still busy. Well, he supposes, at least that means Mark is home.

The doorman calls up, and a moment later Eddie is being waved along to the elevator. This, he decides, has to be an excellent sign, until he realizes that Mark would hardly make the doorman do the dirty work of sending Eddie away. That would make the doorman's life difficult, and Mark, for all his fussiness, seldom makes trouble for anyone but himself.

Only when he's walking down the corridor and raising his hand to knock on Mark's door does he experience anything like true misgivings, but by then he's almost done the stupid thing, so he may as well go through with it. That, actually, is how most of his bad ideas play out.

The door opens, and at first Eddie thinks he must have the wrong apartment. He pulls back to check the number on the door, and, no, this is definitely Mark's apartment, but it's George Allen standing in the doorway.

"Uh-oh," Eddie says, like a fool.

George raises his eyebrows. "Mark's out for a minute. He didn't say he was expecting you."

"He wasn't. It's, uh, a surprise?"

Lula, meanwhile, is losing her mind: twirling in circles, dancing on her hind legs, whimpering pitiably. He picks her up and lets her lick his face, because that's obviously what she wants, and Eddie is not a man to deny a dog anything. "I don't care what Mark says," he tells her. "I refuse to believe you have germs."

George is watching all this speculatively. He's wearing house slippers and a cardigan, which strikes Eddie as odd, almost as odd as George being in Mark's apartment in the first place, but he's more focused on wondering whether the fact that Mark's dog knows him is, in some way, incriminating.

"Make yourself at home," George says expansively, but with a note of broad irony that makes Eddie think he maybe shouldn't help himself to a glass of juice or a slice of the coffee cake he sees through the kitchen doorway. Instead he sits on the couch and scratches behind Lula's ears while she thumps her foot happily against the cushion. George disappears down the hallway toward the dining room.

When Eddie hears George's voice again, he realizes that George must be on the phone. Eddie hadn't realized Mark had an extension in another room. "That's not what Klein said. No, I already told you. I'm writing the story the way I write the story."

When the front door opens, Mark doesn't notice Eddie at first. He looks good. He always looks good, to be fair, but after not seeing him for two weeks, all the things that go into Mark looking the way he does stand out in sharp relief. His hair is coal-dark against the paleness of his skin, and even from across the room his eyes are startlingly blue. His cheekbones and his jaw look both delicate and sharp. He's wearing what Eddie recognizes as Mark's idea of casual clothes: cotton slacks, loafers, a sky-blue oxford with the sleeves rolled up to the precise middle of his forearms.

"You've got company!" George shouts from down the hall.

Mark scans the living room and visibly startles when he sees Eddie.

"Sorry," Eddie says. "I called, but the line was busy. And I really—" He can't say that he really wanted to see Mark, but he supposes that much is obvious from the fact that he's sitting on Mark's sofa.

Mark shifts a paper sack of groceries from one hip to the other, regarding Eddie with an unreadable expression. He disappears into the kitchen and comes back a minute later without the groceries. "I need to walk Lula."

At first, Eddie doesn't get it. Is this Mark's way of getting rid of him? Or is Eddie supposed to stay here while Mark walks the dog? Then Mark jerks his chin toward the door. "Want to come with me?" he asks pointedly.

"Yeah, sure," Eddie says, probably too enthusiastically.

"What are you doing here?" Mark asks once they're on the sidewalk.

"I missed you."

Mark sighs, all put-upon, as if Eddie wanting to see him is the most exhausting thing in the world.

"And you probably missed me, too," Eddie adds.

"That's not the point," Mark says, which is true enough.

"Did you really think that two weeks was going to do anything? Do you really think I'm so dumb that I don't know what I'm feeling?" Eddie's trying not to sound frustrated, and it isn't working. "Or do you think I'm some kind of genius who was going to be able to solve our problems in two weeks? Because either way, Mark, you don't know me at all."

Eddie knows the route of Lula's walk, so he's surprised when Mark turns toward the park entrance and unlocks the gate. It's the middle of a weekday morning, and the only people here are a couple of mothers with kids who are too young for school and an old woman knitting something out of white yarn. They have no trouble finding an empty bench out of earshot of anyone else.

"I didn't think either of those things. I just thought that if you realized you didn't really want to be with me, then we wouldn't have a problem anymore. Or, well, you wouldn't, at least." And that's Mark, only putting his affection in the gaps.

The trees were heavy with bright green leaves the last time Eddie visited this park; now yellow and brown fleck the treetops. "It's been months. I know what I feel. And—not to be insulting—but I think I know what you feel, too, because if you didn't want me here, you wouldn't have me here. I don't know how it'll work, and I don't have a plan, but what I do know is that I want to do it anyway."

Mark doesn't say anything for a while. "George asks about you every day."

Eddie hadn't expected any kind of straightforward sense from Mark, but he also hadn't expected to hear that George Allen is asking about him, so he takes the bait.

"What's George doing at your apartment anyway? I'm surprised he's not still in the hospital."

"He's staying with me for a while. He's on his feet, but he can't really do much for himself yet."

"My grandpa was in the hospital for months after his heart attack, and he was younger than George." Eddie doesn't add that his grandfather had died anyway.

"He knows it's probably safer to just stay in the hospital until—whatever. He knows. But he likes his job, and he wants to keep doing it."

"Are you going to be okay?" Eddie asks. "I mean, if something happens to him." He hopes he's not making a mess of this. "You lost someone not long ago. Are you going to be okay when—if—he . . . you know."

"George knows he's probably at the end, and he knows how he wants to spend his time. I want to help him with that. Not everybody gets to wrap things up on their own terms."

"Well, it's nice of you," Eddie says, even though *nice* hardly covers it.

Mark sniffs, because he can never take hearing that he might be kind. "It really isn't. He's good company. Besides, I partly invited him so I couldn't cave in and ask you to come over. So, no, it's not nice at all."

Eddie knocks his shoulder into Mark's. "Sure it is. That just means you were trying to be good to me." Mark makes a disgusted noise. "Besides, your plan's shot to hell, because George probably put two and two together, what with me showing up and being Lula's best friend."

He expects Mark to be annoyed—justifiably annoyed. But Mark starts laughing. "Oh my God. There's one person in the world who knows, and it's a man with one of the most widely read sports columns in the country."

"Actually, it's two people."

"You mean Lilian? If we're counting people I've told, then it's up to four."

Eddie didn't even know that Mark *had* four people, but he's positive that Mark telling *anyone* is a good sign.

"I took you at your word," Mark goes on, evidently mistaking Eddie's silence for reproach.

"I'm so glad you did," Eddie says. "I told my mom. But she doesn't have a newspaper column, so she barely counts."

Something happens to Mark's face. It's some awful mixture of sympathy and dread and guilt, and Eddie never wants to see it there again. Lula stops sniffing the trash can and lets out a growl, like she's ready to attack whoever's bothering Mark.

"No, Mark, no, it was fine. She's fine. She says hi, okay?"

"Why would you do that?"

"I needed to know. I needed to know if it would change anything. I knew she wouldn't hate me or stop talking to me—"

"You didn't. You couldn't. Nobody knows that in advance."

Eddie isn't sure it's possible to explain unconditional parental love to someone who may never have received it, and maybe Mark's right, maybe it could have gone wrong. "I was as sure of her as I could be of anything. Anyway, that wasn't what I was worried about."

"It should have been."

"What I was worried about was whether she would hate that part of me. Or be disgusted by that part of me."

Mark's turned ninety degrees on the bench, facing Eddie, his expression unreadable. "And was she?"

"No."

"You're lucky." Mark says this with an edge of rebuke in his voice, like you might address a child who ran into traffic and narrowly escaped disaster.

"I know, Mark," Eddie says gently. "I know."

"It could have blown up in your face."

"I know. But I had to. Everything between her and me would have been worthless if she couldn't accept that. Don't you see? You've told me yourself how much you hate keeping secrets."

"Yes, well, that's me. I want *you* to be safe!" Mark gets to his feet and glares down at Eddie. Eddie grins up at him, hearing the fondness mixed in with the anger.

"Yeah, my mom had a couple choice words about that particular hypocrisy."

"Oh my God, she's as silly as you are." Mark strides off in the direction of a garbage can that Lula's straining to reach, and Eddie follows.

"Did you really tell her about me?" Mark asks a few minutes later, after letting Eddie ramble a bit about this movie with talking, flesh-eating plants he saw with Rosenthal and Varga in Los Angeles.

"My mom?" Eddie laughs, remembering how he had talked his mother's ear off about Mark. "Yeah, Mark, I sure did."

Mark goes quiet, and it takes Eddie a minute to register that this is a pleased quiet, not a grumpy quiet. He wants to say that it's nothing, of course he told his mom. But there's no *of course* about it for Mark, is there? He remembers how Mark had looked back in that hotel room in St. Louis when he'd asked whether he could tell Lilian about them. At the time, Eddie thought Mark had the same expression that guys get when they're about to ask to borrow an awful lot of money—conscious that they're imposing and a little ashamed about it. He supposes that's how Mark *would* feel about it after the life he's led.

"I told her that you made a really half-assed attempt to break my heart," Eddie says, "but that I'm not having any of it."

Two days later, Eddie calls Mark first thing in the morning. "Do you have an hour or two?" Eddie asks. "There's something I want your opinion on."

"What kind of something?"

"You'll see. I'll be at your place in a cab in half an hour."

When Mark gets into the cab, he slides Eddie a suspicious look but doesn't ask any questions. Eddie's already given the address of their destination to the cabbie, so Mark can only look out the window as the cab turns onto Fourteenth Street.

"This is close enough," Eddie says when they're stopped at a red light at Sixth Avenue. "We can walk the rest of the way."

A few minutes later, Eddie's pushing open the gate and knocking on a door bearing a brass *2*.

"She said that if nobody answered, I should let myself in." As promised, underneath the doormat is a key.

"It needs a coat of paint," Eddie says when he opens the apartment door for Mark. "And the rooms are tiny. But it's not bad. At least I think it isn't, but I want your opinion before I sign the lease."

The previous morning, Eddie thought this apartment was perfect. It's small but bright, tucked into a corner of the city that most people will never find. It's like something out of a storybook, like he went around a corner and discovered himself in another world.

But now, he tries to view it through Mark's critical eye. There are bricks missing from both fireplaces. The kitchen is cramped. The wood floors are scuffed. Through the open window, he can hear children playing loudly at a nearby playground.

"What's the rent?" Mark asks.

"$160 a month."

"You could get something for half as much up by the stadium. And it'll take you forever to get to the stadium."

"It's a little over half an hour on the Seventh Avenue line. I tried it yesterday." He's thought it through. He even talked it over with his mother. "I figure there are plenty of subway lines around here, so if the city ever gets around to building a new stadium, I'll be able to get there from here without too much hassle, wherever it is." He doesn't add that it's only a twenty-minute walk from Mark's apartment, a distance that Lula could easily make.

Mark goes through the apartment, opening the door to one bedroom and then the other. The larger of the two is scarcely bigger than Mark's maid storage room, but Eddie measured and it'll fit a double bed and a couple of nightstands. The smaller bedroom is just about big enough for a desk and chair.

"But why this neighborhood?" Mark asks as he inspects the kitchen cabinets.

"I came here the other night because I wanted to—never mind, it sounds stupid. The point is that I wandered in here—"

"Tell me the stupid part."

"I wanted to be around queer people," Eddie says, his face heating. "I know I can't really be a part of all that, not now, at least. But I needed to feel like I wasn't alone." Mark doesn't say anything, but he's obviously paying attention—no cabinet can be that interesting—so Eddie goes on. "I've been thinking about what you said about hiding, and how nobody can really know you if you're hiding a part of yourself—"

Mark spins around to face him. "I never said that."

Eddie's pretty sure that he did, actually, or at least that he strongly implied it, but now isn't the time. "Well, I said it, then. Even if nobody here knows I'm queer, maybe I don't have to hide it from them. Maybe when I walk down the street, people won't automatically assume I'm something I'm not. I won't be pretending." He rubs the back of his neck. "It's not enough, but it's something."

Mark's lips are pressed together into a tight line, and he's looking at Eddie with an awful sort of sympathy. He knows how Eddie feels—of *course* he does. "I'm sorry that this isn't easier for you. I wish—"

Eddie, to his mortification, feels his eyes get hot. He holds up his hand to stop Mark, knowing that if Mark says one more gentle word that'll be the end of Eddie's weak grip on composure.

Mark crosses the room in two strides, and for a moment Eddie thinks he's going to hug him, which will be awful, because then Eddie really will cry. But instead Mark kisses him, hard and almost angry. It's nothing like any kiss they've shared before. It isn't careful and it isn't kind, and the only heat in it is fury. Eddie has no idea what it means, but he wraps his arms around Mark and kisses him back.

Finally Mark pulls away and stares at Eddie, a little out of breath, his mouth red and wet.

"I want you," Mark says, angry and ragged, fondness always shored up by something bracing.

Eddie wants to ask what Mark's going to do about it, even if it might give Mark a chance to talk himself out of doing what he wants, but then he realizes that this *is* what Mark's going to do about it.

Eddie likes things to be settled, quantifiable, definitive; he makes a living playing a game where fans use statistics for fun. He wants to know what formula to use, like if he divides the number of times Mark has casually touched his arm in the past half hour by the number of times Mark's frowned at him, he'll know whether this is going to work out. Maybe he just wants to hear, from Mark's mouth, that they're together. But maybe Mark knows something that Eddie doesn't—that saying something isn't the same as actually doing it. And right now, in this empty apartment, Mark is doing it.

They stand there for a moment, both a little out of breath, the truth hanging there, fragile but undeniable. Mark steps back and clears his throat.

"It's not hypocrisy," Mark says. "Me wanting you to be safe, but also wanting to be open myself. I don't know what it is, and I know it doesn't make sense, but it's not hypocrisy."

Eddie's pretty sure it's the definition of hypocrisy, but that it's rooted in the same kind of concern that makes his mom scold him for smoking all of two cigarettes a year. He's going to let Mark love him however he needs to. "This place is very private. I don't think you could find anywhere more private on this entire island."

Mark's eyes go a little wide, like maybe he understands this isn't just about real estate. "It's charming," he says, gesturing at the room around them but not taking his eyes off Eddie. "You should take it."

The landlady shows up a few minutes later, flustered and with tales to tell of stolen hubcaps and the city going to hell in a handbasket. Eddie signs papers and writes a check while Mark pokes around the apartment some more.

"Did you want to get some lunch?" Eddie asks when they've hailed a cab.

"I have to make lunch for George," Mark says, which doesn't answer Eddie's question. "Do you think you can come upstairs?" He sounds genuinely uncertain.

"George already knows we're friends," Eddie says. "Another couple minutes isn't going to tell him anything new. And if he's figured out about us, then lunch isn't going to make it worse. Besides, I don't think he's going to make trouble."

"You're too trusting."

Eddie shrugs. Mark's not wrong. But if Eddie wants to navigate a path that avoids both the dangers of openness and the restrictions of secrecy, he's going to have to take some risks, and this is a risk he feels comfortable with. "I think that's one of the things you like about me."

Mark looks away quickly, so Eddie bets he got that right.

"Anyway, want to pick up sandwiches and get one for George?"

Mark stuns Eddie by reporting that he has food in his refrigerator and intentions to cook it. And, sure enough, when they get to Mark's apartment and Eddie demands to see this sight with his own eyes, he finds a package wrapped in brown butcher paper in Mark's refrigerator and four potatoes sitting on the counter.

"George can't have too much sodium," Mark says as he unwraps the meat, revealing four chicken breasts. "So I've only been using a tiny bit of salt while cooking. If I don't put in any salt at all, he refuses to eat it, like Lula when I buy the wrong brand of dog food. And then if he doesn't eat what I cook, he has the delicatessen send over a sandwich, which is nothing but sodium."

As he speaks, he takes out a knife and trims some of the fat from the chicken with more deftness than Eddie expects. In fact, nothing could be more obvious than the fact that Mark's done this before, and not just for the week or so that George has been living here. With practiced motions, Mark cracks an egg into one bowl and scoops flour into another; into the second bowl he adds the tiniest pinch of salt and a few shakes of pepper.

"You can *cook*." Eddie feels like he's uncovered a deep, dark secret.

"I can't be bothered to cook for one."

With that one sentence, Eddie can see years of dinners cooked and shared, and then all of it taken away. He already knows that Mark must have grieved—must have *been* grieving, the whole time they've known one another—but this might be the first time Mark's *let* him know it. He's pretty sure Mark will crumble into dust if Eddie tries to say something kind, so Eddie just brushes Mark's shoulder with his own. "Do you have an apron?" he asks.

Mark glares at him—he's probably never gotten a stain on himself in his life—but there's something relieved behind the sharpness, like he was worried for a minute that Eddie was going to offer condolences.

"I mean for me," Eddie clarifies. "So I can help."

Mark points at a drawer, and Eddie retrieves a plain red cotton apron. Then he begins chopping potatoes.

Once the potatoes and chicken are sizzling on the stove, Eddie washes his hands. As long as Eddie can hear George nattering away on the telephone across the apartment, he knows the coast is clear, so he steps behind Mark, wrapping his arms around Mark's middle, and kisses his neck. "You're a good man."

"Take it back."

Eddie smiles against Mark's warm skin. "Never."

George doesn't look too surprised that Eddie's staying for lunch, and spends the meal complaining about the entire Robins front office.

Later, George takes a nap. Eddie does the dishes over Mark's protests, then kisses the edge of Mark's mouth when it's time to leave.

CHAPTER TWENTY-EIGHT

I could use your help," Mark says.

"Are you actually calling me?" Eddie asks, looking at the receiver in surprise. They've known one another for going on five months, and this is the first time Mark's called him. "Do you need to be bailed out of jail? Ransom money? Just say the word."

Mark sniffs. "You gave me your new number. Excuse me for putting it to good use."

Yesterday afternoon, Eddie had the phone line in his new apartment connected, and the first thing he did with it was call Mark. Currently, his apartment contains nothing but his new telephone, a mattress, and two suitcases. He doesn't even have hangers.

"George wants a couple things from his apartment, and I could use some muscle," Mark says.

Eddie says that of course he'll help, and Mark reads him an address. When Eddie gets there, Mark's waiting out front, reading a book, leaning against the building with his legs crossed at the ankle the way Eddie's seen him so many times.

Eddie has to make sure he isn't smiling too broadly. He has about a dozen questions that all boil down to: *Are we together now?* But he doesn't ask, because he's afraid that if Mark notices that they're really doing this, he might back off again. Instead he's just camped out in Mark's life, taking up space, showing Mark that there *is* space for him. For both of them.

"So what are we getting," Eddie asks when they're in the lobby.

It's a normal-looking apartment building, not so different from the place Ardolino rents or many of the other high-rise apartment buildings he passes on the street. It's probably where middle-class New Yorkers live—dentists and school principals and, apparently, syndicated columnists. It's an entire economic class away from whoever lives in Mark's building. "What did William do for a living?"

"What?" Mark asks, turning to him. "Twelve," he tells the elevator operator.

"His job?"

"He was a lawyer." The elevator opens and they get out. "For his family's business."

Eddie, who's seen the surname on the mail that still arrives at Mark's apartment, realizes that this is a family business in the same way that DuPont or Kellogg's is a family business, and all the secrecy makes a lot more sense.

"I don't mind you asking, you know," Mark says. "The only reason I don't talk about him is force of habit. And, well." He gestures back and forth between them. "I don't want to make things strange."

"I like when you tell me things."

That's apparently too much earnestness for the moment, because Mark briskly announces "Here we are!" and proceeds to unlock the door to what must be George's apartment.

The first thing Eddie notices is that this place is crowded. It's jammed full of stuff. There are photographs all over the walls, needlepoint cushions strewn across the furniture, ashtrays and clocks and coasters and little lace doilies. It looks like Eddie's grandparents' house, only scaled down. There are decades of living crammed into this apartment.

"What does George need?" Eddie asks, not quite able to imagine how they'll find anything.

"More clothes, some books, a couple other things. He had a suitcase with him when he had the heart attack, because he was on the way to the airport to travel to Pittsburgh with the team. But he's tired of wearing the same five things, and he's already read everything in my apartment that he considers worth reading. I have a list. You find some suitcases and I'll start on the books."

In the bedroom closet, a row of dresses hangs above dusty shoe-boxes, a couple of collared shirts shoved to the side of the rail. It's been two years since George's wife died, but then again, why should George have bothered to throw her things out? Those dresses aren't hurting anyone.

Eddie's seen every inch of Mark's apartment and knows that, barring a couple sweaters that are about three sizes too big, the only clothes there are Mark's. He imagines Mark packing up William's clothes, but then very deliberately leaving an entire bookcase full of history and law books.

"You find the suitcases?" Mark calls from the bedroom doorway. Eddie goes over and kisses him.

"What's that for?"

Eddie reaches out and adjusts Mark's glasses, which the kiss has made crooked. "What, I need a reason now?"

Half an hour later they've packed several changes of clothes and a suitcase full of books. Eddie peeks at Mark's list; everything is checked off. But extra clothes and something to read is what you'd pack for a road trip, not what Eddie would bring along to where he might be living out the rest of his days.

"Do you think we ought to bring some things he likes? Or the things he's used to?" Eddie asks, gesturing around. The apartment is full of stuff that somebody must have liked.

"Photographs, maybe?" Mark suggests.

"I think I saw some albums on the bookcase in the bedroom," Eddie says. "I'll go grab them." He comes back with four photograph albums and a framed picture of a middle-aged woman that was sitting on the nightstand.

Mark runs a finger along the silver frame. "Good idea." He glances around at the photographs on the walls. "Is there another empty suitcase?" Eddie watches as Mark plucks from the wall a framed black-and-white wedding portrait and a Kodachrome snapshot of a woman on vacation, a bright scarf tied under her chin. Then he snatches up a quilt from the sofa and a needlepoint cushion picturing a black-and-white cat.

Eddie goes into the kitchen and takes the coffee mug that's sitting upside down in the draining rack. Next to the stove is a recipe card box, the kind his mom has. He takes that, too.

"We ought to clean out the refrigerator," Eddie says.

They dump spoiled food into a bag and drop it into the trash chute in the hall. Eddie washes the dishes that were sitting in the sink. It's this bizarre funhouse mirror of domesticity, the inverse of housekeeping—they're taking a home apart so the bare bones of it can be reassembled somewhere else.

He remembers doing this with his mom after his grandmother died and his grandfather moved in with them. And then he remembers when his grandfather died and he and his mom carted all his old clothes to the secondhand store. It feels like breaking a taboo to think that someone's going to clear out this apartment when George dies. But that's the point, isn't it? That's why Mark's doing this. The only way George can spend the time he has left doing what he wants is by acknowledging that his time is finite.

"It doesn't feel like enough," Mark says. "I mean, if I were to move out of my apartment, I'd want . . ." His voice trails off, and Eddie is left wondering what, exactly, Mark would want. When you've built a home—when you've built a home *with someone*—how do you go about making a home somewhere else, without them? "Or maybe I wouldn't. Maybe there's something to be said for closing the door and starting fresh."

"My stepdad moved into the house my mom and I had lived in

with my dad," Eddie puts in. It's not the same, obviously—they had done that so Eddie wouldn't have to move. But eight years later, they're still there, and now it's definitely Eddie's stepdad's home, too. "I can't remember him bringing anything other than a record player and some books."

"How did your dad die?"

"Hit a tree on the way home from the bar," Eddie says, and then immediately feels guilty. "I don't remember him ever being drunk around me, even though he must have been. He was a good dad," he adds a little defensively.

Mark stops what he's doing and looks at him. "You have good memories?"

People say all kinds of things when they find out about his dad, but that one's new, and Eddie likes it. "Yeah. Honestly, all my memories of my dad are good." He doesn't know if he's forgotten the bad times—there must have been bad times—or if his parents just kept him sheltered, but he's not sure it matters. The fact of having had a father—however flawed—who loved him is probably built into Eddie.

He's worried this is all too morbid, but when he looks at Mark, there's a small smile on his face. There's also dust on his forehead, cat hair on his pants, and smudges all over his glasses.

"I really love you," Eddie says without exactly planning to. He half expects Mark to become extremely busy somewhere else in the apartment or to start a fight about why Eddie is wrong, but instead Mark's face goes a mottled red. "What, like that's news?" Eddie asks, trying not to laugh. But he hasn't actually told Mark before, not in so many words.

"It's not news," Mark says, scathing and fond, and starts filling an old milk crate with record albums.

The next day, Eddie shows up at Mark's apartment with a bag of groceries that, thanks to the rain, is about to fall apart. This time, he isn't showing up unannounced, because he called that morning and told George to expect him.

"What's all this?" Mark asks.

"I'm using your kitchen. I'm about to riot if I have one more restaurant meal, and I miss my ma's cheesy potatoes. There'll be enough for you and George to have some."

"Does your new apartment not have a kitchen?" Mark asks, waspish as ever.

"I haven't bought any pots or pans yet."

Mark stares at him, but Eddie just unpacks the groceries as if showing up at a friend's apartment to use their kitchen is perfectly normal.

"Help yourself," Mark finally says, with an eye roll that Eddie can practically hear. But he lingers in the kitchen as Eddie starts rummaging through cabinets on a quest for a cutting board and a big enough pot. "The pots are under the counter."

Eddie slices the potatoes, browns some ground beef for chili, then takes out another pot for the potatoes.

"I didn't know you could cook."

"I really can't," Eddie says. "I can only cook the kind of thing my mom would have me make when she was working late, and I had to start supper. Basic survival stuff."

"I'm watching you make a béchamel sauce, right in front of my eyes."

"If you say so."

"George is at the doctor. His niece is driving him. He won't be back until one."

"The food will take over an hour to cook anyway." Eddie pours canned tomatoes into the pot with the browned beef.

"I mean," Mark says pointedly, "we have two hours."

Eddie tries to bite back a smile, something that's never worked for him even once in his life. He sets the lid on the simmering chili and puts the potatoes in the oven. "Half an hour until I have to check these," he says. "So act snappy." He turns around, his arms folded across his chest.

Mark steps forward, looking annoyed and turned on, two things Eddie hadn't even known went together until he met Mark Bailey. Mark hooks a finger into Eddie's belt. "I'm not doing this in the kitchen." But he kisses Eddie anyway.

In the bedroom, Mark is impatient and testy, demanding that Eddie take his clothes off but not giving him enough space to even reach his buttons. He's clinging and cranky, and that's when it registers for Eddie that Mark missed him.

"You missed me," Eddie says, because it's not like he was going to be able to hold that back for more than two seconds anyway.

Mark glares at him.

"I missed you, too," Eddie says.

Mark glares harder, but is distracted long enough for Eddie to get rid of both their shirts. Mark prods him on to the bed, making impatient little noises. Eddies stretches out, crooking an arm behind his head and just enjoying the sight of Mark wanting him. It's full daylight, and the room's brighter than it's ever been when they've done this. He wants to memorize every detail—the chest hair that narrows before leading into the waistband of his pants, the pinkish brown of his nipples, the slight softness of his belly.

It's the first time since Eddie came back from Omaha, and he doesn't want to cook up a story about how this *means* something, but it does, at least to Eddie.

Eddie pulls Mark into the bed on top of him and then rolls them both over. He's noticed that Mark likes that, likes being— not pushed around, exactly, but likes feeling Eddie's strength. And

Eddie likes it, too, likes the way Mark goes quiet and pliable for a second. Likes, maybe, the suggestion that Mark trusts him.

Now he uses his body to cage Mark in, to pin him down a little. They're only kissing, rubbing up against one another a bit, just because they can. "Just like that," Mark says. "You're lovely." And Eddie goes molten.

He's pretty sure he could get off just from listening to Mark say things like that. He'd always kind of known he liked that, but he hadn't really had an opportunity to put it to the test. Mark figured it out, which is so embarrassing, but somehow being embarrassed makes it even better.

It's *some* compensation that he also knows what Mark likes: the moment Eddie shifts from being interested to being desperate, all the dumb shit Eddie says in bed, the way Eddie holds on tight after they're done.

"Love you," Eddie says, mostly to watch Mark turn red. He doesn't expect Mark to say it back—partly because it's extremely obvious that Mark does, and partly because Eddie's not sure it even matters.

"Can we . . ." Mark starts, the words disappearing into Eddie's jaw.

"Sure," Eddie says, not knowing what he's agreeing to and not particularly caring.

"Just—you said." Mark is barely audible. "If you still, I mean. Would you let me . . ."

Before Mark can tie himself up in knots, Eddie rolls onto his stomach. "That the idea?"

Mark skims a hand down Eddie's back, then kisses his neck. "I don't know what you like. I mean—not like this, at least."

"Oh, you know me," Eddie says airily. "I just care about quality."

Mark lets out a laugh that's really just a breath of air.

Eddie takes hold of Mark's wrist and tugs him forward so he's more or less sprawled on Eddie's back, then kisses the palm of Mark's hand. "Have you done this before?"

"Not a lot. Not often enough to feel like I know what I'm doing." He sounds annoyed and embarrassed, the words landing in Eddie's hair.

"You seem like you know what you're doing in the other, um, direction," Eddie says, his body warming as he remembers Mark whispering instructions and praise. "So maybe just do to me what you like done to you? And we can go from there?"

"Hmm," Mark says, like he's not sure about that.

"I want you to," Eddie says, and he's pretty sure the only reason his face heats is because he's catching some of Mark's bashfulness. "I've been thinking about it. A lot." He can feel Mark react to that, so he keeps going, murmuring details of fantasies and ideas and things he makes up on the spot, until he more or less goads Mark into getting the slick out of the nightstand drawer.

It's warm in the bedroom, even warmer with Mark pressed up behind him. Like this, they're so close they can't do much more than rock together.

"I love you," Eddie says, and Mark may not say it back, but Eddie can feel how he responds, the impossible yielding of his own body, a sound like a sigh.

Afterward, Eddie washes up, throws on some clothes, and stirs the chili. Mark's still in bed, and Eddie's happy to take the hint and get back in with him. On the way to the bedroom, he crosses through the dining room. On one side of the table is a sensible black typewriter and a disturbing confusion of paper. On the other is a mint green typewriter and a neat pile of typed pages with Mark's handwriting all over them. A telephone sits in the center of the table. It's like a minia-ture newsroom.

Eddie knows that Mark's revising his magazine feature, which is due any day now. He hasn't dared ask anything about it. He knows it's about the team, and that's bad enough. But now he glances at the papers on Mark's side of the table.

He picks up one of the pages without thinking, mainly because he likes to look at Mark's handwriting, likes everything about Mark to the point that it's worrying. The first thing he sees is his own name.

He flips through the rest. His name is everywhere, like it's been shaken out of a pepper mill and scattered over the papers. Worse, Tony Ardolino's name shows up even more frequently.

"What's taking you so long," Mark calls from the bedroom.

Eddie thinks about putting the papers back and pretending he never saw them. If what he and Mark are doing is too fragile to name, then it's definitely too fragile to talk about this.

Still. There's no way Eddie can get back into bed without know-ing. He goes to the bedroom door. "Whatever you're working on in the dining room. Is it for the magazine?"

Mark pulls the sheets up to his chest. "It's a draft."

"Mark. What exactly is this article about?"

Mark doesn't say anything, and Eddie's heart starts to race. "If you're trying to get rid of me by writing something that'll upset me, you know that's shitty, right? You know that embarrassing me in the press is pretty much my nightmare. I don't think you'd do that." He doesn't think Mark would deliberately hurt him, but Mark has spent the entire summer telling him that he's dangerously naive and too trusting.

Mark grabs his glasses off the nightstand and puts them on. "That's not what this is. I mean, at first I thought you'd see I wrote an article about your slump, and you'd be upset—because you would be, no matter now *nice* the article was—and that would be the end." He says *nice* like it's some new sin he just discovered.

Eddie swallows. "When did it stop being like that?"

"Pittsburgh," Mark says miserably. "Maybe Cincinnati."

So, around the time they started sleeping together. Mark had been planning an exit strategy before they started sleeping together, and abandoned it as soon as they did start sleeping together. "Really poor follow-through on your part," Eddie says. He sits on the edge of the bed and puts his hand on Mark's knee. "Why did it change?"

Mark glares at him, but at the same time tangles his fingers with Eddie's. "Why do you think? Look, the article is still about you, at least partly. But I don't think anything in it will upset you. I don't want it to upset you. I rather desperately want you to like it, which is one of several excellent reasons why I'll never write about you again. It goes to press in a few weeks, and then we can fight about other things, like normal people."

Eddie feels himself grinning at this vision of the future that Mark's evidently planning. "You thought you'd just slip that into conversation—"

Mark covers his face with the hand that isn't still holding Eddie's. "Shut up."

"And what about Tony? I saw his name a dozen times."

"More than that," Mark says. "Definitely more than that."

"Is he going to be upset?" A pit opens in Eddie's stomach at the idea that Tony might think Eddie talked to Mark about him.

Mark looks up. "Eddie, he knows. I interviewed him. I interviewed a bunch of people, entirely on the record."

"When?"

"Over the past few weeks."

"Can I read it?"

"No," Mark says immediately. "I mean, of course you can, but it's a draft. You can read it now, but it's an embarrassment, and I'll have to hide in the bathroom."

There's pink on Mark's cheeks. Eddie's rarely seen him this flustered. All at once, Eddie realizes—this isn't Mark being cagey because he feels guilty. It's Mark being cagey about feeling exposed. He's sure of it. He knows it in the same way he knows when Rosenthal needs second base covered: intuition, instinct, and lots of practice.

It's just like before, when Mark was prickly and cranky about getting Eddie's clothes off, and it turned out that what he wanted was something almost startlingly gentle. Eddie cracked the code in that hotel room in Cincinnati. When Eddie needs reassurance and affection, Mark gives it, wholeheartedly and without reservation. But when Mark needs it, he hisses and complains.

Eddie doesn't know what's in this article, but he knows Mark's feelings are all over it. He doesn't know how—the New York *Chronicle* may be a progressive paper, but it's not publishing gay love letters. Still, somehow Mark's written something very much like that.

"Oh," Eddie says. "Yeah?"

Mark looks like he wants to quarrel about it, but then just pulls him into bed, obviously thinking that sex will distract Eddie from pursuing this conversation. Mark is correct.

"God, you're sweet when you wanna be," Eddie whispers, then kisses Mark before he can protest.

Later, after they've made themselves presentable and cleaned up the kitchen, George comes home, accompanied by a middle-aged woman who fusses over him until he finally tells her to go home.

"I'll take you to the doctor myself the next time, if you like," Mark offers an exhausted-looking George.

"No, it makes her feel useful," George says. "It's my good deed for the day."

"You're a regular humanitarian," Eddie agrees, bringing George a bottle of ginger ale.

"Pour it into a glass!" Mark calls from the kitchen. "We have standards in this household."

George and Eddie shrug at one another, but Eddie gets out a pair of glasses.

Mark isn't doing much to stop George from jumping to conclusions. Eddie guesses that Mark is trying to see if Eddie's scared off—trying to see if Eddie runs away. He'd probably say that he's waiting for Eddie to come to his senses.

Mark pointedly sets the table for three, like he's daring Eddie to stay for lunch—which is mighty rich, seeing as how Eddie *made* lunch. If anyone's making a dare here, it's *Eddie*. But he remembers the rule: Mark's only prickly when he needs reassurance.

Eddie stays.

CHAPTER TWENTY-NINE

In the next day's doubleheader, Eddie gets a double and a home run in the first game and then a single and a triple in the second game. The Robins win both.

After, Eddie gets cornered by a scrum of reporters. He keeps repeating variations of the same line: his coaches and teammates have been working with him, and he's so grateful for their patience and for the support of the fans. That has the benefit of being true, at least, so he doesn't feel completely ridiculous saying it over and over again.

"Relieved," Eddie says, when a reporter asks how he feels. The home run could have been a fluke, but his other hits were solid line drives: a little scrappy, a little ugly, but they got the job done, and the ball did exactly what Eddie wanted it to do. They feel like the kind of hits he can replicate.

"Did you know that in the past three weeks you're batting four hundred?" asks a reporter.

Eddie did know that, because there will always be a running column of long division in the back of his mind, a calculator spitting out numbers without Eddie's input. He's trying to figure out how to answer honestly without looking like an egotist—*Why yes, thank you, I'm very aware of my success*—when another reporter chimes in with his own question.

"Did you know that if you only look at the past month, you're leading the league in triples? And that nobody in the teams you've faced has hit a triple?"

Those two statistics take Eddie by surprise, mainly because who the hell counts triples. "You mean in the past month nobody's got a triple against us?" Eddie asks.

"I mean nobody has ever scored a triple when you're on the field," the reporter clarifies. "Not in the two seasons you've played in the major league."

"That's got to be the weirdest stat I've ever heard," Eddie says. "Who's tracking this?"

It's a genuine question, but everyone laughs.

"You've only committed five errors so far this season. And you're third in the league in double plays."

"I guess I'm pretty lucky in my teammates. Rosenthal deserves half the credit there," Eddie says, because that's the right answer. And it's partly true—fielding the ball isn't something he's doing on his own. He knows for a fact that all five of his errors were in the two weeks after being traded to the Robins, when he was still figuring his teammates out. Now—thanks to hours of practice and even more hours spent playing the game—he can predict where they're going to be and what they're going to do.

Eddie knows that there aren't any reliable statistics to measure a player's fielding abilities. And for a sport like baseball, where every goddamn thing you do gets put on a scorecard and assigned a number, that can be frustrating. Eddie knows he's a good short-stop, and he knows that these reporters are trying to come up with numbers to prove exactly how good a shortstop he is. He also knows that earlier this season, nobody would have wasted their time trying.

Ardolino comes up and slings an arm around Eddie's shoulders. "O'Leary here has ESP, but for baseballs," he says, his voice going extra-folksy. "He just always knows where that thing is gonna be."

"Oh, for Pete's sake," Eddie says, his face heating, and that's the exchange that winds up on everybody's television that night.

"O'Leary!" a reporter calls out. "What do you think caused your slump in the first place?"

Eddie's best guess is that the shock of the trade broke something inside him, in the same way that dropping a watch might make it stop telling time. His mom thinks Eddie was afraid to fail on a national stage, which might be true but doesn't sound right to Eddie. About half the reporters in this room have written at least one column hinting that Eddie got distracted by life in the big city; the other half strongly implied that he was loafing. Eddie doesn't think it matters; what matters is that he figured out how to hit the ball again, and that's because his teammates helped him. Before he can think up a suitable answer, Ardolino speaks up.

"Come on," Ardolino says, already steering Eddie away. "That's just how baseball is sometimes." Then, lower, so the press can't hear, and maybe Eddie's not supposed to hear, either, "That's how everything is sometimes."

~

When Eddie gets back from a short road trip, he calls Mark, but the line is busy, presumably because George Allen never hangs the damn thing up. He stops by his new, still-empty apartment long enough to drop his suitcase just inside the door, then turns right back around.

He feels around in his pocket. He still has the gold key holder, but he doesn't dare use it—whatever they are to one another, it doesn't mean Eddie can let himself into Mark's apartment without an invitation.

Today when the door opens, he's especially grateful he didn't use the key, because the living room is full of old men.

"Am I crashing a party?" Eddie asks, his voice low. "Maybe a meeting of the oldest living veterans of the Civil War?"

"Now that you're here, the average age in this apartment has dropped all the way to sixty-five," Mark murmurs. "Every ancient sportswriter in the tristate is in my living room, and every last one of them showed up with a box of Entenmann's coffee cake." He points into the kitchen, where a stack of white boxes sits on the counter.

Eddie doesn't know if Mark honestly doesn't recognize these men or if he's playing it cool, because they aren't all sportswriters. There are two old ballplayers—one a former Giant he recognizes from a sepia-toned photograph that still hangs in the Polo Grounds, and another who played on the Dodgers in the twenties. They both retired before Eddie was born, and they're both in Cooperstown.

"Should I leave?" Eddie murmurs.

"I'm afraid you're going to have to go shake hands."

Eddie does as he's told, feeling faintly hysterical over the idea that he's touching the hands of living legends. Well, legends he was not entirely sure were still living until about five minutes ago.

What's even weirder is that they know who he is.

"Got a kick out of watching you play this year," says one of the writers.

"Sure, if you like watching terrible baseball," Eddie says.

"I don't mean June. I mean since then."

What follows is a group of old men going on about how the season's nearly over, and the Robins are currently not dead last in the league. It's such an embarrassingly low standard, but maybe a fair one to apply to expansion teams. What's more, there's something fond and protective in these men's voices. He's heard the same thing from fans waiting outside the stadium for autographs, and he's heard it shouted from folks in the stands. Rooting for a team doesn't always mean that you need them to win; sometimes you just want to see them fight, do their best, or even just keep showing up. Sometimes you want to look at a guy and say: *Well, he's fucked, but he's trying.* These are old men; they've all had their share of losing, and maybe they know what they're talking about.

"They think you're here for an interview," Mark says when Eddie escapes into the kitchen. He's scooping coffee grounds into the biggest percolator Eddie's ever seen. "So make an appearance, then join me in the dining room." When the coffee is ready, he hands Eddie the pot. "Do me a favor and bring this out to the living room? They'll get a kick out of having Eddie O'Leary play waiter."

"O'Leary," says one of the old men when Eddie's topping off his cup. "George's got a question for you."

"Why baseball?" George asks. "I used to ask all the players, and I don't know when I stopped. But why play baseball for a living, when it's a career that isn't going to last forever, will never pay you big bucks, and keeps you on the road half the year? You could earn more selling Buicks or repairing furnaces."

"My mom's asked me that a dozen times. A hundred times," Eddie amends, deciding that this is not the time to point out that he's already making a fair bit more than your average Buick salesman. "Part of it's just ego, right? Not everyone's good enough, so if you *are* good enough, you want to show the world. And part of it's that there aren't a lot of jobs where thousands of people cheer for you."

"They boo, too," George points out.

"Not as much as they cheer." That's something Eddie's learned over the past few months. Once New York decided they didn't hate his guts, they cheered for him even when he struck out. He doesn't get it, and probably never will, but it sure makes his job more pleasant. "Why, what do most guys say when you ask them?"

"Women, fame, playing a game for a living," George says without missing a beat. "And drinks on the house. But you're a Boy Scout, so I knew that wouldn't be it." George is giving him a very deliberate look, and Eddie realizes that George is doing him a favor: he's giving a room full of sportswriters a reason why Eddie doesn't chase after women. He feels his face heat. A blush will only cement that innocent reputation, so he doesn't try to hide it.

"I guess there's another reason," Eddie says. "How many people get to have a job that makes folks happy? I know I've got to be the thousandth person to say this, but I really get a thrill when I look into the stands and see some kid with their mom and dad, and I know that this is a happy memory they're going to keep. There are people watching the game in bars, talking to one another about it. I guess I like being a part of that."

"If you think that's not going verbatim in next week's diary, you have another think coming," Mark says, emerging from the kitchen.

The truth is that Eddie hadn't thought about any of that until the last month or so. Before then, he only played baseball because of the first reason he just gave George: He was one of the best in the world, so he had to show everyone. Now it's complicated. He'd keep doing it even if he weren't the best. Hell, he kept at it even when he was one of the worst.

"I think I like making people happy," Eddie says, and it's probably something he ought to have figured out years ago, not just as the words leave his mouth. It could be a stadium full of fans, or a city full of people who need someone to root for, or it could just be the man standing next to him, and maybe that's enough.

~~

It starts with a Phillies batter getting hit by a wild pitch, escalates with Rosenthal getting beaned one hundred percent on purpose by the Phillies' pitcher, and ends with a bench-clearing brawl.

"You *idiot*," Mark says when Eddie comes over late that night. "Sit down so I can look at it."

Mark may not be brawny, but he's mean, so when he pinches Eddie's arm, Eddie does as he's told.

"The team doctor already looked at it," Eddie says as Mark prods

Eddie's swollen eye, peering at it like he's going to find something interesting in there.

"The *team doctor*," Mark scoffs, as if Eddie had said one of the hot dog vendors did the exam. "You just had to be the first one off the bench. And let me tell you, you have no idea how to throw a punch. None. A disgrace."

"What, are you going to show me how?"

"I've never hit anyone in my life, but I'm tempted tonight," he says, glaring at Eddie.

Eddie starts laughing. He had a couple beers in the locker room after the game, and his mouth hurts too much to eat, so he's tipsy enough to appreciate the sentiment behind Mark's grumpy cat routine.

"You're going to get fined," Mark says. "You'll get in trouble."

"Oh no, I'll get in trouble," Eddie says. "Wonder what that's like."

Mark snorts, two-thirds of the way to a laugh, then goes over to the refrigerator. He takes out some ice, wraps it in a dish towel, and flings it at Eddie. "I suppose your teammates are pleased with you."

"Ardolino wants to kill me, but that's just because Miss Newbold wants to kill him, and the commissioner has wanted to kill *her* since March." Actually, Ardolino had clapped Eddie on the back a few times and muttered something like *Jesus Christ, kid, somebody needs to teach you how to fight.*

"How's Rosenthal?"

"Fine. X-ray was negative, and he'll play tomorrow." Eddie grabs Mark's wrist. "I'm fine."

"You have one face. One! Try not to put it in front of any more fists."

They both know that Eddie's never going to sit out a fight, not when one of his teammates has been deliberately hurt. But they also both know that isn't the point. "I'll stay in one piece," Eddie says.

Mark pours them both some bourbon. "The Phillies," he sniffs, handing Eddie a glass, and Eddie can't tell if Mark thinks he ought to have started a brawl with some other, worthier team or if Mark is going to set fire to Shibe Park the next time he's in Philadelphia.

"How's George?" Eddie asks.

"I helped him into bed after the seventh inning. He volunteered to show you how to make a fist. The old lady upstairs could probably give you some pointers, too. Also the baby across the hall, and maybe we could find some nuns—"

Eddie pulls him into his lap, and he comes willingly, wrapping his arms around Eddie's neck like he was waiting for it. Eddie kisses him. It hurts because his lip is swollen, and Mark has to know it, but he kisses Eddie fiercely. Eddie takes Mark's glasses off and kisses him some more.

"I love you," Eddie says without really pulling away, so the words are half swallowed by Mark's mouth.

"You're a nightmare," Mark returns, in precisely the same tone of voice. Eddie can feel that he's smiling.

CHAPTER THIRTY

Two singles, a double, and a home run later, the Robins have beaten the Braves. Eddie isn't expecting Mark—he doubts Mark even has press credentials anymore—but there he is in the locker room. Eddie's pretty sure that everyone will excuse his grin as the natural result of an excellent game.

"I brought George," Mark explains, gesturing to another part of the locker room where George Allen is surrounded by people wishing him well. "He watched the game from the lower deck. I'm not working. I don't even have a notebook with me." He lowers his voice. "I am so happy for you."

"It's just one game."

Mark scowls. "You've gotten on the board in ten straight games. It's a streak. I can count, you know. The season's nearly over, and you're ending strong."

"Don't jinx me."

"Ballplayers." Mark sighs. "What are you doing tonight?"

"You tell me." The truth is that Eddie really ought to find someplace with late hours where he can buy dishes and some other things for his still mostly-empty apartment, but if Mark's asking him to do something, he's not going to say no.

"I wondered if you might like a picnic."

"Sure," Eddie says, even though it's currently ten o'clock at night, and he can't think of a single place in the city where a midnight picnic wouldn't be a sure sign of a death wish. But Mark could say that his idea of a date is a picnic in the middle of the Harlem River Speedway, and Eddie wouldn't ask any questions.

"In your apartment, I mean," Mark says. "I know you don't have furniture. But we could sit on the floor? I have chicken salad and some decent bread."

"I like chicken salad and decent bread. What about George?"

"He's going out to dinner with a friend, who will make sure he gets home all right. He has the neighbor's phone number if there's an emergency. And I gave him your number, too, just in case. I mean, I didn't tell him it was your number, obviously, I'm not insane, but—"

Eddie knows he's grinning. "It's okay, Mark."

"It'd better be," Mark says darkly.

They sit on opposite sides of the cab's back seat on the way to Mark's apartment, but occasionally Eddie looks over and catches Mark doing the same thing.

"It'll just take a minute," Mark says when he lets himself into his apartment. "I have everything in the refrigerator, all ready to go."

Lula sniffs Mark's shoe before greeting Eddie like a returning war hero. At this point, Eddie's pretty sure she does it just to be a little shit.

"Oh, wait," Mark says as he's taking a paper sack from the refrigerator. "You probably don't have any wine, do you?"

"I don't even have any glasses," Eddie admits. "Not so much as a coffee cup."

"I have fourteen wineglasses. I have no idea why. You might as well take a few. They're on the top shelf. You'll have to move some things around, but you can probably reach them."

Eddie suspects that Mark knows exactly how he acquired fourteen wineglasses. He also suspects that it's no small thing for Mark to give away anything from this apartment. He reaches into the top cabinet and moves aside a baffling array of cake pans, but instead of wineglasses, he sees rows of identical jars.

"What on earth are you doing with twenty jars of cocktail cherries?" Eddie asks. He takes one down to read the label, but it's in Italian. The contents are clearly cherries in some kind of syrup, but they're not the kind you get on top of your sundae at the Howard Johnson. "Were you getting ready to outfit a bunker?" He turns to hand the jar to Mark, who takes it like he's being handed a live grenade.

"I wondered where he kept them," Mark says, staring at the jar. "God, I had almost forgotten. Hadn't thought about that in months." He looks at Eddie. "You can't get them in America," he says, as if this explains anything. "But William made sure I always had three in my drink. I figured he must have had a case imported, but I could never find where he kept them. Well, shit." He blinks a couple of times and clenches his jaw, and Eddie doesn't know whether to hug him or pretend he doesn't notice what's happening. "I suppose that's what I get for not cleaning out my cabinets."

"Hey," Eddie says, putting a tentative hand on Mark's shoulder. He isn't really sure what to do. Should he offer to leave? He has a sneaking suspicion that when you're ready to cry about your late lover, you don't want your current lover cluttering up your kitchen. And for Mark, who's private by nature and cagey by default, it has to be that much worse. "Want me to take off?"

Mark stands up straight and adjusts his glasses. "Of course, you don't need to stick around. I'm not being much fun."

"That's not what I meant." Eddie realizes that Mark isn't going to tell him what he needs because Mark probably doesn't know the answer—it's not like Mark's been in this exact situation before, either. So Eddie puts his arms around Mark, jar of fancy cherries and all, and holds him tight. "It's sweet," he says after a minute.

"What is?" Mark asks, his words muffled by Eddie's suit jacket. One of his hands is fisted tightly in Eddie's sleeve.

"That William kept those around for you. It's just really sweet. He obviously loved you a lot. I mean, you probably don't need me to tell you that," Eddie adds hastily. He feels Mark nod, so he figures he hasn't gotten things too wrong.

Mark is definitely crying now, and all Eddie can do is hold him almost painfully tight.

"God, I'm sorry," Mark says a few minutes later, pulling away and wiping his eyes with the cuff of his shirt. "I offered you a picnic, and instead you're getting whatever this is. Really, you can leave. You don't—"

"Mark. Shut up, okay?" Eddie says gently. "Do you really think I'm in this for the food? I'm here for you, and this"—he gestures at Mark and then at the cabinet with the cherry jars—"is part of you."

And that must have been all wrong, because now Mark turns around and puts his forehead against a cabinet door. He's making wet, snuffling noises. "I swear I'm okay. It's been months since I've had this happen. I'm fine."

Eddie comes up behind Mark and wraps his arms around him again. "Do you want a drink? Water? Something stronger?"

"Stronger," Mark mumbles, and Eddie sets about pouring some gin and tonic into a glass. "Do you want some of the cherries in there, or do you want to save them?" There's a good chance Mark will keep all twenty jars forever, and there's also a chance he's going to spend a few months putting five cherries in everything he drinks and then crying about it. Eddie figures either of those is pretty reasonable.

"There's probably some of those little cocktail swords in a drawer somewhere," Mark says in between sniffles. Sure enough, Eddie finds several, and they look like silver rather than the usual plastic ones you get at bars. Eddie should have guessed. He takes one of the jars down from the cabinet so Mark can keep clutching the one he has, spears a few cherries onto the stick, and puts it in the glass. A couple ice cubes, and it looks like a proper mixed drink. Then he pours some gin into a glass for himself and gently steers Mark toward the couch.

Mark drains half his drink in one go. "It's a hell of a thing, crying on your shoulder about . . ." He holds up his glass. "It's unfair for me to put you in this position."

"Stop," Eddie says. It's unlike Mark to be aggressively apologetic, especially when there doesn't seem to be anything to apologize for. "Wait. Am I supposed to be jealous?"

Mark shoots him a look that manages to be wry despite the tears. "I think most people might be. Jealous or just annoyed."

Eddie's not sure about that, but what does he know. When he thinks about that poor man, clearly in love with Mark but too paralyzed by fear to give him the one thing he needed and instead hoarding cocktail cherries, jealousy is the last thing Eddie feels. And as for disappointment . . .

"I'm just glad you were loved."

Mark makes a shocked little sound, then finishes his drink and rests his head on Eddie's shoulder. "Thank you," he says, his voice very quiet.

"Fuck that, don't you dare thank me."

That, for some crazy reason, starts Mark laughing. He might be sobbing, too, actually, but whatever he's doing, he's doing it into Eddie's shoulder and with Eddie's arm around him.

"Another drink?" Eddie asks when Mark's subsided, all his weight sagging against Eddie's body.

"Keep 'em coming."

Mark's drinking on an empty stomach, so two drinks—and ten cherries—later, he's as tipsy as Eddie's ever seen him.

"We got that table at a church sale in Greenwich," Mark says, sending a disorganized gesture in the direction of the little table that does nothing but hold mail. "The chairs are from an estate sale in Pennsylvania," he says, pointing to a pair of chairs about as comfortable as a stone bench. "It was what he'd grown up with, and he wasn't having anything but the best."

"What about that painting of the ship?" Eddie asks. "The one that looks like someone dumped paint onto a canvas?"

"The Motherwell? Oh, that's mine. Does it look like a ship to you? I always think it looks like a vase tipped sideways. William saw a church. Of course, it actually *is* paint dumped onto a canvas, more or less."

Mark goes on about art galleries and Russian painters and the difficulties of getting large canvases through customs, things Eddie does not care about even a little, but he thinks he'll always greedily soak up every detail Mark gives him.

"Do you have a picture album?" Eddie asks.

Mark does indeed have a picture album, which means Eddie gets to see Mark young and shining with happiness in France, in Italy, and in the familiar box seats at the Polo Grounds. He sees Mark with his hair too short ("It was 1954, Eddie; I was certain I'd be *arrested* if my hair touched my ears") and Lula as a puppy. Eddie needs to stop himself from imagining Mark—or William?—pasting these photographs into the album, and then never showing it to anybody at all, or he's going to start crying, and the crying portion of this evening is officially over.

They hear a key twisting in the lock and voices in the hall, so they have time to move apart, even though they were only sitting on the sofa, a photo album spanning their laps. By the time George and his friend—a writer Eddie recognizes from the other day in Mark's apartment—come in, Mark's already at the door. Eddie isn't sure what he's supposed to be doing, so he hangs back until the writer leaves, then goes over to give George his arm.

"I thought you were going out," George says to Mark.

"Change of plans."

"You look like shit," George says, because of course he's noticed Mark's bloodshot eyes and the fact that he isn't steady on his feet.

"You say the nicest things."

George turns to Eddie. "What happened to him?" He probably thinks Mark's been mugged.

"I'm fine, George," Mark says. "I just saw a jar of cherries and had a nervous breakdown about it."

"One of the typists at the *Chronicle* wears Ruth's perfume. Takes me like a punch to the chin every time."

"Still?" Mark asks, audibly horrified.

"Yeah, but it's not such a bad punch anymore. Almost nice, really."

Mark snorts. "Want a drink?"

"Doesn't look like you two left anything for me."

"Ha ha. Eddie's sober."

"Not really," Eddie points out. "Not at all."

"Spend the night on Mark's sofa," George says. "Don't try to get home in this state. You have a game tomorrow, and you don't need to trip on a curb or wander into the river."

"Yessir," Eddie says.

George looks between Mark and Eddie. A man doesn't spend over half a century in the news business if he's not in the habit of noticing things: the rumpled state of Eddie's collar, the dampness on his shoulder where Mark rested his head. He doesn't look surprised by what he sees.

"You wouldn't be the only one," George says when Mark goes into the kitchen. "Or the first one."

Eddie can't pretend not to understand what George means, not after hearing Ardolino basically say the same thing a few weeks ago. It's something that Eddie must have known, on some level. He can't possibly be the only queer man in baseball. But he's not sure how much comfort this gives him, since whoever else is out there is hiding, too. What matters more is that George said it, and that he said it loud enough for Mark to hear. Eddie doesn't think Mark looks at George as a substitute father, not exactly, but he suspects that it means something to Mark to have George's approval.

Eddie washes out the glasses while Mark gets George settled in bed, and when Mark comes out, he looks a bit less ragged than he did earlier.

"I did you out of a picnic," Mark says.

"Don't worry about it."

But Mark gets a container of chicken salad out of the refrigerator and starts slicing a loaf of bread. "You can't go to bed on an empty stomach."

"I don't have to stay here tonight, you know."

"I'd like you to." And that's Mark asking for something, actually asking. Eddie tries not to look too pleased.

The sandwiches sober them up a bit, so by the time they wake Lula up for a two A.M. walk that she probably would just as soon have skipped, they're more or less steady on their feet. On the way back inside, they both wave at the doorman, and Eddie acknowledges something he's been trying for a while now not to think about. The doormen, not to mention the neighbors, probably had their suspicions about Mark and William. And now they probably have the same suspicions about Eddie. George knows, the neighbors know, Eddie's mom and probably his stepdad know. Mark's friends know. Ardolino probably knows—about Eddie, if not about him and Mark being together. And if Ardolino knows, so does Price.

Eddie's relying on the goodwill—or just plain aversion to trouble—of a lot of people. He's relying on the probability that Major League Baseball would move heaven and earth to avoid one of its players being exposed as homosexual. He probably ought to be more worried.

A few weeks ago, Varga was riding the subway at night and got held up by a couple of kids with a knife. They asked for his wallet, and he handed it over. There had been over two hundred dollars cash in there, because Varga had been on the way home from a good day at the racetrack. But he told the locker room that he hadn't even been mad about it. "Take my money, use it in health, and get that knife away from me," is how he described his attitude toward his muggers. That's sort of how Eddie feels now. The fact that he even has to worry about being found out is a knife to his throat—it's frightening and wrong and not even remotely fair—and if one day the price he has to pay to make it go away is his career, he'll pay it with no regrets.

"You were right, you know," Eddie says when they're on the elevator. "There's a real risk that I'll be found out. I need you to know that I know that. I'm not an idiot, and I don't have my head in the sand."

He halfway expects Mark to find something to quibble over, but he looks almost relieved. "Okay," he says. "Good."

"Ardolino and Price probably know," Eddie says.

"Ardolino has said a few things to me."

"What did he say?" Eddie asks, imagining any number of horrible things Ardolino might have said to Mark.

"Put your claws away. He hinted that he knows about us. I didn't confirm, just acted like I had no idea what he was talking about."

"If I can't play anymore," Eddie says when they get out of the elevator, "I guess I'll go to college. Figure things out there." He'd told himself the same thing when he was in the thick of his batting slump, and it had felt like such a consolation prize. It still does, but he'll take it anyway.

"That's what most people do in college."

"Okay," Eddie says as Mark unlocks the door. "I'm going to have a few good years doing what I do best. Then I'll go to college and, I don't know, coach high school baseball or something."

"Well," Mark says quietly. "Probably not that."

"What do you mean?"

"If, in this scenario, you're quitting baseball because of queer rumors, then nobody's going to let you do anything with kids."

Eddie already knows that's how the world works, but now he's swept up in a surge of anger, the same anger that usually has him breaking bats or yelling at umpires.

"In that case," he says, seething, "I'll do something else."

"Television," Mark says decisively. "You have the looks, and there are loads of us in television."

Eddie has no idea if that's true or just Mark trying to make him feel better, but it doesn't matter. He'll figure something out. He bumps his shoulder into Mark's.

"Seriously," Mark says. "You could be the man who says things like 'Old Rusty McGraw is swinging from the heels this afternoon.'"

"Is that supposed to be what I sound like?"

Mark waves a hand. "It's what they all sound like."

Inside, the apartment is quiet. Lula curls up by the door. Mark disappears and returns a moment later with a glass of water and a bottle of aspirin.

Then Mark steers Eddie toward the little room off the kitchen. It's been cleared out. There's no sign of skis or luggage or stacks of boxes. Instead the narrow bed has been made up, and there's a postage stamp of a rug on the sliver of exposed floor.

Mark picks up the pillow and fluffs it, then carefully folds back the sheet and quilt. "It might be asking too much of George to expect him to look the other way if you're actually sleeping in my bedroom."

It's a guest room. Months ago, Eddie had suggested that it would be perfectly unremarkable for Mark to have a friend spend the night; Mark had responded as if spending the night under his roof was the same as Eddie taking out a full-page ad announcing his preference for men. Mark is—if not letting down his guard, then acting like it's not unreasonable for Eddie to let down his.

"You made a room for us," Eddie says, stating the obvious.

"Whether it'll fit both of us is very much an open question," Mark says dryly. There's nothing Eddie can do for it but shut the door behind them and take the half step that brings him to Mark.

"Thanks," Eddie says, and kisses Mark lightly.

"I had hoped—I had planned to spend the night with you. Properly, I mean."

"We'll have other nights." He kisses Mark again. "We have time."

A shiver runs through Mark, and Eddie pulls him close. Maybe Mark will never quite believe that they do have time; he'd been wrong about that once. But he clearly hopes they do, and that's enough for Eddie. It's more than enough.

He starts on Mark's buttons, his hands getting tangled with Mark's. There's nowhere to put their discarded clothing, so it all lands on the floor. When they're down to their underwear, Eddie lies on the bed, moving to the far side so his back is against the wall. There might be enough room if they sleep pressed together, Mark's back against Eddie's chest, the weight of Eddie's arm keeping Mark from rolling off the mattress. But that apparently isn't what Mark has in mind, because he pushes Eddie onto his back and starts kissing him.

There isn't any real heat in the kiss, no actual urgency, even though Mark keeps touching Eddie's arms and chest, like he's taking inventory of his favorite places. Eddie slides a hand into Mark's hair and with the other rearranges him so he's fully on top of Eddie. Now Eddie's pressed into the mattress, Mark a satisfying weight on top of him.

After a while, Mark's kisses slow down. Eddie pulls the quilt over them both as Mark presses his face into Eddie's neck.

It's a shitty way to sleep. Eddie's gotten used to sleeping on buses and trains and airplanes, on saggy hotel mattresses and that chair in the clubhouse that's been there since the Wilson administration. But sleeping with Mark's chin digging into his collarbone is an entirely new level of discomfort, and Eddie doesn't even begin to mind. He's going to be tired and very possibly hungover for tomorrow's game, and he doesn't even care.

CHAPTER THIRTY-ONE

"Eight-letter word for excessively large, fourth letter *O*," Price says when Eddie finds him in the clubhouse.

Eddie thinks about it. "How many letters does *humongous* have?"

"Not eight."

"So," Eddie says, settling into the chair next to Price's and lowering his voice. "I heard Ardolino is going to meetings. Like, meetings for people who—"

"I know what meetings are," Price says. "Where'd you hear that?"

"He told Mark."

"You have a problem with him going to meetings?"

"No! I just—do you think they'll work? You said he tried in the past, but do you think this time it'll work?"

Price frowns at him. "A year or two off the bottle isn't nothing, O'Leary. Those times he quit, it did work. It just didn't last. If you're asking whether I think these meetings will make it so he never has another drink, I don't know. I hope so, for his sake. But even if he falls off the wagon, he can try again. And he can keep trying."

"And that's it? He keeps trying?" It's incredibly unfair that Ardolino has to spend the rest of his life making that kind of effort, possibly failing, and trying again.

To his surprise, Price grins at him. "Eddie, baby, that's what we're all doing."

Eddie doesn't know whether it's a bad sign that Mark's chosen a public setting to do this. They're at a Chinese restaurant on Third Avenue, and Eddie's halfway through his bowl of noodles when Mark hands him a sheaf of typed pages clipped together in one corner.

"This is it? The article?" Eddie asks, even though he knows the answer.

Eddie's been telling himself that it'll be fine, but the truth is that he can't imagine an entire article—there have got to be thirty double-spaced pages here, for chrissakes—about his team that will be anything other than nauseating to read.

Eddie puts his chopsticks down and looks at the papers. He can't believe Mark expects him to sit here and read this while Mark is across the table, pretending to eat noodles and tearing his napkin into ever-smaller pieces.

"There a reason we're doing this in public?" Eddie asks.

"I wanted Chinese food." Mark nudges him under the table. "I marked the parts that are about you. Purple ink in the margins."

Eddie pages ahead to the first sight of purple.

> In June, it looked like the story of the season was a loudmouthed shortstop getting his comeuppance. That, it seemed, was the best this new franchise could hope for, the only kind of story it deserved. And then, right before our eyes, the villain of the piece turned into someone worth rooting for, someone, at least, you don't want to see in the pillory.

His eyes drift down the page to a quote from Rosenthal.

> "He runs three miles a day and spends an hour in the weight room, even on the road. One of these days he'll

get hit by a car jogging around the stadium at night, and then Ardolino will have to change the lineup, and we can't have that," said second baseman Buddy Rosenthal, who, along with O'Leary, makes up the Robins' double-play duo. "It's like nobody told him you just don't have to be in such good shape to play baseball."

"I don't run every day," Eddie points out. When he glances up, he sees Mark with his fingers wrapped tightly around his chopsticks. "Just most days."

"Tell that to Rosenthal," Mark says. On a good day, Mark is wound pretty tight. Today he's a rubber band about to snap.

Eddie turns the page and finds even more about all the effort he put into his game and how little he had to show for half the season.

"You wanted to avert your eyes," said veteran sports reporter George Allen. "You wanted to throw a sheet over the kid every time he left the dugout."

"Jesus Christ, George," Eddie mutters. "Pull a punch, already."

Mark taps Eddie's plate with a chopstick. "Keep reading, keep reading."

O'Leary's real sin was not being the hero we wanted. He's not Mantle. He's not DiMaggio. There's something about him that resists the pedestal, but maybe the time for pedestals is over. This summer, nobody in the stands at the Polo Grounds was looking for a hero, and nobody was trying to rewrite a tired old myth. Instead, people showed up for the sheer pleasure of rooting for someone to defeat—or maybe just withstand—not a

> rival team, but a seemingly inexplicable piece of bad
> luck. Maybe when we watched this man go to the plate
> again and again, we saw something familiar, and we
> wanted better for him because we wanted better for
> ourselves.

"Mark," Eddie says. "This is—this is nice." It's an understatement. Anyone who's read a single paragraph written by Mark Bailey before today will be able to look at this article and see the difference. There's little of the sharpness that was in the *Esquire* articles or the book reviews.

"Shut up," Mark mutters. He pulls his sweater over his hands and sulks. It's the first cool day of fall, and he's wearing a cable-knit sweater the color of cigarette ash. He looks soft and warm, and Eddie just really, really loves him. "Finish reading it, okay?"

Eddie opens his mouth to say that he wants to eat his dinner, finish their conversation about what movie they're going to see tomorrow, and then go home and watch Mark bully George into eating something with vitamins. But Mark is obviously nervous—he needs to know that Eddie's okay with this article, and apparently neither of them are going to have any peace until that happens.

Eddie gently kicks Mark under the table, then goes back to the beginning of the article. There are two other stories twisting together with the story about himself.

> Somewhere, in between the city's refusal to build a
> stadium and a shortstop's record-breaking batting
> slump, a veteran player came out of retirement to drag
> a brand-new team kicking and screaming into exis-
> tence.

"You can't just slap a uniform on a bunch of guys and call them a team," said Tony Ardolino. "That's not a team. That's just people wearing the same outfit."

"He said he needed a year," said Constance Newbold, who acquired majority ownership of the Robins after the death of her father.

Left fielder Buzz Castaneto of the White Sox played with Ardolino for four years. "He always says it isn't a ball club until somebody posts bail," said Castaneto.

Mark goes on to write about Connie Newbold, who went to Giants games with her grandfather, played baseball in college, and persuaded her father to bring a National League team back to the city. He writes about the men who wouldn't work for her in the same way he writes about the people Tony Ardolino knocked off barstools—there's something matter-of-fact but lethal, a delicate turn of phrase that slices the jugular. It's all that elegant nastiness Mark carries around like a concealed weapon. A current of anger runs through the article, weaving it together—Connie Newbold's anger at the men who told her she should let someone else run her team, Tony Ardolino's anger at the bigots who make his teammates' lives harder, and Eddie's simmering anger at himself. Maybe, also, the city's anger at losing two teams a few years ago.

"I love it," Eddie says. "You had to have known that I'd love it."

They're leaning across the table in order to speak quietly, maybe just a little too close.

"I knew nothing of the sort," Mark says. "You're the same man who called me up at eight o'clock in the morning because I wrote down something funny he said."

"You knew I'd love it," Eddie repeats, because this article is filled with—fondness, and respect, and *Mark*. "You knew. You just wanted to make sure *I* knew."

"I knew," Mark agrees. His cheeks are flushed and his eyes are bright, and Eddie hears everything Mark isn't saying.

Eddie heads uptown to the stadium to clear out his locker for the winter. The Robins' last game was two nights ago in Cincinnati, and they finished the season almost in the middle of the heap—a hell of a lot better than anybody could have predicted at the beginning of the season, and decent enough that Eddie's downright optimistic about next year.

He's feeling cheerful when he waves hello to the security guard at the Polo Grounds, even though it'll be another five months before he sees most of these guys again, even though he knows he's going to be bored out of his mind inside of a week. Even though he knows they aren't all coming back next year.

When he walks into the locker room, everyone falls silent in a way that they haven't done since June. Varga, Rosenthal, and half the bullpen are huddled around a copy of a magazine that has Eddie's face on the cover.

Somehow it hadn't occurred to Eddie that Sunday magazines hit the stands on Saturday.

"Were you going to tell us about this?" Varga asks.

"About the article? You all know about the article. Half of you are quoted in it."

"No, dummy. About—" He picks up the magazine and flips a page. "About how you 'resist the pedestal.' What the fuck, man? That's mean. I thought you were friends."

"It's low," agrees Rosenthal.

"Cold," says Luis, who's appeared out of nowhere.

Eddie starts to laugh. "It's fine. It's really fine. He means that nobody needs to think I'm perfect in order to root for me."

Rosenthal frowns. "If you say so."

"I don't think he knows much about baseball," Varga says. There's a murmur of assent. "Does he?"

"We don't talk much about baseball," Eddie says, because he doesn't know what else to say, and it only belatedly occurs to him how weird it is to admit that he doesn't talk about baseball to someone whose entire reason for being around Eddie, as far as the team is concerned, is to listen to him talk about baseball.

"That's enough," Ardolino says, emerging from his office. His voice has the loud peremptoriness perfected by coaches and kindergarten teachers. "Let me read this fucking magazine." He holds out his hand, and Rosenthal puts the magazine into it.

Everyone falls quiet while Ardolino skims the article. Eddie's not sure he's ever seen Ardolino read anything other than a scouting report or a racing form.

"O'Leary," Ardolino barks after a minute. "My office. As for the rest of you, you're goddamn babies. Reporters write shit. It doesn't mean a thing. Fuck, O'Leary's the only one who seems to have figured that out, even if he did learn it the hard way."

Eddie's about to point out that he's not so sure he did learn it, but Ardolino takes his arm and all but drags him into the office.

"I've already read it," Eddie says, sitting in the empty chair. "I'm really not upset. All he means is—"

"I know, Eddie. I wanted to get you out of there before you made a scene defending your—defending Bailey."

Eddie barely has time to register the use of his first name before he understands the rest of what Ardolino said. "Oh," he says, feeling his face heat. He was already almost positive Ardolino knew, but having confirmation doesn't make it any less awkward.

"'I don't talk to him about baseball,'" Ardolino says, obviously imitating Eddie.

Eddie slumps in his seat. "Well, I don't."

"I'll bet you don't."

Ardolino closes the venetian blinds that cover the window between his office and the clubhouse. The magazine, resting on the manager's desk, is folded back to the first page, and Eddie glances down at Mark's byline and the now-familiar text of the article.

"Who else knows?"

"Just me and Price." Ardolino sighs. "And we can both keep a secret."

Eddie has a lot of questions he wants to ask Ardolino. He knows from Mark that Ardolino is probably going to retire over the winter. Miss Newbold will appoint him as her proxy to the board of directors, a move that might infuriate people even more than when she was on the board herself.

Idly, Eddie picks up the magazine and turns the page. He's read the article, but he hasn't seen the photographs. There's one of himself from a little over a year ago, and he's momentarily taken aback. The person in that photo is a kid. He had such a simple, uncomplicated life—he was good at baseball, friendly with his team, and fond of his mom. But it was a life that couldn't grow in any direction. It didn't allow for failure, didn't allow for honesty. He was carefree, but maybe because he didn't know what was worth caring about.

Now he knows who he is and what he wants, and he knows exactly how high a price he's willing to pay for those things. He's tired and he's angry, and his contentment is something heavy and sharp, a prize that he fought for. He wouldn't exchange it for anything.

"You okay, kid? I mean, about this"—Ardolino points at the magazine—"and in general?"

Eddie's not sure exactly what Ardolino is asking. Does he want to know whether Eddie's going to start making life difficult for the team with his rampant queerness? Is he asking whether Eddie wants a trade? He takes a chance that Ardolino means exactly what he's saying.

"I'm okay, Tony." Eddie grins. "It's a great city, and I hope I get to play here for a long time," he says, meaning it for the first time. "This is a team with a great future."

Part VII
FALL & WINTER

EPILOGUE

October

Mark gets to Eddie's apartment early that same evening. He's been early perhaps twice in the past decade, and he hopes Eddie appreciates it. He hopes Eddie's in the mood to appreciate anything, that his teammates haven't raked him over the coals for any perceived complicity in the article. He hopes Eddie doesn't blame Mark. He hopes a lot of things, which is upsetting and very unlike him, but there you have it: he's ruined.

The sky is darkening for no good reason, and Mark's regretting not bringing an umbrella or at least a raincoat. Lula seems to be aware of this lapse, and occasionally throws Mark a highly judgmental glance that he can't even contradict. She's perfectly right.

Finally Eddie rounds the corner and spots Mark and, of course, breaks into the most obvious smile in the world, not that Mark's in any position to judge, seeing as how he's met Eddie's ante and raised it with an asinine little wave.

"Did you bring Lula as a human shield?" Eddie asks.

"Obviously."

Eddie unlocks the door. His key is tucked inside Mark's gold key holder, and every time Mark sees it, he wants to protest that Eddie simply cannot walk around with something that has another man's initials engraved on it. But Eddie likes to give Mark what he wants, and apparently that means he won't be any more secretive than he absolutely has to be. Mark suspects he'll never stop being equal parts appalled and pleased.

As soon as the door is shut behind them, Eddie's kissing Mark.

"Everything's okay?" Mark asks.

"Yes." Eddie's smiling. "They got mad at you for writing mean things about me."

Mark leans back, outraged. "They *what*? *Mean*? That thing is a fucking love letter. Jesus."

"They might not be the greatest readers," Eddie says, gracefully eliding over the *love letter* part, because that's just the kind of sickeningly decent person he is. "Anyway, congratulations on the article. I got you something."

He goes over to the kitchen counter and brings back a box a little bigger than his hand. It's wrapped in pale blue paper and tied up with a bow.

"It's not much." Eddie scrubs a hand across his jaw. "It might be a really bad idea, actually. I swear I'll throw it out if you think it's creepy."

Mark, having never received or even contemplated a present that could be described as creepy, and intrigued by the possibility, carefully unties the bow. He slides a fingernail under the Scotch tape, loath to tear the paper.

"The lady at the store wrapped it," Eddie explains. Mark had already guessed that Eddie didn't have hidden depths as a wrapper of presents.

The box inside is plain white, and when Mark takes off the lid, he sees a single cup: a teacup, and beneath it a saucer. Gingerly, he takes it out. It's duck-egg blue, with a gilt rim and handle. On the inside, in the same gold, is a sprinkling of stars. Probably from the twenties, if Mark has to guess. It's pristine, unchipped; the finish is uncracked. Likely the rest of the set was lost or destroyed, and this is what's left. "It's beautiful," Mark says. "Perfect."

"Or, possibly, deranged. Take your pick. It's the cup from the book."

"I know. You got me a cup from a book about a haunted house."

"I got you the creepiest possible cup."

"That only adds to its charm," Mark assures him. But it's not just a cup from a scary book. He's sure Eddie knows this, but when poor doomed Eleanor imagines being loved, being cherished, having a home where she belongs, she thinks of her cup of stars.

"A pair of golden lions is hard to come by," Eddie says, confirming Mark's suspicion.

"I'll keep it here," Mark says. "For when I stay. You can make me coffee and bring it to me in bed."

"Pretty optimistic to think I'll ever get around to buying a coffee maker."

Mark already bought a coffee maker; it'll be delivered tomorrow, once he's far enough away that he can't be thanked. "Pfft. You're a man of leisure for five months. And right now, you have a bed and a dog bed." Mark had needed a moment to himself when he realized Eddie's second purchase for his home was not a table or chairs or a proper set of hand towels but a bed for Lula, bought for the princely sum of ten dollars at Gimbels. "Clearly you have your priorities in order."

November

It's only when their entrées arrive that Mark starts to panic.

They're out to dinner with Lilian and Maureen, and Andy and Nick. It's late, well past midnight, and the early edition of the *Chronicle*—with a banner headline announcing a newly elected president—is already being bundled into delivery trucks. They had been out celebrating with a bunch of *Chronicle* staffers, so they're all fairly tipsy by the time they manage to find a restaurant that's still open.

When the waitress brings their dinners, Andy and Nick set about wordlessly shuffling food between one another's plates the way they always do—a tomato salad exchanged for a dinner roll, a baked potato divided in two. Lilian stands up to show off the stitching on her new suit—a suit that Mark covets, and which undoubtedly came from a men's tailor. It would not take any great powers of discernment to identify their table as extremely fucking queer.

Mark excuses himself from the table. Lilian finds him outside the men's room, where he's fumbling with a match.

"Give it to me," she says, taking the match from his hand and the cigarette from his mouth.

"We're all very gay."

"Well spotted," Lilian remarks, lighting the cigarette and passing it to Mark.

"The waitress recognized Eddie."

"He just signed a menu for her."

Mark lets out a wordless wail. Lilian, horrifyingly, takes his hand. He gives her a look that he hopes conveys *I may be a wreck, but I don't need anything so tedious as physical comfort*, but he doesn't pull his hand away. They both know you can be happy and afraid all at once; maybe that's easier to do when you aren't alone.

Back at the table, Eddie raises his eyebrows, a wordless *Are you okay?* Mark nods, which is a lie, then shrugs a single shoulder, which is less of a lie, but Eddie understands anyway. Under the table, he squeezes Mark's knee.

Somebody pushes their glass of wine toward Mark, and he drinks it without hesitation, then leans back in his seat and lets the giddy optimism at the table seep into him. Andy's going on about the electoral college, and—yep, here comes a pencil, a napkin pie chart's on its way—and Eddie glances at Mark like *We're talking about this later.*

He remembers watching Eddie's midnight batting practice in New Jersey, when he listened to the crickets and felt the thrum of satisfaction from Eddie's teammates as they watched him finally have some luck. Mark had thought: *Those guys are in this with Eddie, they're his team.* Now he looks around the table and thinks maybe this is something like that.

The happiness is rolling off Eddie in waves, and Mark realizes—probably months after he should have—that Eddie's getting something out of the risks he's taking. Dinner in a restaurant with friends. Cans of Lula's dog food cluttering up his cabinets. The dubious pleasure of Mark's company in Omaha over the upcoming Thanksgiving weekend.

Later, they walk home, a box of cake tied up in string swinging from Eddie's hand. The wine must have gone to Mark's head, because the act of ordering a dessert to go and carrying it home feels impossible, like two men have never before obtained cake together.

Maybe they really are on the precipice of something new and wonderful; maybe this election means that a lot of people want things to be better in the same way that he and his friends do. Maybe whatever changes the next decade brings will be good ones.

Eddie grins at him. "There you go, then," he says, and Mark realizes he said all that out loud. Eddie gently swings the box of cake into Mark's leg, then nudges him with a shoulder.

December

They tiptoe into the apartment, Mark shutting the door quietly as Eddie picks Lula up before her nails can clack on the parquet.

George is sleeping. He's been unwell, or more unwell than he already was, and spends half the day asleep.

Silently, they shrug out of their coats, and Eddie hangs them up while Mark pokes his head into George's room to let the visiting nurse know that she can go home. When he's given her cab money and shut the door, he finds Eddie in the dining room.

"What're these?" Eddie asks, gesturing at a stack of brittle, yellowed newspaper clippings.

"Careful. The *Chronicle* archivist will push me out a window if I lose any."

Gingerly, Eddie picks up an especially aged-looking clipping.

"That's from 1911," Mark explains. "It's the first I could find with George's byline, but the earlier ones would have gone uncredited."

Eddie reads it. "*The Trolley Dodgers beat the Boston Rustlers by two runs.*" And the byline isn't George Allen, but J. Apfelbaum.

"That article probably won't go in the book," Mark says. "I just brought it back for George to see. It's the only one I could turn up with that name."

"Book?"

"Well, I hope it'll be a book. I'm working on a proposal. Half a century of sportswriting. The best of George Allen's columns. I'll write an introduction."

"You know, when I met you, you were basically unemployed, and here you are writing every day like an honest worker of the world."

"The thing about writing is that in order to produce something anybody will be interested in reading, you have to be interested in writing it, and I wasn't interested in anything at all for a while there." It's strange to admit that out loud, even though Eddie already knows it.

"But now you are? And the thing you're interested in is sportswriting? That's a far cry from architects and—who was the woman you interviewed for *The New Yorker*? And what about that article you wrote about the art dealer?"

"You read those?" Mark had *murdered* that art dealer—and rightly so, he was a shameless grifter—but he can't imagine anyone reading that article and thinking it was a good idea to let Mark come within ten yards of them with a reporter's notebook.

"I was curious. It was right after I met you, and I wanted to know more."

"Did you like those articles?" Mark asks, not sure he wants to know.

"I could hear your voice," Eddie says. "So of course I did."

While Mark was writing the magazine article about the Robins, he felt something creeping into his usual voice, something open and trusting, as if he'd joined the sort of church where they play the guitar and hold hands. Instead of the merciless pinning down of character that he used to consider his driving strength, he tried to capture his subjects with a soft-focus lens. Partly that's because he will never do anything to harm Eddie O'Leary, but it's also because he wanted readers to feel at least a shadow of what he felt during the season he spent with the Robins. He wanted them to experience the loyalty of the fans he saw in the stands and in the bars. He wanted them to know what leadership looks like in the flawed persons of Tony Ardolino and Constance Newbold. He wanted them to look at Eddie and see not the face that will inevitably be plastered all over ads for shaving cream and canned soup, but a person.

He knows you can't be a decent writer if you use kid gloves, but he thinks you can be both honest and generous, and he also thinks this isn't something he would have been capable of two years ago.

"Do you know, I made my mom mail me the clippings because I was too chicken to go to the public library."

"Jesus. And she let me write about you? And *you* let me write about you?"

"I trusted you by that point," Eddie says, as if that covers it, as if that's all that needs to be said. "I was in love with you by that point."

Mark wants to throttle him. "Likewise," he manages.

"Yeah?" Eddie sounds like he's trying very hard not to seem invested in the answer.

"It's hard to say exactly when, but I think I was pretty far gone by the time I kissed you. I don't think I'd have worked up the nerve if I hadn't loved you, at least a little."

A fleeting look of shock passes over Eddie's face. Not, surely, at the sentiment, but because Mark said it aloud. Mark doesn't mean to be stingy with his affection, not with Eddie, never with Eddie—and he doesn't think he is, exactly, but he should give Eddie more. He already knows that he'll always give Eddie more.

"And now?" Eddie asks, schooling his expression into something he probably thinks looks innocent.

"I love you." He kisses Eddie then, because otherwise that phrase is going to linger in the air, true but somehow inadequate. He has a professional aversion to phrases that refuse to get the job done. "I'm going to keep loving you," Mark says, and that's much better.

January

There are six cardboard boxes sitting next to the front door of Mark's apartment, and he doesn't want to talk about it. William's old law books are going to the ACLU, and his history books are going to Nick. Everything is neatly labeled.

Mark arranges some of George's books on the empty shelves. George takes one look at them and says, "Maybe don't get too used to me being here," and then Mark has to turn abruptly away and make sure the books' spines are even.

Eddie comes over to eat leftover braised beef. He glances at the boxes, glances at the mostly empty shelves, and doesn't say a thing.

Over the past few weeks Mark's started to imagine selling the apartment. Just as a thought experiment, he imagines living somewhere else. It doesn't feel like a loss, or at least not the kind of loss it might have six months earlier. Maybe this apartment felt so necessary because it was the only place he could be himself, the first place he was wanted. But right now, he carries those things with him. He might not need the apartment as a reminder.

He doesn't say any of this. But he starts to get rid of things. He sells the skis—he never liked skiing, and the idea of Eddie flying down a mountainside at terminal velocity is enough to make Mark want to burn the entire state of Vermont to the ground. He gives William's collection of green Jasperware to the one sister William actually liked, accompanying it with a letter he hopes is gracious.

What's left is furniture, which Mark knows how to sell when the time comes, and the things he loves and won't part with: his books and clothes, Lula's dog bowl, some art, his typewriter, the last remaining jar of cherries.

"What if I get traded?" Eddie asks when they're washing the dishes.

"You're not getting traded." The Robins are setting about building a team around Eddie. He's not going anywhere.

"But what if I do?"

"I can do my job anywhere."

Eddie turns the sink off and looks at him. Mark continues to look intently at the saucepan that he's scrubbing.

"What does that mean?" Eddie asks.

"It means I can fly to New York whenever I need to show my face, and the rest of the time I can live in Wichita or Sioux Falls—"

Eddie kisses him. "They don't have teams in Wichita or Sioux Falls, unless you think I'll be playing in the minors."

"I'd go with you to the minors, too," Mark says, his hands wet and soapy on Eddie's collar. He would move to Sioux Falls for Eddie O'Leary. It's an outrage.

"Really?"

"I have no idea how we'd sell the idea of you bringing along a roommate, but we can cross that bridge later. Poor Lula, being carted off to the provinces," he adds, mainly to make Eddie laugh.

"Really?" Eddie repeats, like he's not getting it.

"Would you rather I didn't?"

Eddie's eyes go wide, amused. "Are you stupid all of a sudden?"

"Eddie. I will go literally anywhere you go."

They rinse some more dishes. Or at least Mark does. Eddie just kind of watches him.

"What if there are rumors—like, outside baseball? Public knowledge. In the newspaper. Do we have a plan?"

This is the worst-case scenario, the one they haven't talked about, although he's sure Eddie's thought about it as much as Mark has. Mark's plan is to take Eddie someplace where they've never heard of baseball. Edinburgh. Sydney. Perhaps a mountaintop. "I will chloroform you and take you someplace safe," Mark says.

"Lilian's place on Fire Island?"

And, okay, that actually makes more sense than a mountaintop and probably wouldn't even require chloroform, but Mark's keeping his options open. "Sure," Mark says, trying to look reasonable.

"You're very romantic," Eddie says, and Mark suspects he isn't even joking.

February

Mark knew this was how it was going to end, but when the visiting nurse puts her hand on his arm and tells him, he's shocked anyway.

"Is there someone you can call, Mr. Bailey?"

Of course there is. She dials the phone for him, and doesn't look twice when twenty minutes later a professional baseball player arrives, out of breath and still in a pair of pajama pants. Eddie calls George's nieces, the funeral parlor, the *Chronicle*. He pays the kid next door two dollars to walk Lula, and then makes scrambled eggs for Mark.

It's cold at the cemetery. Eddie's hand periodically finds its way to the small of Mark's back, a glancing touch.

"He would have been glad that everyone came," Mark says in the cab home, because the funeral had been a full house. There were nieces and cousins and old friends. There were the reporters and athletes who made their way to Mark's apartment during George's months there, several ballplayers who were still in town over the winter, approximately half the *Chronicle* newsroom and masthead, and dozens of people Mark has never seen before.

Mark knows George had a full life, a good life, and now he's being buried next to his wife. It's all exactly what George wanted, maybe what anyone would want. But it's still an end. And maybe Mark was foolish to get attached to someone he knew wasn't going to be around for long, but that's the point, isn't it? Nobody's really around for that long.

When they get in the cab, Eddie pulls off his glove and wraps his hand around Mark's.

March

It's a month," Eddie says. He's said this fifteen times in the past twenty-four hours. Spring training starts in two days. His apartment is in shambles. It looks like he's never packed a suitcase in his life. Mark already knows he's going to have to mail all the things Eddie forgets.

They're in bed, Eddie sprawled out on his stomach and Mark still half on top of him, pressing bruising kisses into the back of his neck, taking a proprietary pleasure in marking him up. He'll have to stop once the season starts, because he doesn't want anyone wondering where the marks are coming from, but for now he can be as extravagant as he pleases.

He starts kissing his way down Eddie's spine. Eddie whimpers into the pillow.

"It's only a month," Mark agrees, speaking the words into Eddie's skin.

"Fly out for the exhibition game in Miami," Eddie says.

Mark already booked a room at the nicest hotel he could find, but he's not telling Eddie. "Shut up and let me—just let me."

"I'll call you every night," Eddie says the next day as Mark drives him to the airport. He's crammed into the passenger seat of Mark's Renault in a way that can't be safe. Mark's coming around to the idea of buying an American car.

"I know you will."

"Show Lula my picture so she doesn't forget me."

Mark tries to roll his eyes but can't keep a straight face anymore.

"I knew I could make you smile," Eddie says.

"What?"

"You've been moping."

"I—" Mark's ready to deny it. "Okay, fine, yes, I've been moping."

"You wouldn't let go of me this morning in bed."

"I don't even like you." Mark pauses to honk at some jackass who's parked in the departures lane. "While you're gone, I'm moving into your apartment." He hadn't actually planned on telling Eddie, just bringing his things over and never mentioning it.

"Of course you tell me when we're in a moving vehicle and I can't even touch you. Don't bring that uncomfortable chair, all right?"

"I'm buying six more uncomfortable chairs just like it," Mark says. "Twelve more."

"Can't wait to see where you think you're going to put them."

"I'll stack them on your side of the bed."

Eddie swiftly grabs Mark's hand off the gear shift and presses a kiss to his palm. "So—tonight, should I call you at your number or mine? I mean—ours?"

"Ours," Mark says. "Call me at ours."

Acknowledgments

Nothing could have prepared anyone in my life for a solid year of baseball fun facts. I cannot overemphasize just how much I've put my loved ones through regarding the architecture of stadiums that no longer exist, the pittance most ballplayers made before unionization, and the evergreen iniquity of team owners. You never know the depths of someone's love for you until they feign interest in the biography of Mickey Mantle you're reading.

Miranda Dubner, Megan Tomkoski, and Katie Welsh read early drafts of this book for baseball fact-checking and also general hand-holding and reassurance. Any baseball errors are my own fault but also baseball's fault for being so weird (which I mean in the most affectionate sense). The members of the WWYM Discord were tireless when it came to suggesting titles, sorting out punctuation issues, and aiding and abetting all my more dubious impulses.

My agent, Deidre Knight, has had my back with this book and all the books that came before it. I'm so grateful to Sylvan Creekmore for helping shape this story into what it is, and to everyone at Avon who worked on this book.

I mined the work of Roger Angell and Jimmy Breslin for vibes in re the 1962 Mets and the strange catharsis of rooting for an objectively awful team. Despite the fact that I used the names of actual teams, the ballplayers in this book are completely fictional. I'm sure the actual 1960 Phillies never did anything wrong in their lives. (This is probably a good place to note that in a universe where there's a 1960 National League expansion, there would have needed to be a second new team in addition to the Robins; assume this team exists and is so boring that nothing about it or its city ever needs to be mentioned in the pages of this book.)

About the Author

CAT SEBASTIAN writes queer historical romances. Before writing, Cat was a lawyer and a teacher and did a variety of other jobs she liked much less than she enjoys writing happy endings for queer people. She was born in New Jersey and lived in New York and Arizona before settling down in a swampy part of the South. When she isn't writing, she's probably reading, having one-sided conversations with her dog, or doing the crossword puzzle. Cat is the author of many series, including the Turners, Seducing the Sedgwicks, the Regency Impostors, and the London Highwaymen.

DISCOVER MORE BY
CAT SEBASTIAN

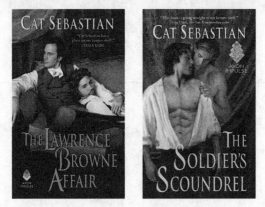